About the Authors

Tara Pammi can't remember a moment when she wasn't lost in a book, especially a romance which, as a teenager, was much more exciting than mathematics textbooks. Years later Tara's wild imagination and love for the written word revealed what she really wanted to do: write! She lives in Colorado with the most co-operative man on the planet and two daughters. Tara loves to hear from readers and can be reached at tara.pammi@gmail.com or her website tarapammi.com

Maya Blake's writing dream started at thirteen. She eventually realised her dream when she received The Call in 2012. Maya lives in England with her husband, kids and an endless supply of books. Contact www.mayablake.com/
twitter.com/mayablake
facebook.com/maya.blake.94

Louise Fuller was a tomboy who hated pink and always wanted to be the prince. Not the princess! Now she enjoys creating heroines who aren't pretty pushovers but strong, believable women. Before writing for Mills & Boon, she studied literature and philosophy at university and then worked as a reporter on her local newspaper. She lives in Tunbridge Wells with her impossibly handsome husband, Patrick and their six children.

Passionate Encounters

March 2022
Tempted by the Boss

April 2022
Second Chance Seduction

May 2022
**Consequences of
One Night**

June 2022
Risking It All

July 2022
A Price Worth Paying

August 2022
Revenge is Sweet

Passionate Encounters
Revenge is Sweet

TARA PAMMI

MAYA BLAKE

LOUISE FULLER

MILLS & BOON

First Published in Great Britain 2022
by Mills & Boon, an imprint of HarperCollins*Publishers* Ltd,
1 London Bridge Street, London, SE1 9GF

www.harpercollins.co.uk

HarperCollins*Publishers*
1st Floor, Watermarque Building,
Ringsend Road, Dublin 4, Ireland

PASSIONATE ENCOUNTERS: REVENGE IS SWEET
© 2022 Harlequin Enterprises ULC

Sicilian's Bride for a Price © 2018 Tara Pammi
Signed Over to Santino © 2016 Maya Blake
Revenge at the Altar © 2018 Louise Fuller

ISBN: 978-0-263-30565-4

MIX
Paper from
responsible sources
FSC® C007454

This book is produced from independently certified FSC™ paper to ensure responsible forest management.

For more information visit: www.harpercollins.co.uk/green

Printed and Bound in Spain using 100% Renewable electricity at CPI Black Print, Barcelona

SICILIAN'S BRIDE
FOR A PRICE

TARA PAMMI

For my very own hero, my husband Raghu.

Twenty is nothing—I could write a hundred heroes inspired by you.

CHAPTER ONE

DANTE VITTORI STARED at the legal document that had been delivered an hour ago. The floor-to-ceiling glass windows that made up three whole sides of his office on the forty-sixth floor of Matta Towers in Central London cast the luxurious space in an orange glow, thanks to the setting sun behind him.

Vikram Matta—his mentor Neel Matta's son and Dante's best friend—was now legally dead.

He felt a twinge in his chest for exactly one minute.

He'd learned that grief, like regret, was a useless emotion. He'd learned this at the age of thirteen when his father had killed himself instead of facing lifelong incarceration for his Ponzi scheme that had fleeced hundreds of people. He'd learned this when his mother had simply changed her name back to her Sicilian father's and married a man he approved of within a year of his father's death.

Giving in to his emotions would have crushed Dante back then. Vikram was gone; he'd made his peace with it a long time ago.

Quickly, he rifled through the documents, to ensure he hadn't missed anything.

He was almost to the last couple of pages when he stilled.

Voting Shares of the Deceased

The hairs at the back of his neck prickled. His mind instantly rewound back to the conversation he and Vikram had had with Neel when Neel had found he hadn't much time to live.

Neel Matta had started Matta Steel, a small steel manufacturing business, almost forty years ago, but it was Dante who had grown it into the billion-dollar conglomerate it was now. Against his own brother, Nitin's wishes, for the first time in the history of the company, Neel had granted his own voting shares to Dante, an outsider.

He had made Dante a part of his family. And now Matta Steel was the blood in his veins, his mistress, his everything.

Instead of wasting time grieving after Neel's death and Vikram's horrific plane crash, Dante had taken the company from strength to strength, cementing his position as the CEO.

But with Vikram's voting shares being up for grabs now...

His secretary, Izzy, came into the office without knocking. Being another alum of Neel Matta's generosity, Izzy took for granted a certain personal privilege with Dante that he didn't allow anyone else. Neither did he doubt that she'd interrupted him for a good reason.

The redhead's gaze flew to the papers in front of him, clear distress in those green eyes for a moment. But when she met his gaze, she was the consummate professional.

Of course Vikram's death had touched her too, but like him, Izzy was nothing if not practical.

Pushing his chair back, he laced his fingers at the back of his neck and said, "Spill it."

"I heard from Nitin's secretary, Norma, that he's thinking of calling an emergency board meeting with special counsel present."

Neel's brother was so predictable in his greed and deception. "I was expecting that."

"I wasn't sure if you had realized it has to do with Vicky's voting shares being up for grabs now."

"I did." Izzy was both competent and brilliant. And utterly loyal to him. The one quality he knew he couldn't buy even with his billions. "Tell me your thoughts."

She took a seat and opened her notebook. "I pressed a little on Norma and learned that he means to go over the bylaws in front of the board and direct the conclusion that Vikram's shares—" an infinitesimal catch in her throat again "—should go to him, since the bylaws state that the voting shares are to be kept in the family."

"Except when Neel modified them to grant me his shares." They had been a gift when Dante had made a big business win. Neel had been paving his way into retirement, wanting to slow down and let Dante take over. Instead his heart disease had killed him in a matter of months.

"He means to censure that as an aberration on Neel's part due to his ailing health."

Dante smiled. "It's an allegation he's continued to make for nigh on ten years now, even though I have held the controlling stake in the company."

"Also, he's conveniently forgotten Ali."

For the first time in years, Dante found his thoughts in sudden disarray.

His mentor's rebel daughter had always been the one thorn in his rise to success. The one piece of trouble in Neel's life that Dante hadn't solved for the man he'd worshipped. The one element he'd never quite figured out properly.

"No, he hasn't." Alisha's scorn for her father's company wasn't a secret.

He stood up from his seat. London's night was glittering

into life all around them. "Nitin's counting on Ali simply refusing to have anything to do with the company, as always. Which means he can inherit all of Vikram's shares."

"Can't you contest that?"

"I can, but if he gets the board on his side and they rule that the shares go to him, there's not a lot I can do. He'd own the majority. Unless I got…" He trailed off, an idea occurring to him. "Nitin needs to be taught the lesson that I own Matta Steel. Irrevocably."

"I'm assuming you've already come up with a plan for that."

He had. A brilliant one. He hadn't put his heart and blood and soul into Matta Steel just so he'd have to defend it every other year.

Again, that twinge of doubt pulled at his chest. He flicked it away. There was no room for emotions in his decision. The only thing he would never violate was Neel's trust in him—and that meant keeping control of Matta Steel.

Alisha had never wanted to be a part of her papa's legacy. She had turned her back on everything to do with the company and Neel and even Vikram when he'd been alive.

She'd had nothing but resentment for Dante for as long as he could remember. And he would feel no compunction in taking the things he wanted—the things that she scorned anyway—off her hands, forever.

All he needed was leverage.

Everyone had a price and he just needed to find Ali's. "Find out where she's holed up now. She could be anywhere."

Izzy jerked her head up, shock dancing in her green eyes. "Ali?"

There was reluctance, maybe even unwillingness in her stare.

"Yes. Find Alisha," he said, simply dismissing the un-asked question in Izzy's eyes. He pulled his jacket on and checked his phone. No reason for him to miss out on his date with the latest Broadway actress touring London.

He reached the door and then turned. "Oh, also, call that PI for me, won't you? I want to have a little chat with him."

"Which one?"

"The one I have on my payroll to keep track of Alisha's movements."

"But you never look at his reports." Izzy's accusation was clear. He'd never given a damn about Alisha except to have someone keep an eye on her, for the purpose of ex-tricating her if she got herself into trouble.

For Neel's sake.

"I didn't need to, until now. She's been safe, mostly, *si*?" It was a miracle in itself, since she traveled through all the hellholes of the world in the name of her little hobby. Izzy didn't need to know he read every single one of those re-ports. On any given day, he knew how and where Alisha was. "Now, however, I need a little bit more info on her."

"Dante—"

"None of your business, Isabel." He cut her off smoothly and closed the door behind him.

Izzy had been the one constant person in his life for so long, from the moment he had come to live with Neel all those years ago, yes. But it didn't mean he invited her into his private thoughts or that he considered her a per-sonal friend.

Dante Vittori didn't do relationships, of any kind.

"There's someone here to see you, Ali."

Alisha Matta looked up from her crouch on the floor of the Grand Empire Palace restaurant. Her shoulders were tight from supporting the weight of the camera and her thighs burned at her continued position. Ignoring her friend Mak's voice, she kept clicking.

She'd been waiting all morning in the small kitchen of the crowded restaurant, waiting for Kiki to come home.

The pop of the flash of her Nikon sang through her nerves, the few moments of clarity and purpose making the wait of the last three months utterly worth it. "To your right, look into the camera. No, jut your left hip out, you're gorgeous, Kiki," she continued the words of encouragement. She'd managed to learn a little Thai in the last year but her stuttering accent had only made Kiki laugh.

The neon lights and the cheap pink linoleum floors became the perfect background as Kiki shed her jeans and shirt in a move that was both efficient and sensual as hell. Her lithe dancer's body sang for the camera.

But even the perfection of the shot couldn't stop the distraction of Mak hovering.

"If it's John, tell him we're done," she whispered.

"It's an Italian gentleman. In a three-piece Tom Ford suit that I'm pretty sure is custom designed and black handmade Italian loafers. Gucci, I think."

Ali fell back onto her haunches with a soft thud, hanging on to her expensive camera for dear life. Mak was crazy about designer duds. There was only one Italian gentleman she knew. Except, if it was who she thought it was, he shouldn't be called a gentleman. More a ruthless soul in the garb of one.

"Said his name was…"

Ali's heart thudded in tune with the loud blare of the boom box. "What, Mak?"

Mak scrunched his brow. "You know, the guy who wrote about all those circles of hell, that one."

"Dante," Ali whispered the word softly. How appropriate that Mak would mention Dante and hell in the same sentence.

Because that was what her papa's protégé represented to her.

The very devil from hell.

Princesses in glass castles shouldn't throw stones, bella.

Okay, yes, devil was a bit overboard because he hadn't actually ever harmed Ali, but still, Ali hated him.

So what was the devil, whose usual playground was the London social circuit, doing on the other side of the world in Bangkok?

The last time they had laid eyes on each other had been when she'd learned of Vikram's plane crash. She closed her eyes, fighting the memory of the disastrous night, but it came anyway.

She'd been so full of rage, so vulnerable and so vicious toward Dante. For no reason except that he was alive while her brother was gone. Gone before she could reconnect with him.

"He doesn't look like he's happy to be kept waiting," Mak interrupted her trip down a nightmarish memory lane.

Ali pulled herself up.

No, super busy billionaire Dante Vittori wouldn't like waiting in the ramshackle hotel. How impatient he must be to get back to his empire. To his billions.

How dare Ali keep him waiting while each minute of his time could mean another deal he could broker, another billion he could add to his pile, another company he… She smiled wide.

She'd make him wait.

Because Dante being here meant only one thing: he needed something from her.

And she would jump through those nine circles of hell

before she did anything that made his life easier. Or calmer. Or richer.

Slowly, with shaking fingers, she packed up her camera. She pulled the strap of the bag over her shoulder, picked up her other paraphernalia, kissed Kiki's cheek and pushed the back door open.

The late September evening was balmy, noisy and full of delicious smells emanating from all the restaurants that lined up the street.

Her stomach growled. She promised herself some authentic pad thai and a cold can of Coke as soon as she got to her flat. Thwarting Dante and a well-earned dinner suddenly seemed like a highly pleasurable way to spend her day.

Just as she took another step into the busy street, a black chauffeur-driven Mercedes pulled up, blocking her. Ali blinked at her reflection in the polished glass of the window when the door opened. Out stepped Dante.

In his crisp white shirt, which did wonders for his olive complexion, and tailored black pants, he looked like he'd stepped out of a *GQ* magazine cover and casually strolled into the colorful street.

His Patek Philippe watch—a gift from her father when he'd welcomed Dante onto the board of Matta Steel, yet one more thing Papa had given Dante and not her—gleamed on his wrist as he stood leaning carelessly against the door, a silky smile curving that sculpted mouth. "Running away again, Alisha?"

He was the only one who insisted on calling her Alisha. Somehow he managed to fill it with reprimand and contempt.

All thoughts of pad thai were replaced with the cold burn of resentment as that penetrating gaze took in her white spaghetti strap top and forest green shorts and traveled from her feet in flip-flops to her hair bunched into a messy bun on top of her head. It was dismissive and yet so thorough that her skin prickled.

Chin tilted, Ali stared right back. She coated it in defiance but after so long, she was greedy for the sight of him. Shouts from street vendors and the evening bustle faded out.

A careless heat filled her veins as she noted the aristocratic nose—broken in his adolescence and fixed—the dark, stubble-coated line of his jaw and deep-set eyes that always mocked her, the broad reach of his shoulders, the careless arrogance that filled every pore. He exuded that kind of masculine confidence that announced him as the top of the food chain both in the boardroom and out of it.

And his mouth... The upper lip was thin and carved and the lower was fuller and lush, the only hint of softness in that face and body. It was a soft whisper about the sensuality he buried under that ruthlessness.

Her heart was now thundering in her chest, not unlike Mak's boom box. Heat flushed her from within. She jerked her gaze to meet his, saw the slight flare of his nostrils.

Christ, what was she doing? What was she imagining?

Ali moved her tongue around in her dry mouth, and somehow managed to say, "I have nothing to say and I want nothing to do with you."

To do with you...

The words mocked her, mocked the adolescent infatuation she'd nursed for him that she now hated, morphing into something much worse. Everything she despised about him also attracted her to him. If that weren't a red flag...

He halted her dignified exit with his fingers on her wrist, the calloused pads of his fingers playing on her oversensitized skin.

She jerked her arm out of his grip like a scalded cat. His

mouth tightened, but whatever emotion she had incited disappeared behind his controlled mask. "I have a proposal that I'm sure you would like to hear."

God, how she wanted to do or say something that made that mask shatter completely. How she wished she could be the one who brought the arrogant man to his knees. Her sudden bloodthirstiness shocked even her.

She'd always liked coloring outside the lines, yes, but not to the point of self-destruction. And that was what Dante made her do. Always.

At some point, hating him had become more important than trying to build a bridge to her father, than reconnecting with Vikram.

No more.

No playing to his point by doing something he would hate; no trying to stir up that smooth facade and burn her bridges.

You're a necessary nuisance, Alisha. I put up with your mind games for his sake. Only for his.

A calm filled her at her resolution. "What do you want from me?"

A brow rose in the too angular face. There was that tightness to his mouth again. In a parallel universe, Ali would have concluded that that assumption pricked him. In this one where she knew Dante Vittori had no emotions, she didn't.

"Why are you so sure that I want something from you?"

"You're thousands of miles away from your empire. From everything I know, there's no steel plant in this area, nor a lot of demand for it. Unless you're scouting the area to build a new plant with cheap labor, then you're not to check up on me."

"I've always known where you are, Alisha."

She swallowed.

"However much you like to pretend that there are no ties between us, however far you run in pursuit of your little hobby, you are, at the end of the day, his daughter."

His statement put paid to any emotional extrapolation she was still stupid enough to make from his previous one. As if he worried she might read too much—or anything at all—into him keeping tabs on her.

He had always been loyal to her father; would always be loyal to him. Keeping track of her fell somewhere under that umbrella. Nothing at all to do with the woman she was.

Nothing.

"I'm not interested in trading insults with you," she said, unable to stop her voice from cracking. "I'm not... I'm not that impulsive, destructive Ali anymore."

"That would be a nice change of pace for us, *si*? So we'll have dinner and not trade insults tonight."

"I said no insults. That doesn't mean I want to be anywhere near you for more than five minutes." It was her own confused emotions and this...blasted attraction that made her want to avoid him even now.

"Ah..." With a graceful flick of his wrist, he made a big show of checking his watch. "That lasted about thirty seconds." His gaze caught hers. "I'm not and have never been your enemy, Alisha."

And just like that, her attraction to him became a near tangible thing in the air. Her hating him became the only weapon in her armor. "Eating out is a pleasure for me and somehow I don't see that being the primary emotion if we're forced together for too long."

A calculating glint appeared in his eyes. "There's something you want in my grasp. When will you learn to act guided by your goals and not by your emotions?"

She could feel herself shaking. "Not everyone is an am-

bitious, heartless bastard like you are." There went her resolution to be polite. "Just tell me what your proposal is.
Now."

"It has to do with your mother's charity. That's all you'll
get now. My chauffeur will pick you up at six for dinner. And, Alisha, dress appropriately. We won't be eating
hunched over some street vendor's stall in the market. Neither will I appreciate the half-naked, wrapped-around-a-
has-been-rock-star look you sported the last time around
for my benefit."

How she wished she could say it hadn't been for his benefit, but they both knew it had been. Her eighteenth and
his twenty-eighth birthday party would be etched on her
memory forever.

"Arrogant, ruthless, manipulative, controlling, yes, but
I never thought you were a snob," she threw back at him.

"Because I want to have a civilized dinner at a place
where you won't throw things at me?"

Another bad night. Another bad memory.

No, it was time to rewrite how Dante saw her. Time to
stop expecting things from him from some unwritten script
in her own head. "One dinner. No more."

She'd almost walked away.

"Why does it bother you so much to be around me?"

Her face burned and it had nothing to do with the last
of the day's heat. "It doesn't."

"*No?* Isn't that why you avoid your family home, why
you never come to London? You avoid your extended family, your old friends, you move from place to place like a
nomad."

You took everything that should have been mine, she
wanted to say, like she'd done once. But it wouldn't be
the truth.

Dante hadn't taken anything her father hadn't been more

than happy and willing to give him. Dante hadn't shattered her family. Her father had.

But when it came to him…she was still that morass of anger and attraction and something more that she was terrified to discover. "That mansion, even London, they haven't been home to me in a long time."

That silky, slick smile tugged up the corners of his mouth again. "It's a relief to know then that your life's not revolved around avoiding me then, *si*. See you tonight, Alisha."

He was gone before she could blink, before she could counter the arrogant assumption. As she went home, Ali couldn't shake off the sense of dread that settled in her gut.

She and Dante couldn't stand each other. So why the hell was he insisting on an intimate dinner? And how would she get through it without compromising her dignity?

CHAPTER TWO

OF COURSE THE infuriating man couldn't simply text her the name of the hotel when he'd ordered her to dress appropriately, Ali thought, as the black Mercedes weaved through the heavy traffic, leaving the bustle of the city behind.

But having known Dante since the age of twelve, Ali had made a guess.

Dante was a man who expected, no, *demanded* the best of everything in life. He had a reputation for being a perfectionist with his employees but then no one complained because he rewarded hard work and ambition. God, she'd really gone looking for reasons to hate him back then.

The luxury Mercedes pulled smoothly into the courtyard of the latest on-trend, five-star resort that had been renovated last year to look like it could proudly belong in any posh European city, with the boat-filled canals of the Chao Phraya river offering a lovely view. The seafood at the restaurant was to die for, Mak had informed her, and he'd heard it from one of his many connections in high places.

Okay, so the worst thing that could come of this meeting was that she could walk away having had a delicious dinner at a lovely restaurant. And to prove to Dante that she could fake class and poise with the best of them.

She smoothed her hand over her stomach as she stepped out of the car and was pleased with the light pink sheath dress that she'd chosen to calm the butterflies. In the guise of studying the hotel's striking exterior, she took a moment to study herself in the reflection of the glass facade.

Her long hair, freshly washed and blow-dried to within an inch of its life, fell to her waist like a dark silky curtain, her only jewelry a thin gold chain with a tiny diamond disappearing into the low V-neck of her dress. The linen dress was a cheap knockoff of a designer brand she couldn't afford on her erratic income. But she looked like a million bucks, the fabric clinging to every dip and rise of her toned body as if it were custom designed for her.

The light pink was set off perfectly against her dusky skin and she'd let Kiki do her makeup—smoky eyes, gold bronzer and pale pink lip gloss. Tonight, she would be the sophisticated, poised Ali her mother had raised her to be, even if it killed her.

Another glance at the financial papers of her mother's charity hadn't changed reality. Other than a huge influx of cash, there was nothing anyone could do to save it. So, if Dante had something that could help, Ali would listen. She would treat this as a meeting with a professional.

Her beige pumps click-clacked on the gleaming cream marble floor as she walked up to the entrance to the restaurant. Soft yellow light fell from contemporary chrome fixtures. Beige walls and cream leather chairs gave the restaurant an utterly decadent, romantic atmosphere. Her belly swooped as Ali caught sight of Dante's bent head, the thick jet-black hair glittering in the lights.

Gripping her clutch tighter, Ali looked around. Every other table was empty. She checked her knockoff watch and saw it was only seven in the evening, nowhere near closing time.

The setting was far too intimate, far too private. Just far too much a scene plucked right out of her adolescent fantasies. But before she could turn tail and run out of the restaurant, that jet-black gaze caught her.

The mockery in those eyes made Ali straighten her shoulders and put one foot in front of the other.

He stood up when she reached their booth—a cocoon of privacy in an already silent restaurant. He'd exchanged the white shirt for a slate-gray one that made his eyes pop. With his jaw freshly shaved, thick dark hair slicked back half-wet, he was so…no, handsome was a lukewarm word for Dante's fierce masculinity.

The scent of his aftershave, with an aqua note to it, was subtle, but combined with the warmth of his skin, it sank into Ali's pores. Every cell in her body came alive.

"Where is everybody?"

"Everybody?" he said, standing far too close for her sanity.

Ali sat down with a plop, hand smoothing over her stomach. "Yes, people. Other Homo sapiens. Who might want to partake of the delicious food I've heard they serve here."

There was no mockery now when he looked down at her.

Heat swarming her cheeks, Ali ran her fingers through her hair. "What?"

His gaze swept over her face, her hair, the low V-neckline, but went no farther down. A shiver clamped her spine. "You clean up nice."

"Oh." The one syllable hung in the air, and she looked away, pretending to smooth her dress, putting her clutch down.

He took his sweet time sitting down, not opposite her, but on the side of the table, to her left. Ali shifted her knees away to the far right.

"If you scoot any farther down, you'll fall off the seat. Why are you so jumpy?"

Ali stilled, clasped her restless fingers in her lap. "I'm not."

"*No? Really?*"

His accent got thicker any time he got a little emotional. It was one of the tells Ali had picked up a long time ago. Pulling herself together, she met his gaze. Did he really have no idea what being near him did to her equilibrium? Did he really not feel the charge in the air around them, the pulse of undercurrents in every word, every look…? God, how was it that she was the only one who felt so much?

Not that she wanted Dante to be attracted to her. Her shoulders shook as a shiver of another kind traveled down her spine.

"If you're jumpy around me, it means you've arranged a little something for me. A surprise."

Ah…that was what he attributed it to. She closed her eyes and counted to ten. She couldn't even blame him because back then she'd been a little devil all right.

She'd lit sparklers in his room one Diwali night that had put holes in the new suit her papa had bought him. And that had almost lit the entire house on fire.

She'd taken a hammer to his new cuff links—Vikram's present—and minced them to so much dust.

Oh, and let's not forget the documents for an important merger she'd taken from his room and shredded.

When he'd brought his girlfriend to meet her papa… Ali groaned at the memory. And those weren't the half of all the destructive things she'd done to show how much she hated him.

She cleared her throat. "I told you. I've changed." When he raised a brow, she sighed. "I didn't know where we were dining. How could I arrange anything? I was just surprised to see no other patrons, that's all."

"I had my secretary book the entire restaurant for us." When her mouth fell open, he shrugged. "If you were going to cause a public scene—which given my knowledge of your character seemed like a high probability—I wanted to minimize the public part."

"Fair enough," she replied back with all the sass she could manage. Other people would have been a buffer, other people would have distracted her from this…whatever made her skin prickle with awareness.

Luckily, before her sudden awkwardness could betray her, the maître d' arrived.

"A bottle of your best white wine and the shrimp salad for both of us."

Ali lifted her chin. "I don't want shrimp."

"No?"

His fingers touched her wrist, and again, Ali pulled back as if he were a live current.

His jaw tightened, a flare of heat in his eyes. "Even though it's what this restaurant is famous for and you made that soft moan when your eyes came to that item on the menu?"

Her cheeks aflame, her heart pounding, Ali stared down at the menu. The words blurred, the tension between them winding round and round.

"Madam?" His expression set into a pleasing smile, the maître d' spoke up. "If you don't want the seafood that Mr. Vittori has ordered," he said, "might I suggest something else?"

"No." Ali took a deep breath. It wasn't the poor man's fault that Dante was playing with her. And she had played into his hands like she was still that irrational, impulsive hothead who wanted to hurt him for everything that was wrong in her world. "I'll have the shrimp, thanks."

"Don't," she simply said, once the man left.

Don't manipulate me. Don't rub me the wrong way. Just don't...be in my life.

Dante leaned back, his stare intense. "Don't make it so easy."

Before Ali could launch into another argument, he placed a rectangular velvet case on the table. Ten minutes into the dinner and she felt like she was already emotionally wound up. She fell back against her seat. Of course, he was the master manipulator, playing on weaknesses, while he had remained untouchable.

"What now?"

"Open it."

Just get it over with. Just get it over with. And walk away.

Ali opened the clasp. She caught sight of the tiny, exquisitely cut diamonds set into flowers with such delicate white gold that it always took her breath away, as it glittered under the soft lights. She rubbed the necklace back and forth with the pads of her fingers, compulsively, a balloon of ache in her chest. As if the gentle love of the woman who had worn them might have rubbed off on the stones.

It had taken everything she'd had in her to sell her mother's precious piece.

She pulled the box to her and clasped it so tightly that her knuckles showed white.

First, he had dropped the word about her mother's charity, now the necklace. Dante never did anything without some kind of payoff. He hated her just as much as she did him, and still he had sought her out. The hair on the nape of her neck prickled while her belly went on a swan dive.

"Why do you have this? What do you want, Dante?"

What do you want, Dante?

Dante stared at the tears shimmering in Alisha's large brown eyes, his breath punching into his throat.

It *was* the equivalent of a punch to his gut. He had borne enough of those in Sicily in his teenage years. Boys he'd known all his life had turned against Dante overnight; calling him names, roughing him up.

All thanks to his father's crime.

Those boys' punches had lit a fire in him back then, fueling his ambition to build a name for himself, separate from his father's. They had turned his young heart into a stone that never felt hurt again.

He had craved a fortune and a name all of his own. He had decided never to be weak like that again; never to be at anyone's mercy, least of all be controlled by a woman's love. And he had turned it into reality.

But the candid emotion in Alisha's face as she touched her mother's necklace, the havoc it wreaked on him, was a thousand times worse than any harm that had been inflicted on his teenage self.

When he'd delved into those reports on Alisha, he'd been shocked to find that Alisha had visited London several times over the last five years.

She'd had to go to London to deal with problems concerning her mother's charity. She had even spearheaded a charity gala to raise money. He'd been looking for leverage and he had found it.

He wasn't cheating Alisha out of anything she wanted. He was, in fact, proposing he give her what she wanted out of it, the one thing she held precious in return for what he wanted.

No, what threw him into the kind of emotional turmoil that he'd always avoided like the plague was that he was involving *her* in this play.

Alisha, who was a mass of contradictions, who he'd never quite figured out, who'd been the kind of flighty, selfish, uncaring kind of woman he loathed, was an unknown.

From the moment she'd come to live with her father, Neel, she'd hated Dante with an intensity that he'd first found amusing and then dangerous. Even worse, she'd always incited a reaction in him that no one else provoked.

But all this was before the changes in her the last six years had wrought.

Cristo, the sight of her walking into the back alley a few hours ago—the white spaghetti top plastered to her breasts, her shorts showing off miles and miles of toned legs, the utter sensuality of her movements as she pushed away tendrils of hair falling on her face, the sparkle of the fading sun on her brown skin...

The shock in her face, the greedy, hungry way she'd let those big brown eyes run all over him...even that hadn't made a dent in the need that had pulsed through him.

Dios mio, *this was Neel's daughter.*

She was forbidden to him. And not just because he was determined to take the last bit of her father's legacy from her. But because, with everything he planned to put into motion, Alisha would be the variable. His attraction to her was a weakness he couldn't indulge, much less act on. There were only two positions for women in his life: colleagues like Izzy and a couple of his business associates, women whose judgment he respected, women he genuinely liked; and then there were women he slept with who knew the score, and didn't want more from him.

Alisha didn't fall into either of those camps.

"Dante? What the hell are you doing with my mother's necklace?"

"I bought it back from the guy you sold it to." He made a vague motion to her tears, more shocked than discomfited by them. He'd never seen her as anything but poised to fight her father, him, Vikram, with all guns blazing. Never in this…fragile light. "Looks like I made the right call in thinking you would like it back. Why did you sell it?"

She took another longing look at the box before pushing it back toward him. "For a pair of Jimmy Choos."

"Don't be flippant, Alisha. I never understood why you were always so determined to be your own worst enemy."

"I have no idea what you're talking about. And really, did you invite me to dinner just to point out my flaws?"

He forced himself to pull his gaze from the way she chewed on her lower lip. Suddenly, everything about her—her mind, her body, *Dio*…everything—felt fascinating. Everything was distracting. "I know your mother's charity is failing. Why didn't you come to me for help?"

"Why didn't I come to you for help?" Some of that natural fight in her crawled back into her shoulders. He liked her better like that. He didn't want a vulnerable Alisha on his hands for the next few months. She laughed. White teeth flashed in that gamine face. "Have you met me? And you?"

Despite himself, Dante smiled.

He'd forgotten how witty Alisha could be, how she'd always laughed in any situation, how even with all her tantrums and drama she'd made the house lively when she'd come to live with Neel after her mother's death. Even with grief painting her eyes sad, she'd been so full of life, so full of character, even at the age of twelve.

He'd never gravitated to her, true, but when she'd blossomed into a teenager, it had seemed as if her hatred for him had grown too. The more he had tried to fix things between her and her father, the more she had resented him.

Her gaze slipped to his mouth for a fraction of a second. Every muscle in him tightened. "I'd starve before I take anything from the company. Or you."

He was far too familiar with that spiel to question it now. "What did you need the money for?"

"If you know I sold it, and to whom, then you know why. Come on, Dante, enough beating around the bush."

The waiter brought their food and she thanked him.

She dug into the food with the same intensity with which she seemed to attack everything in life.

Dante, mostly because of the jet lag, pushed his food around. He watched her as she sipped her wine, her tongue flicking out to lick a drop from her lower lip.

He wanted to lick it with his own.

The thought came out of nowhere, hard and fast. He pushed a hand through his hair and cursed under his breath. *Maledizione!* In all the scenarios he had foreseen for this, he hadn't counted how strikingly gorgeous Alisha had become. Or the intensity of the pull he felt toward her.

Whatever tension had been filling up the air, it now filled his veins. And he realized it was because she wasn't focused on him anymore.

Not so with him. Not even the constant reminder, the ironclad self-discipline that made him a revered name in his business circles, the one that told him this was nothing but a quid pro quo, could distract his gaze from the expanse of smooth brown skin her dress exposed. He took the wine flute in his hands, turned it around and around, watching his fingers leaving marks against the condensation.

He wanted to trace his finger against the slope of her shoulders to see if her skin was as silky as it looked. He wanted to touch the pulse at her throat, to sink his fingers into her silky hair and pull her to him, hold her against his body as he plundered her mouth...

She put her fork and spoon down, and took another sip of her wine. Then she leaned back all the way into her seat, her head thrown back over the top. The deep breath she took sent her chest rising and falling.

Basta! He needed to direct this conversation back to his plan.

"Tell me what you've been up to in the last few years." The words slipped out of his mouth. She looked just as shocked as he felt. "You know, other than living like a hobo and moving around every few months."

She shrugged, and the simple gold chain she wore glimmered against her throat, the pendant dangling between her breasts playing peekaboo with him. "You don't have to pretend an interest, Dante. Not now."

"You're his daughter. I've always been interested in what you do with your life. Until I realized my interest only spurred you toward destruction."

"Water under the bridge." She put her napkin on the table, her expression cycling from wariness to fake cheer. "Thank you for the dinner. That was a treat, even with your company. And on second thought, thanks for buying my mother's necklace back." She took the velvet box from him and put it underneath her clutch on the table. Waggling her brows, she leveled a saccharine smile at him. "You must know me well to give me a present I would so appreciate."

Being on the receiving end of that smile was just so… jarring. "You mean to sell it again, don't you?"

"Yep."

"That will only take care of the payroll for another month. I've seen the financials, Alisha. The charity will be bankrupt in a month."

Her mouth tightened. "I'll find a way. I always do."

"Or you could just ask me for help."

"I told you, I don't want your money. Or the company's or Papa's. I need to do this on my own."

"Does the charity home really mean that much to you?"

"It does. It's where Mama grew up. I spent so much time there with her. Some of the happiest moments of my childhood were there."

"If you really want to save the home, put aside your irrational resentment of me and I will funnel some much needed money into it."

"And what do I have to do in return?"

"Marry me."

CHAPTER THREE

MARRY ME...

Marry Dante...

Ali's mind went into a loop over that one phrase, like one of those gramophone records her mama had had.

Marry Dante, marry Dante...

Dante, who thought she was selfish and spoiled.

Dante, with whom she reverted back to that lonely girl come to live with a distant father, distracted brother and a resented changeling, after her mama's sudden death.

With Dante she would always be her worst self.

Panic skittled over her skin like a line of fire ants crawling up her legs. She needed to marry Dante like she needed a hole in her head. It would be like all the bad decisions she'd ever made steamrolled into one giant boulder that would chase her for the rest of her life.

A hysterical sound released from her mouth.

"Alisha?"

She brought her gaze to his, stood up from the booth, picked up her clutch and turned. "You've gone mad."

"Alisha, wait."

Nope.

She didn't want to hear more. If she did, he would rope her into it.

As a master strategist, he wouldn't have sought her out across the world, wouldn't have approached her if he hadn't already figured out a way to make her agree. And she needed to flee before that happened. Before their lives were even more tangled. Before she betrayed herself in the worst way possible.

Dear God, when it came to him, all she had left was her pride.

"Alisha, stop!" His arm shot out just as Ali got ready to sprint across the restaurant if necessary.

Long fingers roped around her wrist and because of her desperate forward momentum, her foot jerked to the side. Pain shot up through her ankle and she fell back against him.

The breath punched out of her as he anchored her by throwing his arm around her midriff.

Unstoppable force meets immovable object...

"What happens when they crash, Alisha? Who gets destroyed?"

The world stopped tilting at that silky whisper as she realized she'd spoken out loud. And yet, the explosion his touch evoked continued to rock through her body.

The scent of him was all over her skin, filling each pore, drowning her in masculine heat. His legs were thrown wide, the tensile power of his thighs just grazing the back of hers, his chest pushed up tight against her back. Her chest expanded as she tried to stop the panic. On the exhale, the underside of her breasts fell against his steely arm. A soft hiss of warm air bathed her neck, making it a thousand times worse. Or was that pleasure skittering across her skin?

An onslaught of sensations poured through her, her skin prickling tight, and yet, a strange lethargy crawled through her limbs. She wanted to lean into him completely, until her bottom was resting against his hips. She wanted to feel him from chest to toe against her back, she wanted to rub herself against that hard body until he was as mindlessly aroused as her. Until that iron will of his snapped like a thinly stretched rubber band.

As if he could guess the direction of her thoughts, his fingers tightened around her hip, digging into her slightly to keep her still; to keep her from leaning back and learning his body's reaction to her.

Because, really, in what universe did she imagine Dante would want her back with this same madness?

She groaned—a feral, desperate sound. Why was it that everything she did came back to taunt her a thousand times worse?

"Because you don't think before you do," came the voice at her ear. Ah…perfect! Of course, she'd said that out loud too. "You're impulsive, brash and if I hadn't caught you, you would have fallen flat on your face."

"Kissing the floor sounds like a better alternative," she said, her words throaty and whispery.

"Will you sit down and listen if I let you go?"

As if operating on an instinct that defied rationality, her fingers clenched over his wrist.

She opened her eyes and swallowed hard. Since he'd undone his cuffs earlier, her palm rested against a hair-roughened wrist. She rubbed the skin—the rough texture, the plump veins on the back of his hand—the startlingly sensual contrast between her and him inviting her along further and further.

It was the sharp inhale followed by another curse that pulled her out of the fog.

Her chin flopped down to her chest. "No. I don't want to hear anything you say. I don't want to be near…you in this moment, much less in the future."

The vulnerability she fought every waking minute, the longing for a deeper connection in her past, with anyone related to her past, pervaded her in his presence.

This was what would happen if she agreed: every look, every touch would wind her up; lines between want and hate, reality and fantasy would blur…until she attacked him—claws and all—just to keep herself tethered, to keep herself together. Or until she gave in to this inexplicable yearning she had felt for him for so long.

The stiffness of her posture drained away and she leaned back against his chest. She let herself be weak and vulnerable for five seconds.

Both of his arms wound around her. He held her gently, tenderly and that…that was more than Ali could bear. That uncharacteristic moment between them, the mere thought that he could pity her uncontrollable attraction to him, snapped her out of it.

She wriggled in his embrace and he instantly let her go.

Pushing her hair back, she fought for composure. The glass of cold water down her throat was a much needed burst of reality. When he sat down, when she had her wits together again, she looked back at him. "Tell me why."

"Vikram's been declared legally dead."

Gray gaze drinking her in, he paused. Ali looked away.

That he knew what her brother meant to her, that he had seen firsthand that night her grief, her regrets, it was something she couldn't erase. This nebulous connection between her and Dante—despite the knotted history of it—was the only thing she had of her past. And however far she ran, it seemed she would never be free of it. "And?"

"Your uncle will contest for his voting shares and might win. I'd like to crush his little rebellion with as few resources and as little time as possible. I have a huge merger coming up with a Japanese manufacturing company that I need all my energies focused on. Thousands of jobs and thousands more livelihoods depend on that merger. He's well-known for his ability to create PR damage."

So that was what he'd been counting on—that Ali's loathing of her uncle was greater than her combined loathing of her papa and Dante.

Her uncle had driven a wedge between her parents, though Ali knew it had been her father that had finally broken them apart.

Her father's ambition. Her father's unending hunger for success.

Just like the breathtakingly stunning man sitting across from her.

"I never realized what a true legacy you are of papa. Not Vicky, but you."

"Vicky always blazed his own path."

She nodded, the depth of her grief for her brother a hole in her chest. At least that was one thing she couldn't blame Dante for. Her brother had been a technical genius with no interest in his papa's company.

"If I marry you, I can transfer my shares to you and the eventual fate of Vicky's shares won't really matter. You can continue to be the master of Matta Steel." Even she couldn't dispute the trailblazing new heights that Dante had taken the company to since her father's death.

"*Si.* Your vow not to touch a penny of your father's fortune will not be broken since the voting shares are yours through your mother. Monetarily, they don't have much value, since they can't be sold off, or transferred to anyone outside marriage. So this is a good deal for you."

He had a well-rehearsed answer for every contentious point she could raise. "What do I get in return?"

"Money to throw into the drain that is the Lonely Hearts Foundation."

She refused to bite into that judgmental tone. "As much as I want?"

"A pre-agreed upon amount, *si.*"

"I want a check—from your own personal fortune," she added, determined to wring every drop of blood from him, "for that amount. If I agree."

There was a glint in his eye and a slick smile around his mouth, arrogant confidence dripping from every pore. *"Bene."* A regal nod to her request. "From my personal fortune, *si*?"

And whatever she demanded would be a drop in the ocean for him.

"We can't annul or end the marriage for three years or they will revert back to you. We'll both sign a prenup. At the end of the three years, a substantial amount of money will be settled on you."

"I don't want a settlement, I don't want a penny from you. And I won't—"

"Don't be foolish, Alisha. Throwing away your inheritance when you were eighteen was one thing but—"

"—under any circumstances sign a prenup," she delivered that with all the satisfaction of a well-placed right hook.

Shock etched onto those arrogantly handsome features.

It wasn't wise tweaking the tail of a tiger, especially when he was so royally wound up. But if she expected an outburst, a small glimpse of his infamous Sicilian temper that cowed all his employees, Ali was disappointed. Only a small tic in that granite jaw even betrayed how...thrown he was by her coup de grâce. Since he had dropped the whole thing on her with the sensitivity of a bulldozer, she'd pulled that out pretty fast based on that instinct she'd honed for years to annoy the heck out of him.

But now she realized how much she needed that illusion of control over...this. The only way she could keep the balance in this relationship of theirs was not to give him everything he wanted.

"Why not sign the prenup? All it does is give you money I know you won't touch."

She smiled, thoroughly enjoying herself. "Is that praise I hear for my principles?"

"If you think mucking around through life, running from your own shadow is principled, all power to you. I call it a juvenile need for petty revenge you've yet to outgrow. And I keep waiting for you to wake up from this…protracted dream of yours, for the thud of reality to hit you.

"I know spoiled princesses like you like the back of my hand. There will be a day when you'll crawl back to the luxury of your old life with your tail tucked between your legs. Because, really, what have you achieved in the last six years, except to sell off your mama's jewelry piece by priceless piece?

"Sign the prenup. When that day comes, you'll be thankful to me for giving you that option to fall back on."

Wow, he wasn't pulling his punches. Somehow, Ali kept her smile from sliding off her face.

His matter-of-fact assessment of her stung more than it should. She'd seen that same lack of respect, that same exaggerated patience in her father's eyes on the eve of her eighteenth birthday.

As if dressing like a skank and making out with a former junkie rock star in front of their esteemed guests was all he had expected of Ali. And before she could change his impression of her, before she could apologize for her share of mistakes, he'd been lost to her.

But, if it was the last thing she did, she resolved to change Dante's opinion of her.

Not because she wanted his approval—okay, she did, in some throwback to her angsty, unwise, earlier self—but because she wanted to prove him wrong. She needed to bring that arrogance down more than a peg or two. Really, she was doing a public service on behalf of all the women of the planet.

She needed to find some kind of closure for all the painful history between them. She longed for the day when she could look him in the eye and feel nothing.

No attraction. No wistful ache. No emotional connection whatsoever.

"No. No prenup. Let's not forget I'm doing you a favor. I know you're used to people bending over backward for you but I—"

Dark heat flared in his gray eyes. "Do you really want to threaten me about what I can or can't do with you, Alisha?"

Ali jerked back, the temperature cocoon soaring from arctic cold to desert hot within seconds. Red-hot images of herself doing his bidding, forbidden images of their limbs tangling…the heat between them was a near tangible thing in the air.

Did that mean he felt it too?

Walk away now, Ali. Walk away before you're far too tempted to resist.

But the thought of being able to save the charity that meant so much to her mother, the thought of returning to London, the thoughts of being grounded for a while, the thought of proving to Dante that she wasn't a car crash in the making won out. "I want your word that this agreement is only on paper. That you won't use it to manage me, to manage my life in any way."

His fingers roped over her wrists like a gnarly vine. That accent slipped in through his soft words. "Do not think to play those silly games with me that you did with your father, Alisha. I will not let you drag my name through mud like you did his. No splashing yourself all over the media with some ex-junkie. No sneaking out behind my back with another man. At least not when you're in London."

"If you're not careful with your threats, you're going to sound like a real fiancé, Dante." Whatever his conditions, she knew she'd have no problem keeping them. Like she'd already told him, her days of doing things to wind him up were over.

But she wouldn't let Dante have all the power in this relationship. "Let me get this straight. If I give up men for three years, will you do the same? Will you be celibate for three years?"

"I won't be the reason my name or this agreement of ours gets dragged through the mud."

"That's not really answering the question."

"My name, my reputation…they mean everything to me, Alisha. I built them brick by brick from nothing. Away from the shadow of my father's crime.

"I created a new life from the ground up. I built my fortune, I made my reputation anew after everything I had was destroyed in a matter of days." Ali shivered at the dark intensity of his words, the specter of his past almost a live thing between them. With his ruthless ambition coating every word, it was easy to forget what had brought Dante to her father at all. What had built him up to be this man she saw now.

"You put one toe out of line during any of this and your precious charity won't get a penny."

CHAPTER FOUR

SHE WAS LATE.

Of course she was. It was his own fault for assuming Alisha could ever be a headache-free zone for him. What he should have done was show up at the dingy flat she lived in, insist she pack up and drag her to the airstrip.

Instead, he'd given them both a few days to gain perspective. To make sure he could think, away from the distraction of her...presence. Of her outrageous demands. Like the demand that he forward a sum of ten thousand pounds as the first payment.

Already, his lawyer was freaking out at the massive risk Dante was leaving himself open to by marrying her without a prenup.

And that was before the man found out what a firecracker Alisha was.

But for all the threats and warnings his lawyer had screamed over the transatlantic call, Dante couldn't see her using this marriage to fleece him, to build her own fortune. He couldn't see her dragging him into some kind of court battle—but threatening to sully his reputation in a rage, yes.

That he was more than ready for. In fact, the idea of sparring with Alisha now, the very idea of going toe-to-toe with her sent a shiver of excitement through him. *Cristo*, his life was truly devoid of fun if a battle with Alisha filled him with this much anticipation.

He'd called it her protracted, rebellious phase—he had thought her a spoiled princess but he was beginning to question that. He had had his chauffeur drive him past her flat, he'd seen where she waitressed sometimes. And she'd lived like that for more than five years.

Common sense pointed out that she wasn't going to come after his fortune. Or Matta Steel.

The realization both calmed and unnerved him. Because, for the first time in his life, he had a feeling that reassurance came mostly from a place of emotion, despite the logic of it too. But he was determined to keep control of the situation.

If she thought he was handing over that amount of money without asking questions…if she thought he'd let her play him, play fast and loose in London, if she thought being his wife in name was just the latest weapon she could use against him…

It was time to reacquaint her with her adversary and set the ground rules for this…agreement between them. He refused to call it a marriage, refused to give his suddenly overdeveloped sense of guilt any more material to chew on.

Which was why he was waiting in Bangkok to accompany her back to London in his private jet rather than have his security bring her. He was also determined to accompany her because her return to London would definitely be commented on by the press, and once they announced that they had married, even their planned civil union without pomp and fanfare would still occupy the news cycle for a couple of weeks at least.

Thanks to his father's notoriety during his life and the spectacle of his suicide during his incarceration alongside Dante's swift rise through the ranks of Matta Steel to the position of CEO, there was plenty for the media to chew on. They were always ready to find some chink in his personality, some weak link in his makeup to crow that he was his criminal father's flawed son.

Sometimes they did get their hands on a juicy story from a woman he'd dumped—for the simple reason that she wanted more from the relationship and he didn't. Dante didn't care a hoot about a tabloid feature.

But this…agreement with Alisha would be no small step in the eyes of the media and the world. As such he needed to make her understand the importance of her behavior in the coming months.

The stubborn defiance in her eyes, the stark silence she'd subjected him to through the drive back to her flat hadn't been lost on him.

Alisha didn't respond well to threats.

He remembered the two-day disappearance she'd engineered when, on Neel's instructions, Dante had tried to enroll her in a boarding school in Paris a couple of months after she'd first come to live with her father.

Fighting the near constant hum of his attraction to her had briefly made him forget that.

This was a business deal and he couldn't antagonize Alisha any more than he would lose his temper with a new business partner. There had to be a way to get her to behave, to cooperate without letting the full force of his contempt for her to shine through.

The one thing he knew for certain was that he couldn't punish her for his own attraction to her, for his lack of self-control. And as much as his mind and body were bent on reminding him that she had fancied him once, he refused to go down that road.

No.

After the first hour, he stepped out of his car. The unusually heavy wind roared in his ears and he pushed up his sunglasses even though the sun had yet to make an appearance on the chilly late September morning.

Patience had never been his strong point. And yet he had a feeling that it would be stretched to the limit in the near future. A few months with Alisha was bound to turn him mental in his thirties.

He continued to wait and was just about to call her when a caravan of cars—really, a who's who of colorful vintage cars in different stages of deterioration—pulled up on the long, curving road that led to the airstrip.

Laughter bubbled out of his chest. He sensed his security team giving him sidelong, concerned looks. Well, no one ever made him laugh like Alisha did. Neither had a woman tested his control, or called forth some of his base instincts with a single smile like she did.

How fitting that the drama queen arrived in a ramshackle entourage of her own.

The caravan came to a stop with a lot of screeching noise that confirmed his suspicion that all three cars were on their last legs. But what crawled out of the cars was even more shocking. A surprising number of people clambered out of those small cars, a torrent of English and Thai flowing around. Car trunks were opened and suitcases and bags in different colors and makes pulled out.

Emerging from the third car, dressed again in short shorts that should have been banned, and a chunky sweater that fell to her thighs, almost covering the shorts, was Alisha. Loose and oversize, it fell off one shoulder almost to her bicep, leaving a hot-pink bra strap exposed.

And there was that same black camera bag—heavy from the looks of how the wide strap pulled over one shoulder and between her breasts.

Hair in that messy bun. No jewelry. Combat style boots on her feet.

No makeup that he could see. In fact, in the gray morning light, she looked freshly scrubbed, innocent and so excruciatingly lovely that he felt a tug low in his belly as surely as the sun peeking through the clouds.

Her wide smiles and husky laughter made her eyes twinkle. She stood among the loud group like sun shining on a vast field of sunflowers, every face turned toward her with genuine affection, long limbs grabbing her, hugging her, men and women kissing her cheeks. A sense of disbelief went through him as he spied a sheen of tears as she hugged the man called Mak.

And then she met his eyes.

Current arced between them even across the distance. As one, the group turned their gazes on him. Instead of surprise or curiosity, there was a certain knowledge in the looks leveled at him, knowledge about him. A certain warning in the looks, a subtle crowding around her, as if Alisha had imparted her opinion of him.

Out of the blue, for the first time in their shared history, he wondered what Alisha thought of him. What was behind all that…resentment of him? Did she still believe he'd stolen her legacy?

That hum began again under his skin as she pushed away from the crowd.

His breath suspended in his throat as the subtle scent of her skin teased him. He felt an overwhelming urge to bury his nose in her throat; to see that gorgeous, open smile leveled at him.

"Do you have the money ready?"

"All ten thousand pounds, *si*," he responded, a hint of warning in his tone.

She pulled out a slip from the back pocket of her shorts, the action thrusting her breasts up. He gaped like a teenager until she said, "Please have it transferred to this bank account."

He looked at the slip of paper with a routing number and an account number and raised his brows. "Whose account is it?"

"Kiki and Mak's joint account." She sighed at his silence. "You can't place conditions on how I use the money. No micromanaging my life."

"You're not doing this to piss me off, are you?"

She rolled her eyes. "No. As much as our shared history gives you reason to believe that, I'm not."

He took a step toward her. "Are they blackmailing you? Whatever it is, I'll take care of it. What was it, Alisha? Drugs they hooked you into? Naked pictures?"

"What do you mean, naked pictures?"

Her shock was so genuine that it took Dante a couple of seconds to speak. "Who do you think took care of that junkie rock star before he could sell your pics to every tabloid magazine?"

A frown tied her brow, her gaze staring at him unseeingly. "Richard threatened to sell naked pictures of me? Did you see them?"

"Of course I didn't look at your pictures," he snapped. "He gave us enough proof to show it was you."

He pushed a hand through his hair, the very prospect of that idiot taking advantage of a young Ali turning him inside out even now. It was the one time in his adult life that Dante had lost his temper and given in to the urge to punch the man's pretty face.

Vikram had had to restrain him physically.

"So did you pay him?" Ali asked softly.

"I don't respond well to threats, just like you. He gave me the flash drive with the pics on it and I smashed it with a paperweight."

She laughed, the sound full of a caustic bitterness. "Wow, you really don't think much of me, do you?" Her mouth trembled. "Mak and Kiki are the last people who would blackmail anyone. For the first year, when I moved here, I didn't pay for anything. Board or food. Whatever I pay them, believe me, it's very little in return for what they did for me."

Would the woman never develop a sense of self-preservation? "It's not a hardship to be kind to an heiress, Alisha. A payoff is usually expected at some point."

Hurt painted her small smile, her eyes widening, even as she bravely tilted her chin.

He had hurt her. The realization sat tightly on his chest.

"They don't know who I am, Dante. When you showed up at the restaurant a week ago, it was the first time I told either of them who I was."

"Alisha, I don't—"

"And if you say some stupid thing like I haven't earned it to give it away, believe me I did. Mama earned each and every one of those voting shares. She lost Papa to the blasted company. And all she got were those in return. So, yes, she paid for them. And y'know what? I paid for them too because I should've grown up with my father and brother and Mama in the same house. I shouldn't have had to wonder why Papa barely visited me. Vicky shouldn't have had to wonder how Mama could have so easily given him up. I shouldn't have had to wonder why it took Mama's death for him to be in my life.

"I shouldn't have to wonder what I lacked that meant he chose…" Her chest rose and fell, a haunting light in her eyes. "I paid for those shares, Dante. And I want some good to come out of what I'm signing up for with you. Something to ground me when you drive me up the wall over the next few months. That money will be a nice deposit for the business Mak and Kiki want to begin." She swallowed and met his gaze. "They welcomed me with open arms when I desperately needed friends, when I needed to be loved."

The vulnerability in her words struck him like a punch to his solar plexus, bringing in its wake a cold helplessness.

I'm not that impulsive, destructive Ali anymore.

Her words from a week ago haunted Dante as he watched her climb the steps to the aircraft. Maybe she wasn't that same old Alisha anymore. But as far as he knew, people didn't really change.

A reckless Alisha wouldn't have visited London three times and tried to patch up her mother's favorite charity.

A spoiled Alisha wouldn't have lived in anonymity when she could have simply used her father's name to live in luxury.

So maybe he hadn't known Alisha at all.

Maybe he didn't know the woman he was marrying after all.

CHAPTER FIVE

ALI STARED MINDLESSLY as she stepped onto the flight and elegant luxury met her eyes. Every moment she spent with Dante, the past relentlessly pulled at her. Along with all the moronic decisions she'd made in anger, in hurt, coming back to take a chunk out of her ass.

From the moment she'd stepped out of the car, she'd been aware of his eyes on her every second. His silent scrutiny, the way his gaze devoured her expression made her skin feel stretched tight. Any hope she had indulged that that pulse of attraction at the restaurant was just a heightened reaction because she was seeing him for the first time in six years died a quick death.

Even with her friends surrounding her—she still couldn't believe how many of them had showed up—she'd been aware of him.

It was as if, overnight, she'd developed an extra sense. A sixth sense that evolved to keep her in tune with Dante's every move, his every look, his every breath. And now they had twelve hours of flight in the enclosed space together, and the fact that the interior of the aircraft was much more expansive and luxurious than a commercial flight made no difference whatsoever.

Feeling hot and agitated, she tugged at the hem of her sweater and pulled it up in one quick move.

Like her, Dante also shed his jacket with a flick of those powerful shoulders.

Trying to look away was like the earth trying to pull out from its orbit around the sun. The cabin shrunk around them, and her breaths became shallow. Even before take-off, oxygen was in short supply.

Instead of his formal attire, which was second skin to him, today he wore a sky blue polo T-shirt that made his gray eyes pop.

If virility needed a picture in the dictionary, Dante would be perfect.

For virility see Dante Vittori.

Just the sight of his biceps and thick arms with a dusting of dark hair was enough to send her belly swooping. The blue denim clung to his tapering hips and powerful thighs. Ali sighed and pulled in a long breath. God, this was going to be a long flight. She couldn't take this much of him—the proximity, the constant awareness, the constant tugging in her belly urging her to look at him, to breathe him in.

And she craved more.

It wasn't just the physical attraction.

When she'd first moved in with her father after her mama's death, Dante had made quite the impression on her.

He'd been serious, brooding, off the charts handsome, and the worst of all: so close to her father—something she'd desperately needed but hadn't had. Her papa's eyes had been so full of pride for his protégé's achievements, his single-minded focus, his ambition.

At thirteen, she'd been hormonal, lost and he had been a hero, the golden son who had gotten everything she'd coveted. The one man who seemed more confident, more powerful, more handsome than any she'd known. She'd left London five years before because she'd been lost, grieving, sick of the imbalance in the dynamic between them.

Yet, it seemed nothing had changed.

Would he always be like this to her—this magnetic, confident embodiment of the perfect man? She looked up and found his gaze on her. Clearly disapproving. "What? Why are you giving me the stink eye?"

"The stink eye? What are we, six?"

"I could be six. You're what…a hundred and thirty now?"

The soft material of his T-shirt stretched taut across his wide chest and hard abdomen, mocking her words. "I'm old because I don't engage in childish behavior and language? Because I show up on time?"

"No, you're old because you…" Her words veered off as he walked closer, the very air filled with his dark masculinity. "You were probably born old with no sense of humor and an exaggerated sense of your own importance."

He raised a brow.

Heat rushed up her neck. "Okay, fine. I was two hours late, but I'm not really sorry. I told you I couldn't make a seven a.m. flight. You went ahead anyway. We planned Kiki's birthday party four months ago and it had to be this morning."

"You couldn't have had it last night?"

"She works nights. So it's your own fault if you waited for two hours. I told you, Dante, this whole thing…isn't going to be all by your rules. You're going to have to treat me like an adult."

"*Bene.* As long as you conduct yourself like one."

"Fine."

"Now that we have gotten that out of the way, I have some things I would like to discuss."

Ali folded her arms and tilted her chin up. "*Fine*. But first you have to feed me. I haven't had anything to eat since yesterday afternoon."

"No wonder you look like a bag of bones."

"I'm sorry I'm not curvy enough to fit your standards."

He sighed.

Ali scrunched her nose. "Hunger makes me cranky."

His mouth twitched. "Is that an apology?"

"Of sorts."

He nodded and like magic, the flight attendant arrived with a tray.

Ali dug into the bowl of creamy penne pasta with a delicate white wine sauce. The soft clink of the silver utensils filled the silence, which had an almost comfortable quality to it. It was only when he looked at her, as if he meant to see into her soul, as if she was endlessly fascinating, that she got flustered. Great, all she had to do to keep her sanity was avoid looking at him. "Okay, talk."

Dante seated himself in the opposite seat from Alisha and stretched his legs the other way. He'd stared earlier, his thoughts going in an altogether wicked direction when she'd removed the sweater and it had made her nervous. Which in turn had made her flippant. How was it that it had taken him that long to figure out that that was Alisha's default when she was unsure of herself?

"A team is airing out Matta Mansion as we speak. It's quite a drive from my flat in central London but it should work. You'll make it your home base for the near future and I can visit you there. There'll be a certain amount of media coverage on this so Matta Mansion will provide the perfect cover. My PR team's drafting a statement to announce our engagement."

"I don't want to live there."

Dante gritted his teeth, determined not to lose his temper. "Alisha, you just promised that you wouldn't fight me on every single thing."

"And you said you wouldn't railroad me. I can't…" Distress filled her eyes and his retort died on his lips. "I won't go back there. Not without Vikram and Papa. Not to an empty house…" She looked away, her profile lovely as she swallowed.

Dante sat back in his seat, fighting the urge to pull her into his arms and soothe her. *Cristo*, living with Alisha would be like riding a never-ending roller coaster. One moment he wanted to throttle her, one moment kiss her senseless and the next hold her tight.

He wanted her where he could keep an eye on her. Especially because of the media storm she didn't understand would hit them. "That only leaves my flat."

The devilish imp was back in her eyes when she turned to him. "I never thought I'd see the ruthless Dante Vittori scared."

Again, that overwhelming sense of relief poured through him. The vulnerability in her eyes sometimes made him feel like that adolescent youth again—powerless and all too aware of his own needs. And in its wake came the most overwhelming urge to hold her and kiss her until it was gone from her eyes.

Pure lust, he could handle. This…dangerous urge to play her hero—no!

"Scared?" he asked.

"The idea of me in your flat terrifies you to your hardened soul."

He laughed and the sound of it was a shock to his own ears. She dug her teeth into her lower lip, but couldn't quite arrest her smile either. "Fine, the flat it is. But—"

"I'll respect the rules of your domain. I'll control the

urge to have orgies every night. I'll be mindful of your pristine reputation and the shadow I could cast over it as your wife. How was that?"

He was still smiling. "That sounds like you drafted it."

"All night," she retorted, the irreverent minx. "Anything I missed?"

He shook his head, all the threats and conditions he meant to impose on her disappearing from his mind. She was a live wire, he didn't forget that for one second. Nor could he think. Because of the manifesto she'd read him, his ordered and peaceful life would remain that. And yet, he couldn't muster a sense of dread over it. He couldn't bring the words to his lips to kill that wide smile. He couldn't contain the little flare of excitement in his blood every time she leveled those eyes on him, every time she fought with him, every time she looked away but not before he saw the interest she couldn't hide in her eyes.

This was a dangerous high he was chasing, and *Dios mio*, where was his sense of self-preservation? So when he said, "What about you?" his voice was harsh.

She raised a brow. "What about me?"

"Any demands or expectations?"

"Not really. I'm…excited to put your money into the charity. I have some contacts I would like to network—"

"For what?"

"For my photography," she said, her smile dimming. "I'm going to see if I can sell them in the market for a penny a piece." Shift to sarcasm. It was like watching a panorama of emotions. "Oh, I also need a studio—a darkroom essentially." Back to a practical survival instinct he couldn't help but admire. "All in all, I'm looking forward to being back in London."

"You develop your own prints?"

"Yes."

"I'll arrange it."

"Thank you. Between the charity and the darkroom, you won't see me. Your perfectly ordered life will remain just the same."

Put like that, she sounded so sensible that Dante wanted to believe it. He not only had to believe it, he had to keep it like that. There was no feasible route his fascination with her could take.

No other outcome was possible between them. No other.

Ali had no idea if it was the unusually long-lasting peace on the flight or being back in London under the same roof, but the moment Dante showed her into the guest room, she made the connection she'd missed earlier.

What he'd said had been eating at her.

Richard had tried to blackmail Dante for those pics... great judgment call, Ali!

She finished her shower in a hurry, and pulled on the first pair of panties, shorts and T-shirt she could find in her bag. Hair wet and dripping down her back, she barefooted it to Dante's door.

He opened on the first knock, his hands pulling his T-shirt from those jeans. The slab of abdominal muscles she spied before she jerked her gaze to his almost made her forget why she sought him out. Almost.

She stepped back as he closed the door behind him.

"Alisha? What is it?"

"You said 'us'. You told Papa about the pictures Richard claimed he had, didn't you?"

It had been exactly around that time that she'd been summoned into her father's study and while her father had sat silently in the corner—his disappointment a noxious cloud in the air—Dante had informed her that she wouldn't be going away as apprentice to a world-renowned photographer as planned. Or at least, the exorbitant fee she'd needed to pay wouldn't be coming from her father's bank account.

Vikram, as usual, had been absent, working in his lab, and her father had refused to talk to her that evening, even as she'd pleaded with him to rethink his decision. That was the last time she'd talked to her father.

Dread coursed through her that she was once again locking herself in that bubble with Dante, her mind and body constantly battling it out.

Dante stilled. "What?"

"That's why he…cut me off. Refused to pay the fee for that apprenticeship. You told him and I lost a chance at the one thing I wanted to do most in the world. Being accepted into that program…it was the one thing that got me through so much. Through Mama's death, through being thrust into living with you three strangers…and because of you, I lost the opportunity to learn, to see if I could follow my passion.

"Did you hate me so much, Dante? Yes, I made impulsive, rash decisions, but you know what the worst part of it was? Papa died thinking I was determined to shame him in front of the world."

Tears filled her eyes. She swiped at them angrily. Regrets were useless. The past was done.

His fingers on her arm turned her, his grip a vise. Ali couldn't look up, everything in her cringing that he saw her like this. The last thing she wanted was his pity.

"Alisha, look at me. Alisha!" His growl filled the space between them. "I didn't tell Neel, okay? I just dealt with Richard. Vicky told your father."

She blinked. "What? Why?"

"Vicky loved you and…he was worried for you. He felt guilty for neglecting you for so long, for being preoccupied with his lab. He convinced Neel that separating you from the heiress label would cut off all the hangers-on and leeches. Maybe ground you a little. Give you a chance to see the reality of your friends. I…"

"What, Dante?"

"I tried to persuade Neel not to do that."

"I don't believe you."

He flinched. Just a tremble of that upper lip, but it was there. "I told you, I'm not your enemy. You reminded me of someone I despised for so long. You were spoiled and immature and rebellious, but I didn't hate you.

"I knew photography meant everything to you, how *not*…miserable or angry or rebellious you were when you walked around clicking away on that old camera. I tried to convince Neel that he could pay the fee and still cut you off from the rest of your trust fund. He wouldn't listen. I think he felt you'd pushed him too far that time."

Ali nodded, her chest so tight that it took all her wits to keep breathing. Dante had supported her. Dante had intervened on her behalf. "That's funny, isn't it? All the tantrums I threw for his attention, all the really bad decisions I made because I was so lost…and he punished me for the one thing I didn't do by taking away the most important thing to me. I beat myself up every day that I didn't take the chance to get to know him, that I ruined our relationship. But he didn't even try to get to know me."

"I think you reminded him too much of Shanti. He never got over the fact that she left him."

"That's not my fault. I was a child, and so was Vicky."

Something dawned in those jet-black eyes. He ran a hand over his face, exhaling a long breath. "He was a good man, but not perfect." Suddenly, his head jerked up, his gaze pinning Ali to the spot. "What do you mean he punished you for something you didn't do?"

"I don't know what Richard showed you but I never

posed for any pictures naked. And even if I had, even if I had made bad choices, I didn't deserve to be punished by Papa and Vicky and you for it. You three had each other. Who did I have?"

He jerked back, a whiteness around his mouth.

She'd shocked him—with the truth or with her tears, she had no idea. But for once, it didn't feel good to shock Dante. How could she think anything but hurt and destruction could result from this stupid agreement?

Ali was almost out of his sight when she stilled.

I knew photography meant everything to you.

No, no, no.

He couldn't have, could he?

She didn't want to ask, she didn't want to know. But the question would eat her up.

Dante reached for her, his fingers drawing circles over her wrist. "Alisha, what?"

Just weeks after that scene with her father, mere days after she'd moved out of the mansion once and for all, she'd received the camera. One of the costliest professional cameras on the market—almost forty thousand pounds even five years ago, it had arrived by a special courier.

With no message.

It was not the most expensive thing she'd received in her life, thanks to her father's birthday gifts every year. But it had been the most thoughtful present anyone had bought her, the present that had brought her more joy, more peace than anything else.

She'd simply assumed at the time that it was Vicky's gift. She'd even texted him thanks but had never received anything back. She'd attributed it to her brother's usual neglect of any communications.

"My Nikon XFD45…"

He didn't quite shy away his gaze from her but Dante

released her instantly. "There's nothing to be achieved by raking over the past." He patted the pad of his thumb under her eyes, a quick, feathery stroke, something dark flashing in his eyes. "You're tired. Go to bed."

Ali pushed into his personal space, heart racing. "Dante, who bought that camera for me? Who sent it to me?" And when he opened his mouth to blurt out some nontruth, she covered his mouth with her palm. "Please, Dante, the truth."

He pushed away her hand from his mouth. His nostrils flared, emotion glinting in his eyes.

"I did. I saw how you cried that night. I argued with Neel to no avail. And when I went to your bedroom and found it empty, I knew you weren't coming back. Days later, it wouldn't leave me alone so I ordered the camera."

Words of gratitude hovered on her lips. She'd always viewed him as the enemy, had hated him on principle, but this one gift…it didn't negate all the barbed history they shared. And yet, suddenly, Ali felt like the ground had been stolen from under her.

"Why didn't you—?"

"I felt guilty that evening. Powerless to right what I thought was a needlessly harsh action against you." His mouth took on that forbidding slant she knew well. "Of course, you pushed and pushed and pushed me…yes. But after I realized you were…" It was as if he couldn't put into words what he felt. "Buying that camera for you relieved my guilt. Don't read too much into it, Alisha."

For once, Ali didn't balk at his dismissal. She was more than ready to leave behind the cutting awareness of being near him, of the seesaw of her own emotions.

But as she dried her hair and crawled into bed exhausted, her heart refused to believe the perfectly rational explanation Dante offered.

He'd asked Papa not to take away the photography program from her.

He'd checked on her, even if it had been out of guilt.

He'd bought her that camera, knowing how much it would mean to her.

Maybe he had cared about her a little. Maybe Dante wasn't...

That sent a sharp spike of fear through her rambling mind, had her sitting up in the bed even as her eyes burned for sleep.

This whole idea of a platonic marriage between them, her very sanity, hinged on the fact that Dante was an unfeeling, ambitious man.

If that fell apart, what else was left to protect her heart from the intimacy of the next few years, from her foolish attraction, from her own endlessly naive heart?

CHAPTER SIX

THUD. THUD.

"Alisha?"

Thud. Soft *thud.* Followed by a curse in Italian.

"Alisha, fifteen minutes or I break down this door."

They were tight, softly spoken words, and yet filled with that controlled fury they made Ali jump. She stepped out of the hot shower that she'd been standing under for far too long. She shivered and grabbed two towels—one for her hair, and one for her body. Her cell phone chirped and she glanced at the time and grimaced.

She glanced at the date and grimaced a little more. Any more grimacing and her face was going to be permanently frozen into a…grimace.

Today was the morning of her wedding. To Dante.

She was marrying Dante today.

Or Dante was marrying her?

Ten days of repeating that to herself hadn't made it any easier to face today.

She hurriedly toweled down her body, threw on panties, tugged on denim shorts and a loose T-shirt, just as the knock came again.

Toweling her hair with one hand, she opened the door.

Dante pushed inside.

The towel fell from her hands while her heart thudded against her rib cage. Ali rubbed at her chest and stared at him, a prickle of heat flushing all over her and pooling between her legs.

She groaned and closed her eyes. But nothing could erase the sight of him from her mind. Strikingly handsome didn't do him justice at all.

Black jacket that defined his powerful shoulders; white dress shirt that stretched against his broad chest; black pants that molded to his powerful thighs; jet-black hair slicked back, gleaming with wetness. A smooth shave of that sharp, defined jawline that she wanted to run her tongue along; dark eyes—penetrating and gorgeous, glimmering with interest and intensity.

He was too much.

This was far too much for anyone to bear. If she'd known all her bad decisions and all the pain she'd caused her papa and her brother and Dante could come back to her in this form... Karma was indeed a bitch.

Ten days of being back in London, ten days of seeing Dante every morning, impeccably dressed in a three-piece suit—sometimes he was ready to leave for the day when she was getting ready to crawl into bed after hours spent in the darkroom—had taken a toll on her mental health.

It was too much Dante to stomach on any given day.

Furthermore, he'd been determined to oversee a wardrobe upgrade for her because no, he still didn't trust her not to play some cheap trick to embarrass him. They'd also been forced together while he explained in detail the legalities of transferring her voting shares that he insisted she understand, and because of her ill-thought-out idea of coming to him with some financial questions regarding her mom's charity—the only time she sought him of her own accord. Yes, they had spent far too much time, far too close to each other.

In the blink of an eye, she could now recall a hundred different expressions he wore.

With one breath, she could remember the scent of him.

At the drop of a hat, in the middle of the night or day, whether she was at the Lonely Hearts HQ or in her darkroom, she could conjure the curve of his mouth when he smiled, the laconic glint in his eyes when she was flippant, the way his nostrils flared and his jaw tightened when she annoyed him.

It was as though her mind was happily compiling a database of Dante-related details to draw upon whenever and wherever it wanted.

As a teenager, it had been an inexplicable obsession, a weird love-hate relationship, a mild form of nauseating hero worship. Within a few days of returning to London she'd learned that she knew nothing of the real man beneath the insufferable arrogance and ruthless ambition. It was only after she'd burst the bubble of illusion had she realized the safety there had been in it.

Now she saw a complex and interesting man. She saw that beneath the ruthless ambition, there was integrity and a moral compass that no one could shake. Beneath the rigid discipline and control, there was a man who knew every single employee by name and their family conditions. There was a man who saw more than profit margin, much as he coated it with what he called simple business tactics. This was the man her father had nurtured and loved.

Where had all the animosity she'd nursed and tended to with such care for almost ten years gone? Was she so pathetically deprived for affection that the stupid camera incident had changed the entire dynamic between them?

It was now replaced by an awkwardness filled with anticipation, tension and lot of tongue-tied staring on her behalf. Like now.

She opened her eyes and caught him doing a leisurely perusal of her T-shirt sticking to her still damp body. Her meager breasts looked round and high, her nipples clearly distended with wetness. Jerkily, she tugged the shirt away.

His jaw tightened, that infinitesimal flare of his nostrils freezing her midaction.

He was just as aware of her as she was of him. Was that possible?

His ankles crossed, he was a picture of masculine arrogance and yet there was tension around that mouth, a wave of something radiating from him, filling the air around them.

Awareness pounded into her, stronger and sharper than an IV of caffeine. He did notice her. He wasn't immune to her. He was…attracted to her?

She swayed on her feet and he was instantly there, anchoring her, a warm marble slab to her touch, his heartbeat a thunder under her skin. She snatched her arm away just as he raised his own.

"You're not ready." Gravelly and husky, he sounded unlike himself.

The moment stretched as they stared at each other, the world outside held at bay. Her skin pulsed, her breasts falling up and down as if she were running.

She wanted to reach out again and touch him. She wanted to run her fingers over that defined jawline, press her tongue against the hollow of his throat, unbutton his shirt just a little and slip her fingers inside until she could feel the sparse hair that dotted his chest—she'd snuck a peek when he'd come in from a run one morning. She wanted to check for herself if his heart was thundering like hers was, run her hands down, down, down until she could trace his hard abdomen, down into his trousers until she could see if he was—

The sound of his curse, gritted out with near-violence sent a blast of heat up Ali's chest and cheeks. "I'm ready, okay? Just…" She rubbed a hand over her forehead, lowering her tone to normal. "As ready as I'll ever be for this. So let's get this over with, please."

He pushed a hand through his slicked-back hair, making it flop forward. "What you're wearing is not…appropriate. Only you can make an old T-shirt look like it should come with a red-hot warning."

The words fell from his mouth fast, totally unlike him. By the skin of her teeth, she somehow, somehow, managed to ignore the rough texture of his tone.

"Not this again, please." She pushed her hand through her hair, realizing it was dripping wet. "All we'll do is sign papers in front of two witnesses. The registrar will make us repeat those vows—which I've learned by heart, okay? I'll sign my name, you'll sign yours. *It will be over.* Nothing changes between us. Everything remains the same." It had been her mantra since she'd woken up at five in the morning.

When he stared back at her with infinite patience, she let her anxiety seep into her tone. "Don't make it harder than it has to be, Dante."

"There'll be press waiting outside the registrar's office."

Ali sank back. "What? Who could have leaked it?"

His hands smoothed over his jacket and he almost seemed reluctant to speak. "I invited them."

"Why?"

"Have you seen the headlines since we returned?"

"Yes."

Just as he'd predicted, there was far too much interest in his every move.

The rebel Matta heiress engaged to her father's protégé and confirmed billionaire bachelor Dante Vittori was far too juicy a story. All her previous transgressions had already been dragged into the spotlight again to contrast her record with Dante's pristine reputation.

There was no doubt in anyone's mind that she was the lesser one, the one found wanting in their coupledom.

A half laugh, half bark tore out of her chest as she remembered the headline that had described Dante on an online gossip site that Ali should've known better than to click. Consequently, she'd fallen into the internet hole of Dante's love life over the past ten years.

Models, actresses, there had even been one popular daytime talk show host. When she'd dug herself out of the hole, like everything related to gossip sites on the net, Alisha had felt like a pervy spectator with ringside seats to his love life.

What was worse was that old feeling of inadequacy, the sense of not being good enough, that had plagued her all her adolescent life and driven her to make horrible choices. Really, it was mind-boggling how she could believe she wasn't enough of a woman for a fake marriage to the perfect male specimen that was Dante Vittori.

Fake marriage, people!

"Isn't it bad enough that my reputation precedes me? Bad enough that every stupid online magazine is speculating that you're somehow saving me by marrying me. Old friends are calling me with all kinds of questions."

He frowned. "Why didn't you tell me? Have they been harassing you?"

"Mrs. Puri, our old housekeeper, called the other day and asked me if I was pregnant. And then blessed you in Hindi for two whole minutes for your loyalty and refused to stop giving me tips on how to be a good Indian bride.

"When I pointed out that you were Sicilian, she went off about how Sicilian men, like their Indian counterparts, expect a traditional, biddable wife. She had the gall to tell me that I was lucky to have caught a handsome, loyal man like you despite all my flaws. I wouldn't have been surprised if there'd been smoke coming out of my ears."

Of all the reactions she'd expected from him, it wasn't the hearty laugh that shot out of his mouth. His eyes lit up as if there was a light behind them, and his teeth flashed white in his olive face. Her fingers itched for her camera. She wanted to capture him in that moment forever. Like a hundred other moments. "I adored Mrs. Puri. How is she?"

Ali glared at him even as parts of her down south melted at how gorgeous he looked. How carefree and approachable and affectionate. "She's happy and cozy in Cambridge with the huge pension you settled on her. Why didn't you tell me you did that for all of Mama and Papa's old staff?"

An uncommunicative shrug. "What else did she say?"

He was still smiling and it felt like the sun was peeking through the gloomy October morning.

"I'm glad you think my life is funny. They think you're coming to my rescue. That my life went off the rails again because of something I'd done, and you, for the sake of Papa, are sacrificing your demigod-like virility on the altar of my thoughtless recklessness. I don't want to give them more—"

A feral smile playing around his mouth, he threaded his hand through her hair and tugged her forward. Mouth dry, heart palpitating, Ali went, like a bow flexing in the hands of a master archer. "Sacrificing my demigod-like virility at the altar of your thoughtless recklessness? Only you can come up with such outrageous descriptions."

She licked her lips and his gaze arrested there. "The legion of your female admirers saddened by our engagement give complete credence to my statement."

He traced his knuckles against her cheek, a thoughtful curiosity in his eyes. It was barely a touch and yet all of her being pulsed beneath that patch of skin. Slowly, he released her hair and the progressive loss of his addictive scent and his warmth made her want to weep.

"Just the idea of our engagement did that. There's no way to stop the press from following this story like rabid dogs when it comes out that we've married so quickly. They will hound me, but I'm used to it. They'll make your life hell. This way, we give them what we want. We control the narrative. A quick statement from us and a couple of orchestrated shots means the story doesn't take off in a hundred different ways."

"I don't want to pretend anything."

"It'll just be a photographer and one journalist from a reputed online website. They won't even be allowed inside where we sign the papers. Dress like you mean it. Turn the world on its head. Think of it as armor, Alisha. Dazzle them so much that they don't wonder the why of this anymore. Surprise them with all the changes you've made."

"The changes I've made?"

"Haven't you made changes? I barely see you during the day and you're at that studio most nights. Be smart about the publicity you'll garner over the next few months. Use this opportunity. Use me."

Her gaze drifted to his broad shoulders. "Use you?" she whispered, a veritable cornucopia of forbidden, erotic messages downloading into her brain for using him.

"Si." An unusual smile curved his lips. "Being my wife will automatically give you unwanted attention. People who want to get to me will clamor for your attention first. Invitations for lavish dinners and charity events will flow. Make connections. Use these people to build up the charity. You can either hide over the next few months or you

can use the time to achieve your goals. It all depends on how you choose to look at the situation."

Put like that, it made so much sense to her.

He was right. It was inevitable that his reputation, his high connections would overshadow her life for a long while. So why not make use of it all for a good cause?

A bright energy infused her veins. For the first time in her life, there was someone who understood her, who encouraged her. On an impulse, she threw herself at him. Arms wrapped around his neck, she pressed a hard kiss to his cheek. It lasted only a few seconds, half a minute at the most.

And yet, she couldn't forget the steely cage of his arms around her waist, the rough smoothness of his cheek, or the way everything in her body felt loose and heavy at the same time.

Pulling away, she refused to look at him.

In her wardrobe, she pulled out a cream, knee-length, silk sleeveless dress, one of the classiest creations she'd ever seen.

The dress slithered over her skin with a soft whisper. But she couldn't get the back zipper all the way. Fake it 'til you mean it. That was what she was going to do. With the world and with Dante.

Face frozen into an unaffected smile, she walked back out and presented her back to him. "Zip me up."

An eon seemed to pass before he tugged the zipper up, and another eternity when the pads of his fingers lingered on the nape of her neck. While he watched, she finished putting the final touches on her face. A dab of eyeshadow, the perfect shade of red lipstick and then hands on his arm, she pushed her feet into three-inch stilettos.

"Do I look good enough to be Mrs. Vittori now?"

A fire licked into his eyes. His arm rose toward her

face, slowly, his features tight. But it fell away before it reached her mouth.

She saw the bob of his Adam's apple, the controlled tremor that seemed to shake his powerful body. "Forget all the rubbish the media writes about my affairs, the compare and contrasts, *si*? You're beautiful, and talented, and you could take any one of those women single-handedly."

Any other day, she'd have preened under his praise. But today, it served as a much needed reminder. The research into his love life was a reminder.

He'd never even had a girlfriend for longer than three months.

But for those voting shares, for the sake of the blasted company, he would sign his name next to hers on a piece of paper without even a prenup.

That was like a tiger willingly walking into a cage.

Until she had arrived back in London, until she had heard all the hoopla about his billions, until she had read about his rigid but straightforward tactics when it came to the company, she hadn't appreciated what a big thing that was.

He had billions, an empire he had built piece by piece over the last two decades and he was leaving it open to attack, making it vulnerable by marrying her without the prenup.

Like an eager puppy that returns again and again for affection, Ali couldn't help but think that it was because he trusted her not to come after his fortune.

Maybe just a little bit.

Being the one woman that ruthless Dante Vittori trusted beyond anyone or anything was bound to go to the head of even the most sensible woman between sixteen and sixty, any woman who had a working vagina, any woman who could appreciate having a little glimpse into a powerful and striking man like Dante.

And Ali had never been rational or sensible when it came to Dante.

For a quiet, civil ceremony, there were too many people waiting in the registrar's office. Somehow, Ali had made it without hyperventilating through the ride.

Izzy's gaze sought hers but Ali didn't meet it. There was only so much acting she could do and quiet Izzy would know in a second how this affected her. She and Marco, Dante's head of security, were to be the two witnesses.

Three men stood in the outer office, a lot of paperwork in front of them, and Ali realized they were lawyers. A tall woman and two men stood behind her—the gossip columnist and her team.

"Come," Dante whispered at her ear and Ali followed him inside.

Somehow, she made it through, smiling, shaking the kind registrar's hand. She even laughed vacuously at some thin joke.

And then it was time for the vows.

When the man asked her if she wanted to add anything personal to the preexisting set of vows, Ali wanted to run away. This was wrong. All wrong.

She felt the warmth of Dante's body by her side before he turned her toward him. And slowly, the declaratory words came, more easily than she had thought they would, his gaze holding hers, anchoring her, his broad shoulders her entire world.

"I do solemnly declare that I know not of any lawful impediment why I, Alisha Rajeswari Matta, may not be joined in matrimony to Dante Stefano Vittori."

Steady and clear, she finished her vows.

When Dante spoke, with no inflection or tone, his gaze fixed, each word swept through her with the force of a thunderstorm. Ali trembled all over.

And then he was finishing... "I call upon these persons here present, to witness that I, Dante Stefano Vittori, do take thee, Alisha Rajeswari Matta, to be my lawful wedded wife."

My lawful wedded wife... The words clung to her skin, as if tattooed there.

She took the pen from the waiting registrar and scribbled her name in a flourish.

A second time.

A third time.

By the fifth time, her fingers shook. Sweat beaded on her upper lip. Ali had no idea how she kept it together when, with each scribble of her name, it felt as if she was twining her fate with his.

Okay, yes, she'd never really given much thought to families and weddings in the last few years.

A wedding had always been some future affair, a loving marriage a dream she had put on the back burner while she figured out the hard path she'd chosen for herself. While she figured out how to save her mother's charity. While she made something of herself that would have made her mama and papa, and maybe even Dante proud.

Which was also why it had been so easy to say yes to this blasted arrangement.

But now her breaths rushed in and out, fast and shallow. She focused on them, willing herself to calm down. It didn't help. Her hands trembled. The next few months would be hard enough without lying to herself.

Being Dante's wife—even in name only, even temporarily—meant something to her. Because he was the one man she'd always...what? Admired? Wanted? Lusted over?

What was it that she felt toward him?

Dante went next.

Despite the misgivings in her tummy, she watched mesmerized as he signed his name with a flourish. No shaking fingers for him.

Because this whole thing meant nothing to him.

Except the company, Dante cared about nothing and no one. That had to be her mantra for every waking minute and disturbingly dream-filled nights. She walked as if in a trance as the registrar wished them well and they walked out into the lounge. With people, waiting and watching them.

"Izzy, give me the rings."

Her mouth fell open. "You didn't…"

His big palms landed on her hip, and pulled her up toward him with the slightest pressure. Heat from his hands burned through the silk of her dress, stunning her, stealing her breath. Her hands were trapped between their bodies, on his chest.

His nose was buried in her hair as he whispered, "Stop looking as if you were trapped in a nightmare." A thread of impatience and something else colored his words. He shifted her hair away from her neck. She knew he was using the thick curtain of her hair to hide his words but still she trembled all over. His breath was warm over her bare neck, sending silky ripples down her spine. "Do a better job unless you want to confirm *I'm* sacrificing myself."

He tugged her fingers up and slipped two rings onto her left ring finger, as casually and as intimately as if he were buttoning her shirt.

The camera went click, click, click, in tune to her thundering heart.

The solitaire diamond in its princess setting winked

at her, the accompanying platinum band beautiful in its simplicity. The rings felt like a vow, a bond tying her to him.

Tears filled her eyes and she hurriedly blinked them back.

God forbid that camera had caught those tears. They would say she'd cried and gone down on her knees at his feet out of gratitude or some such.

He opened her palm and dropped another ring there. Fingers shaking, Ali somehow managed to hold the ring in two fingers. He extended his hand to her. For the life of her, she couldn't come up with something casual to say, to shrug off the moment.

She looked down at his hand. Blunt, square-tipped nails on elegantly long fingers. Such a small detail. Such an intimate detail.

The Dante database in her brain pinged. God, she was going mental with this. Holding his fingers, she slipped the ring on.

"Now, if we can get a couple of shots of you two kissing," the beige pantsuit said with a smile, "our readers are desperate for more about you two. It would be icing on the cake."

The rest of the reporter's words drifted away into nothingness as Ali's gaze jerked to Dante's.

Shock pulsed through her. Jet-black eyes held hers, curiously devoid of anything. No mockery, no warning. Just waiting for her to follow his lead.

He had known this was coming, had known what the reporter would ask. He'd probably planned it out in his diary the day he'd proposed this arrangement. And yet, he'd left her in the dark.

If he kissed her, if he even touched her, there was no way to hide her desire for him. To hide this madness he stirred up in her. And the thought of rejection in his eyes, or even worse, pity...

But he didn't give her a chance to protest.

Or to think.

Hands on her hips tugged her forward. Dark, fathomless eyes held hers as he bent his head toward her.

Ali could feel herself falling into those eyes, drowning in their intensity. Swimming in the dark depths. Terrified that she'd betray her own longing, she closed her eyes.

Every other sense magnified a thousand times. The world around them—the reporters, the witnesses, the dingy old walls, everything melted away.

Only Dante remained.

"Put your arms around my neck." He sounded needy, husky, hanging on the edge of desperation. She refused, or couldn't curb, her overactive imagination. Her hands crept around his neck.

He smelled like heat and masculine need and dark desires. His hands patted her back, as if to soothe her continuous tremors, up and down until suddenly they were digging into her hips.

His breath hit her mouth in soft strokes, the knot in her belly winding and whirling upon itself.

And then his lips touched hers in a soft, silken glide. Just there and gone, before she could pull a breath. Ali jerked at the contact, nerve endings flaring into life. She tried to jerk away from his hold.

His curse filled her ears. "Shh...*bella mia.*"

One hand settled at the base of her neck, holding her still and he pressed another of those featherlight kisses.

Tease and torment.

An infinitesimal moment after an eternity of longing.

It wasn't enough. A feral groan rippled up through her body as he pressed another kiss. Ali opened her mouth.

And the careful swipe of his tongue against his own lips became something else.

Acting on an instinct as old as time and space itself, she slid her tongue against his lush lower lip then dug the tips of her teeth into it.

The tenor of the kiss changed from one breath to the next. Rough hands moved from her hips to her buttocks, cupping, kneading, pressing her close. The sound that tore out of his mouth was growly, hungry, and it lit a spark of hunger in her body.

Ali pressed herself into him and trembled all over again.

He was aroused. He was aroused. Dear God, he was aroused.

His erection was a brand against her belly, his hard thighs cradling hers. His hands crept into her hair, pulled at it until her head was tilted at the perfect angle. Until her mouth was open for his assault.

Dante's mouth. On hers.

Feral. Hungry. Ravenous.

Hot. Hard. Wild.

It wasn't how she'd imagined it would feel. It was a million times better.

He plunged his tongue into her mouth, sliding it against hers, licking, nipping, biting. And then he did it all over again. Again and again.

There was no sense of that self-control, the self-possession that he was known for in his kiss. A torrent of Italian fell from his mouth, gliding over her sensitive skin. Her breasts were heavy, her nipples peaking at the constant rub against his chest.

Her hands clutched his biceps when his tongue swooped in, licking, stroking, nipping and repeating the sensual torture all over again. His hands roamed all over her, kneading, stroking, kindling the spark into an unquenchable fire.

He didn't let her gasp for air. His mouth rubbed up over hers again and again.

Until she was trembling like a leaf against him. Until there was wetness against the soft folds of her sex. Until she splayed her leg around his lean hips and sank into him. That contact was like a jolt of electricity. Liquid fire in her veins.

Until a cough and a whistle and a "Hot damn, they're really into each other" punctured the moment.

Dante wrenched his mouth away from hers, his hands on her shoulders firmly setting her back from him. His breath was harsh, his mouth swollen and dark pink.

Ali had no idea what he barked at Izzy and the rest of them. Had no idea what was up, what was down. Had no idea if she was walking or floating.

She went where he took her.

The hard slam of the door woke her up and she looked out at her surroundings. They were back in his chauffeured limo, cut off from the world. He sat opposite her.

Color burned in those high cheekbones. "It shouldn't have gone that far."

The cutting coldness in his tone pushed Ali out of the sensual fog. She licked her lips and tasted him there. And liked it far too much.

She knew how he felt. She even agreed with him. No good could come out of this attraction. This mutual attraction. This red-hot attraction that wasn't all in her head.

Dante wanted her. Her mind was stuck in that loop.

"If you blame me for it, I'll sink my nails into your pretty face." Good, she sounded steady. Like her knees weren't still quaking. "You orchestrated that whole thing there, so don't you dare blame me if it went off your precious script."

Something dawned in his eyes. For the life of her, Ali didn't know what. Even his remoteness now, as if that kiss hadn't made even a dent in his self-control, couldn't douse the feral satisfaction that ran through her.

The dynamic between them shifted and swirled in the luxurious interior of his car.

"One kiss doesn't mean anything, Alisha."

She fell back down to earth with a vicious thud even as she told herself the same thing. "No, it doesn't."

But it meant everything.

The taste of him lingered on her lips, the press of his fingers on her hips a burn.

It meant Dante saw her as a woman.

It meant Dante wanted her desperately.

It meant Dante and his self-control could go on a hike when she was near.

It meant for the first time in her life, the power in their relationship was fluid.

She wasn't foolish enough to pursue this thing, but man, it felt good to have it. She let a sassy smile curve her mouth, determined to come out on top. No matter that she would relive that kiss a million times from here to the end of eternity.

No matter when she went to bed tonight, her wedding night as it turned out, she was going to play that in her head while she got herself off. In the twisted world that they were inhabiting right now, she actually had the right to him, didn't she?

Lawful wedded husband and wife and all that...

"What are you thinking?" he asked, that something flashing in his eyes again. And this time, Ali recognized it for what it was.

Dante's desire for her, despite his self-control.

"That after my X-rated dreams about you for so long,

this time, I have real material to work with tonight. Conveniently, my wedding night," she said, brazening it out.

The curse that fell from his mouth was filthy and long and ricocheted around the leather interior. It was music to her ears.

Ali laughed, the power that rocked through her washing away the sense of inadequacy that had haunted her for so long.

Color bled into his high cheekbones, his eyes filled with dark desire as he held hers. He was imagining what she'd said, he knew that, she knew that.

Ali refused to look away.

"Alisha, if you—"

"What's in my mind is not in your control, Dante. Let it go."

Another short, pithy curse this time. "You really thrive on it, don't you? You have to control everything around you."

He nodded and looked away. "*Si.* It's… I can't undo it now. This is a marriage on paper, Alisha."

Warning reverberated in his words and hit her right in the solar plexus. But nothing could take away the high she was riding. "You said to control the narrative, *si*? So, I've got it. You fell in love with me on one of your visits while trying to pin me down all these years. Desperately. I led you on a merry chase all around the world and finally, I let you catch me.

"That kiss says that perfectly. I want to be the star of this story. I want to be the woman who brought Dante Vittori to his knees in love. And when this is over, I will be the one who walked away. Capisce?"

She stared at him defiantly, daring him to contradict her. Seconds felt like eons. Whatever vulnerability she had felt earlier, whatever emotion had gripped her, lifted as she wrested control of the situation.

She would be the one to walk away, she'd make sure of that. And in the meantime, she was going to have a hell of a lot of fun poking the sexy, gruff bear.

His gaze searched her, as if he was seeing her for the first time. As if she'd morphed into something he didn't understand right in front of his eyes.

And it was a power trip for her.

CHAPTER SEVEN

THE TASTE OF Alisha's mouth—so potently sweet, so addictively warm—clung to Dante's lips even a fortnight later. Through meetings with the Japanese team over negotiating a multibillion-dollar contract supplying steel spread over ten years, through board meetings that he and Ali attended together to present a united front to Nitin and the rest of the board members, through endless evenings when Dante caught her in the sitting room of his flat before she disappeared into the darkroom on the lower floor.

She'd been so dainty, so fragile, trembling like a leaf when he'd clasped his arm around her waist, when he'd pressed his palm into her slender back to pull her closer... but her passion had been voracious, honest, a force of its own.

He'd just meant to touch his lips to hers in a quick press. He'd meant to keep it platonic.

But thinking Alisha would behave when she could wreak mischief on the whole situation, when she could use the moment to challenge him, to pay him back for surprising her with the press, had been his first mistake.

Imagining that the attraction between them would wither away if he continued to ignore it, his second.

Just as Dante had predicted, the media and the world exploded at the shots he'd had his PR team release.

The Kiss, as it was being referred to by the entire world, had taken the media by storm.

Except the kiss hadn't turned out to be the perfectly set up shot he'd planned. No, it was a minute-long clip that had gone viral already on a million websites, as one of the most candidly romantic shots.

Especially because he looked ravenously hungry for her, because in his adult life, he'd never once lost himself in a woman like that. Ali had gotten what she wanted. The whole world believed she'd brought him to his knees.

Dante couldn't even blame the press for sensationalizing the story. The defiant tilt of Ali's chin as she pressed herself to his body brazenly, the hunger and passion in that moment... His lower body tightened every time he watched it—like a teenager watching his first porn video.

One glance at the clip and he had an erection.

Dios mio, it consumed him night and day. It came to him when he saw her lithe body in those skimpy clothes she paraded around in in the flat. It came to him when they were forced into physical intimacy at any public outing they had to attend as a couple.

It came to him when he simply looked at her mouth.

His entire adult life, he'd thrived on control in every aspect of his life and that meant his libido too. The women he'd chosen to take to his bed—he'd never let lust drive those choices. His affairs—even the short-term ones—hadn't involved wanting one woman so badly.

They had been more of a quest for release.

Wanting Alisha of course fell into none of the principles he lived by. If it had been just a physical attraction to her—if it was a matter of an itch needing to be scratched because of their history, because, in his entire life, Alisha was the one woman who never seemed to be cowed by him, who challenged his control, who with delicious defiance came toe-to-toe with him—it would have been different.

If she had continued to tease and torment him, if she had used the knowledge of his desire for her as some kind of weapon—damn it, it almost seemed like he half expected and half wanted her to do it—then it would have been another matter altogether.

No, the equally ferocious depth of her desire for him had been a one-off.

In a strange role reversal, she seemed to be the one conducting herself perfectly, a charming socialite wife, a smart charity hostess in the public eye and a polite, courteous stranger under his roof.

The charity was growing from strength to strength now that she had thrown herself into it. She had used the news of their engagement to raise its profile, make connections. Her photography she still held pretty close to her chest. He was getting more and more curious about it, he'd even told her he wouldn't comment on or mock something that was simply a hobby, but she refused to let him see even a single portrait.

An empty attraction to a woman he didn't quite admire or even like was an easy matter. But the more days that passed by, the more he saw a different side to Alisha.

The way she'd thrown herself into it over the past couple of weeks was eye-opening.

He'd even dropped in one afternoon, with a valid reason in hand—more papers to sign confirming that she was releasing the voting shares to him—at the office space she'd rented. Alisha had been deep in conversation with the new accounts manager she'd hired, looking at a presentation he knew she'd slaved over for the last week about expansion plans she wanted to take up in the next two years with the new infusion of cash—a dream that her mother, Shanti, had put on hold after she'd left Neel.

He'd found himself smiling when he dropped by in the middle of the day sometimes and found her at the piano, playing old Hindi melodies that he'd heard Neel play many years ago. And when she wasn't working on the charity, she escaped into her darkroom. He'd been tempted, more than once, to ask her if she was hiding from him. From them.

But asking her meant acknowledging what they were both trying to deny. It meant asking himself a question he didn't want to probe within himself.

Restlessness plaguing him, he walked to the portrait that hung on the wall in his office. He and Neel had been interviewed for a *Business Week* article and had posed for the picture.

He looked at the man who'd given him the chance to make something of himself. The man who'd taken him at his word, the man who'd seen and nurtured his work ethic and not the dark shadow of his father's crime. Neel had given him a chance at a second life, a better life, a new path.

Alisha was Neel's daughter.

And so Alisha would always be forbidden to Dante, especially for the sort of relationships he had with women.

He had easily bartered for her voting shares because those shares would be used to drive the best interests of the company, but kissing her, touching her, thinking these thoughts of her...

There was a spike in his heartbeat when his phone rang and Alisha's face lit up the screen. He let it go to voice mail.

Two minutes later, a series of pings came through. An almost juvenile thrill went through him at the thought of those waiting texts.

Spending tonight @ MM

He frowned. MM meant Matta Mansion. The house where she'd refused to stay just a few weeks ago.

The next text was a series of emojis with cake and wine bottles and champagne glasses.

FYI Getting drunk. Won't return tonight. Don't freak out. Send Marco tmrw morn. Good night, Dante.

And then a kiss emoji.

He smiled, her irreverence coming through in her texts.

But he didn't know whether it was simply an FYI as she claimed, or a red herring to hide what she was really up to. He hadn't missed the fact that she'd been unusually subdued yesterday night too.

He noticed the missed calls from his mother. She called him only a few times a year.

Hurriedly, he looked at the date. He left the office, even as reams of paperwork awaited him, without second thought.

He couldn't leave her alone, tonight of all nights.

With its white marble facade and once beautifully maintained grounds, Matta Mansion greeted Dante like an old friend. *Dios mio*, he shouldn't have let the house fall into such a state of neglect.

Even though Shanti had already been gone for years with Ali in tow, he knew Neel had kept it in great condition with the hope that she'd come back to him.

Dante had moved out after Vikram had died in that crash and Ali had left London. Neel had treated him as another son, but it hadn't felt right to be there without them.

A lot of good things had happened in his life here. He'd found solid ground to stand upon, belief in himself after his life crashed and burned, all thanks to Neel's generosity.

But Alisha… For the first time since she had walked into the mansion—a thirteen-year-old girl with a haunting ache in her eyes and a defiant distrust of her father, her brother and himself—he saw it from her point of view.

How scared and lost she must have been. How, lost in his own grief, every action Neel had taken regarding her had been neglectful and alienating and sometimes downright cruel.

Neel had never hugged his daughter. He'd never reassured her that he wanted her in his life. And when she'd started acting out, he'd cut communications, he'd had Dante implement his decisions for Alisha.

Dante had been blind to it all.

His wife, Shanti's, death had hit his mentor hard. Dante had never pried into why she'd walked out on Neel with her daughter in tow. He had automatically assumed that it had been somehow Shanti's fault.

God, even then, he'd been a distrusting cynic.

You three had each other. Who did I have?

They were there for me when I was lost and alone.

Those words haunted Dante as he slid his Mercedes through the electronic gates and into the courtyard.

She had no good memories of this place. And yet, she was here tonight.

For once, Dante wanted to be what Alisha needed. He wanted to care for her.

What he felt in his chest didn't feel like some misguided sense of loyalty. The knot of anticipation as he walked in through the foyer and took the stairs up the winding staircase didn't feel like responsibility.

The thrill that coursed through his blood, the swift punch of desire tightening every muscle as he opened the door to her old bedroom and found Alisha on the floor, leaning against her white princess bed, her head bowed, her knees pulled up to her chest, didn't feel like pity for a girl he should have tried to understand better back then.

She'd turned on the lamp on the side table next to her and the soft pink walls created a glow around her leaving the rest dark. A bottle of Scotch and a couple of glasses lay in front of her. In her hand was a framed photograph of her mother, more on the floor.

Of Neel with Dante and Vikram.

Of Neel with her, both of them stiff and unbending.

Of Dante and her, at one of the parties that Neel had insisted on throwing.

She looked so painfully alone that a wave of tenderness swept through him. But even that couldn't arrest the swift rush of desire.

A pale pink spaghetti strap top and shorts, her usual attire, bared her shoulders. In the glow of the lamp, contrasted by the surrounding darkness, her skin, silky and smooth, beckoned his touch. Her hair rippled every time she took a long breath.

Unwilling to disturb her, he looked around the room he hadn't entered in years.

A room of her own, built with a domed ceiling and fairy lights, handcrafted furniture custom ordered for her, couture clothes and jewelry, antiques, priceless Indian pieces acquired at royal auctions, modern, light pieces that Shanti herself had favored—Neel had given Ali everything a princess would expect.

But not what she'd so desperately needed.

Affection. Understanding. Love.

Suddenly, in this room she'd perceived as a cage, Dante saw Ali for who she truly was.

The glimpses of vulnerability beneath the brazen facade, the reason she was slaving to save her mother's charity, the very reason she'd accepted his proposal... Ali lived and breathed emotion as much as he scorned and avoided it.

But even that didn't send him running.

She looked up at him, and her eyes grew wide. The long line of her throat was bare, the pulse jumping rapidly. "What are you doing here?"

"I wanted to see—"

"If I was dragging your good name through mud and dirt, emboldened by my father's Scotch? Throwing a wild party with a lot of naked people gyrating on the floor?"

Once those taunting words would have riled him no end. Now, all he saw was the vulnerability she hid under the affected defiance. He removed his jacket, draped it on the bed and joined her on the floor.

She stared at his feet and then up, her gaze touching every inch of his body. *Cristo*, had she any idea what she was doing to him?

"You remembered to take off your shoes and socks?"

Something mundane. To fill the silence. "Of course. This was my home for years."

"I...want to be alone. Now that you have confirmed that I won't cause any bad PR, you can leave."

He undid his cuffs and rested his hands on his knees. Her eyes followed his every move, her disbelief and something else coloring the silence. "I thought I should join the celebration. How many did we celebrate together?"

"Seven, eight?" Her fingers were tightly furled in her lap. She crisscrossed her legs, giving him a view of her toned thighs. Feeling like a Peeping Tom, he looked away. "I hated each and every one of them, just so you know. That first year, I thought at least for my birthday, he would be mine, just mine. Instead he forced me to share it with you."

"Neel held me up as an ideal, demanded that you treat

me like the demigod I am and so you hated me on principle."

She made a sound that was half snort and half laugh.

He liked that sound. He liked when she was her flippant, brazen self.

The moment made the thick mass of her hair hit his neck and his shoulders. The side of her grazed him and he tightened every muscle in his body to minimize the contact. He tensed against the pleasure barreling through him.

Still, he didn't leave.

"It wasn't all just on principle, Dante. You…you made it—"

He took her hand and squeezed, guilt sitting on his chest like an anvil. He'd been the recipient of a self-indulgent parent's neglect and yet he hadn't seen the same in her plight. "I'm sorry for not seeing how alienated and alone you felt in your own home, thanks to me."

The stillness that came over her was like a seismic shift. Except she didn't explode. He saw the sheen of tears in her eyes and turned away. She wouldn't want him to see her like that.

A strange, unbidden, unwanted sentimentality swirled through him tonight and he didn't want to feed it any more fuel. Seeing Ali in pain, he was sure, would qualify as fuel.

"I… It wasn't all you," she whispered. "You just made an easy target. I despised you because you were so close to him and I took every chance I could to show you. And him."

"Your father was a man with a great vision. But he wasn't perfect. I've been blind to that."

Another stretch of silence.

"I'm sorry I was so horrible to you. That I burned your Armani suit with those Diwali sparklers, and for shredding important contracts."

"What about the terror you unleashed on my girlfriend? Melissa? Melody?"

"Meredith," she corrected with a smirk. "She deserved it. She was horribly snooty." When he looked at her, she turned her face away. "I had the most humongous crush on you, which is really twisted given how much I hated you."

"I'm not sure if I guessed that or not. You were…hard to understand."

Her shoulders shook as she laughed and buried her face in her hands.

"Pour me a glass, *si*?"

Her fingers trembled as she lifted the decanter and poured him a drink. He took the tumbler from her hands before it slipped to the carpet and turned so that he could better see her.

Her skin glowed golden, the thin bridge of her nose flaring. Her mouth…just the sight of her lips sent desire crashing through him. *When had want become need?*

He raised his glass. "Happy birthday, Ali. What are you, eighteen now?"

"I'm twenty-six," she said, bumping him with her shoulder. "You, on the other hand, are what, a hundred and twenty?" When he didn't answer, she clinked her glass against his. "Happy birthday, Dante."

He took a sip of the Scotch.

They stayed like that for he didn't know how long. That current of awareness still pervaded the air, but there was also something else. A comfortable silence. All that shared history finally untangled enough to realize that there was a bond between them.

A new beginning, maybe. A fragile connection.

Something he hadn't known weighed on his chest for so long seemed to lift. She was her papa's legacy even if she desperately denied it. And she'd always been his responsibility, even before he'd made her take his name.

The Scotch was both fiery and smooth as it went down her throat and settled into a warm fire in Ali's veins. It seemed to open up her senses even more, as if the awareness of Dante sitting next to her, his thighs grazing hers slightly, the masculine scent of him—sweat and cologne and him an irresistible combination—wasn't enough.

The last thing she'd expected when she'd texted him was to see him here. All day she'd been in a melancholy mood that she hadn't been able to shake. The charity gala her team was putting together to raise more funds or even the meeting with an agent she desperately wanted to sign— nothing could hold her interest. In the end, she'd called in sick to both, and drifted from place to place all over London, ending up at a quaint coffee shop she used to visit when she'd shared a flat nearby with two girls.

She liked to think of it as her grounding year.

She'd moved away from Matta Mansion, walked away from her father and Vicky and Dante. It had been the hardest thing she'd ever done but also the most liberating.

But even the coffee shop that was like a warm, old friend hadn't been able to chase away the blues.

She was lonely.

She'd been lonely for a long time now, ever since her mother's death. The last few years had been better. She'd surrounded herself with friends who cared about her. She'd filled her days with meaningful charity work wherever she lived, in those lulls between her photography stints, but being back in London was unsettling.

No, it wasn't London.

It wasn't even this house that her father had built for

her mother when they'd been newly married, where painful memories dwelled.

No, this ache in her chest, this constant thrum under her skin, was because of the man next to her. But she couldn't take a step toward him, she couldn't bear it if he rejected her, even if this time she wanted to be with him for all the right reasons. She wanted to be with him as a woman who understood herself and her desires and her own shortcomings.

She liked him. A lot.

She liked her father's protégé who was ten years older than she was and knew all her flaws and vulnerabilities.

She liked the man she'd had a crush on for years.

She liked the man she was married to. If it weren't so tragic, it would be comic.

Her thoughts swirled, her senses stirred. It was exhausting to feel like this all the time. She couldn't—

"Are you going to tell me what brought you here tonight?"

She whirled the glass in her hand, watching light reflect and refract through the golden liquid. "Do you really want to know?"

"Yes, Alisha. When I ask you a question, usually it's because I want to know the answer."

"I don't... I was feeling melancholy. So I took the bus around most of London today, just...reminiscing. I ended up at this coffee shop I used to go to with friends after I left...to live on my own. I ran into my ex there."

He didn't move or even bat an eyelid. But she sensed the stillness that came over him as surely as if a cold frost had blown into the room. "Jai?"

He didn't remember his own girlfriend's name but he remembered Jai? "Yes."

"Ah…you're pining over him." Was there an edge to those words that she could detect beneath the control?

"It was a shock to see him, yes. But out of all the decisions I made then, Jai was… He was a good influence on me. He made me see that just because I didn't do that apprenticeship didn't mean I had to give up photography. When he saw me today, he gave me a quick hug, all open smiles. Talked about his start-up, congratulated me on my news—"

"Your news? Did that agent sign you on? Why didn't you tell me?"

Putting her glass away, Ali stood up, scooted onto the bed and leaned against the headboard. Dante stood up in a lithe move, a tic in his tight jaw as he looked at her.

"What? I'm getting a crick in my neck turning to see your face and my bottom is falling asleep on the floor." She patted the place next to her on the bed and smiled, faking a brazenness she didn't feel. "I won't bite, Dante."

He said nothing. Just stared at her for a few more seconds, then sat down near her feet.

"I haven't heard from the agent. I actually haven't sent him my portfolio yet."

"Why not? You've been in your darkroom for hours and hours this week." He took her hand in his. "You are scared of being rejected."

She shrugged. Yes, she was. "No one's ever seen my work."

"And you'll never know where you stand unless you send it." He looked at her hand in his, his voice husky, his head bent down. Her fingers itched to sink into his hair. "What was Jai congratulating you about then?"

"Our wedding. He was congratulating me on…" She compulsively turned the ring on her finger. "This." Jai had been genuinely happy for her, that she'd finally achieved her heart's desire, he'd said.

When she'd looked at him blankly, he had smiled understandingly.

You think I didn't know? I liked you, Ali, really. But even for the few months we were together you had too much baggage. Too much... You were fixated on him. On Dante. He was all you talked about. His personal life, his relationship with your father, his relationship with you. It was clear that Dante would always be the primary man in your life. You were half in love with him, as much as you continuously claimed that you hated him.

She'd always wondered why Jai had ended their relationship. But she'd moved on easily. She'd wanted to travel, she'd wanted to focus on photography. Today, his answer had shaken her.

She'd been fixated on Dante back then, yes, but that wasn't love. What the hell did she know about love anyway?

For the rest of the day, Jai's words had haunted her. Now she saw it.

The melancholy that had gripped her, it was an ache to be with Dante.

To spend time with him in comfortable silence like now, or trading snappy comebacks, to discuss stoicism and pop culture—three guesses who was into which—to laugh with him, to understand what drove that razor-sharp mind and fueled that ambition, to touch him, to have the freedom to run her hand over his cheek whenever she wanted, to sink her fingers into his thick hair, to press her mouth to his in a quick kiss every time he got that brooding look in his eyes...

To be just a woman with him. A woman he liked and respected and wanted. Their lives were intricately twined now, for the first time seeing each other clearly and her feelings consumed her.

She pressed the heels of her palms to her eyes. "You were right. I... I think I'll move back here. There's just more room here and once the novelty of our announcement dies down, it's not like the media can see if we're spending our nights together in one room. I mean, in the same house. We both work insane hours anyway."

In the dim light of the lamp, his scowl was downright ferocious. "What?"

"As big as your flat is, it's...like living in each other's pockets. This way, we'll have more freedom, more...space."

"More space to do what, precisely? See your ex again? Should we expect him to come knocking on the door any moment now? Is that why you wanted me to leave?"

She jumped off the bed, fury burning away that achy longing. "That's unfair. The last thing I'd do is have a secret affair while the whole world is crowing about our wedding as the most romantic thing in the decade. Not that you deserve my...fidelity. I just can't do this anymore."

She turned to leave the room, to leave his unfair comments to himself, but he grabbed her arm.

Ali ended up against him, his legs straddling her hips, her hands on his chest. He rubbed her back gently, his breath feathering over her forehead. The scent of him made her skin tight. The incredible warmth of his body made hers hum.

She wanted to stay like that the entire night. An entire lifetime.

His hands were gentle as he clasped her cheek, a slumbering warmth in his eyes. "If it's the agent, I'll make some calls. If it's the charity that worries you, don't. And if it's the media scrutiny that's bothering you, it will die down soon.

"You're...you're so much his daughter, Alisha. Driven

and grounded. I was wrong to think you were a spoiled princess. Whatever the problem is, I'll fix it. I owe it to Neel to do right by you."

Just like that, he tramped all over Ali's budding feelings. She didn't want his loyalty or his sympathy because she was her father's daughter. She wanted him to see her. Alisha. "It's you." The words tumbled out of her mouth. "You make this all strange and wrong and hard. I feel like I signed away more than those blasted voting shares."

Shock filled his eyes. Slowly he pulled his hand away. "I would never harm you, Ali."

She nodded. He didn't get it. He would never get it. Ambition and goals and reputations, those things he understood. Matters of the heart were a different matter.

She was terrified that slowly, irrevocably Dante was stealing hers. And if she didn't stop it, if she didn't steel herself against him, if she was foolish enough to offer it to him, he would crush it into a thousand pieces.

Still, she asked. "Are you happy to pretend that kiss didn't change anything between us?"

After a long time, he blinked slowly, tension pulling at his mouth. "Yes."

She fisted her hands. "I don't have your self-control, nor do I want to suppress every little thing I feel when I genuinely like you. I can't live with you and pretend as if I don't want to do this."

"Do what?"

"This."

She pressed her mouth to his, every breath in her bracing for him to push her away. His lips were soft and firm. Scooting closer on her knees, hands on his shoulders, she tasted the skin just under his ear, felt the shudder that moved through his hard body.

He tasted like heat, like heaven, like homecoming.

When he gripped her hands to push her away, she trailed her tongue up to his jaw, alternating with nips and bites until she reached the sexy hollow of his throat. She pressed her tongue against that hollow, feeling his pulse inside her. Feeling the power of his body inside her. "Tell me the truth just once. Tell me you don't want me and I'll do whatever you ask. I'll never talk about this again."

Without waiting for an answer, she nipped his skin, hard, long, with her teeth. He growled, a drawn-out erotic sound. The tips of her breasts grazed his chest and she let his hard body take even more of her weight. Tipsy, drunk, delirious, she felt a buzz at his harsh breaths. She pushed her hand down his broad chest, over the hard ridge of his abdomen to his belt and below. His breath was like the bellows of a forge in her ears.

Her hand found the waistband of his trousers and then the zipper. Belly clenching, she traced the hard ridge pressing up beneath the fabric. Up and down, just with one finger, until he grew harder and longer beneath her touch. Nerves tight, she covered him with her palm. His shaft twitched against her hand, making her mouth dry.

God, an incredibly unbearable erotic rush filled her very veins. He was that hard for her. She could have died and gone to heaven, just for that.

He gripped her wrist like a tight manacle, stilling her. But he didn't push her away. And Ali pushed her advantage.

Sinking her fingers into his hair, straddling his hard thighs, she pressed shamelessly closer. Their mingled groans rent the air as his hardness pressed against her sex at just the right spot.

Rough hands tugged her by her hair and then he was kissing her with a ferocious hunger that matched her own. Teeth banged as he plunged his tongue inside her mouth and dueled with hers. His tongue thrust and withdrew from her mouth, making her sex clench. Whorls of sensation built in her lower belly. The kiss whipped her senses into a frenzy.

Mouth open, he left damp patches on her throat. His lips soothed while his teeth bit, and soon Ali was sobbing for more. She pulled his hands from her hips to her breasts, the tips aching for his touch. "Please, Dante...more."

She didn't care that she was begging. That she was raw and vulnerable and all the things she'd promised herself she wouldn't be with him. But whatever madness had her in its grip seemed to hold him too.

Still holding her gaze, he brought his mouth down to her neck, to the upper curve of her breasts. "Pull your T-shirt up."

Fingers trembling, Ali did it. He traced the seam of the white lace with his tongue, a dark fire in his eyes. Transfixed, Ali watched as his rough mouth found the peak jutting up lewdly against the thin silk fabric.

His fingers were so unbearably gentle when he pulled the lace cup down. Her breast popped out, jutted up by the tight wire of her bra, the peak tight and begging for his attention.

Breath hung in her throat as he closed those sinuous lips around it. She jerked her hips against his when he pressed his tongue against her nipple and grazed his teeth over its surface.

She moaned, and twisted her hips in mindless abandon when he sucked her nipple and the curve of her breast into his mouth. The pulls of his mouth, the thrust of his hips, the press of him against her core...sensation upon sensation built in her lower belly. She was moaning, she was panting. He used his teeth against the plump tip and Ali felt like she was lifting out of her body.

She thrust against him, shameless in her pursuit for release, her thighs in a death grip around his hips, her fingers holding his mouth to her chest, her heart beating like a fluttering bird against its cage.

Relentless waves of pleasure beat down over her, drenching her sex in wetness. Her throat felt hoarse from all the screaming. She hid her face in his shoulder, a strange joy fluttering through her veins.

A torrent of curses ripped from Dante, puncturing the deafening silence around them with a contained violence. He dislodged her onto the bed.

He ran a hand through his hair, standing against the door, his chest heaving, a sheen of perspiration on his forehead. His hair was sticking out at all angles because she'd pulled and tugged at it to her heart's content while he'd made her body sing.

"*Cristo*, this is your childhood bedroom, in his house!"

The aftershocks of her orgasm unfurled through her pelvis even as tears filled her eyes.

No, damn it, she wasn't going to cry. She'd wanted what had happened, she wanted a lot more. But neither was she going to enter into a cycle of self-pity. She wasn't going to beg him to give this thing between them a chance.

She'd shown him, told him what she wanted. Now, it was up to him. She had far too much self-respect to beg a man to act on what he clearly felt for her.

Ali pulled herself up on the bed.

His head jerked up at that moment, the shadow of his hunger for her still in his eyes.

Dark color slashed his razor-sharp cheekbones as that hot gaze drifted down to her breasts. Her nipples were swollen and tight from his fingers, from his mouth. His evening shadow had left a mark on the upper slopes.

Chin tilted, Ali faced him. Her insides were a gooey, painful knot, while her hands shook. Holding his gaze, she hooked her bra together and pulled the straps into place, adjusting the cups at the front. It was a push-up bra, designed to create cleavage.

And still, he stared. She looked around for her T-shirt and pulled it on. Then she raked her hands through her hair, hair he'd tangled by pulling it while he plundered her mouth.

There wasn't a part of her body on which he hadn't left an impression. Just the memory of his erection rocking into her was enough to send a sweet ache between her legs.

"Ali—"

"It happened. I'm not sorry it did. With all the pheromones running wild in my system right now, I think it's impossible to regret that." She held his gaze, for the first time since she'd seen him as a thirteen-year-old, hiding nothing from him. "It was the most amazing experience of my life with a man I like, I respect and I want. Don't cheapen it, don't tell me why it's wrong. Don't take this away from me."

He walked toward her with each of her words. Ali flinched when he clasped her cheek reverently, when he rubbed his thumb over her lower lip. "Do you know, that's the first time in a long while that I've forgotten what I stand for? Seeing you come apart like that..." Naked desire filled his eyes. "I've never lost my mind like that. I've never wanted a woman so much that it's messing with my work, never. The passion in your kiss, the honest desire in your eyes, the sounds you make when you climax...they will haunt me for the rest of my life. For all my fortune, you're the one thing I can't afford."

Ali braced herself, like a leaf in a cool autumn wind. Whatever emotion she'd spied in his eyes drained away, leaving that cool, unflappable mask. "You and me, this can't go anywhere. I don't do relationships and doing this

with you, when I know I can't give you anything else…
that will just make me the kind of man I spent my whole
life trying not to be."

"What kind of a man would that be? A man who feels
emotion, a man who clearly cares for those around him, a
man capable of far more than he lets himself give?" Ali demanded. Her own strength surprised her. But then, Dante
had always been capable of pushing her.

His eyes flared, something almost like fear in them.
God, she was being delusional. What could a man like
Dante fear?

"I deserve at least an explanation after that orgasm you
gave me."

This time it wasn't fear, but self-disgust. "If I take you
tonight, just because I want you, because you want me,
knowing that all I can give you is a cheap, torrid affair
under the guise of this marriage, it's a betrayal of all the
trust your dad gave me."

"Papa has nothing to do with this."

"Neel will always have everything to do with me and
you, Ali," he shouted the words at her. Self-disgust painted
his features harsh. "If I screw you against the wall, here
in his house, it makes me the same selfish bastard as my
father was."

"Jesus, Dante, your father fleeced thousands of euros
from innocents. How can you say you're the same?"

"I'll be the same because you're innocent and I'll have
given in to my basest desires. And all I'll do is take what
you give and then discard you when I tire of you. What I
want from you—the only thing I want from you—are those
voting shares. And you've already given them to me."

The cruel finality of his words pierced Ali like nothing
else she'd ever experienced. How could it hurt so much
when it was what she'd expected?

When she didn't really know what she wanted from him?

It felt like giving up but she nodded anyway. Survival instinct took over.

She stiffened when he took her hands in his and pulled her into his arms. The tenderness of his embrace stole her breath. Earlier, it had been the way he'd played her body, made her mindless, and now this side of him...

Who knew there was so much depth to the hard man he showed the world? Who knew that even his rejection would only make her like him even more?

She felt his mouth at her temple, the long breath he drew in her hair, the slight vibrations that seemed to shake his shoulders. Her arms went around his waist loosely, for he was the safest place she'd found in a long time. "I understand why you want to leave the flat. But for now, for tonight, will you please come home with me, Alisha? I can't... It would eat me up to leave you here. Do this for me. *Por favor, bella mia.*"

Ali laughed into his neck, even as her tears seeped out and soaked into his skin. Raw vulnerability cloaked her and still, it seemed what had happened, what he said couldn't happen, couldn't puncture the bond that had formed between them.

"What?"

Tilting her head back, she looked at him. Stared into his eyes. Her chest ached at the concern she saw in them. How had she ever thought him uncaring? "I didn't think you knew that word."

He smiled back at her, lines at his eyes, teeth flashing. "I know it." His gaze swept over her face, as if he couldn't help himself. "I just didn't think there would come a day when I would say it to you."

Still smiling, Alisha withdrew from his hold. Shying her gaze away, she packed up her things into her tote bag. "Just for that, I'll make sure you say it again and again to me. In fact, I'll make sure, somehow, I make you beg, Dante."

She walked out of her teenage bedroom without looking back, feeling as if she'd grown a thousand years in just one evening, wishing Vikram was here to hug her, wishing Papa was here to hold her in her confusion, wishing she weren't falling for Dante.

Wishing, once again, in the very same house like she'd done all those years ago, that she could change Dante's mind, that she was enough, wishing he cared about her more than he did.

CHAPTER EIGHT

IT SEEMED TO Dante that the universe or some karmic superpower was conspiring against him.

What he'd done with Ali, to Ali, in her bedroom, of all places... The memory of her flushed face, the image of her lush breasts in his hand, the sensation of those brown tips so hard on his tongue, the wildness of her body as she rocked into him and found her pleasure... *Dios mio*, it haunted him in the fortnight he'd spent in Tokyo on business.

Even in his dreams, Ali was there, taunting him, teasing him, the trusting smile on her lips, the raw desire in those eyes just as arousing as the invitation of her naked limbs.

Until he'd driven her to his flat that night, and bid her good-night at her bedroom door, he'd been terrified that she would refuse him. That he had crossed a line he never should have, that she wouldn't forgive him for his seesawing behavior.

No trip had ever felt so long. Because he'd never had anything to come home to before.

When he'd returned late at midnight, she'd already been in her bedroom. Somehow, he'd buried the urge to knock, to check that she was really in there. Even though his security team had assured him that she was.

This morning, he had another important meeting with the shareholders. He canceled it.

There was a ruckus involving the Japanese firm and some

miscommunication about production schedule and delivery dates between his team and their team. A ten-billion-dollar contract and thousands of new jobs hinged on the deal he had negotiated.

Instead of the usual urgency to smooth out the knots, all he felt was a strange tiredness for his job. *Cristo*, he'd been working nonstop for almost twenty years and this morning he wanted to damn it all to hell.

It had taken Izzy a few tries—at the end of which she'd remarked on his distracted mood—to tell him that all of his management team was sitting on tenterhooks, waiting for his wrath for such a major communications blunder. They were right, he didn't tolerate sloppiness or inefficiency in himself, or his teams. They went through rigorous training and usually his employee base, especially the upper management team, were people who'd been with him for years. And if a mistake of this proportion had been made, the person responsible would have informed him of it immediately and taken corrective steps.

In the end, Dante had figured it out.

It was all Nitin's doing. His petty little revenge was causing havoc. He had been attending meetings he hadn't been invited to behind Dante's back, promising to take the lead on communications and then dropping the ball, leaving some unsuspecting newcomer to take the fire all the while their Japanese client waited for an important communication. It was exactly the kind of games that had made Neel distrust his brother wholly, that had made him try to keep Nitin's corporate decision-making ability severely limited.

That Dante had unequivocally taken a controlling stake in Matta Steel after acquiring Ali's voting shares was a bitter pill for Nitin to swallow.

It had taken Dante longer than it would normally have taken him to figure it out, and to come up with a strategy for how to react appropriately. That morning he'd skipped his usual run, poured himself coffee—coffee he'd automatically made to Ali's liking—and sat at the breakfast bar waiting for her to show up.

Izzy's shock had been palpable on the video call when he'd informed her he intended to work from home that day. Especially with the situation being what it was at work.

But for the first time in his life, he couldn't focus on work. He couldn't think of anything other than facing Ali this morning. Of how to make her stay. He didn't want her at the big, empty mansion with all the sad memories dragging her down. He wouldn't have a moment's rest thinking of her there alone. The loneliness in her eyes—it was the same thing he'd spied in his own eyes before he'd come to live with Neel. But where he had channeled all the powerlessness and the rage he'd felt back then into ambition, into freezing his emotions, Ali was the opposite.

She lived bravely. Everywhere she went, she spread her love and generosity around.

The protectiveness he felt toward her was so new and so intense that he felt a restless urgency in his veins. The idea of her leaving this flat, of leaving London while he'd been gone had consumed him.

The sound of her bedroom door opening jerked his head up. Instead of the shorts and sleeveless T-shirts he'd come to expect from her, she was dressed formally in a fitted dress shirt that hugged her high breasts, a lovely contrast against her brown skin, and black trousers that showcased her long legs. Pink stilettos added a pop of color—that signature Alisha layer to her serious outfit. Her hair fell like a silky curtain to the middle of her back, light gold tints in it catching the weak sun filtering through the high bay window.

Those strands had felt like pure raw silk in his hands that night and he had to fist his hands to fight that urge now.

He watched silently as she placed her jacket and a portfolio bag on the sofa in the living room. There wasn't even a token protest in his mind that he was obsessed with her. Then she checked her cell phone and slid it back into her bag.

She pulled out her left hand and stared at her fingers. She fiddled with the two rings, the princess-cut diamond glittering at him even across the distance. Every muscle in his body knotted as he forced himself to stay quiet.

She pressed a hand to her nape, giving him the lovely lines of her profile. With a soft sigh, she took both the rings off her finger, stared at them a little longer and then slipped them into her handbag.

A roar of denial built through him. He wanted to demand she put those rings back on, he wanted to sink his fingers into her hair and hold her for his kiss, he wanted to throw her over his shoulder and claim his right over her mind, body and soul...

The force of those urges left him stunned.

In just a matter of seconds, he saw his whole life—the life he'd methodically created for himself, the future he'd always envisioned—fall apart like a stack of cards.

He wanted Alisha with a depth of desire he couldn't understand.

He wanted his rings on her finger.

He was already obsessed with the way she leveled those beautiful eyes at him—sometimes in fury, sometimes with laughter, sometimes with such naked, honest desire that it felled him at the knees.

He didn't want her running away again from the charity, from London.

He didn't want her alone in some corner of the world.

He didn't want her running away from him.

And the only way he could have her, was if she was truly his wife.

* * *

Ali walked into the kitchen and stilled at the sight of Dante sitting at the gleaming quartz breakfast bar. Usually he left for work at the alarmingly inhumane hour of six thirty having finished his run, his breakfast and his shower.

She devoured him openly, like soil deprived of water, unable to tear her gaze away since he'd been gone for a fortnight. Dark shadows hung under his slate-gray eyes. He'd obviously showered because his hair gleamed with raven-black wetness but strangely, he hadn't shaved yet. She knew he shaved twice a day and judging by the thick bristle covering his jaw, he'd missed more than once.

His lovely mouth was hidden and yet Ali liked him like this. He looked gruff and approachable and sexy. She could go on a discovery path, trailing her mouth over that bristle looking for the mouth that kissed so well. That tasted like heaven and heat.

His pale gray shirt was untucked and a couple of buttons were undone. When he stood up, she saw that he was wearing dark jeans and the denim molded enticingly to his hard thighs. Her mouth dried, and every promise she'd made to herself that she wouldn't moon over him like a lovesick teenager died an instant death.

"*Buongiorno*, Alisha."

Deep and husky, the sound of his voice was so good to hear. She'd desperately missed it and him. But seeing him when she couldn't touch him was just as bad an ache.

"I don't think I've ever seen you without a close shave," she said, her voice barely rising above a whisper. "Although the lumbersexual look works too."

Only when his brows raised and his eyes came alive with a fiery glint did she realize what she said. Heat filled her cheeks. "You surprised me. Izzy said you wouldn't be back until Sunday."

"I cut the trip short. I tried not to wake you last night."

"I heard you though, so—"

"So it's not really a surprise to see me this morning then, is it?" He had her there. "You look tired. Lovely but tired."

"I haven't been sleeping well. Been working a lot. How was Tokyo?"

"Same old stuff. Lots of meetings from dawn to dusk, then dinner, then more work. And few hours later, this morning, the same old fires again."

She'd never heard him sound so…dismissive of work before. Never seen him looking anything but perfectly put together in his Armani three-piece suits. Almost as if the power was a cloak he wore to hide the complex man beneath.

She frowned, even as she greedily swept her gaze over the way the tight denim clung to his thighs. She knew the power in those thighs, remembered how they'd clenched rock hard when she dug her nails in. "You're wearing jeans. And you didn't shave. It's nine thirty and you're still here. Your laptop is not even open." She rattled off one thing after the other, trying to arrest the pure longing coursing through her. "I know because I checked the time before I came out. I've been awake since five thirty and I took extra long in the shower because I know you don't leave until six thirty and I made sure that…"

"Made sure that you didn't come out until I left?"

His gaze held hers and all the air left her lungs. She licked her lips and a fierce fire awakened in his eyes. The memory of what had happened between them that night charged the air. Her breasts ached for his hands, and wetness pooled between her thighs.

"Yes. I have a big day."

His elegantly long fingers stilled in the process of pouring coffee from the French press in his hands. The slosh of the liquid made him look down. He shook his fingers and pushed them under the tap. Ali didn't move even as she wanted to go to him. She would beg again, and she'd promised herself she wouldn't.

"There's burn cream under the sink," she offered.

He turned the tap off and looked sideways at her, his mouth twitching. "Are you not going to move from that spot?"

"I have to leave."

"Without your coffee first?" The teasing tone of his words, the way he was looking at her, Ali was terrified and ready to run. This was pure torment on so many levels.

"Where are you off to?"

She checked the platinum wristwatch—her mother's old watch that he'd found in her father's things and had had fixed for her. So many small things he had done for her. The camera, the studio, this watch…and yet he denied her with his words. "I'm meeting with that agent this afternoon."

He smiled and it lit up the entire room. "Good. That's good. Give me fifteen minutes to deal with something and I'll drive you."

Alarm bells went off in her head. And her body. The last thing she needed was continued exposure to him. He was her kryptonite, he always would be. And wasn't that just pathetic?

"Why?"

"For moral support."

She glared at him. "Because you think my work is so bad that he'll automatically reject me?"

He raised his hands, palms up in an "I surrender" gesture. "Are you always going to twist my words and fight me for the rest of our lives?"

The rest of their lives…it was like a punch to her midriff. There was no rest of their lives, not if she wanted to be sane. Once she saw this agent, she would know what to focus on next. Her career at least would always provide an escape from London. And from him.

"You think you're not good enough—for your papa, for the charity, for the agent. For the world. Not me. You made that decision all by yourself."

"That's not true," she offered as a token protest, the depth of his perception stealing her breath.

He was right. Despite her mama's best efforts, she'd always wondered why her papa had given her up. Why Vikram had simply abandoned her.

Why her papa had never loved her like he did Vicky and Dante.

Why, why, why, why had she so easily assumed it was she that lacked something?

Not good enough for Dante either.

That was what she had thought that night at the mansion.

Why assume that Dante didn't want to be with her because she was not good enough?

Was that why she was ready to run away again instead of standing and fighting for the most real relationship she'd ever had in her life?

The questions came at her like missiles while he simply watched.

"Why do you want to come with me?" she said, going on the defensive. It was her one remaining coping mechanism. "When just a few weeks ago, you called it my fun hobby?"

"*Mia dispiace*, Ali. I was wrong about you on a lot of levels. I've seen you slog in the darkroom for hours on end. And I'm assuming at least some of it wasn't just to avoid me. *Si?*"

"*Si.* I've been working on this collection for a long time now and it's finally coming together. I develop my own prints and it's time-consuming."

Tenderness she'd never thought him capable of shone in his face. "Will you forgive me for mocking your passion? For—?"

"For being an arrogant jackass for as long as I've known you?" she added with a smile of her own.

His chin hit his chest in a mockery of remorse, his palm went to his breastbone and he glanced up at her through those long lashes that should have made him look feminine and instead made him stunningly gorgeous. She laughed out loud.

Who knew the man could be just as dramatic as her?

"*Si*, I forgive you. I… We were both wrong on many things. I didn't realize how many things we even have in common."

Like their ambition to prove themselves to the world, their loyalty and their love for her father and…

"Yeah? Like what?"

She blinked at the sudden intensity of his question. "Like our love of cheese. I mean, come on, that's a solid basis for a lifelong relationship." Her words drifted away onto a whisper as she realized what she was saying.

He didn't want a relationship with her.

Only her voting shares—no one could blame Dante for mind games at least. "It's not necessary. I've been doing things alone for a long time."

"I don't want that to be the case anymore. I want to come with you because I remember how nervous I was the first time Neel asked me to handle a client all on my own. I was—" he scrunched his brow and she wanted to kiss the line he got between his eyebrows when he did that "—twenty-three, twenty-four…and I was so determined to make a good impression that I almost sent out contracts with the wrong dates on them. I'd like to be there for you, Alisha."

"Because you owe it to Papa?" She folded her hands, hurt splintering through her. "This sympathy thing is getting old fast."

She got out nothing else for he covered the distance between them. The scent of him had her swaying toward him. She wanted to bury her face in his neck, she wanted to breathe him in until he was the only one in her world. "No. I'm not doing this for Neel. Or for the company. Or any*one* or any*thing*. I want to do it for you."

"Don't you have to work?" she said, his words weaving magic into her soul.

"I thought I'd take the day off. After your meeting, we can go out for lunch."

"Lunch? Dante, I told you, I don't want to—"

He bent and kissed her cheek and every molecule in Ali's body stilled. The contact was soft, tender, his beard a rough rasp in contrast. Her knees shook beneath her and she had no choice but to anchor her hands over his shoulders.

She felt the tremble that went through him as he wrapped his fingers around the nape of her neck. "I promise you, *bella mia*. Tonight we'll talk and if you still want to leave the flat, we'll discuss our options. But you can't just leave London." The emotion in his eyes was a hot burn against her skin, stealing away her protest. "I would never hurt you, Ali, you know that, *si*?"

Ali hid her face in his chest and nodded. Even knowing that, it wasn't in his hands. For all his good intentions, he would hurt her. Because he was becoming more and more important to her, no, *essential* to her and she had no way to stop that.

She was just about to pull away from him when the front door to the penthouse opened. They turned like that together, surprised, since security hadn't even called to announce the arrival of any visitors.

An older woman and a younger woman—the former clearly Dante's mother from the strong resemblance between them—walked in. The security guard placed a collection of designer luggage discreetly behind them and left with a nod at Dante.

Both women stared at the way she was half leaning into Dante, her body pressed into his side with his fingers around the nape of her neck. As if walking in on a married couple in an intimate embrace was a shocking sight.

For all they knew, she and Dante could have been having sex on the living room sofa or at the breakfast bar, or standing up against the back wall, or...

Coloring at how quickly her thoughts had gone in that direction, Ali tried to move away from Dante but his arm held her rigidly, his fingers digging into her hips. He relented a little when she gasped, but his arm stayed around her waist, pressing their sides together. He seemed oblivious to her discomfort as he stared at the woman standing behind his mother.

"*Buongiorno*, Dante," the striking beauty said, tilting her chin up in a silent challenge. A torrent of rapid-fire Italian fell from her mouth.

There was a thread of something, a possessiveness, an intimacy, that brought Ali's spine straight. She glanced between the woman who had to be Dante's age and Dante, who still looked at her as if he was seeing a ghost.

The woman had exquisite features, was dressed in the height of haute couture in a beige-colored pantsuit that clung to her voluptuous curves and looked as if she had just walked off the pages of a fashion magazine instead of a long flight.

A surge of something unpleasant rose in Ali's chest. Without thought, she covered Dante's fingers with her own. To pull him back to the present, she told herself.

The words rang hollow, even inside her own head. Good Lord, the last thing she was going to do was fight over him when he'd been clear about what he didn't want from her.

And it didn't look like he was even going to introduce her to his guests. Neither of the women so much as looked in her direction.

She went on her toes and said, "I'm going to leave while you…deal with them. Enjoy your day off." And since her mama had taught her manners, she smiled at the two women. "I'll see you later."

His fingers fanned around over her hip as he pulled her even closer. The press of his chest against hers made her breathless. "I told you I'd drive you to the meeting." He bent and rubbed his nose against hers. "Don't run away, Alisha."

Her heart beat double time, a whisper of hope and joy threading through her.

The other woman spoke again, in Italian, something to the effect of she'd been looking forward to seeing Dante or spending time with Dante. Ali frowned. "Are you doing this for…her sake?"

He scowled. "What?"

"Did you take the day off for them?"

"I had no idea my mother was on a flight to London." When that melodious voice piped up again, he cut her short with one look. "Ali doesn't understand Italian. Please speak in English, Francesca."

Francesca's smile dimmed at the edges as she nodded at Ali, as if she were the bloody queen of England granting a peasant a great honor. "Hello, Alisha."

"Hi, Francesca."

"Aren't you going to welcome us, Dante?" Sylvia Ferramo asked.

Ali knew very little about his mother, even for all the sensational coverage of his father's crime all those years ago.

Sylvia looked no older than forty-five at the most. There was a delicacy to her expression, a fragility to the bones of her face as if she would break at the lightest whiff of air.

Finally, Dante addressed his mother. "Since you decided to take the trip *without* informing me, Mama," he stressed and the woman colored, and the tight grip on Ali's heart released, "I'm sure you do not require me to invite you in. You can breakfast with us and shower if you'd like. I'll ask my assistant to book you a suite at Four Seasons."

"No," Sylvia said, walking in and reaching for his hands. "I'm seeing my son after a long time, *si*?" One arm still around Ali's waist, Dante bent only after she tugged at him so that she could kiss his cheeks. He offered no embrace and even worse, he radiated a brooding tension that clearly discouraged her from coming closer. "Francesca and I will not mind sharing a room here. Our visit is short and I, especially, want to see more of you than I would at some luxury hotel."

He still said nothing. Ali had never seen him so shocked, or so intentionally rude. Hoping to cover up the protracted silence, she offered her hand to Sylvia. "Hello, Mrs. Ferramo. Please, stay for as long as you like. I'm gone for most of the day anyway and in fact, if it gets too tight here, I can just bunk out on the sofa in my studio on the forty-eighth floor."

"You're not going anywhere," Dante commanded, just as Sylvia shook her hand.

Though there was no warmth in her eyes, her smile was polite and open. She examined Ali as if she were a foreign insect. As if she could weigh just from one look whether Ali was good enough for her son. "I was quite surprised to read about your wedding in the news. I have no idea why my son chose to hide his bride from me. Or why it all happened so quickly."

This time, there was no mistaking the implied innuendo in her words. "Mama, if you want to spend time with my wife and me, without being invited in the first place, then you will at least be civil. You'll keep your numerous innuendos and suggestions and caustic remarks to yourself. Alisha is mine to protect and I will not tolerate the kind of poison you're so good at spreading here, capisce?"

Mine to protect. Her heart crawled into her throat.

Her cheeks paling, Sylvia nodded.

"Now let me show you to your rooms."

Feeling like a fourth wheel who didn't understand the undercurrents, Ali picked up her handbag and portfolio from the sitting lounge. The coffee would be cold now anyway. She didn't miss the longing, doe-eyed look Francesca cast Dante either. The woman had come with the express purpose of renewing a friendship, even knowing that Dante had a wife of barely a month.

Maybe because Dante had told her how it was between them?

She came out into the foyer and pressed the button to call the elevator. This was good. Francesca and his mother were exactly what she needed until she figured out her next step.

"Where are you going?" Dante said right behind her, and before she could respond, he took her portfolio from her. "I told you I'd take you to the meeting. And before you ask again, for God's sake, I didn't invite my mother, or Francesca."

"So, is she the blast from your past?"

"What?"

Very much not the question she needed to ask. "Never mind. It's not my business."

Holding her gaze, he put her portfolio down with the utmost care and then advanced on her. Like a frightened rabbit, Ali stepped back until her bottom hit the back wall.

Leaning forward, he caged her on all sides. He was all over her and yet he wasn't touching her at all. "Ask me, Ali. Anything."

She wanted to ask him why he was so cold toward his mother, or why he never mentioned her. Or why she'd not been a part of his life for all these years. Why a man who'd been so devoted to her father, who'd grieved Vikram and who cared about Ali, didn't care about his own family.

Instead, she asked the question she knew would devour her for the rest of the day. "Who is she?"

"The girl I wanted to marry a long time ago. She broke it off and, with hindsight, I'm glad she did. And she's firmly in the past."

"So that…thing between me and you back there was petty revenge?"

"Nessuno." The foyer rang with his denial. "I would never, never use you like that."

"Then what was it?" She closed her eyes. Their relationship was like a minefield—so many unexploded and untouchable subjects. But one touch and the passion between them ignited. One step and their bodies would connect and it would be heaven and she was shaking for the effort it took to hold herself back. "Don't play games with me, Dante. I'm not as strong as you think."

"I think you're the strongest, bravest, the most beautiful woman I've ever known." His breath caressed her cheek, sending sparks swooping down her skin. "Ali?"

"Hmm?"

"Don't you want to wait until tonight to know?"

She opened her eyes and as she saw her reflection in his gray eyes, Ali knew. It was too late for her. "Know what?"

With each word, he moved closer, until his nose was buried in her neck. Until she felt the tension swathing his powerful frame. Until he was everything, her entire world.

"I want this…us to be real." He lifted her left hand and stared at her bare finger. "I…want you never to take off your rings again. I want to take you to bed and stay there for a month. I want your loyalty and your fidelity. I want you to be my true wife."

"And what do I get?" she whispered automatically, mesmerized by the intensity of his expression, unable to kill the hope fluttering in her chest.

To belong to Dante, to be his in every way…

He smiled then and it was a thing of wicked beauty. "I never intended to marry, you know. After the thing between Francesca and me. Never. But you… I don't think I can go another day without making you mine. You will have everything I have to give. My fortune at your feet, my body and my fidelity. It'll be my privilege to call you my wife, my privilege to take care of you, my privilege to give you all the pleasure you could ever want."

Not love. Everything but love.

She knew him well and she knew that he hadn't left the word out on purpose. For a man who'd never meant to marry, for a man who had a long-standing mistress in Matta Steel, of course, love wasn't a priority.

Love wasn't even in his thoughts.

He hadn't said he wouldn't love her either. God, was she clutching at straws?

He touched his forehead to hers and let out a long exhale. "Say yes, Alisha, and you'll never be alone again. You'll never want for anything."

Before those words could sink in, before her world could tilt back to its right axis, he pulled away. His gorgeous eyes shimmered with desire, his hands tucked into his trouser pockets pulled at the front, calling her gaze to his arousal.

A soft sound fell from her mouth as desire hit her hard and fast. She fisted her hands, fighting the urge to trace the shape of him, the urge to beg him to take her here, in the foyer, while his mother was in the next room.

"*No.* Don't take another step. Be my wife and I'm all yours."

Ali cursed as even now he denied himself and her.

"This is the only way this is going to happen." He ran his palm over his jaw, devouring her with his gaze, his shoulders tight. "In fact, I'm shocked at how long it took me to realize how perfect you and I will be. I'd like to think even Neel would have approved. I want you and I like you and I want to protect you. We know each other. The fire we have…is no common thing. Together, we can build a good marriage based on respect and a bond that will never break. Together, we'll be his legacy."

She spoke through panic, from the same desire running fierce in her veins. "If you say marrying me is paying his debt to you, I'll never look at you again."

"No, *cara mia*. It's not a debt. But I'm a man with principles and as much as I want to be inside you right now, it won't happen. You are not any woman. You'll never be just any woman to me. Be my wife, Alisha, give me your vows truly. Promise me your commitment. There will be no cheap, dirty affair so that you can scratch an itch and run away when it suits you. Or when it gets hard. Or when it gets old.

"For once in your life, have the courage to stay.

"It has to be all the way between us, *tesoro*. All or nothing."

CHAPTER NINE

Come to me, Alisha.

DANTE'S TEXT FROM two hours ago drummed in her head as Ali finally rode the elevator to the penthouse. It wasn't lost on her that he hadn't explained his disappearance for most of the evening, with Francesca in tow, after stealing the ground from under her with his announcement.

He didn't say please.

He didn't cajole or persuade even.

He just commanded her as if she were his to command. As if there was no doubt she'd accept this. As if she was so desperate to be with him that she would simply breeze into being his wife.

And this was how their relationship would be too, she had no doubt. He might as well have said *Give me your heart and soul* outside the elevator earlier in the day.

Oh, but she desperately wanted to belong to him. Not because she'd spent her whole life looking for a place to belong. But because he was what she'd been searching for.

Because he was right, she was tired of running away. Of being scared.

She wanted to stay and fight for him, for this, for them.

But incensed by his arrogance, she'd texted back.

Say plz.

His silence for almost a half hour had killed her. She'd just stared at her phone waiting, watching, desperately yearning.

Sitting in the quiet blackness of her darkroom, the *ping-ping-ping* of her cell phone had set her heart thundering in her ears. Her fingers shaking, she'd looked at the texts.

Just "please", cara mia? Come to me and I'll go down on my knees for you.

You're mine, Alisha. So stop playing games.

Take one step toward me and I'll give you heaven.

The possessiveness, the promise, the passion… She had trembled at the picture he painted, laughed at how, even in his texts, he was so… *Dante*.

Because what he did give was absolute. It was in his actions, it was in the way he gave everything to her father's legacy and it was in the way he cared about his employees. In the way he'd gotten to the core of her in mere weeks. In the way he'd prodded and pushed her into being her best.

She could tour the world another decade and she'd never find a man like Dante.

So there she was, standing outside his bedroom door while her future waited on the other side. The rectangle of light peeking from under the door made her pulse dizzy. It was half past one in the night and finally, thankfully, the flat was silent.

Of course, Ali could never forget the fact that Sylvia and Francesca were just a few doors down, after refusing again his offer that they'd be more comfortable at the Four Seasons. For her part, Sylvia seemed desperate to make a connection with Dante and Ali couldn't begrudge her that.

She'd give anything to see her papa or Vikram just one more time and say sorry for all the hurtful things she'd done. But Dante's ex was another matter altogether.

Ali had ended up going alone to the meeting with the agent. Because something had blown up with the Japanese merger and Dante had had to leave. She hadn't pinned her hopes on him coming and yet she'd been disappointed.

She'd been waiting on tenterhooks most of the evening for Dante and Francesca to return from some urgent meeting. During dinner, Sylvia having grilled Ali enough to last a lifetime, about Papa and Vikram and their wedding, he hadn't offered any more info on the big secret meeting.

Now here she was, outside his door, her heart battering against her rib cage. But if she didn't go in, she'd never forgive herself for chickening out, for not even giving them a chance.

Gathering a long breath, she twisted the knob, walked in and closed the door behind her.

He was sitting at his desk, the lamp playing with the planes and hollows of his face. He was still in his white dress shirt, unbuttoned all the way now, and black trousers. His hair stood out at all angles, making even more of his high forehead and the slashes of his cheekbones.

The air around him thrummed with palpable tension, and Ali saw there was nothing in front of him on the desk except the phone.

She hadn't texted back after his messages, which had been a half hour ago. And as he stared at her, she saw in his face the same desperation she felt, the taut need, the uncertainty in the tight line of his mouth.

His gaze swept over her from top to bottom—from her hair in that messy topknot to the tight stretchy sweater dress.

She leaned against the door, digging her nails into the wood grain. "Did you think I wouldn't come?"

He shrugged and the action parted his shirt wider, giving her a peek of his defined pectorals with flat brown nipples and tight abdominal muscles. She licked her lips, imagining running her tongue against that rock-hard band.

He made a low, growling sound that went straight to her sex.

"Tell me."

"I wasn't sure you'd come." He ran his hand through his hair as if the admission cost him.

She thought it would make her feel better, less vulnerable to see that he hadn't been sure of her. She didn't. Suddenly, she wasn't interested in power games with him. Not anymore. "Why didn't you come to me then? Why this mindplay?" A raw vulnerability filled her, coating her throat with tears. She wanted him so much. She ached to be held by him, she longed to belong to him.

"Isn't it enough that I've been yours for the taking from that first evening in Bangkok? Enough that I came back to the flat against every rational instinct? Enough that I waited all evening, after you disappeared for the evening with your ex?

"What do I have to do—crawl to you on my knees to make you understand that this isn't just an itch? That this is not a phase or a stopgap or a..."

He pushed off from the desk, reaching her before she could blink. His hand went around her neck, pulling her to him. His mouth took hers in such a roughly erotic kiss that her throat dried, her breath stuttered, her belly swooped. She gasped and he swooped into her mouth with a mastery that made her sex clench and throb.

"It had to be your choice, Alisha. Do you not see, *bella mia*? This is far too important to me. This is..." he whispered against her mouth, his gaze so intense that she felt stripped to the bone. "This can't be some boardroom deal where I use your weakness against you to make you surrender. This can't be a taking. I needed you to come to me, to choose this on those conditions."

He clasped her cheeks and peppered kisses all over her face, a desperate intensity in his words. "This is the first time in my life I've waited, and wanted, not knowing what the outcome would be. But now that you're here, *cara mia*, you'll never have to take that step again.

"I'll forever cherish what you give me. You've undone me, *tesoro*."

His teeth bit, his tongue stroked, his body pressed her against the wall until every inch of his hard body was plastered against hers. His unrelenting chest crushed her breasts. His lips—God, his lips—nipped and rubbed until Ali was nothing but a quivering mass of sensations. Until hunger for more consumed her.

His deep groan soothed and excited at the same time. And then his tongue was inside her mouth again, laving at her with rough, long strokes. She stroked hers against his and then sucked on it. His arms around her tightened, one hard thigh wedging between hers.

Hardness and heat, he was hers. Tremors swept through her.

His mouth moved to her jaw. He licked her earlobe before his teeth bit down on the tender flesh. Ali jerked and rubbed her core against his thigh.

"Wait," he said, jolting his lower body away from her, his glorious chest falling and rising. "Francesca…her ex pumped all her money into some get-rich scheme and she came here for my help."

"She came here for more than that, believe me."

"We spent all evening with my team of lawyers and PIs to figure out how to help her. And I did it tonight because I want her out of here as soon as possible. Whatever she and Mama thought about coming here, I have no interest in her." He took her hand up to his mouth and kissed her palm. "You're my wife and tell me you believe me that I'll never look at another woman like that again. My word means everything to me."

Ali nodded, feeling a catch in her throat.

He gathered her into his arms, his forehead brushing hers. And sighed. "Tonight is your lucky night, *cara mia*."

"Why just me?" She dug her teeth into his chin and he jerked. "I'm a good lay too, you know. If you want proof—"

He tugged at her hair roughly, thrusting his tongue in, murmuring something in Italian that she was pretty sure meant her mouth was going to get her into a lot of trouble. Or that he was going to shut her up the only way he knew.

He was hot, rough, thrusting in and out with his tongue. His hands moved compulsively over her back, her waist, coming to rest on her buttocks. In a rough movement that betrayed his lack of control, he pulled her up until his erection pressed up against the V of her legs. Their groans rent the air, the hard ridge of his shaft a perfect fit against her soft core. "I forgot to buy condoms." His hands snuck under her top and her belly clenched at the rough contact of his palm. "So, it's all you tonight."

Ali shivered at the wickedness in his tone. "As exciting as that sounds, why do you not have condoms here?"

"I don't bring lovers here. You're the first woman who's lived in this flat, who's come into my room and who's going to share my bed."

"That makes me feel special," she said flippantly. Because flippancy had always been her default response when she was protecting herself from hurt.

"You think I do this lightly?"

Ali shook her head. The one thing she'd never doubt

was Dante's word, his commitment once he gave it. "Two lovers. I'm clean and I'm on the pill."

His eyes took on a thunderous look, as if he didn't like hearing that. He rubbed his jaw, and studied her. "Five. I'm clean."

That unpleasant feeling gripped her and she tried to chase it away. He was hers now. "Five? Maybe you forgot how to count because I can recount off the top—"

"Rumors and gossip? I took Matta Steel to a net worth of five billion dollars in ten years. I don't have time to have as many affairs as the media hints."

"Is… Francesca one of those five?"

The shutters that fell down in his eyes were instant. He let her go and Ali missed his warmth like a limb. "Let it go."

"How would you feel if Jai was in the flat, two doors down?"

"I'd throw him out by the scruff of his collar."

"Even though I repeatedly told you he was out of my life?"

He rubbed his face again. "This will never work if we don't trust each other."

"I do trust you. It's just that…you know everything about me. All my weaknesses. I know nothing about you."

"You haven't let me see your work."

"So earn that right, Dante."

"Francesca's parents broke off our association the minute the news of my father's crime came out. We'd been together for most of our lives. When I asked her about her parents' decision, she said she was abiding by it. She didn't want to marry a man whose father's crime would always cling to him. Who owed millions to people, who could never leave that infamy behind."

"She broke your heart."

He looked up and shook his head. "*No*. Funnily enough, by that time, I'd been dealt much worse."

Maybe Francesca hadn't broken his heart but she'd made him close himself off. Ali went to him, hating the distance he put between them. "I'm glad then that she has such a fickle heart. Because now you're mine.

"One woman's discard is another woman's hero."

A white smile flashed in his dark face, lust turning his eyes impossibly darker. "I'm no hero, Ali. Heroes don't exist, *cara mia*. Only men with weaknesses and men without."

She didn't like the gravity of his tone. The shadow of his father's dark past was in his eyes. Twining her arms around his neck, she rubbed herself against him shamelessly. His erection was a brand against her belly. "Fine, you're no hero. You're the perfect man with the perfect hard-on and I can't wait—"

He tucked a swath of hair behind her ear. "I need to learn what turns you on. I need to make you scream. I need to lick every inch of you. Then, if you're still willing, then I will be inside you, *cara mia*."

Heat scoured her cheeks and Ali tugged her gaze down to his neck. "Oh, God, you're going to be all methodical and in control, aren't you?"

His laughter surrounded her even as his words wound anticipation tighter and tighter inside her. She snuck her fingers into his hair, pushing away the thick lock that fell onto his forehead. He looked down at her and smiled and in that smile, Ali found the entire world. The thing that she'd been searching for through the years and continents—a place to belong. A place to call her own.

This man was worth staying still for. Worth fighting for. It felt as if she'd been waiting her whole life for this moment. With this man. Every choice she'd made had led her here. To tonight.

To Dante.

Dante moved away from Ali. Every muscle in him curled tight with a hunger he couldn't deny anymore.

It felt right. All the way to his bones.

Her soft voice, full of vulnerability tugged at him. Reaching for the wall behind him, he turned on the overhead ceiling lights and the room was instantly ablaze. And in the middle of the room, leaning against his king bed, stood Alisha.

The cashmere dress she wore hugged every swell and dip of her body, the peach tone setting off her dusky skin. The dress ended inches above her knees, while her legs were clad in knee-high brown boots, leaving miles of toned thighs on display. Her breasts jutted up high and firm and he knew, just knew, that she wasn't wearing a bra.

After years of self-discipline and having sex for the simple release it provided, tonight he wanted to gorge on her.

Now that she was here, he wanted to take his time. He wanted her limp and damp and blown apart. He wanted to drown her in so much pleasure that she'd forget any other man's name. He never wanted her to feel as if she'd made a compromise with him. She would never want for anything as his wife. Not for riches, not for security and not for pleasure.

He ran a hand over his jaw, feeling the scratch of his stubble. "Stay there while I shave. I won't be long."

"No, don't." The tip of her tongue swept over her lush lower lip and he felt that hesitant stroke lower on his body. The very thought of her hands on his shaft, that tongue wrapped around his hardness sent him to the very edge he'd talked himself away from just now.

"No?" he said, raising a brow. Silky, hoarse, his voice sounded so unlike him. "Tell me why not."

"I… I like your stubble."

He had no idea how he managed to stay still, all the way across the room. How he managed to hang on to the last thread of his control when all he wanted was to splay her legs wide and pound into her. "Why?"

She tucked her hand into the cowl-neck of her sweater dress, as if she found her very skin restless. As if she couldn't wait to shed it all. "I want to feel it against my skin."

Desire slammed into him anew, a fever in his blood. "Where, Ali?"

She lifted her chin, his equal every step of the way. "Here." She rubbed her cheek. "Here." Her pink-tipped fingers rubbed the nipple poking against the dress. "Here." Her palm swooped down over her belly. "And here." Now her palm was between her thighs.

His mouth dried out. "Pull your hair down."

Hands raised into that mass, she pulled at the clip and it all came tumbling down in glorious, silky brown waves that framed her lovely face. And then she shook her head in that classic feminine gesture that drew his balls tight. He wanted to feel that hair on his belly and lower, he was going to fist his hands in that heavy mass and hold her still for him while he thrust into her wet heat.

Cristo, there were a thousand things he wanted to do to her. Inside her. With her. An eternity wouldn't be enough for all of it. "You'll feel it, *tesoro*, against your skin." He let his gaze rest on the jut of her breasts, her flat belly, to her thighs. "Everywhere."

Brown eyes widened into deep pools, and a soft mewl fell from her mouth. "Any other requests from my sexy wife?"

"Take your shirt off," she commanded him, in a tone that thrummed over his skin.

He shrugged it off his shoulders. It fluttered to the floor in a whisper. Her gaze moved over him hungrily, from his throat to his shoulders to his nipples, to the light sprinkling of hair on his chest, and then to the line of it that disappeared into his jeans.

And then strayed over the bulge in his pants.

Again, her tongue came out and licked her lower lip. His shaft lengthened, almost painfully hard now.

"Take that dress off," he said, struggling and failing to remove the rough need in his words. "Leave your boots on."

Her gaze gleamed. His breath hung on a jagged edge when she picked up the hem and pulled it over her head. Lust slammed into him like the side of a mountain. A growl escaped his throat—half pain, half pleasure at the breathtaking sensuality of her body.

She wasn't wearing a bra. Her breasts were small and high and round, the brown nipples puckered into tight knots. His mouth watered. Miles of smooth brown skin shimmered flawlessly under the bright lights. Silky hair fluttered over one side of her shoulder, beckoning his touch.

Her chest curved sharply into a narrow waist, small enough for him to wrap his hands around and flared into wide hips, followed by long, shapely thighs and legs, legs he wanted wrapped around him while he plunged into her.

Dios mio, she was a red-blooded male's wet dream. And she was his.

Only his, forever. This night and all the nights to come.

"Now the panties." His command rolled out of a dry mouth.

He thought she would refuse him, on principle. She'd always hated that he ordered her around, that he knew what was best for her.

"No arguments?" he said, goading her, wanting her to fight him. Needing something to fracture that utter surrender in her eyes. In her body.

"I've no problem following your commands when I know you have my best interests at heart."

A shudder went through him at the arrogant confidence in her voice, the husky timbre of it. Chin tilted up defiantly, gaze burning bright, she tucked her fingers into the thin seam of her panties and rolled them down.

She had to lean back against the bed to pull them over her boots and her hair fell forward like a silky curtain, covering her breasts from his view.

Skin clammy with need, he took her in, as she threw the panties at him, a wicked smile curving her mouth. The fabric fell to the ground as he moistened his lips.

His gaze went from her flat belly to the V of her pelvis, down to the black curls hiding her sex from him. She was gloriously sexy.

He shook with the need to just take her right there, standing like that, her eyes wide and swimming in desire. But not tonight. He would do that another night. He would take her without preamble, he would reach for her one night, kiss her awake slowly and she would welcome him and he would be inside her while they were laughing with each other, in the kitchen, in the living room, in the shower.

But tonight, he intended to take it slow if it killed him. He sat down on the leather recliner. "Come here to me," he growled out, patting his lap.

And she did, her hips swinging with each step, her breasts swaying up and down, her mouth curved in a teasing light. She came over to him with such naked want in her eyes that his erection pushed against his trousers. When she stilled in front of him, her knees hitting the recliner, he leaned forward. His hands filled with her buttocks, he pressed her forward into his face. The scent of her arousal seeped into him like a drug. He shook from the force of his desire. He licked around her navel, breathing her in.

He left his trousers zipped, for he needed every ounce of control he had to bring her to climax first. For the first time in his life, Dante had nothing left because Ali had undone him.

Simply by giving him everything she had with such trust. Such open affection. Such…

It was a gift, he knew, and he promised himself he'd cherish it even if he couldn't return it in full measure.

"Climb into my lap. And straddle me."

Ali barely heard, much less understood Dante's words beneath the rushing in her ears. Knees shaking like Jell-O, she climbed up onto the recliner, while his hands traveled over every inch of her bare skin.

Cupping her buttocks, smoothing over her hips, tracing her rib cage, palming her breasts, then sweeping between her inner thighs without really touching her where she needed to be touched. Next they were at her back, pushing her down and forward. She sank into his lap and the feel of his hard shaft against her sex was like electricity in her veins.

Instantly, mindlessly, she moved over him and his growl ripped through the air. Rough hands gripped her hips, staying her. "Don't move, not yet. I want to come inside you."

"Yes. Please," she whispered on a dry mouth.

He tongued her nipple. A wet lash. Her back arched into the hot caress. Murmuring in Italian, he repeated the soft flicks of his tongue over and over again, until she was panting. Sobbing. Shaking. She dug her fingers into his thick hair and held his head to her breast, demanding more. Needing more. His teeth nipped before he closed his lips over the peak. "Every night after that time, I dreamed of this." He rolled her nipple in his mouth, pressed his tongue against it again and again before he sucked on it.

Fire burst through her belly.

Sensations poured over her like warm honey, beating on her, sending arrows of shooting pleasure down to her lower belly. And just when she was at the edge of mindless ecstasy, when she could taste the pleasure on her tongue like bottled lightning, he stopped.

Made her come down from the edge.

He repeated the torment again and again, until her skin was clammy with sweat. Her thigh muscles were trembling. And she was shaking with need. She looked down into his dark eyes. "You want me to beg, don't you? This is payback for all the trouble I caused you all these years?"

Rough hands stroked her bare back, down the line of her spine to her buttocks, up and down soothing her. He pressed a fierce kiss to her mouth, tongue and teeth whipping her into a frenzy again. His hand shook as he pushed back damp hair from her forehead, desire and something else in his eyes. "I like seeing you like that. Desperate for me. My name on your lips like a chant. Your eyes hazy and clouded. Your body so achingly gorgeous and mine to play with. It's like a drug, *cara mia*. Building you up, seeing you crave me like that… You give of yourself so boldly, so completely, so…generously. I promised myself I would have you limp and screaming my name for hours." Huskiness filled his words.

She rocked into him, craving his hardness at the apex of her thighs, delirious with need. Mindless for his possession. "Inside me, Dante, now, please."

He lifted her onto her knees. The rasp of his zipper, the sliding whisper of his jeans were havoc on her skin. His erection released up toward his belly, thick and long with veins she wanted to trace with her tongue. She licked her dry lips, and he growled. "Not tonight, *cara mia*."

Ali shook with violent need when he took himself in hand. "Lower yourself, slowly."

She lowered her hips and he rubbed the length of him against her wet folds. Pleasure knotted in her pelvis and she jerked at the overwhelming sensation.

His dark gaze stayed where he could see their bodies straining to join. "Do it again," he commanded and she did.

Once more, again and again, she pressed the plump head against her clit. And the next time she did it, he thrust his hips and he was inside her.

Ali gasped at how embedded he was inside her like this, stretching her to the hilt.

Sweat beaded on his forehead, the thick corded muscles of his neck standing out in stark relief. "*Maledizione*, you're so tight."

"It's been a long time. And now I know why I didn't even miss it. I was waiting for you, Dante."

A stillness came over him. "Ali, I don't deserve—"

"Shh…" she whispered and took his mouth in a soft kiss.

Stiff at first, slowly he melted into it as she tangled with his tongue just the way he liked. She ran her hands all over his warm, damp skin, loving the tight clench of his shoulders, the taut skin stretched over his chest. "You know, Jai was right. I didn't realize it for so long."

He scowled and cursed.

She wrapped her arms around him, loving the warmth and hardness of him surrounding her. "I've always had a thing for you. I've always weighed every man I meet against you. I don't even know when…"

His hands in her hair jerked her head back roughly. His nostrils flared and he rotated and thrust his hips at the same time. His thumb found her clit and pressed. On and on he worked her, with his shaft inside her, his fingers on her clit, as if he meant to make her mindless. And without warning, Ali came, liquid lightning splintering through her belly and lower.

His dark gaze devouring her, he kept thrusting, and the waves came and came, drowning her, dragging her.

She fell onto him, moaning, chasing the high still. "When what, Alisha?" he demanded, a craven starkness in his voice. "When what?"

"I don't know when it happened. Or maybe it was already there and it's only that I just see it now."

He stood up with their bodies still joined, his hands on her buttocks and he brought them to his bed. Pleasure began fluttering through her pelvis again when he kept her at the edge of the bed and started moving inside her.

There was an angry glint in his eyes, color burning beneath those cheekbones. The tenor of his thrusts quickened, his fingers painfully digging into her hips. She loved it, she loved that he was selfishly chasing his climax, that he wasn't clad in that cloak of control.

Ali pulled herself up on her elbows and met his mouth. "For years, it was easy to hide behind my hate." She dug her teeth into his lower lip and pulled. And in reward, his hips flexed and rotated.

Feral want painted his features with a harshness. His shoulders stood out in stark relief, a tremor in his skin when she claimed every part of him.

His nostrils flared as he dragged her even closer, pushing her thighs indecently wide with his shoulders.

He was glorious and she was the only one who could give him what he needed. She locked her legs at his buttocks and gave herself over to his rhythm.

Sweat beaded on his throat and then he pistoned once, twice, thrice, with a jerking motion. A growl fell from his mouth as he came—an uncontrolled, raw sound. She licked the sweat at his neck and bit his shoulder hard. "I love the sound you make when you come undone. I love how you know me so well. I love you, Dante. I'll always love you."

Smiling, Ali fell back against the sheets, her pelvis sore from the pounding, from the way he'd used her, her thighs trembling and aching. Her heart was so overflowingly full. He'd lost control there at the end because of what she'd said. And she reveled in it even as he remained silent. Even if every second of that silence pierced her.

She closed her eyes and turned her head away.

But not before she saw the shock in his eyes. And the stillness that came over him. And the way his entire body shuddered, his chin jerking as if she'd somehow dealt him a lethal blow.

For once, she didn't care what he was going through.

She was in love with him and there was a certain freedom in admitting that. In saying that out loud. In flinging her heart wide open and embracing what she felt.

In lying, satiated, next to the man she loved.

CHAPTER TEN

PINK DAWN WAS sweeping its fingers through the sky outside his bedroom, the world, the city pulsing into life as Dante came awake. For the first time in his life, he felt no rush to meet it. No urgent meeting, no PR emergency could wrench him away from the warm bed, the haven of his room, from Ali.

Two short weeks into his relationship with Ali, their true beginning, and it seemed like it had been two lifetimes. The first couple of days, he'd braced himself for some... flash of reality maybe, something to make him pay for the out-of-body experience he'd had with her that first night.

He kept expecting her to demand something, anything, in return for the declaration she'd made so boldly, so brazenly, so unflinchingly.

After all, he had countless memories of his mother declaring her love for his father, and then demanding a gift. A more expensive car, a diamond bracelet, a better flat... as if her love was a transaction. As if no word or deed was ever enough.

And his father, falling deeper and deeper, had never realized that whatever he did would never be enough for her.

A knot formed in his stomach every time Ali kissed him, or laughed at him, or just plain looked at him. An expectant bracing to see what she would ask of him. Of what she'd demand that he couldn't give in the name of love.

It would be an awkward conversation, a hurtful one, but he'd been prepared to have it. She also seemed to have no expectation of hearing him return her declaration.

Because he couldn't love her. There was no force on earth that could propel him to open himself up to that kind of vulnerability, that kind of weakness, no way he would give her that power over him.

But she asked nothing of him, except his body. She was insatiable, just as much as he was and every night she came to him with that same naked desire in her eyes. She explored his body as if he was a sumptuous buffet she intended to gorge on, with her mouth, tongue, fingers.

She demanded her pleasure from him and took such effervescent delight in his pleasure, in seeking and discovering new ways to break his control, to bring him to his knees.

She asked nothing of him except his laughter, his company, his opinions. She didn't seem to have a plan beyond giving herself to him and simply expecting him to enjoy being with her. It was as if she'd reached through the fortress he'd built around his emotions and he found himself opening up.

This wasn't a transaction to her. Her love, or even her admission of it didn't demand a price.

She just gave. It just was.

I love you, Dante.

He couldn't tell himself it was from the sexual high she was floating on for he had never seen such clarity in her eyes. Such courage.

It had been like looking at the sun. He'd never thought giving could be as powerful as taking. And yet Ali managed to do just that, with him.

No, she had gazed into his eyes, both vulnerability and boldness in the tilt of her chin, her body thrusting up toward him, matching his hunger with hers, milking his shaft with her heat, her mouth against his chest, his heart thundering away under her touch, aching endlessly, craving more and more. She whispered those words like a benediction. Like a promise.

Just the memory of her was enough to send blood pooling in his groin, for that thrum to fill his blood. The sheet tented in front of him and he reached out a hand for her.

Cold, empty sheets greeted his hand. He frowned just as he heard the continuous *click-click* of a high-speed camera. With a curse, he sat up in the bed.

Dressed in a sleeveless T-shirt that stuck to her breasts and pink panties with cute bows on the sides, she was switching on the overhead lights. Dante blinked as bright light pierced his eyes. "Turn off the lights, *cara mia*. And come to bed."

She didn't answer. The sound of the shots she took pinged over his skin.

"Sit up for me, won't you, Dante? Please."

He sat up, almost unconsciously, the command in her voice driving his movements. She sounded nothing like the Ali he knew. "Push your hand through your hair."

Again, he found himself doing it before muttering, "I'm no model, Ali."

She dug her teeth into her lower lip, a frown on her face. "You're the sexiest man I've ever photographed and believe me, I've shot attractive men before."

"Naked?" he asked, possessiveness and something much baser filling his chest.

"*Si*, naked. Raise your arm, *por favor, caro mio*. I want the birthmark under your bicep in the shot. It's the only imperfection I've found so far in your body."

He smiled, the cajoling tone of her washing away anything else, the heat of the memory when she'd traced that and the small mole on his right thigh with her tongue filling his veins. "Make me a deal I can't refuse."

Warmth flushed her cheeks as she lowered the camera for the first time since he'd woken up. A wicked smile curved her lips. "I'll go down on you."

His erection twitched under the sheets and she licked her lips. He groaned.

"Altro," he said, knowing there was nothing in the world he would refuse her.

"You always ask for more," she pouted. "I'll let you go down on me."

As bold as she'd been the first night, it seemed there were depths to Alisha he would never learn. Hiding her face in his chest, she'd confided one night that her experiences had been few and not really of the adventurous type.

He let his gaze run down her belly to the V of her thighs, the pink silk barely covering her mound. His mouth watered at the very prospect of latching his lips over her sex, of thrusting his tongue into her tightness while she screamed his name. Of holding her down while she writhed under his mouth.

She clutched her thighs close as if she could hear his thoughts and he laughed. *"Altro."*

"I will let you see my work," she said softly. "But you have to promise me that you won't…that you will not… It's my heart and soul, Dante."

Warmth unlike anything he'd ever known spread through his chest. "It would be my honor to see your work. And my privilege to pose for you," he added and saw her smile widen, reach her eyes, and just like that, another layer of ice around his heart seemed to thaw.

That tension faded from his body. They would have the marriage he wanted. They would have everything together without the emotional transaction of love coloring every exchange.

"Okay, now, raise both your hands for me, please," she commanded and he happily played along.

A week later, Ali waved at Izzy as she passed her desk and without knocking, pushed open the door to Dante's office on the top floor of Matta Towers.

Standing against the far wall, with his back to her, he didn't hear her arrival. Ali took the time to study him, her heart pounding away. She'd never visited Matta Towers, even when her papa had been alive, on principle.

Vikram had invited her, several times. She even remembered Dante inviting her once, going as far as saying that Neel would be happy to see her there. She, intent on cutting off her nose to spite her face, had refused. Because she'd been waiting for her papa to invite her.

Now, she would wait forever.

And she didn't want to let him make the same mistake.

His suite was vast with a stunning view of the London skyline, a dark mahogany desk, as imposing as the man himself, taking center stage. Creamy leather sofas sat in the small sitting area to the left, and to her right was another door through which she knew was his personal suite. Where he had probably been sleeping for the last three nights, because he certainly hadn't come home.

When she had called his cell phone and asked after the first night, he'd informed her, almost politely it had seemed, that the Japanese merger was taking all his time. Having heard of the passive-aggressive communication misfire her scheming uncle had taken part in, almost bringing the deal to a halt, she knew that he was telling her the truth. Not that she thought Dante would lie to her. If he was bored with her, or if that initial frenzy of desire they had both been drowning in receded, he would tell her.

She had a feeling it was to do with the frequent bouts of his mother's crying in the evenings, in the confrontations she seemed determined to have, regardless of the fact that it embarrassed Ali and infuriated Dante. Thank goodness Francesca had left after the first few days.

But the wretchedness in Sylvia's eyes tore at Ali and she couldn't just watch anymore.

"Dante?" she whispered, bracing herself for that consuming gaze.

He turned and just like that, pure longing filled her. He looked sharp and arrogant as usual, but there were dark shadows under his slate-gray eyes. Warmth flicked into life in his tired eyes and her heart ached.

She thought he might ask her to come to him. Or he would come to her, take her in his arms and kiss her senseless. After all, it had been three days since he'd touched her or kissed her or even held her. She missed him like there was an ache in her chest.

But he did no such thing. The warmth of that smile dimmed as he pushed his hands into his trouser pockets and leaned back against that wall.

In that moment, Ali realized something. He never touched her outside the context of sex. As insatiable as his passion was when he wanted her, he wasn't the demonstrative kind in public. But his stance clearly said that she was interrupting. He confirmed it when he said, "I have a meeting in fifteen minutes. Why didn't you tell me you were coming all the way over? I would've told you I was busy."

She swallowed, refusing to take his words as the complete dismissal they were. He wasn't going to get out of it that easily. This wasn't even about her, she reminded herself. It was about him.

And his mother and his past.

Brazening it out with a wide smile, she covered the distance between them. Before he could push her away, she went on tiptoes and kissed his mouth softly. Slowly. Pouring all the love in her heart into the kiss. For all the hardness of his body, she was amazed how soft his lips were, and for all his dismissive words, how he let her do what she wanted.

She traced the sharp angles of his face with her mouth—the blade of his nose, the high planes of his cheekbones, the hollows of his cheeks, his tight brow. Sinking her fingers into his crisp hair, she tugged and pulled. He came to her, willingly, giving in. She traced her way down to his neck, licked his pulse, pressed her tongue into the hollow of his neck. The familiar taste of skin, the scent of him calmed the furor in her blood. "Didn't anyone ever teach you that was the proper way to greet your wife after not seeing her for three days?"

After what seemed an eternity, the stiffness left his shoulders. A familiar shudder went through him. He pushed off from the wall with a soft growl, his hands sinking into her hair. "No, this is how I would greet my wife," he said, and bit hard into her lower lip. When she gasped at the pain-pleasure, he licked the hurt away. He took over the kiss with utter possession that sent currents arrowing toward her sex.

Wet, warm and wanton, she clung to him for breath, clinging to him for everything he could give. Hands around his shoulders, Ali rubbed herself against him mindlessly, desperate for more. His hands were at her buttocks again, his mouth at her neck. "I'll ask Izzy to postpone the meeting for another half hour. I need to be inside you, now."

She had no idea how she found the strength to say no; to pull away when all she wanted was to feel him inside her, to feel the closeness he allowed only during sex, to feel as if everything in her world was right again. "No, Dante, I didn't come here to have sex."

He released her so fast that she'd have fallen back if not for his swift reflex. His chest rose and fell, his mouth narrowed. Eyes glittering, he rubbed the back of his hand over his mouth. As if he wanted to wipe her taste away. "Then what was the point of the kiss, *cara mia*? To prove that you can fell me to my knees in a matter of a few minutes?"

She flinched at the soft cruelty of his words.

"I wasn't aware that we're supposed to keep track of who breaks whom. I never… I kissed you because I missed you. And that turned into something else, because it always does when we kiss. Or have you been sleepwalking through the last few weeks?"

Color washed over his cheeks. "I… I don't have time for this. Go home, Alisha."

He never called her Alisha like that anymore, the very word dripping with contempt and exaggerated patience. As if she was being purposely troublesome.

Which in itself was a clear sign that he wasn't all right. A month ago, she was sure he wouldn't have lost his temper like that with her. But neither was she going to think of his nasty words as some sort of progress between them.

She folded her hands, the hurt cycling to anger. "But you have time to have a quickie with me against the wall? And after? You'll make me clean myself up in the bathroom and send me home with a pat and some cash?"

The curse that fell from his mouth sounded downright filthy. He bent toward her, fingers coiling in her hair, his breath coating her face. "Don't cheapen it. It's never like that between us."

"You're the one cheapening it."

"Ali…" He sounded distressed, at the end of his rope.

"Please leave. I… I'm not in a place where I can handle this in the right way. I don't want to hurt you, *cara mia*."

"Then don't hurt me. Don't dismiss me as if I'm a nuisance. The whole reason I risked the rush-hour traffic is to see you. You're upset about something. I get it. But being nasty to me is unfair. Maybe you're not used to relationships with give-and-take. But you don't get to order me around like I'm some disposable member of staff.

"You don't get to make me do all the emotional work, always. And just because I love you doesn't mean I'll let you walk all over me."

The effect of her ultimatum was ruined when tears filled her eyes. Pushing away from him, she angrily swiped at her cheeks. God, did he have any idea that he could destroy her with one harsh word?

She had almost reached the door when she heard him say, "Don't leave, Ali. Don't let me chase you away."

Hand on the knob, Ali stilled. Loving him did make her vulnerable, but not weak. She felt him at her back and the entirety of her being wanted to lean into his waiting arms, to take the only comfort he offered in his touch, to lose herself in the fire between them. "Don't. Touch me."

The sharp inhale of his breath, the stillness, conveyed his shock.

"*Mia dispiace*, Ali. It seems I'm always saying sorry to you. Turn around and look at me. Please."

She turned but couldn't manage to look at him. Instead, she made her way to the sitting area, took a bottle of water from the small refrigerator and gulped the cold water down. She found him sitting at the two-seater and chose a sofa opposite him. His mouth narrowed but he didn't say anything.

"Do you accept my apology?"

"I don't know," she said with a shrug. "I came because she's leaving, Dante, your mother's leaving in a few hours."

Any tenderness that had returned to his expression faded. His face became that stony mask again. "I know."

"I feel sorry for her. She seems so desperate to make a connection with you. I'd give anything to see Papa again, to tell him how sorry I am, to tell him that all I ever wanted was to love him, and to have his love in return. Can't you forgive her for whatever she's done? For yourself, at least? It's clear it hurts you to see her."

He didn't say anything for so long that Ali braced herself for another cutting remark. His gaze grew distant, tight lines fanning out from his face. *"Nessuno."* The refusal rang around the silence like a pistol shot. "I don't think it's even a matter of forgiving her because I don't feel anything for her. Even before my father was incarcerated for his crime, she cut all ties with him. Took her maiden name again. Within months, she had married her second husband. She urged me to change my last name too."

The utter lack of emotion in his eyes terrified Ali. It seemed that he really wasn't acting from a place of anger but nothingness.

Forgetting all her vows to herself, she went on her knees in front of him and took his hands in hers. He was cold, as if the past hadn't quite left him. "It makes her weak, yes, but not a monster, Dante."

"But he did it all for her. He was so in love with her, he so desperately wanted to please her that he cooked the books, embezzled from hundreds of innocents."

Ali fell back onto her haunches. "What?"

"She's from a wealthy Sicilian family with old ties to Mafia. He was a humble accountant. My mother…on the outside, she's a delicate flower but on the inside, she's spoiled, privileged. She is insidious with her demands, with what she thinks is her due. She was in a rebellious phase when she met him and he fell hard for her.

"Soon, I came and then reality descended on her. There were no cars, no villas, no jewelry, nothing exciting about being a mother at twenty-two. She grew up like royalty. Her discontent was like cancer and he…for her, he was determined to do anything. Which he did. Our wealth grew exponentially over a few years. Cars, mansions, a jet-setting lifestyle, he lay everything at her feet, her utter slave.

"I'm not justifying the number of innocent lives he ruined but *dios mio*, even at the end, he didn't regret it."

"You can't blame her for what he did. They were both weak." Fury filled her for between them they had distorted his view of love. And for that, she didn't want to forgive either of them.

He looked down at Ali, frowning. "You're right. It was his lack of a moral compass. But every time I see her, I can't forget that after everything, she didn't even have compassion for him, much less love. He rotted in that jail cell and when she refused to even visit him… When he heard that she'd married again, he hanged himself."

He rubbed his forehead with his fingers, and Ali's heart ached for him.

"When I see her, I remember his face. He was such a fool in love. To this day, I can't understand how a sensible man could lose himself like that. His love for her was his biggest weakness. It led to the destruction of countless others and himself. It's poison…" he said in a voice that was so full of bitterness that Ali thought she might choke on it.

Dante thought love was poison. A weakness. She felt as if someone had dropped a huge boulder on her chest, crushing the very breath out of her.

She had known he didn't believe in love. But to think of it as poison…

When he pulled her up, Ali went into his embrace and buried her face in his chest. "She doesn't deserve your tears, Ali. Or your sympathy." He seemed to hesitate, his mouth buried in her hair. "You were right. I don't do well with emotions. I will learn, *tesoro*, to be a good husband, to communicate with you. Never to hurt you like that again. We'll have a good marriage based on mutual respect and passion. When the time is right, we'll have a big family, if that's what you want. But you should know…" A tremor coated his words. "I will never allow myself to feel like that, never put my faith, my life in the hands of love. I can't change for you. I can't be anything other than what you see. Don't ask it of me."

Having dealt her that soft but final statement, he left her standing alone in what used to be her papa's office, her heart breaking softly.

For the young man who'd never had the chance to believe that love wasn't always a poison, or cancer. For a young man who didn't understand that even as he wreaked immense hurt on her, she still loved him with every molecule of her being.

That she could no more stop loving him, that she couldn't stop hurting for him any more than she could stop breathing.

Dante returned home that night, feeling like the lowest of the low.

His feet automatically took him to the guest room. His mother had left then. He stood in the center of it, the faint scent of gardenias filling his nostrils. For as long as he could remember she'd worn that scent. For as long as he could remember, she'd been a fragile beauty with no spine, letting the world sway her back and forth.

And to think he'd once assumed Ali was a spoiled princess like her and Francesca. He'd called her a pampered princess, once he'd even called her a waste of space.

No, his wife was a lioness with a heart of gold. And he'd hurt her tonight.

Unable and unwilling to face her reaction to his blunt words, he had left her alone in his office.

Dios mio, he couldn't bear to hurt her any more than he could love her. And the warring instincts constantly ate away at him.

She had come to offer comfort and he'd crushed her heart. But seeing his mother these past few weeks, dealing with the guilt in her eyes, reliving the worst years of his life all over again…he felt as powerless as that sixteen-year-old.

Left with the legacy of his father's crime and his death.

Left with discovering how, through the weakness they called love, they had fractured their family, his faith in them, his faith in everyone and everything.

For all the billions he'd amassed, for all the stains he'd removed from his reputation, Dante felt like a jerk, a weak man unable to stop wreaking hurt on the one woman who thought him worthy of her adoration, who refused to stop looking at him as if he were a hero.

He'd had Izzy schedule the meeting on a different floor, hiding away like a coward. Not that he'd been able to focus on a single word.

Maledizione! Enough was enough. He didn't intend to let the past rot his future with its poisonous fingers. He and Ali, against all odds, had made a fresh start and he intended to have a full life with her.

He would spend his life earning that adoration in her eyes. He meant for them to be consumed by the fire between them, again and again. For it was the one place where he could give of himself completely.

A sudden desperation gripping him, he checked the room she'd occupied when she'd moved in. There was no way he was going to let her spend the night in a different bed. She belonged with him. He switched on the lights in that room and found the bed neatly made, bare of any of her things.

Panic like he'd never known unfurled in his belly. Had she left him? Had he broken her heart? By the time he walked to his bedroom, his heart was thudding against his rib cage.

The bedroom door swung open wide and there she was in the middle of his bed, illuminated by a pool of light. Tenderness and relief and desire, a knot of emotions crowded in his throat. There was a rational voice crowing too but he couldn't even hear it.

She lay on her tummy, her leg splayed, her round buttocks thrust up, her face to the side, taking up most of the bed, as she always did. Moving to her side, he pushed the silky strands from her back and placed his palm on there. Just touching her calmed the wild need inside him. Just breathing in the scent of her, of seeing her in his bed night after night…desire crawled through him, sinuous and hard, as it always did.

He stripped and crawled into bed. Fear beat a tattoo in his head that he was far too deep already. But it didn't stop him from kissing the smooth skin of her back.

From shifting the thick curtain of her hair to the side until he could kiss the shadows under her eyes. Shadows he knew he had put there.

From inhaling the scent of her deep into his lungs until she was a part of him.

From drawing a wet trail of kisses down to the round globes of her buttocks.

From turning her lithe body to the side until her back was resting against his chest.

From slipping one arm under her heated flesh until he reached the round fullness of her breast.

From rubbing his cheek against hers, against her shoulder, every inch of her he could reach like a starving man.

From whispering a torrent of mindless Italian at her ear, from threats to promises to pleading.

From smiling when she woke up with a soft mewl and when her sleep-mussed eyes alighted on his.

From saying "I'm sorry" a hundred times.

From the hardness in his chest melting when her mouth curved into a soft, welcoming smile.

From rubbing her plump nipple back and forth between his fingers.

From growling when she pressed herself into his touch wantonly.

From kissing the graceful curve of her neck.

From digging his teeth into the soft muscle of her shoulder.

From growling like a Neanderthal when she pressed her bottom into his groin, rubbing against him, until he was rock hard again.

From peeling her panties away from her legs like a man possessed.

From the utterly masculine grunt that escaped his throat when her wetness coated his fingers.

From nudging her upper leg up and away, from opening her wide for him, from pushing into her wet heat and lazily thrusting up into her until the restless beast in him calmed again.

From trailing his other hand down her silky body until it reached her clit.

From whispering, "Yes, again, *cara mia*," like a man possessed when she pleaded with him that her sensitive flesh couldn't clench and fracture again after her first release.

From the desperate need that crawled through his legs toward his spine when she turned and looked into his eyes,

and said against his plundering mouth, "You can be selfish, Dante. You can take me once without thinking of my
release. I'm more than happy for you to use me for your
pleasure. As you want it, whenever, wherever."

From his chest cracking wide open.

From the cold sweat that claimed his skin as he worked
his fingers and himself in tandem, determined that she
would fly with him again.

And when she came with his name on her lips, and her
muscles clenching and releasing around him like a silken
glove, he couldn't stop himself from pushing her facedown
onto the bed, from pulling her up onto all fours and thrusting into her from behind.

He couldn't stop his heart from aching, his body from
shuddering again and again when she turned toward him,
an impish smile around her mouth and said, "Harder, Dante.
Deeper, please. I want to come again. With you."

He had no idea how he managed to bring her to climax
again. All he knew was that she fell apart and he lost even
the semblance of control. For the first time in his life, nothing mattered but his own release. Nothing mattered but the
burn riding up his thighs and pooling in his balls.

Nothing mattered except losing himself inside her.
Hands fisted in her hair, teeth sinking into her shoulder,
he drove in and out of her, working himself to the edge.

His climax when it came was the most powerful thing
he'd ever experienced. The most raw, honest, revelatory
moment in all his life. The most he had ever shared of himself, the most he had ever taken of someone.

He flopped onto her body, resting his weight on his elbows, his harsh breaths making her hair fly under him,
their sweat-slicked bodies gliding and sliding against each
other. Still, he wasn't satisfied. She was so fragile, so delicate beneath him. "Ali, look at me."

Hoarse. Raw. Uncivilized. Each word of his felt different. Felt new. He felt different. Somehow less, not enough for her.

She turned, her chin resting against the white sheets. Her hair flew away from her face as she blew at it, and then, after the spine-tingling experience they had just had, after the rough way he had used her, somehow she managed to smile at him. A gloriously warm smile that made her eyes shine and her mouth wide. "Hi."

A single, weightless word that lit up an incandescent joy in his chest.

When he finally noticed the uneven rhythm of her breath, he tried to move off her.

She shook her head.

"I'll crush you," he whispered, undone by the smile, by the warmth. By her.

"Not just yet."

"I'm sorry for earlier. For…leaving you like that."

"As long as you find your way back to me, we're okay, *si*?"

"Si."

And then she tugged his head down to her and took his mouth in a wet, open, raw kiss that made him semi-hard between their bodies again. Her smile was pure wickedness. "That was fantastic, mind-blowing. You give good sex, babe. You're always worth the wait."

Like a teenage boy, he could feel himself blushing. He rubbed his thumb over her lip. "I didn't hurt you?"

"No, but it's your turn to compliment me. I know how fabulous I am but a girl needs compliments now and then."

He knew she was teasing but he couldn't laugh. He couldn't imagine life without her now. He rubbed his fingers over her shoulder and placed a reverent kiss to her damp skin. Emotion was hard for him, and words to express what he felt, even harder. "I'm glad I blackmailed you."

She flipped herself onto her back under him, and the rasp of her breasts against his chest made them both groan. And then her hands clasped his cheeks, her eyes shining. "I'm glad I caved."

With that simple statement, she rolled over to her side, pulled his arm over to kiss his palm and nestled into him as if she belonged there.

His wife was the bravest woman he'd ever met. And he, a powerful, arrogant thirty-six-year-old who ruled his life with precise ruthlessness, was terrified of what else she would unleash on him.

Of what else she would ask of him that he couldn't, wouldn't be able to give. Of what he'd do the day she realized that finding his way back to her simply wasn't enough.

CHAPTER ELEVEN

ALISHA STARED AT her reflection in the mirror, her eyes wide at the outrageously sexy outfit she'd chosen for the party tonight.

And this dress she'd had specially commissioned from an up-and-coming British-Indian designer was it. It was an extravaganza for a woman who'd lived in jeans and T-shirts for a decade but Ali wanted to make her parents proud tonight.

She wanted the world to know of her happiness.

She wanted to share it with these people who'd been part of Matta Steel for generations.

She wanted to embrace her part in her papa's legacy.

She wanted Dante to be proud to call her his wife.

The wide, ruffled skirt of her mauve *lehenga* had layers upon layers of ruffles, giving her the fairy-tale princess look that was all the vogue on the runway this year. But the true genius of the outfit was in the *choli* and the *dupatta*.

When the designer, Maya, had showed the sketch to Ali, her first impulse had been a resounding no. It bared too much, it was too risqué. As far as she knew, a traditional *choli lehenga* was a wide, full skirt with a blouse that bared her midriff, yes, but covered everything up front with a silky *dupatta* to trail from her shoulder.

But since Ali had asked for a modern take on it, for something that was traditional and yet looked sensual,

Maya insisted she give it a chance. And when Ali had tried it on, it had looked simply stunning.

The blouse was strapless with gossamer mauve sleeves hanging low on her arms leaving her entire neck and shoulders bare. But the silky blouse cupped her breasts from beneath, like a lover's hands, leaving the upper curves bare. Since she didn't have big boobs, it wasn't so much the cleavage that was outrageous but the way it covered only the lower half.

The *dupatta*, which was a silky shawl in the same mauve, shimmered with intricate silver thread work, hung from one shoulder.

At Ali's insistence, Maya had hitched it across her chest and pinned it to the skirt. So the effect was the mirage of the *dupatta* covering her torso on one side while her breasts played peekaboo on the other.

Big chandelier earrings hung from her ears while she left her hair down to show off the new haircut. She had made her eyes up into a subtly smoky kohl look and had dusted dark blush onto her cheeks. A light pink shimmering gloss on her lips and she was done.

She was ready to meet the world.

And she was ready to meet her husband whom she hadn't seen in three weeks.

She had so much news to share with him, so many plans to make, so many things to look forward to that she felt as if she was bubbling over with happiness.

Ali had wanted to shock and surprise Dante but she was the one who got the surprise of the century as she stepped out of the chauffeured Mercedes that evening.

Matta Mansion glittered like a new bride on the night of the Diwali party, decorated with hanging lights everywhere. Focus lights from the grounds made the white marble fa-

cade glitter like an Indian palace of old. The gardens beyond had been decorated with fairy lights, every brass and
copper artwork that had been the highlight of her mom's
art collection polished to a sheen.

Ali walked into the ballroom and gasped. Thousands
of red, earthenware *diyas* with cotton wicks had already
been lit and cast shadows on walls. She had no idea how
Dante's staff had managed to lay their hands on so many
of them. No idea how he'd found out all the lovely Hindu
traditions that surrounded the festival of Diwali and had
them implemented. Especially when he'd been in Tokyo
for three weeks.

A small trio of players were seated on a divan behind
the main dais, decorated with flowing silks, playing *sheh-
nai* and *tabla*. The scent of fresh flowers filled every nook
and cranny. Just the delicious aroma of all the sweets the
chefs had laid out on the massive buffet table had her mouth
watering.

Ali stood on the second-floor balcony and looked out
over the gardens. In another hour, every inch of space would
be crammed with guests Dante had insisted they invite.
Dusk was just an hour away. Once everyone was here,
Dante would welcome them all.

They would light some sparklers and then there would
be a feast.

Tears filled her eyes as unbidden, a memory came to
her, drowning her.

Of her mama decorating the house just like this when
Ali had been maybe four. Of throwing open the doors to
every member of staff and employee of Matta Mansion. Of
dressing Ali and Vikram in traditional clothes while she
herself had worn a bright red sari and the diamond necklace that Alisha now owned. Of her papa picking her up
and then kissing her mama on the forehead.

"Ali?"

Ali turned so fast that she almost tripped on the hem of her *lehenga*.

Dressed in a conservative black suit with a white shirt underneath, Dante looked suave and powerful and utterly masculine. Air left her lungs in a hurried rush. The platinum cuff links she had left for him on his study table glimmered at his cuffs. That unruly hair was combed back, highlighting the harsh features, rendering him absolutely magnificent.

"You look…incredible."

The husky, rough tone of his words made butterflies flutter in her belly. Suddenly, she was glad she'd gone with Maya's outrageous creation.

His hands landed on her shoulders, the rough pads of them slithering against her bare skin. Dark eyes studied her with lingering intensity. His gaze moved from her hair to her shoulders, lingering for just a few seconds on the way the *choli* cupped her breasts. Her nipples tightened, her blood thick as honey in her veins.

"I should have believed you when you said I'd be floored, Alisha." The way he said her full name made her smile. Exasperation coated his words. "Asking me to foot the bill for that dress is tricking me. It bares too much, Ali."

"It's called a *lehenga*," she said swishing the wide skirt in her hands with a brazen smile. "I told the designer to make it the most spectacularly sexy outfit London has seen in a while. I told her it should befit the wife of a gorgeous, arrogant, wonderful husband. I told her the world should remember the night when Alisha Matta—"

"Vittori."

She blinked. "What?"

"Alisha Vittori. You're Alisha Vittori. Not Matta anymore."

Alisha Vittori.

It was just a name, and yet her heart thudded against her rib cage.

She scrunched her nose and his jaw tightened. "Nobody really changes their name these days."

"Mrs. Puri, in all her omniscience, it seems, was right. I find I'm a traditionalist at heart. I want my wife to take my name. I want the entire world to know that, while you have me wrapped around your finger, I have a claim on you too. I never want there to be a doubt about why I want you as my wife."

The voices downstairs floated away leaving Dante and her alone in their own world. His finger rubbed her collarbone, relentless heat spewing from the small touch.

With a groan, he covered her mouth with his. Completely. Utterly. The kiss was tenderness itself. Soft. Inviting. Opening up the whole world and putting it at her feet.

It seemed as if it was the very essence of the man he was—full of depth beneath the isolation he set upon himself, full of emotion and passion that he was determined to deny. A heart so big and that gave generously while remaining closed off to receiving anything in return.

He venerated her with those soft lips, his eyes shining because she'd given him everything. He knew it, she knew it. The words didn't need to be said. It was as she'd guessed—the only way into Dante's heart, the only way to carve a small place for herself in there, was to surrender everything. To lay everything open at his feet.

She felt as if she was stripped to flesh and bone, all her armor falling away. As if his kiss was what she was made for.

He deepened the kiss, his fingers in her hair, his hold on her heart tightening.

It spoke of things he would never say. It showed her that

she had a place in his heart too, however small. It told her that this arrogant, powerful man was no more in control of the bond between them than she was.

He kissed her as if she were the most precious thing he had ever held. He extracted a tiny velvet box from his jacket and her heart raced.

Every inch of her trembled as he pulled out a delicate-looking necklace. Three diamonds glittered in the middle of the thin chain, while tiny black beads lined up on either side. Ali stood, stunned, as he pushed her hair back and hooked the delicate chain behind her neck. It was a *mangalsutra*, the chain a husband put on his wife in the Hindu tradition.

His fingers lingered at her nape, his chin resting on her head.

She kept her head bowed, fighting the tears prickling behind her eyes. Fighting for breath. Struggling to stay still while the ground rocked from under her.

As if he understood, he wrapped his arms around her and held her tight. Her breasts pressed against his chest, her trembling legs held by the cradle of his powerful thighs.

"Mrs. Puri told me that I wasn't being fair. That your father would have demanded that I do right by you. That I was doing everything by my family's traditions, leaving yours out."

"She called you and took you to task?" Ali demanded. "She worships the ground you walk on."

The few seconds he waited resonated with his reluctance. "I called her and asked her to explain how things had been done with your parents. And she walked me through them. Ali, if you want a Hindu wedding or a reception, or a *mehendi* night or a bachelorette party, whatever you want, I want you to have it. I don't want you to resent me ten years down the line because I cheated you out of some tradition or custom. I don't want you to tell me in thirty years that

I didn't give you a bride's trousseau as custom demands. I want you to have everything you desire, *cara mia.*"

He had the whole mansion looking like it had during her childhood. Like a beautiful bride waiting for her groom.

He had decided that they would resurrect the tradition of the Diwali party, which had been her mother's yearly extravaganza. He'd invited so many of the old staff, Matta employees, charity workers, even Jai.

He had asked Mrs. Puri so that he could do right by her family's traditions.

And he claimed, again and again, that he had no heart to give. That he wasn't a romantic. That he didn't do relationships. That he didn't do love. Her heart seemed to have crawled into her throat and lodged there. Making even breathing difficult.

"Look at me, Alisha," he said in that commanding tone of his.

Chin quivering, Ali did. If he kissed her, she would melt into him. He was everything she had ever wanted and she felt as if she were in some fairyland where all her wishes were being granted. Terror filled her when she thought of that midnight stroke that would return everything back to reality, to a world without him.

"Will you be my wife, Ali?"

She took his hands in hers, tears running down her cheeks, and brought his hand to her cheek. "I don't need ceremonies to define this thing between us. The first time I walked into your bedroom, I became your wife, Dante. You're making me cry and I look like something the cat dragged in when I cry…and—oh, no, my makeup," she wailed.

Laughing, he produced a handkerchief and carefully blotted her cheeks. "You're always beautiful and it will drive me insane the whole evening that other men will see you in that outfit."

"Did Mrs. Puri tell you that according to Hindu traditions, you're stuck with me for seven lifetimes?"

He nodded and there was such tenderness in his eyes that it stole her breath. "I'm hoping that this is the first one. Shall we go down?"

"It's not fair," she whined.

He frowned. "What's not fair?"

"It's been three weeks and I'm dying to get you into bed, or against the wall, and there are all these people waiting for us…"

He pressed a chaste kiss to her temple as if to tease her even more. "Patience, *tesoro*. Remember, good things come to those who wait."

And he was worth the wait.

By the time they had seen the last guest off and were riding the elevator toward Dante's penthouse, it was past one in the morning.

Ali was so tired she felt like she could fall asleep standing up.

His arm around her shoulders, Dante pulled her to his side until all her weight was against him. His mouth was soft at her temple. And then he nuzzled her throat, the gesture less sexual and more tender. "Bed for you, I think. I've been waiting all evening to get you out of your…*lehenga*," he said gingerly, trying out the word, "but I'll do it to put you to bed."

Ali smiled so widely that she thought her mouth would crack. "No, no, no. I have a million things to tell you, plans to make for us and it's been killing me to wait."

His gaze lingered on the shadows under her eyes. "Ali, we can do it tomorrow morning. I'm not going anywhere."

"Please, Dante."

He laughed and pressed a swift kiss to her mouth. "Well, if you ask nicely like that, *si*."

Excitement replacing the exhaustion, Ali hit the number for the floor to her studio. "First thing on the agenda for tonight—do you want to see my work?"

The anticipation and the pure joy that filled his eyes made him look breathtakingly beautiful. "*Si*, please."

She took his hand and dragged him with her. Just as they reached the door to the studio, she halted. "Actually, that's not the first item."

"Ali, I hate that I've made you so insecure with my cruel words, but please, *cara mia*."

"No. It's not that. I… I just… I came up with this during the party."

His smile disappeared. "No, you can't be friends with Jai. I had Izzy invite him because you said he was looking for capital for his start-up and it would be good for him to network and meet some of the shareholders. It's not that I don't trust you, it's just that your ex in your life is not something I can tolerate. Please don't—"

She wanted to argue just for the heck of it. But Dante was taking tentative steps toward communicating his feelings with her and really, she didn't even want Jai in her life. They had nothing in common anymore. Instead she said, "Okay. I won't."

He looked so shocked by her easy acceptance that she laughed out loud.

"Just like that?"

Going on her toes, she whispered, "Today's your lucky day, mister." She swiped her tongue over his lower lip until he opened for her. "I hope you take complete advantage of it. Of me." His answer was to kiss the hell out of her, until she forgot her own name.

He was panting when he pulled away, lust etched on every inch of his face. "If you want me to listen to all the items on your agenda, you had better keep your hands to yourself, *cara mia*."

Out of breath herself, Ali nodded.

It took her several minutes to retrace their conversation. "So, the first thing is that today, I… Having the party at the mansion, it made me realize… I want to live there. I mean, us, I want us to live there. To make our home there, make it a happy place again, fill it with good memories and laughter and…" She swallowed the word *love* at the last second.

"I think it would have made both Mama and Papa and even Vikram happy, don't you think? We can—" heat swarmed her cheeks at the intensity of his gaze "—like you said, when we're ready, we… I do want a big family and the grounds and the house would be perfect to raise an army of kids."

"An army?" he said in such a low voice that she laughed again.

"Si."

"Okay. We'll live at Matta Mansion."

She took his hand and rubbed the palm against her cheek. Her heart was in danger of exploding out of her chest. "Just like that?" she said, trying to breathe over the lump in her throat.

"Today's your lucky day. I hope you take advantage of that, *bella mia*."

I love you so much. The words flitted to her lips but Ali swallowed them away. She didn't want to bring awkwardness to such a beautiful day and she didn't want to make him uncomfortable.

Instead, she just nodded, took his hand and pulled him into her studio.

Dante had no idea what to expect. His disparaging comments before still shamed him. So he had forced himself to keep an open mind, to support and encourage her when she needed it, to catch her if she faced disappointment. Not because he thought she would fail but because art was such a subjective world and he just…he wanted to be there for her.

As Ali turned on the huge industrial-strength lights he'd had the workmen install when he had purchased two flats and had them converted into a large open studio for her, he told himself that whatever she showed him, he would praise her, he would encourage her effort. He would—

A number of blown-up framed photographs stood leaning against the walls all around him.

He found himself at an utter loss for words.

Each print was a candid shot—a starkly beautiful life moment captured in time. One was a naked woman in the kitchen of that restaurant in Bangkok—no hint of vulnerability in her face as she met the camera head-on. One was a woman feeding her child—utter bliss on her face. One was a man on his knees in front of a woman with his mouth on her sex, one of a woman covered in bruises from fingerprints on her neck to the impression of shoes on her belly and it went on and on and on.

Every single one of them was hauntingly beautiful, tender and yet real at the same time—life in all its glory and indignity—and each one spoke volumes of the extraordinary talent and perspective of the woman who had captured them.

Shame and pride warred within him, and still he had no words to say.

"Dante?" she whispered, no tentativeness or need for validation in her words.

Standing amid her black-and-white and color prints, she was a goddess.

He went to her, took her hands, kissed her knuckles. Searched his mind for the right words. *Cristo*, what could he say that would tell her how humbled he felt that she had shared them with him.

"I don't know why you did it, but thank you for buying me that camera all those years ago."

He shook his head, emotion clogging his throat. "Don't… lay this at my feet, *bella*. If I hadn't, you'd have found another way to make it happen. You're…your work is…" he laughed. "Your papa…he would have been so proud, Ali. He would have been elated to see how extraordinary you are."

Tears overflowed in her eyes and fell down onto her cheeks. She came to him like lightning and fire and he caught her in his embrace. Held her while she cried. Glad that for once in his life, he'd found the right words to say to her.

Hoping that every time she came to him for something like this, he had enough to give her what she needed.

Hoping that, for the first time in his life, his past hadn't robbed him completely of his ability to give affection, to receive the love she gave him.

Ali had no idea how long she stayed in Dante's arms like that. All she knew was that life couldn't get more beautiful. Or more giving. He was so solid and real and wonderful in her arms that she never wanted to let go. The moment was so tender and loving and complete she almost changed her mind. Almost.

But she didn't want to start their new life hiding something so important from him. She didn't want to make this decision on her own. She shouldn't have to. Especially since it affected them both. And she was sure, whether he agreed with her or not, he would want to know.

So, as much as she wanted to stay in his arms and beg him to take her to bed, she took a long breath, filled her lungs with the essence of him and pulled back slightly. "Do I look all grungy then?" she said, still trying to find the right words. "I have too much makeup on to be crying every other second."

He didn't smile. A little line appeared between his brows, as if he knew she was delaying. But then, he did know her very well.

"What is the third thing on your agenda?"

She stepped out of his embrace completely and faced him. "My agent wants me to do an exhibit, as soon as possible, actually. Her team is trying to decide which gallery will display it best. And she told me that they're all trying to get it to theirs. It will start in London, and based on the reception, it might…go to other cities, like New York, Beijing. We're still talking about the details.

"It's all happening so fast. I've hired an employment agency and put out ads for employees for the charity too."

"That's fantastic news. The world should see your talent. And it looks like you're doing the best thing for the charity. You can still be involved at a higher level. Are you worried about the travel?"

Ali shook her head and swallowed the misgivings in her throat. "No, no… That's not it. It's just that something else has come up too. Do you remember that photography apprenticeship I had wanted to go on but that never happened?"

He didn't completely withdraw, but his mouth tightened. *"Si."*

Ali looked down at her laced fingers. Christ, why was this so hard? Why did it suddenly feel like there was an ocean between them already? "My agent showed some of my work to this American entrepreneur/philanthropist who puts together teams to work in some of the remotest areas of the world, like Tibet, Bosnia, Haiti. You know, sometimes they're war zones, sometimes it's just a rebuilding effort to clean up after natural disasters.

"Anyway, he got in touch with me a week ago, out of the blue. No introductions. Not his agent reaching out to mine. Just called me one afternoon when I was here and asked me if I could meet him in a couple of hours because he was leaving London that night.

"Two minutes into the meeting, he asked me to join his team on the next expedition. Apparently, he always hires a world-renowned photographer to capture the expedition, sort of to bring those things to the world's notice. My agent told me he's never asked anyone as young as me before, but apparently, when she forwarded some of my work to him, he instantly decided that he wanted me. I've been reading up all about his teams and the trips they take, and I realized what an honor it is to be chosen."

Dante covered the distance between them and hugged her tightly. "I'm not surprised."

Some of her tension dissolved. When he held her like that, it felt as if there wasn't anything she couldn't conquer. "Yeah?"

He tipped her chin up. "You didn't say yes?"

"No. I… First, I was just so stunned. It took me a while to realize what a big compliment it was to my work. Not until I Googled the hell out of him. And then that night, my agent asked me what I was waiting for. I told her I'd have to talk to you. I mean, it's a decision that affects both of us, our life together and I… It didn't feel right to just say yes and then tell you about it afterward. I wanted to talk to you about it. It's been so hard to just sit on it while you were in Tokyo."

Once again, Dante had no words. He kept thinking he had the measure of her and she kept surprising him. His chest felt tight, as if his heart was too big for it. "Ali…"

His hands shook as he gathered her to him. "I'm glad you waited to discuss it with me although it's not necessary. This is your career and I want it to go from height to height until the whole world takes pleasure in your work."

She nodded but her anxiety was like a cloak around her. He hated to see her smile dim. He pushed the hair back from her shoulder and covered the silky bare skin. "What is worrying you? Is there a fee you have to pay? Don't worry about finances or the charity."

"No, there isn't. Of course, I don't get paid either because it's a privilege to join his team."

"So what's the problem?"

"The next trip that he wants me to go on...will leave in a month."

"And?"

"I'll be gone for at least eighteen months. Might be more. If I agree and sign the contract, I'm bound by it. I can't just up and leave if I don't like it. Of course, there will be scheduled breaks but I'm told they won't be long."

It was like a punch to his stomach. He couldn't imagine not seeing her for eighteen months. *Cristo*, he felt like a teenager saying goodbye to his first crush. It felt like a lifetime. "I see," he said, just to give himself time to gather his fragmented thoughts.

Ali hid her face in his chest, as if afraid of his reaction. The graceful line of her profile, the small tremors he could feel in her shoulders… This was the opportunity of a lifetime.

He couldn't be selfish. Her commitment to their marriage, to him, it was more than he'd ever expected to have in life. She was more than he'd ever expected to have. "There's nothing to it but that you go. *Si*, it will be hard not to see each other for that long but I… I'm going nowhere. Our life together is going nowhere.

"Just don't…fall in love with some guy on this expedition." The words fell away before he could prevent them. He cringed at how pathetic and insecure he sounded. But there was no arresting that chain of thought. He pulled her left hand up, the diamond winking at him. "Remember that you belong to me, *cara mia*."

Brown eyes glared at him through thick lashes. "It's not funny, Dante. Do you really not trust me?"

He rubbed his thumb over her cheek, compulsively. "Of course I trust you. You're just…" He blew out a big breath. Damn it, he'd always been strong and he needed to be strong for her in this. He couldn't use her affection for him to sway her. She would come to hate him for it and he couldn't bear that.

"Eighteen months is a long time!" He slammed his head back. That was the exact opposite of what he meant to say.

"Exactemente!" Instead of looking upset, she nodded her head fiercely. "I was hoping you'd say that. I don't think I can go that long without seeing you. No, I know I can't. These two-and three-week trips to Tokyo have been bad enough." She nuzzled into his neck, and he felt the flick of her tongue at his throat. The bite of her teeth at his pulse. He hardened instantly against the soft curve of her bottom and she groaned. "I…was hoping you'd come with me."

Dios mio, when she moved like that, all he could think of was to be inside her. Eighteen months was a long time, his brain repeated the thing on a loop. It took him a couple of minutes to process her last sentence. "What?"

She pulled back so that she could look into his eyes. "You know, like a long honeymoon. Except instead of luxury hotels as you're used to, it will be tents or huts or whatever accommodation they give us. We wouldn't have to be apart at all. I checked with my agent and his team and they said spouses are welcome. Of course they'll expect you to pitch in, but I don't see that as a problem. That way eighteen months will just be a breeze and then we can return—"

"Stop, Alisha! Just...stop talking." He felt as if she'd knocked him down.

She turned those big eyes on him. Expectant. Wide. Full of hope and happiness.

But nothing could stop his answer. "I can't just take eighteen months off. I run a billion-dollar company."

"I know. I mean I'm sure you can stay in contact with your teams even in the remotest areas. The voting shares have been officially transferred so you don't have to worry about a coup or any such thing. Izzy told me how Uncle Nitin tried to sabotage the Japanese deal and how that forced you to finally put him on a leash. So he's not a worry anymore either."

Dante stiffened. "What Nitin almost got away with proves that I need to be at the helm. I can't just walk away."

She leaped out of his arms, as if being near him was unbearable. Shaking her head, clutching her midriff. As if he was supposed to agree instantly to her madcap idea. "No one's asking you to quit Matta Steel. I don't think what you do is easy or small. I know that thousands of livelihoods depend on the company. If you're willing to at least give this thought, I'm sure it'll be a matter of snapping your fingers to have the technology to support it ready."

Dante paced the floor, feeling as if there was some dark force coming at him but he couldn't do anything to avoid it. As if he was losing her, but there was nothing he could do to hold on to her.

What she was suggesting was...unthinkable. The company was everything to him. "I can't go away for eighteen months, Ali. I just can't. What you're suggesting is childish and... I understand you're excited and got carried away but it's not that simple."

"Ask me not to go then. This is a great opportunity to build my career, to bring exposure to my work, yes. But at the end of the day, it is only one way. Ask me to give it up for you, for us, for our marriage and I'll do it. I'll happily stay, Dante. Please, just ask me. Demand it of me."

"*No!* Don't do that, not for me. I don't deserve it. Damn it, Ali... I can't give you anything in return for such a sacrifice." The words piled out of his mouth, a strange tightening in his throat. It felt as if she was cutting his very breath off. Felling him at every turn. Like his heart was in her hand and she was fisting it tight.

"It's not a sacrifice, Dante. That's what you don't seem to understand. I love you. I want to spend my life with you. I want to make our marriage a priority. I just... Don't cut me down at every turn. Please, Dante."

He didn't want her sacrifice. It would choke him for the rest of their lives. "I can't ask you to set your career aside for me. For us."

Hurt made her stomach so tight that Ali felt as if she couldn't breathe. He wasn't even going to consider any option she presented. He refused to take a step toward her, and he forbade her from taking one toward him. She pulled at her hair, fear beating a tattoo in her veins. "So how does this work then? What if, after this trip, I go on another one? How will this marriage work then?"

"You're asking me hypothetical questions to which I have no answers. Matta Steel is my lifeblood. I can't shirk my responsibilities. I can't risk something I have given decades to."

"Won't or can't, Dante?" she said, anger coming to her rescue. "What's the point of being a bloody billionaire if you can't even be your own boss? What's the point of this marriage if we are together when it's convenient for your career and mine? When you won't let me give myself to it completely and neither will you? You would have us live in this strange…limbo just because you fear love?"

A cold frost filled his eyes, turning his gray eyes unbearably distant. Even cruel. He was a stranger again. A man she hated. A man who had not an ounce of tenderness in him. A man who cared about nothing but the company. "Don't make this small thing between us into a transaction, Alisha. Don't twist this into some sort of big, romantic gesture that I'm supposed to do for you to prove what you mean to me.

"You don't get to dictate how this marriage works. Now or in the future. I can't just step away from the company I've given everything to, from the role for which I married you in the first place. I'm not my father. I never will be."

She nodded, suddenly everything so clear to her naively wishful heart. "But I'm not asking you to make a big, romantic gesture. I'm not asking you to give up Matta Steel. I'm just…"

It wasn't that he wasn't even giving her idea a chance. It was the rigidity with which he did it. He'd always draw careful, clear lines between them. Always be a little out of her reach. Always decide what their relationship would be and would not be. Push him a little and he trampled her. Demand a little more than he wanted to give and he would crush her heart.

God, she'd been so stupid. She'd imagined them in some tent under the stars in some remote location, weaving an even stronger bond for life. She'd imagined having him all to herself. She'd built so many castles in the air.

The idea of walking away from their life together before it had even begun made her chest ache. "No. You won't even give this thing between us a chance. God, Dante, you don't even know how to take that I'm happy and what I'm willing to give. You're so terrified that I'll demand some price for not going. For simply loving you. What do I have to do to prove that I won't? How long will I have to worry what I say or do will make you think I'm asking something you can't give. That I'm asking too much of you. It will always be me reaching out. Always be me waiting for you to love me, maybe just a little."

"I can't... I won't be manipulated in this relationship, Alisha."

"Then there's nothing more to be said except goodbye."

"Ali—"

"I'm going back to the mansion. Don't come after me, please. Not tonight. I... I'll leave soon and it will provide you with the perfect excuse to tell your precious media. And don't worry, your reputation will be pristine, just like always. I won't tell the world I fell in love with a man who truly doesn't know the meaning of the word."

Every instinct in her clamored to wait for him. To let him catch her, to let him hold her, to let him chase away the pain in her heart. But he was the one breaking it. He was the one throwing it away, the one who didn't realize what her love truly meant. He would always measure it like a transaction, always think of it as a weakness.

She had put her world, her heart, at his feet. And he had simply kicked it away.

So she held her head high and went back to the elevator.

She'd lived alone before, she'd somehow made it through, and she would do it this time too. Even if it felt like the pieces of her were too many ever to mend again.

CHAPTER TWELVE

SHE WAS GONE.

She'd been gone for over a month.

First, she left the flat, bunking down one floor below him, in the studio he had had built for her. Because he'd been worried about what trouble she would get herself into, and he wanted to keep an eye on her. Because he'd thought Alisha was a liability he was taking on. And he would need to do damage control.

The first couple of days in the flat without her had been his first glimpse of hell. Memories of her seemed to have been absorbed into the very walls, the very fabric of his home.

He'd lived alone for countless years and yet the silence now had a different, haunting quality. So Dante had taken to sleeping at his suite at work.

Then she'd walked up to the flat one evening when he'd returned for a change of clothes.

Clad in that off-the-shoulder loose sweater and some kind of leggings, she'd looked so excruciatingly lovely that it had been a kick to his gut. "You cut your hair," he'd said, unable or unwilling to keep a possessive tone out of his voice.

She hadn't even called him on it. Fingering the wispy ends that framed her delicate face and highlighted those sharp cheekbones, she'd simply said, "It will be easier this way. I won't have time to wash and blow-dry."

And then she'd told him that she was packing up all her work, leaving it with her agent, and that she was leaving the studio too.

That all that open space he'd had custom-built for her, premium real estate in London, was free again, to do whatever he wanted with. He'd been so angry with her.

He had still not understood how she could make a mountain of a molehill, how she was using a small difference of opinion as an excuse to turn her back on her vows, to walk out of their life together.

It wasn't as if he had asked her to turn down that opportunity. It wasn't as if he had told her that he would not wait for her.

No, he hadn't begged, it wasn't in his makeup to do so. But, even in the fury that had gone through him, he'd said he was okay with the kind of life she had described for their future. That even if she chose to go on expedition after expedition, to build her career, to do what she loved, to follow her passion, that it was okay with him. That he would always be in London, that he would always have a place for her in his life.

She looked as if he had swung an arm at her. As if he was speaking in a different language. As if he was the one who didn't know the meaning of compromise.

It wasn't what he wanted out of their life together, it wasn't the picture he had of their marriage. He didn't want her to go off for long months at a time, leaving him behind. But, still, he had taken that step.

She'd looked like another word from him would blow her away, like a fluttering leaf, but she hadn't cried. Funnily enough, he would have felt better if she had cried. Instead, the emptiness in her eyes, the sheer absence of that light that was her spirit, had terrified him.

And then she moved into her papa's home. He knew

she'd been there for three weeks before flying to New York to meet the philanthropist's team. He knew that in just a few days, she would leave for wherever it was that they were going.

Izzy had the information about their destination. He'd ordered her to get as much information as possible from Alisha, but had forbidden her to tell him where she was going. He didn't want to know. He didn't want to know in which part of the world his wife was.

But even after a month of her being gone, he was surprised at how empty everything felt each evening when he came home. He wasn't some romantic fool, some naive idiot in love to expect some kind of miracle to happen. He didn't expect her to be there waiting for him, in tank top and shorts, waiting to tease him, torment him, to love him.

Dios mio, how she had loved him. How she had touched him and kissed him and taken him inside her.

But every night he missed her. He missed her in his bed. He missed her in the kitchen. He missed her in his heart.

So he'd done what he'd always done to protect himself when life dealt him a setback. He'd reminded himself he had what he had always wanted. He was the CEO of Matta Steel.

He had thrown himself into the Japanese merger, worked like a demon for eighteen, twenty hours a day, hitting the bed only when sheer exhaustion claimed his limbs. When he was so brain-dead that thoughts of Ali couldn't torment him. He'd waited to feel that knife edge of desire to wane. Waited for the day when he would wake up and not reach for her. Waited for him to stop expecting her to walk in. Waited to stop holding his breath for her to kiss him, claim him. Like only she did.

Today, this morning, was not that morning.

Tonight, it seemed, was not that night. Grabbing the

keys to her studio, he took the elevator to the floor below. He had a feeling he had left sanity behind a few days ago. That he was on the very edge that he'd been determined all his life to avoid. That despite his every safeguard, despite him breaking her heart, Alisha had brought him to his knees.

He pushed open the door to the studio and turned on the industrial lights. Bare walls and empty floors greeted him.

There was no trace of her in the studio, just as she'd left no trace in the flat. A strange fever gripping him, he walked around until he felt as if the walls were closing in on him. And that was when he saw it, one lone print, framed, blown up, sitting against the far wall, covered by brown paper and tied together with string.

He was so desperate for a glimpse of her work, for a glimpse of her, that he realized he was tearing through the paper with no respect for her work. Breathing hard, he forced himself to slow down. Slowly, he removed the brown paper, picked up the frame and brought it to where he could see it properly.

What he uncovered stole the remaining breath from his lungs.

It was him.

His picture. The one she must have taken before he realized that she was taking pictures of him.

Before he'd been even completely awake. When he'd still been in that moment between sleep and wakefulness, when all his defenses were down, when his heart was as free and light as it had been when he'd been a small boy, loved by his parents.

It had been in that moment when he'd automatically reached out for her, searching for her. She'd zoomed in on his face at the second before he'd found that she wasn't there next to him. And somehow, she'd captured everything he felt for her but hadn't even known.

Such love, pure and complete, such anticipation, such expectation, such utter trust, that somehow when he reached for her, and when he found her, his life would be complete. That he would be complete.

What had she felt when she had developed the print? Why hadn't she come to him with it, why hadn't she shown him what he'd felt and demanded that he acknowledge it? Why hadn't she—?

It will always be me reaching out. Always be me waiting for you to love me, maybe just a little.

Dios mio, she had begged him to give them a chance. She'd asked him for one capsule of time in his entire life and she had promised to give him all of hers. All the moments, all of herself. And he had said no. He'd pushed her away. He'd called her childish, dramatic, he'd told her she was twisting things.

God, he didn't deserve her.

It wasn't his father's fault or his mother's fault, it was his own. He had had love like he had never known before and he had pushed her away. *Cristo*, he'd actually put the company before his wife.

She was right, he was a coward. He had known in his heart that she was everything to him. That if she persisted, she could demand his very soul and he would put it at her feet.

I will not be my father.

God, he'd even given voice to his biggest fear.

From the beginning, she had floored him with her generous heart. She'd captured him with her surrender and Dante found he had nowhere to go, no recourse but to tell the woman that stole his heart that he loved her.

That all the riches in the world didn't mean anything

without her. That for her, he would give up a hundred companies, he would give up everything.

She was everything to him.

New York in December was like a page from a fairy tale.

White blankets of snow covered every building, every street, wherever Ali looked.

Christmas lights sparkled everywhere—on buildings, skyscrapers, trees, awnings of tall apartment buildings, reflected brightly on the white snow-covered ground.

But she'd never believed in fairy tales, not even as a child. Maybe that was what came of living with a single parent, of being the product of a failed marriage.

Even when the city was at its most beautiful, its most brilliant, Ali still saw the broken-down buildings, the cheap housing and poverty, a sharp contrast to the glittering beauty and opulence. She loved walking through the different boroughs, and she'd been going through the rolls on her camera like it was candy. It was such an interesting landscape. So much life to see. To capture.

But, every once in a while, especially when she was being jostled around by typical New Yorkers in Manhattan, suddenly she would spot a well-dressed man—usually in an expensive three-piece suit, his hair jet-black, his profile sharp—and just like that, her heart would crash to a complete stop.

The masses of people around her, the noise, the decadent scents of food and sometimes the nauseous scents of decay, the honk of horns, the chatter in different languages flying back and forth…everything would melt away. She'd still, even with the wind biting her cheeks, and crane her neck to locate that tall man. Every molecule in her body thrumming with hope that maybe, this time, it was not some stranger, not some executive, but Dante.

It happened a dozen times, a hundred times, and yet, she fell for it every single time. Hope, excitement and then the crash of disappointment, followed by such a paralyzing ache in her chest.

She went through her day, meeting with John Carter's team, trying different restaurants in Manhattan and midtown, just living. Slowly, she would build herself back up and then she would spot someone again.

It was a vicious loop that she seemed to be stuck in.

She couldn't wait to leave New York. But Mr. Carter's assistant had only informed her this morning the trip had been indefinitely delayed.

No reason had been given and Ali, for once too distracted, hadn't even asked for it.

In the first week, she'd realized that the scale of these trips was beyond what she'd initially imagined. The logistics were mind-boggling. The question left to her was whether she should stay in New York or go back to London.

New York, her aching heart whispered immediately.

Because New York was an ocean away from him.

Because, as much as it pained her to keep looking for him in a crowd where he would never be, at the end of the day, she had lived through another day without breaking down. Without calling him just to hear his voice.

Without jumping onto a flight back to London to beg him to take her back. On whatever terms.

She couldn't do that. She couldn't always be the one reaching out. Couldn't live with the constant choke hold of worry about what would make him shut down.

Whereas London was full of memories. She wasn't sure she even had the strength to walk away again. It had been hard enough to do it the first time. Pulling her coat together, Ali checked the street sign and sighed. Finally, she had made it to the Plaza.

She'd stay another week and then decide. Right now, it was time to join the living.

She forced herself to smile as she pulled the glass door open.

It wasn't Christmas yet but she knew Christmas parties abounded everywhere.

It would be nice to see the people she would be working with over the next eighteen months. It would be nice to forget the man she had left behind for at least a couple of hours.

She inquired at the reception desk and was directed to a suite on the twentieth floor.

Since the receptionist had immediately turned away to take a call, Ali swallowed her question and made her way to the bank of elevators. She checked her hair in the mirror and straightened the sweater dress she'd worn over black leggings.

In no time, she was knocking on the door. Something didn't feel right. She almost turned away just as the door opened and there was Dante.

A barrage of emotions came at Ali, knocking the very breath out of her. "What the hell are you doing here?"

But she didn't wait for his answer.

She turned away but didn't really make it far before he grabbed her arm and pulled her into the suite and closed the door behind her.

After two months, after searching for that beautiful face in every stranger, the sight of him rocked the ground from under her. Stole her breath. He was wearing a chunky sweater and dark jeans.

Two or three days' worth of beard covered his jaw, giving him a dangerous quality. Hiding that sensual mouth. His eyes glinted with some secret agenda, his shoulders stiff with tension.

In fact, he didn't look like the remote, coldhearted man she'd left behind at all. He looked distracted, rumpled, a little bit broken, as if he were human after all. As if despite his best efforts, she had left a little mark on him.

"*Buongiorno*, Alisha." His gaze swept over her sweater dress clinging to her breasts. A fire licked in his eyes. "You look good enough to eat, *cara mia*. I missed you. *Dios mio*, how I have missed you."

Even with the chill from outside still clinging to her skin, those husky words instantly warmed her up. The emotion ringing in them was a slap to her senses.

She wasn't going to engage with him. She wasn't going to get into a fight. She didn't want to spend a minute more than necessary with him, because at the rate her heart was beating, she was going to collapse on the bed and beg him to give her mouth-to-mouth. "I don't have anything to say to you. Nothing new to negotiate. In fact—" her throat filled with tears "—I take back what I offered. I won't give up this opportunity of a lifetime for you. You don't deserve it. You don't deserve me, Dante."

A bleakness entered his eyes. He ran a hand through his hair, his only tell that he wasn't quite put together. "I deserved that."

"Stop agreeing with me. Stop telling me you missed me. Just…stop."

"Don't cry, *cara mia*. I promised I wouldn't hurt you. I just want a conversation with you. Just half an hour of your time, Ali. Then you can walk out of here. I won't stop you."

Slowly, the shock of seeing him faded, and reality sank in. "Wait, I don't understand. How are you here?"

"I took the jet this morning."

Why was he playing with her like this? Letting her tote fall down to the floor, she leaned against the bed. She rubbed a hand over her forehead. "Why are you here, at the Plaza? John's assistant told me the team was meeting for Christmas drinks."

"That was me. I had John postpone the trip too."

Shock pulsed through her. "What? Why?"

"I had a lot of things to see to. Paperwork…"

"Paperwork, of course. What is it this time, Dante? What else requires signing? What else do you want from me? Because I have nothing left to give you. Nothing."

"Ali, I know I've—"

"This is not fair. I… I can't do this again and again. I can't walk away from you over and over. Don't play games with me."

"I've never played games with you. Not once. Not even in my dreams."

His fingers clasped her chin in a firm hold, his eyes boring into her. He studied her as if she were dessert after a fast. As if he were parched for the taste of her. "I…told John that I want to join the team. But I need a month or two at least to get things in good shape at the company. I can't just… If I need to give this my all—and I desperately want to—I need to make sure there are contingencies in place, in case the teams can't get to me immediately.

"I made three trips to Tokyo to make sure there were no problems with the production line. He twisted my arm of course, until I made a huge donation. But like you said, what's the whole point of being a billionaire if you can't bribe your wife's boss to wait until you can beg her forgiveness? To wait so that I can join her before she disappears for eighteen months and leaves my heart broken? Because it has been, *cara mia*. Without you…"

Hands on her hips, he dragged her to him until she was pressed up against him from chest to thighs. Shaking and shuddering, he was a fortress of heat and desire around her. Relief, it was relief that gripped him, she realized. "I kept dreaming that you had left before I could get to you. I've never felt so powerless…not since the *polizia* came to take Papa away. You were right. What I suggested wasn't a compromise at all. *Dios mio*, one eighteen-month stint is bad enough. If you left me like that again… I'm sorry for not realizing the value of what you gave me. I'm sorry for hurting you so much. For being so…"

His mouth trailed soft kisses all over her face, down her jaw, onto her neck until her pulse was in his lips. Shock and pleasure and hope—all collided with each other in her chest, vying for the upper hand.

Pleasure won and she clung to him like a limp doll, willing him to take her mouth without having to beg for it. Rough hands snuck under her blouse, branding her bare skin.

Words came and fell away from her mouth and Ali stared, hope fluttering its wings in her chest.

She gasped when Dante sank to his knees and buried his face in her belly. Dark eyes, shimmering with wetness, looked up at her. "I'm going with you, just not immediately. Do this trip and return to London or not. Do a hundred trips for the rest of our lives and don't return to London. I don't care. As long as we're together."

"Are you sure? This is not a transaction." A sob racked through her. "It's not a condition to love you. To be with you. It's not… If you ask me to leave with you to return to London today, now, I will. I just… I need to love you in my own way, Dante. Even if you don't. Even if you—"

When she would have interrupted him, he nipped her, effectively silencing her. "I'm in love with you, *cara mia*. We will travel the world so that you can take more of those powerful photographs. We will live like nomads if that's what you want. Our kids will travel with us if that's what you want. We'll never return to London again. Never buy a home. We'll do it all your way."

Ali sank to her knees and burrowed into him. "No. All I wanted was for you to take a step toward me. To let me love you like I want to. To love me back just a little."

"I love you a lot," he said and utter joy spread through her.

"I will make my home with you, wherever you are, Dante. You're my home, don't you see? Always, you've been the place I can land, the person I can love. You're everything to me."

Dante picked his wife up in his arms, his heart bursting with love for his wife.

* * * * *

SIGNED OVER TO SANTINO

MAYA BLAKE

PROLOGUE

CARLA NARDOZZI TOOK the chauffeur's proffered hand, stepped out of the luxury SUV and was immediately bombarded with the sights and sounds of New York City. The journey from her Upper East Side hotel to Midtown had been as tense and chilly as the air conditioning blasting from the vents.

To her right, her father, Olivio Nardozzi, stood stiff and seething.

Carla would've summoned a genuine smile for the driver had she been able to function in anything other than a complete state of ongoing shock.

The past seven days had unfolded in a series of bombshells she could scarcely wrap her head around. Bombshells she'd struggled to navigate without going under until she'd eventually, exhausted, settled in a place of icy numbness. But the biggest trial of all lay ahead of her. Or more accurately, it lay above her, sixty-six floors up in the office of the man she'd hoped never to set eyes on again.

As if pulled by powerful magnets, her gaze slid up the glass façade of the building housing the esteemed J Santino Inc.

An opportunity beyond your wildest dreams.

A once-in-a-lifetime endorsement deal.

A collaboration even a figure skater with your prominence would be insane to turn down.

For the better part of a year, those words had been impressed upon her by her father and her advisors. Lately, they'd been uttered in the solemn, no-nonsense tones of her agent and friend, Draco Angelis, who'd been at a loss as to why she was resisting the life-changing deal.

She'd listened and nodded in all the right places but had

known she would never accept the deal. Never have any-thing to do with the man heading the globally successful luxury goods company.

She'd kept her secret for three years and Carla had had no intention of facing it, or the man it involved, ever.

Until her reality had drastically altered.

A shiver that had nothing to do with the blustery March spring day rattled her bones.

In a few minutes, after long years of strictly regimented avoidance, she would be face to face with Javier Santino.

The man who'd taken her virginity. The man who'd granted her the most sensual, intensely unforgettable night of her life. The man who'd then absorbed her shocked, poorly delivered words the morning after with granite-faced hatred, then proceeded to banish her from his life with the cold in-cisiveness of a scalpel-wielding surgeon.

Years later, Carla still couldn't recall those harrowing hours without the naked blade of fear striking her heart.

It was the reason she'd avoided Javier Santino at all costs. It was the reason this was the last place she would've will-ingly placed herself.

'Come on, the deal isn't going to finalise itself with you standing out here staring at the building.'

The numbness that had wrapped itself tightly around her eased for a cracked moment, replaced with myriad volatile emotions as she stared at her father. Disappointment. Sad-ness. Anger. A deep and painful burgeoning acceptance that Olivio Nardozzi had a vastly differing definition of parental love than most normal fathers had for their children.

Bitterness surged high. 'We wouldn't be here if you hadn't gambled away—'

'Don't start this again, Carla.' He stepped closer on the busy sidewalk so they wouldn't be overheard by the trio of lawyers who'd accompanied them and now stood on the sidewalk, ready to escort her into Javier's presence. 'We have aired this out many times already. I don't particularly want to air it once again, especially in public. You have an image to maintain. A faultless image we have *both* worked hard for. In less than an hour's time, our financial worries will be on their way to being a thing of the past. We have to look forward.'

Look forward.

How could she when her immediate future entailed placing herself in the heart of the lion's den? A lion whose deathly silence had been even more unnerving than the roar she'd expected at any point during these past three years?

Sucking in a shaky breath, she placed one foot in front of the other, walked through the revolving doors and stood in the lift as they were whisked upward.

The office décor of J Santino Inc. was the last thing Carla expected. Sure, the place pulsed with the core efficiency needed to run a billion-dollar enterprise. But while Carla had expected glass and chrome and futuristic art pieces, she exited the lift and stepped into a vibrant foyer with colourful walls, exotic flowers and employees relaxing on lounge chairs and giant futons. Exquisite Latin American art dotted the vast space, and she was unwillingly reminded of Javier's passionate Spanish side.

Closing her mind to it, she followed a statuesque receptionist down a burgundy-carpeted hallway to a set of wide double doors, which swung open with an electric whine.

'Mr Santino will be with you in a moment.'

Carla's heart climbed into her throat as she entered a vast conference room.

Absently, she heard murmurs as her team took their seats, but she couldn't think past the coming meeting, her insides twisting hard as she drifted past sumptuous chairs and a polished cherry-oak table towards wide windows with impressive views of Manhattan.

Would those gold-brown eyes that had snapped cold fire at her the last time they'd seen her still blaze with hatred? Over the last year, since she'd first been approached with the endorsement offer, she'd wondered why Javier Santino would want her anywhere near his company. Sure, her world-number-one-figure-skater status placed her in a certain *would-kill-for* echelon, but there were a few dozen other sports figures in a similar position. Despite her management's insistence that she was being pursued because she was the right person for the job, she'd wondered whether it'd been a carefully set trap.

But not once had Javier attempted personal contact, choosing to communicate through his lawyers and executives. Folding her arms, Carla swallowed and allowed a little hope to grow. Maybe Javier had moved past the events of the morning after their night together. Perhaps the abhorrence she'd glimpsed during their fraught exchange, the deep trepidation that what had happened between them had been life-altering, and the long months following when a peculiar ache had lodged itself in her chest every time his name had crossed her mind, had all been in her overblown imagination.

Javier had moved on to other conquests, and had continued to aggressively pursue his *work hard, party harder* lifestyle if his presence in the tabloids was any indication.

So maybe her trepidation was for nothing, maybe she was just overthinking this—

'Do you intend to conduct the meeting standing up, Miss Nardozzi?'

Carla flinched and turned at the flat, detached tone.

Her breath locked in her lungs, every cell in her body clenching in freeze frame as she stared at the man sauntering down the side of the conference table.

In a dark grey pinstriped suit that accentuated his broad shoulders and a white shirt and navy tie that screamed understated elegance, Javier Santino didn't need the tough lawyers who flanked him to underscore his supremacy and importance. He was *still* hugely formidable and domineeringly sexy. His overpowering masculinity would continue to draw eyes to his sculptured cheekbones and uncharacteristically full mouth, which held a perpetual reddish tinge as if he'd been thoroughly and expertly kissed, long after he was well past his prime.

He stopped opposite her and, even across the vast polished surface, the sheer dominance of his aura slammed into her. Gold-flecked brown eyes pinned hers, one eyebrow lifted in cool, arrogant query.

Deep inside, past the numbness and the fear, something wild and hot and dangerous sparked to life, and she felt the ground shift beneath her feet.

She shouldn't have come... Then again, what choice did she have?

'Very well. I'll take that as a yes.' His gaze conducted an impersonal inspection of her face and body, then swung from her, releasing her from the disturbingly deep frisson that had taken hold of her. Striding to the head of the table, he pulled out a chair, unbuttoned his jacket in one deft move, and sat down. 'Since you also didn't answer my PA when she asked whether you wanted refreshments, I'll assume you don't want any?' Javier continued, the deep, smooth tenor of his voice igniting the flame higher.

Carla swung her head towards the departing PA, her mind unfreezing itself long enough to wonder how long she'd been caught in the dangerous tide of the past.

'No, I'm fine. Thank you.' She raised her voice slightly to catch Javier's PA. The woman turned and nodded with a cool smile before leaving the room.

'Good. Shall we begin?'

The magnetism that had gripped her outside as she'd stared at Javier's building returned full force. Her gaze returned to him, her heart beating faster as she stared at him.

There was no trace of the censure she'd expected, no hot-blooded Latin lip curl or even a hint of the fact that this man had seen her naked once, had done things to her body that still had the power to make her blood pound hot and hard through her veins.

He was going for impersonal. Stony. Businesslike.

As she shakily pulled out the chair he indicated to his right and sat down, Carla told herself it was okay to breathe in relief.

If Javier wanted to proceed with no acknowledgement of their past, then so would she. In fact, it was a brilliant thing. No need for further angst.

'I believe everything's been settled between our lawyers? You're finally willing to agree to the quarterly payment terms and the performance-related incentives stipulated in the contract, correct?'

Carla dragged her eyes from Javier to glance at her father. She spied the haughty desperation there, the silent command that their dirty laundry not be aired. She wanted to rail at him, demand to know what had possessed him to gamble away all her money, to jeopardise everything she'd worked for and bring her to the brink of bankruptcy. She didn't doubt that he'd have another blithe explanation, the callous hauteur he'd often displayed towards her as a child their only means of communication nowadays.

She glanced away again, deliberately numbing herself to the pain and disappointment. Steeling herself, she focused on Javier once more.

'Yes, I agree to your terms.'

'Unless, of course, there's any way you'd reconsider a larger, upfront payment?' her father suggested, squaring his shoulders as he planted his elbows on the table.

Javier's gaze didn't shift from her face. 'No. If you came here under the pretext of signing the final agreement only to try and renegotiate the terms, then you've wasted all of our time. I sincerely hope that's not the case, Miss Nardozzi.' The cold edge in his tone matched the look in his eyes.

Another shiver rippled over her. 'No, the clauses agreed upon are fine.'

Her father exhaled. 'Carla—'

'*Everything* is fine.' She struggled to keep her voice from wobbling through the lie as tension escalated in the room. 'Can we get on with it, please?'

Javier's gaze sharpened. 'You understand that, due to the delay in getting this signed, the cooling-off period will no longer apply? This contract, once signed, will be final and binding.'

Her fingers started to curl into her palms. Inhaling deeply, she placed them on the cool surface of the table and strove for composure. 'Yes. I really don't see why we're going over this again. My lawyers have explained everything to me. I'm ready to sign your document. All I need, Mr Santino, is a pen.'

If she'd been expecting a reaction, Carla realised she would be sorely disappointed. His gaze flicked with almost cruel lack of interest from her to his lawyers. An imperious nod, and the documents were produced and laid out before them. An elegant ball pen bearing his name arrived before her.

Shakily, she picked it up, signed and countersigned where indicated. The contracts were witnessed and exchanged. And her fate was sealed.

She would become the exclusive face of carefully selected J Santino products, called upon for advertising campaigns and publicity events whenever he chose.

It was done. With any luck, she could now negotiate further time with the bank back in Tuscany and save her family home. Not that it'd ever been a real home. These days it was more a showpiece property for her father to bask in the success he claimed she wouldn't have achieved without him.

But it was the only remaining roof over her head. The New York condo was gone, as was the chalet in Switzerland. *Everything* was gone.

Carla set the pen down and stood. 'Thank you for your time, Mr Santino. Now if you'll excuse us—'

'You're not free to go just yet, Miss Nardozzi.'

Her breath stumbled as Javier rose with fluid grace.

She stared up at him, meeting that stony expression once more. 'What…what more could we possibly have to discuss?'

A tight smile pursed his lips. 'It's confidential. Come into my office.' His gaze flicked over the table's occupants in a dismissive glance. 'Alone.'

Without waiting for a response, he headed for a set of double doors opposite from where she'd entered.

Her palms grew hot and she fought the urge to rub them against her thighs. Every instinct screamed at her to get up and walk out. She'd made it this far relatively unscathed. She'd seen Javier again, withstood his imposing presence, heard his voice, inhaled that singularly unique scent without losing her composure. What she'd dreaded most was over.

Yet she couldn't move.

'Now, Miss Nardozzi,' Javier insisted in cutting tones.

The atmosphere shifted again, men in expensive suits fidgeting beneath ricocheting tension.

'Carla,' her father's warning tone rumbled over her.

She ignored him, looking past him to the doors that led to freedom. Could Javier stop her from leaving? From retreating back to that numb place where she was marginally cocooned from pain and betrayal?

Yes. Because she was now bound to him, a contracted employee who couldn't refuse *reasonable* requests.

Swallowing the hysterical laugh that rose in her throat, she stood, ignoring the collective muted sighs of relief that floated round the table.

Carla entered Javier's office and drew to a stunned stop. Unlike the rest of his company's workspace, this was an unapologetically masculine domain. From the massive walnut desk and throne-like armchair set back against a solid wall, to the studded black sofas grouped around a glass and gold TV and entertainment centre on one side, the space shrieked a dominance that made her flesh tighten with acute premonition.

But no.

So far Javier had been cold and brutally businesslike. Uninterested in her, other than as another financial asset for his company. She had nothing to fear.

Behind her the door swung shut, followed by another distinct click.

Her gaze flew to Javier, to the tiny remote in his hand. A second later, he flung the control away, then advanced towards her with slow, precise strides. Her breath uselessly trapped in her lungs, Carla tilted her head to meet his gaze and the blood rushed from her head in a dizzying surge.

Because those mesmeric eyes were no longer cold. No longer impersonal. A very specific, very dangerous light blazed in their depths. A light that threatened to stop her heart altogether.

'At long last, here you are,' he murmured.

The savouring, triumphant statement made every nerve in her body jump.

'Here I am? What does that mean?' she retorted, fully aware her voice was bled of any power.

He stepped closer, amplifying his power and might by a thousand degrees. 'It means I never thought this day would arrive. You won't believe how many times I nearly threw in the towel. But revenge is a dish best served cold. Isn't that what they say?'

Ice filled her veins. *'Revenge?'*

He bent his head closer, as if sharing a salacious secret. 'Luckily, I'm a very patient man,' he whispered. 'I knew, sooner or later, I could count on you and your father's greed to bring you back to the contract table.'

Carla's mouth dropped open, her heart falling to her toes. *'Dio mio.'* Her voice snagged on the words.

He leaned back and smiled. A pure evil smile that drew her dumbfounded gaze to his sensual lips. *'Sì, this* is the expression I've been waiting three years for.'

He'd been scheming. Laying the perfect bait for her

downfall. And like a lamb to the slaughter, she'd walked right into his trap.

Just as she'd been a weak, trusting lamb throughout her father's machinations, childhood fears of abandonment unconsciously stalking her into adulthood so stealthily that she hadn't realised she was being taken advantage of until it was too late. She'd sacrificed herself for her father.

And now she was to be a sacrifice for Javier Santino.

A sheer wall of dread rose before her, every single brain cell frozen as she was caught in suspended animation.

From far away, she heard Javier speak but she couldn't rouse herself from the horror of her circumstances.

Firm hands caught her elbows. Eyes fringed by thick lashes narrowed. 'What is wrong with you, Carla? Or should I call you The Ice Princess? Isn't that what the media calls you? You're certainly dressed for it.'

Numbly, she glanced down at her white palazzo pantsuit. The jacket's severely cut style opened at the elbows when she lifted her arms, and the sleeves dropped almost to the floor. Teamed with a white silk camisole and white stilettos, the ensemble broadcasted a cutting-edge style suitable for a woman at the top of her game. Or so the stylist had insisted when she'd arrived with the clothes this morning. Staring at the get-up, she suddenly saw differently.

White, for innocent sacrificial lambs.

White, for fools.

The hysterical laughter she'd tried to stem bubbled up from her chest and burst free. It sounded strange in the impressive, masculine room. But the crack in her self-control felt good.

So good she couldn't stop laughing.

Javier blinked, then jerked her once. 'Carla!'

Laughter cut off like a light switch. 'I thought I was only Miss Nardozzi to you?'

Puzzlement tracked over his face. 'What's wrong with you?' he demanded again.

'What do you care?' she flung at him.

'I don't, except I'd prefer not to have a conversation with a woman who's acting like a walking, talking zombie.'

'Right in this moment, I wish I were one.'

A dark frown clamped his brow. 'Excuse me?'

Another bubble of laughter bursting free, she shook her head. 'You should see your face, Javier. Is this not going how you expected? Did you expect me to be a quivering idiot in the light of your revelation? Did you—*what are you doing*?' she screeched as strong arms lifted her off her feet.

In half a dozen strides he pinned her against a wall. They stared at each other for a charged, timeless second. Then someone moved. Her gasp was swallowed by the mouth that slanted over hers, the domineering possession so electrifyingly potent, every trace of numbness was instantly zapped from her body.

In its place raw, intense emotion flooded. Every sensation she'd retreated from surged in a tidal wave of feeling, concentrating in that powerful connection of their fused lips. From one heartbeat to the next, they tore at each other. Tongues duelled, groans fought for supremacy, hands searched and groped. And Javier came out on top each time, his indomitable will pounding into her, into the kiss until she was a seething ball of sensation, ready to be done with as he pleased.

Gradually the other emotions receded, leaving her with a deep, decadent arousal she'd only believed existed in her dreams. The realisation that it did not had her surging up on tiptoes, eager to experience more of it.

Javier deepened the kiss, his hands moulding her, his teeth nipping at her full lower lip. Powerful thighs parted hers and he planted himself firmly between them, the evidence of his arousal unmistakeable.

Dio, but he felt glorious. And he made her feel *alive*!

About to spike her hand through his hair, demand more, more, *more*, she was brought back to earth when her arms were wrenched from around his neck and pinned ruthlessly to her sides.

'Do I have your attention now?' he rasped.

White lamb. Sacrificial fool.

She glimpsed the menacing look in his eyes and her insides turned to useless jelly. 'Wh-what do you plan to do to me?'

Teeth bared in a cruel smile, he dropped his head and rubbed the tip of his nose against hers in a gesture so divorced from affection, it staked a cold knife of fear in her heart.

'Where would be the fun in laying it all out for you, Principessa? All you need to know is that by the time I'm done with you, you'll know that you should never have used me the way you did three years ago. Before I'm done with you, Carla Nardozzi, you'll get on your knees and beg my forgiveness.'

CHAPTER ONE

One month later

'SIR, I THINK you'll want to turn on the TV.'

'And why would I want to do that?' Javier Santino drawled, not lifting his head from the graphics spread on his desk. His designers had done an exemplary job, the sample bottles for the launch of his new and exclusive tequila line truly exquisite.

About to reach for the glossy image he'd settled on, he paused when his PA rushed to the far side of the room and grabbed the remote.

Javier sighed. Had she not been ruthlessly efficient, he wouldn't have forgiven her occasional bouts of excitable behaviour. Making a mental note to crush that tiny irregularity out of her, he turned from the view of Manhattan spread beyond his corner-office window and watched her flick on the TV.

'You asked the PR department to alert you if and when any of our clients make the news. They just called. Carla Nardozzi is on every channel.'

Javier froze.

In all his nearly thirty-three years, only two names had possessed the power to stop his breath. For the first three decades of his life, it'd been his father's name. The day after his thirtieth birthday, Carla Nardozzi's had joined the list. Both names sent icy chills of rage down his spine. Both robbed him of the ability to speak.

Three years after the event, his brief dalliance with Carla and how it'd ended still stuck between his ribs like the sharpest stiletto. As much as he detested himself for his weakness, he'd never been able to put it behind him.

It didn't matter that he knew why. The fact that he'd been unable to do anything about it angered him even more. In the grand scheme of things, Carla Nardozzi should be forgettable. A blip in his memory that shouldn't be worth his time or effort.

And yet all efforts to consign her to the *ex to forget* pile had been fruitless. He'd even gone as far as to pull her further into his orbit, just so he could tackle this particular thorn in his side once and for all.

'That will be all, Shannon,' he forced out, his gaze on the pictures flickering on the muted screen. He didn't recognise the building the paparazzi were crowded in front of, but the medical vehicles flashing past had him striding across the room.

His PA's retreat barely registered as Javier activated the sound.

'Miss Nardozzi's condition has now been downgraded from critical to serious but stable. Doctors are monitoring her closely following her awakening from her brief medically induced coma and she's responding well to treatment at this top medical facility in Rome.

'To recap events, Carla Nardozzi was airlifted from her father's estate and training facility in Tuscany following a fall during training. Unconfirmed allegations suggest the world number one figure skater's trainer, Tyson Blackwell, is being questioned by authorities following the accident...'

Javier flung the remote down. 'Shannon!'

The door opened a second later. 'Yes, sir?'

'Tell my pilot to ready my jet. We leave for Rome immediately.'

'Of course.'

Before the door had shut, he was picking up his phone. He knew the number by heart, although these days his dealings with Draco Angelis were more business than pleasure. The reason for it pierced another jagged blade of anger through him. Javier gritted his teeth as he pressed the receiver to his ear.

'You've heard the news,' the deep voice rumbled.

'When did this happen and why wasn't I informed immediately?' Javier snapped.

'Cool it, *amigo*. I've had my hands a little full on this side of town,' Draco responded.

Javier's ire didn't abate. 'You have people in place to ensure the right parties know what's going on. I should be at the top of your list of people to communicate with when it comes to Carla Nardozzi.'

A brief, pregnant pause. 'Agreed. You would've been informed before the hour was out. You just beat me to it.'

'For the sake of our continued working relationship, I'll choose to believe that.'

Draco exhaled. 'Is there anything else going on here I should know about, Santino?'

Javier reined himself in with effort, tightening his control on the emotions rumbling beneath his skin. This was business. Nothing else. 'Aside from the fact that I've invested several million dollars in your client and am about to invest several more? You think I should have to find out about her accident from the media? I don't appreciate being placed in a position where I'm caught unawares by situations like these.'

A deep sigh echoed down the line, and Javier got the impression that the formidable Draco Angelis had something on his mind. 'Point taken.'

'When did all this happen?' Javier was aware of the distinct bite to his voice but he didn't soften his tone. Any hint of softness was seen as a sign of weakness. And he'd sworn an oath a very long time ago never to be seen as weak or gullible.

'Yesterday.'

'And this induced coma?' he pressed.

'It was only overnight until they were sure there wasn't any brain damage. She's awake and the doctors are optimistic she's out of the woods.'

Javier exhaled. He released his death grip on his phone when the plastic creaked. 'I should be wheels up in an hour but I'd appreciate frequent updates on her condition.'

'You're coming to Italy?' Draco's voice expressed surprise.

Javier snapped up his briefcase shut and headed for the door. 'Considering how much I've invested in our mutual client, I believe a personal interest in her recovery is well within my rights. I'll see you in seven hours.'

He hung up and walked past his PA's desk.

'Cancel all my appointments until further notice.'

She opened her mouth then immediately shut it.

In his limo minutes later, he tried to wrestle his fury under control.

So what if Carla Nardozzi had rejected him in a way only the father who'd barely acknowledged his existence had done? After years of biding his time, he'd finally found a way to get his own back. The Ice Princess would be taught a salutary lesson. All he needed was to ensure she got back on her feet in order for him to deliver the punishment she truly deserved.

His emotions had nothing to do with this.

This was a matter of business. And of his pride.

Nothing else.

Carla tried to lift her head off the pillow and was immediately engulfed in a fog of pain and confusion.

'No, *signorina*, don't try and move.'

She relaxed, and the pain receded a touch. But the confusion remained. She'd been sure she was dreaming. And yet the voices and images flitting through her mind had been so vivid, so real.

Her father's voice had been unmistakeable. He'd been there the few times she'd woken up in the strange, sterile room.

But it was the other, deeper voice she'd heard the last time she'd woken that confused her and made her heart race. The change in the lighting suggested she'd fallen asleep some time after hearing *him*.

By all accounts that voice didn't belong here...wherever this cold, grey *here* was.

The last time they'd met, he'd been icily indifferent, a ruthless businessman intent on one thing—getting her to sign along the dotted line.

Or at least, he had been...until he'd had her exactly where he wanted her. Until that kiss.

Like a blurred lens swinging into sharp focus, the memory of the kiss burned bright and insistent. Along with the recollection of the way he'd looked at her afterward.

Javier Santino had looked at her with pure hatred. And she didn't blame him. After what she'd done three years ago, he had every right to detest her. It didn't help that her will power withered away to nothing in his presence. But since that unfortunate day a month ago, she'd summoned enough strength to assure herself nothing would happen.

Javier hated her. She'd dealt his ego a great blow. And a ruthlessly powerful and charismatic man like that would never forget an insult to his pride.

Which bemused her as to why he'd kissed her in the first place.

Or had she kissed him...?

Memory blurred and confusion remounted. Carla lifted her hand to her head. Tracing her fingers gingerly over a particularly sore spot, she gasped as pain ricocheted through her. A dull throb in her other wrist brought her attention to the fact that it was in a cast.

'Where am I?' she attempted, swallowing painfully around a dry throat.

The buxom woman bustling around her paused and Carla noticed her nurse's uniform for the first time. 'In a private hospital in Roma,' she replied, smiling her sympathy. 'You suffered a bad fall and a particularly nasty concussion.'

Of course. Memories of her accident resurged. The row with her father. Then with her trainer, Tyson Blackwell. Her instincts screaming at her in the moments before the accident to walk away. Then the sickening twist and the ice rushing towards her, one arm out in front of her in a vain attempt to break her fall.

She curled her fist and rested it in her lap. 'How long have I been here?'

'Three days. You've been asleep for most of the time since you came out of surgery, but it's great that you're healthy. You'll be on the mend soon. I'll get the doctor now, then you can visit with your family. They've been quite anxious to see you awake.'

'They?' she echoed, puzzled. Her father was her only family. Had been since… Carla swallowed as tears pierced her eyelids, surprising her.

She hadn't cried since that fateful night when she was ten years old. She'd known then that tears would earn her nothing but a sharp tongue and dire punishment and had quickly wised up.

'Sì,' the nurse responded. 'Your *papà* has been here throughout. He left about an hour ago, just before your young man arrived. *He's* been haunting the halls ever since his arrival.' The older woman cast her a sly glance. 'You're lucky to have such a passionate man in your life.'

'I…what…?'

The nurse patted her hand. 'Don't fret. The doctor will be here soon.' She exited, leaving Carla in a deeper state of confusion than before.

Pull yourself together.

Grabbing the remote that adjusted the bed, Carla slowly raised herself up, just as the doctor arrived.

'Signorina Nardozzi, it's good to see you awake.'

Carla nodded a reply, then lay there patiently as she was checked over, the fog clearing with each passing second, and with it a heart heavy with foreboding and regret.

The accident had happened because she'd been fleeing her demons. Pushing herself beyond her endurance in light of what her father had done and their ongoing rowing. Finally understanding why he'd been even more callously demanding these past few months had done nothing to alleviate the pain lodged beneath her breast.

She had well and truly reached a crossroads with her father.

Carla forced herself to listen to the doctor's prognosis. The state of her health was directly connected to her career. Despite the changes she intended to make, she needed to ensure her health remained optimal. The very roof over her head was dependent on it.

'Your father mentioned you're eager to return to training?' the doctor disclosed once he'd reeled out his list of dos and don'ts. 'Your next figure-skating event is in two months, I believe?'

'Yes,' she replied. It wasn't a championship event, but an important one nonetheless.

The portly man frowned. 'I advise against any form of training for a few weeks. Two weeks of total rest if you heal fast enough. Four weeks just to be on the safe side before you begin any strenuous exercise. Your wrist on the other hand will need a little longer than that.'

'What about publicity work—photo shoots and such? I have commitments to fulfil.' Her contract with J Santino Inc. didn't include lying about in hospital beds. She was surprised Javier hadn't sent his lawyers after her already considering the stringent clauses in her contract.

The doctor's frown deepened. 'I strongly recommend that

you take at least two weeks without any stress on your body. After that, perhaps if you agree to engage private care—'

Carla shook her head. 'That won't be necessary. I can take care of myself—'

'She'll have private care from the day she's released. You have my word on that, Doctor.'

Carla's breath caught in her throat at the deep voice that preceded the sleek, powerfully built man who entered the room.

So…she hadn't been dreaming after all.

Javier approached. From the top of his dark wavy hair to the tip of his handmade designer shoes, he commanded a formidable, absorbing presence that reduced the rest of the room's occupants to mere spectators as his intense, dark brown eyes locked on her.

Tongue-tied, she watched him approach with measured, self-assured strides until his broad shoulders filled her vision.

'What are you doing here?' Her vocal cords, rough from disuse, rasped the words.

Javier's eyebrows arched, his gaze cuttingly cynical. 'News of your terrible accident has been all over the media. Your adoring fans are camped outside the hospital. You think me so uncaring that I would stay away at a time like this?'

His voice was smooth. Deep and warm and beautifully nuanced with inflections from his Spanish mother tongue. Mesmerising enough to disguise the vein of cruel cynicism to anyone but her.

Carla heard it loud and clear. It cut right to the heart of her. But she refused to look away. Whatever Javier intended for her—he'd spent the better part of a year dangling the lucrative sponsorship carrot in front of her father just so he could get to her, after all—she would face it head-on. She'd spent far too long bowing her head down. It might have taken her the best part of twenty-four years to stand up for herself. But she was done taking orders from anybody. A part of her regretted that it had taken this long, that her actions might have caused ripples she'd never be able to reverse, but it was better late than never.

'Thank you for your concern, but, as you can see, I'm in private consultation with my doctor, so if you'd excuse me?'

A nervous throat cleared. 'I'm sorry, *signorina*, but I understood from your father that Mr Santino was permitted to be here,' the doctor offered.

She forced her gaze to remain on Javier's. 'The permission wasn't my father's to give.'

Tense silence descended on the room. Javier's eyes gleamed, an almost unholy relish in the mahogany depths before one corner of his mouth lifted. 'Are you suggesting the doctor throw me out, Carla? Or are you not up to dealing with me right now?'

Her stomach hollowed, the unspoken threat in the words gnawing at her. 'I'm up to dealing with anything. I just don't think this is the right time or place. Perhaps you could come back later.' Or never.

His jaw flexed. 'I could, but why bother? I think what the doctor was trying to say was that you need further rest when you leave here. In light of what's happened, I'm prepared to suspend any commitments to J Santino Inc. until you're well enough to commence your sponsorship duties. You'll also have round-the-clock care by medical professionals.'

The doctor nodded eagerly. 'That's a very wise decision—'

'That's very generous of you, but I won't be needing your help with my recuperation,' she bit out, hiding her shock that Javier would be prepared to go to such lengths to help her recovery. She didn't doubt he had his motives for his overt generosity, but they were none she intended to subject herself to.

She held her breath as he moved closer to the bed. She was forced to tilt her head up to look at him; her head swam as the magnitude of his persona hit her full force.

'You may have forgotten the small print in the contract you signed, Carla, so I'll refresh your memory. It included my company, and therefore me, being made aware of and taking steps to ameliorate any new medical issues that might adversely affect our agreement. You being out of commission for several weeks has the potential to reflect badly on our association. Unless I choose to be…magnanimous.'

Carla managed to pry her gaze from the sensual mouth that dripped poison onto her skin. 'I'm sorry that my accident inconveniences you.'

'It's unfortunate, yes, but I'm willing to work with you provided you don't resort to stubbornness. Or perhaps you wish me to get my lawyers to pry that information from the hospital administrators?'

'How dare you?' she breathed.

Javier's narrow-eyed gaze flicked to the doctor and nurse who watched them with unabashed curiosity. 'If you've finished, Doctor, perhaps I can speak to Miss Nardozzi in private? You have my assurance that we'll reach agreement about the best way forward for her aftercare.'

Carla's heart climbed into her throat as the doctor nodded almost reverently before leaving, trailed by the nurse, who most unwillingly pried her eyes from Javier's body.

The moment the door shut behind them, the private hospital room shrank. Every inch of her focus zeroed in on the man who stood watching her in utter, dread-inducing silence, dark eyes piercingly intense.

Slowly, inexorably, his gaze wandered over her, lingering in places that made her breath catch.

She became hyperaware of the thin, insubstantial hospital gown and blanket that covered her body. The almost debilitating weakness in her limbs that had nothing to do with her health and everything to do with how this man made her feel just by being in the same room as her.

It'd been that way from the moment they met, three years ago, in Miami. The weekend from hell was firmly engraved in her mind. A naive twenty-one-year-old, striking out against the rigours that battened her down. A dangerously captivating man who'd represented the exact opposite of the caution she should've exercised that night, he'd been like a blazing comet in her dark world.

Except with morning had come the brutal realisation that she'd risked much more than her independence.

'Suddenly you have nothing to say?'

'I have plenty to say,' she rasped through a painful throat. 'But you seem to be in the mood to throw your weight about. I thought I'd just wait until you tire yourself out.'

A grim smile chased across his lips. 'Have you forgotten, *cara*? I don't tire very easily. Especially when it comes to the things I'm passionate about.'

Raw heat replaced the weakness in her limbs, firing her blood and making her head pound.

He advanced a few final steps, and stared down at her. Then he reached for the water jug on her bedside table. Still keeping his eyes on her, he poured a glass of water, inserted a handy straw and held it to her lips.

'Drink.'

She wanted to refuse. But her throat hurt. She was beyond thirsty. And getting back on her feet as quickly as possible was imperative. She couldn't begin to take control of her life from a hospital bed.

She dropped her gaze from his imperious regard, and parted her lips. Sucking on the straw, she drew the cool water into her mouth and shuddered with relief as the soothing liquid assuaged her ravaged throat.

He let her draw another mouthful, then he pulled the straw away. 'Take it easy, you don't want to make yourself ill again.'

The sound that emerged from her throat felt blissfully less abrasive. 'Your audience is gone. Please stop pretending you care about my health.'

He returned the glass to the nightstand. 'The state of

your health is directly connected to the millions I stand to lose if you don't meet the terms of your contract. Trust me, there's no pretence on my part. Tell me what happened with your trainer.'

Carla frowned as the unwanted memory sliced across her thoughts. She'd let her emotions get the better of her. Had refused to listen to her instincts even though she'd known training with Tyson Blackwell had been a mistake. Hell, her agent and friend, Draco, had warned her repeatedly about Blackwell.

Further regret made her purse her lips. 'He was a mistake that never should've happened.'

The moment the words left her lips, she felt the blood drain from her face. It took a single glance at Javier to see that he was just as affected by the words.

They were almost identical to what she'd said to him three years ago. The dark curl of his unbelievably sensual lips condemned her poor choice of words.

'I… I meant—'

'I'm well aware of what you meant. You seem to make a habit of collecting and leaving a trail of mistakes in your wake. You asked me what I was doing here. It's quite simple, *querida*. It's time to honour the promise I made to you a month ago.'

CHAPTER TWO

CARLA'S STOMACH HOLLOWED. 'What is that supposed to mean?'

He didn't answer for a minute. Instead, he strolled to the single window that let in bright sunlight, glanced out for a moment, then turned.

If anything, his silhouette was even more formidable, his almost god-like stature drawing her gaze to his captivating frame.

'The reason you were chosen to be the face of the J Santino luxury line was because you're an expert at blending the illusion of innocence with ruthless ambition.'

'If there's a compliment in there you expect me to thank you for, I'll need a moment or two to think about it,' she replied.

The haloed outline of his shoulders lifted in a shrug. 'The results speak for themselves. Or at least they used to.'

'Is there a point to all this?'

'Your choices lately have been...disappointing, to say the least.'

'My choices?'

'You dragged out your negotiations with Draco Angelis's agency until he threatened to walk away. I'm guessing you realised, almost too late, that playing hard to get with him would get you nowhere? Then you insisted on associating yourself with a trainer whose reputation should've made you stay well clear of him.'

Carla swallowed hard against the need to tell him why. But she could see no way to set the record straight without pointing a direct finger at her father. And in a way, hadn't she also been at fault for desperately clinging to a familial bond that was only in her mind? 'My last trainer retired. Tyson Blackwell was only supposed to be temporary—'

'He was known to push his trainees too hard. You should've had nothing to do with him,' he cut across her.

Her breath shuddered out. 'I didn't want to. My father made a deal with him without my knowledge,' she muttered.

Disapproval vibrated off him. 'Then you should've hired someone else.'

She wanted to blurt out that she'd said the same thing to her father, instigating yet another row. A row during which she'd discovered she had no choice but to work with Blackwell because there was no money to hire anyone else. A row that set in motion a series of disagreements that still remained unresolved. Ones she wouldn't be able to brush under the carpet this time, even though it meant facing the hard truth—that her father loved the prestige and financial reward she brought him much more than he loved her.

Staunching the anguish before it bled into her voice, she replied, 'We both know why you pursued me to sign with you. So why are we having this conversation?'

'Because aside from our impending *private* matters, your father made an excellent case on your behalf by convincing me you were a good bet.'

'Wasn't it the other way round? Didn't you pursue him because you convinced him you were a good bet for my image?'

'Is that what he told you?' he enquired silkily, his tone taunting.

She pursed her lips and glanced away. When her fingernails cut into her palm, she forced herself to relax her fist. For the past few months, ever since she had broached the subject of untangling her father from his active role as her manager, their relationship had grown more strained than ever. Tensions had increased until an argument last month when he'd branded her ungrateful and irresponsible. Carla hadn't fooled herself into thinking the haggard look her father had worn in the past few weeks had anything to do with familial concern for her well-being. Time and hard lessons had taught her otherwise. But she hadn't known the reason behind her father's almost visceral reaction to her wanting to take a different path in her career. Not until six weeks ago, after the lavish charity event he'd given in their home in Tuscany. A weekend where her eyes had been opened in more ways than one.

Carla steeled her heart against the pain she'd never managed to suppress. Appearances were everything to Olivio Nardozzi, enough for her to know she was nothing but a meal ticket to the man who had raised her. Any threat to the lifestyle her father believed was owed to him had been disposed of with ruthless efficiency the moment Olivio became aware of his daughter's exceptional talent.

It was the reason her father had relinquished control to her when she'd come of age, but had legally tied up his role in her career as her manager. Twenty-one and reeling from her mother's sudden death, she'd fooled herself into thinking that the working collaboration with her father would ease a relationship whose foundations had been decimated when her mother had walked out on them both when Carla was ten.

With the passage of time, Carla had been prepared to forgive the fact that he'd chosen to tie her in knots professionally at the moment when she'd been most vulnerable. She'd chosen to believe that, somewhere deep down, her father had loved her mother and was reacting just as strongly to her death. What she couldn't forgive was her father cunningly plotting three years later to cement a lucrative business association by attempting to marry her off to Draco Angelis.

Willing calm into her body, she lifted her gaze as Javier paced closer. 'So you're here to do what exactly? Ensure I toe some sort of line set by you?'

'Among other things, I intend to ensure this…' he touched a hand to the wound dressing above her right temple '…

and this…' a drift of his fingers over her cast-bound wrist
'…don't happen again.'

Carla gritted her teeth against the heat dredging through
her. On top of everything else, she didn't need the reminder
that this man's touch elicited the most decadent sensation
inside her. She jerked her arm away, hiding the twinge of
pain in her wrist. 'Please don't touch me.'

His fist balled for an unguarded second before he dropped
his hand. She didn't need to look up to know she'd succeeded
in angering him further. 'Your co-operation in seeing to
your own health would help matters proceed smoothly. And
please look at me when I'm talking to you.'

A childish urge to refuse surfaced. Reluctantly she raised
her gaze, squashing the electricity that fizzed through her
when his eyes locked on her. 'As I told you, I'm perfectly
capable of taking care of myself. Once I'm back home in
Tuscany—'

'You're not returning home.'

She frowned. 'Of course I am. It's my home.' Albeit a
home that felt more like a museum and her father's way of
congratulating himself for what *she'd* achieved. But it was
the only home she had left, and the only thing standing between her and losing *that* home was her contract with Javier.

'In Tuscany, the nearest adequate medical facility should
you need one is over sixty miles away. You were lucky this
time that there was an air ambulance nearby when you fell.
Tempting fate again is unwise. Besides, I want you where I
can keep an eye on you.'

'Fine, I'll stay here in Rome. I can rent an apartment
here—' She stopped speaking when he shook his head.

'No. New York or Miami is a much better option.'

'For you, you mean?'

'Of course. As much as I love your fair city, I have an
important launch in a few weeks that needs my attention.
I can't hop on a plane whenever you make an unfortunate
choice. Besides, you were contracted to be in New York for

your sponsorship duties sooner rather than later. And before you trot out an excuse about talking to your father, I already have. He's agreed.'

Bitterness dredged her insides. As much as she wanted to vocally condemn her father, she kept her mouth shut. Doing so would only hand Javier further ammunition against her. She would deal with her father later. 'So do all your clients get this special attention from you?'

'No, *querida*, I reserve this for ice princesses who believe they're above the mores that govern normal human beings,' he drawled.

'I don't—'

'Save the denial. I have first-hand experience of the way you operate, remember?'

The accusation stung deep. Licking dry lips, she shook her head. 'That was a long time ago, Javier. What happened three years ago…that wasn't me… I shouldn't have—'

His hiss of anger stopped her words. 'Stop before you dig yourself in deeper. Our association only requires you to recite rehearsed lines and act as if every J Santino product you endorse is as essential to you as the air you breathe. And when you're healthy enough, that is exactly what you'll do. In the meantime, keep pretending you're the perfect creature the public perceives you to be. But when we're in private, do me a favour and spare me the lies. I find it demeaning and frankly embarrassing.'

The rock that had lodged itself in her throat with each harsh word from his lips almost prevented her from speaking. 'Is your ego so badly bruised that you can't put what happened between us behind you? And don't pretend you're here just to protect your investment. You have over a thousand employees and a team of lawyers who could've relayed your instructions as effectively as you. You didn't need to fly all this way just to…'

'Just to what?' he invited smoothly, his tone almost bored as he flicked a non-existent speck off his sleeve.

'Can you tell me honestly that you don't want to make me suffer for being the only woman who didn't fall for Javier Santino's world-renowned machismo?'

A careless shrug. 'Why would I be bothered about machismo when you fell so readily for something far more... earthy? Much more satisfying?' he taunted.

Her face flamed, memories she couldn't stem rushing to the fore. 'If it was so satisfying, then why do you hate me so much?' she blurted before she could stop herself. Carla berated herself for asking so obvious a question. She knew why he hated her. Still on shaky ground after her first full-on rebellion against her father, she'd fallen headlong into Javier's arms. Only what she'd imagined would be a casual encounter had been *much more*. So much more that she'd been reeling the morning after, desperately aware that what had happened between them was in no way a casual fling. She'd deliberately stricken the heart of his pride, the almost self-destructive trajectory she'd set herself on seemingly impossible to veer from. It wasn't a moment she'd been proud of.

'Hate is a useless emotion, one I don't waste my time practising. Self-respect on the other hand, especially when it reflects on my reputation, is of paramount importance to me.'

She frowned. 'What are you talking about?'

'You may have the public fooled, *chiquita*, but we both know you have no shame. Throwing yourself at a man who doesn't want you is one thing. Throwing yourself at a man who is engaged to another woman is a different matter entirely. I didn't delegate this trip because you need to be made aware of the consequences of a scandal should you choose to be so unwise as to keep pursuing Angelis.'

Carla flinched. 'Draco? I'm not pursuing him. I haven't done anything wrong...' She trailed off, the look on Javier's face inviting her to not bother.

'Are you implying that the pictures of you on social media

actively throwing yourself at him at your father's charity event six weeks ago were fake?'

Flames of guilt lit her insides. 'It wasn't what it looked like…it didn't mean anything.' Draco Angelis was the brother of her best friend, Maria Angelis, and the big brother she'd never had. Sure, at one very brief point during her teenage years she'd fancied herself infatuated with him, and had even used him to protect herself against unwanted male advances a few times. Six weeks ago, with her budding resolve to take a more active role in her life and career still shaky, she'd leant on him more than perhaps had been wise.

Luckily he'd understood and hadn't held her less than stellar behaviour against her, and neither had his fiancée, Rebel Daniels. Watching Javier's expression, she knew he wouldn't be as accommodating of her explanations.

'Things are never as they seem with you, are they?' he confirmed.

Suddenly weary, she sagged against the pillow, her head beginning to throb. 'Think what you will. I don't need to justify my private life to you. If you've finished saying what you came here to say, please leave.'

Silence greeted her response. She didn't need to look at him to know his gaze would be heavy with anger and condemnation. 'Agree to return to New York with me and I will.'

'You make it sound as if I have a choice. Isn't this part of your grand revenge scheme?'

'Perhaps it is. But I'm happy to delay what comes next. As long as I get what I want.'

Carla sighed and squeezed her eyes shut. '*Sì*. You win. New York. Rome. I don't really care. Just leave me in peace for now, if you can bring yourself to.'

Javier stood looking down at her. The soft, delicate arch of her lashes fanned against her cheek as she kept her eyes closed. Her complexion was alarmingly pale, and he experienced a twinge of guilt for wearing her out when she needed to rest. A second later, he pushed the feeling away. He of all people knew just how Carla Nardozzi's outwardly delicate frame hid a core of icy steel. She hadn't risen to number one in her chosen profession by being a wilting flower, no matter how much she outwardly projected an air of shy, innocent fragility.

His jaw clenched as he recalled that her innocence had been real once upon a time. But it had been ruthlessly sacrificed on the altar of what she'd wanted more—the attention of Draco Angelis.

Some men collected virginities as trophies. He'd never been one of them. But his preference for a more experienced bed partner had abandoned him the moment he'd met Carla Nardozzi three years ago.

He gave a grim smile. A *lot* of things had abandoned him during those insane few weeks, including his common sense.

High from closing the deal of a lifetime that had seen him propelled into the echelons of *world richest* the week before his thirtieth birthday, he'd thrown a series of lavish parties in his homes across the world, the wildest and most decadent of which had culminated in Miami, the place he called his true home.

The place he'd experienced Carla.

Javier jerked himself from the memories. The reminder of the gullible idiot he'd been in the days following raked rough and jagged over his senses.

Never again.

It took several minutes to realise she wasn't deliberately ignoring him and feigning sleep. Carla had truly fallen asleep, her breathing soft but deep, the lines of exhaustion he hadn't wanted to acknowledge now smoothing out on her face.

He stepped back from the bed before another guilty twinge lanced him. He'd come to reiterate the message he'd delivered to her in his office a month ago. Standing there watching her sleep—her perfect face relaxed and enthrall-ing—was an inane exercise.

About to turn away, he paused as a niggling thought im-pinged. It was the same sensation he'd experienced when she'd turned up in his New York office to sign the contract.

Despite her spirited words just now, an air of apathy sur-rounded her that seemed at variance with the woman whose ambition had made her competitors cow before her on the ice rink. Magnificence like that didn't happen overnight, and Carla Nardozzi was known for her indefatigable dedication to her discipline. And yet, she'd seemed a shadow of her-self during their meeting in New York. It was that inkling of ennui he'd sensed that had propelled him to get a rise out of her...by kissing her.

It was what was stopping him leaving the room right now.

Having never experienced such an emotion, Javier wasn't sure how to deal with it. And not knowing how to deal with a problem wasn't a scenario he readily accepted.

He told himself it was the reason he was sitting in the armchair in the corner of the room, watching Carla sleep two hours later. After all, he was a firm believer in confronting an issue before it grew out of hand.

He'd confronted the man he'd been told was his father when he was seventeen. And again when his mother had died. Both times the results had been traumatic enough to fell a lesser man. He'd chosen to absorb the experiences as the hard lessons he'd needed to forge his path in life. So what if being termed a bastard by the man whose blood ran through his veins had left an imagined hole in Javier's life for a long time? He'd learned with time that he could live without the soft trappings of family and endless entangle-ments of relationships that were, more often than not, fraught and tedious. The ideal family life he'd envied from afar as a child had proved to be nothing more than a cluster of blood relations fighting over what remained of a once prestigious aristocratic name.

He'd achieved more in his lifetime than his so-called ancestors had managed in several generations.

But the rejection still hurt...

Javier shrugged tense shoulders, ferociously denying the voice in his head, and looked up as Carla murmured in her sleep.

Clinically, he examined her, forcing himself to assess what had drawn him so inexorably to her. She certainly wasn't his type. Slim and far too delicate where he preferred his women curvy and vivacious.

Yet, from the first moment he'd laid eyes on her, he'd been captivated by the combination of ethereal beauty that comprised silky caramel-streaked chocolate hair, vivid green eyes and a figure that begged for masculine hands, *his* hands, to mould and possess.

And despite everything that had happened—her deliberate, callous insults and her flaying rejection the morning after their passionate night together—he couldn't help the rush of heat to his groin as he lingered on her full mouth and the steady rise and fall of her breasts.

He surged to his feet, disgusted with himself for ogling a sick, bedridden woman.

But Carla Nardozzi wasn't just any woman. She epitomised the very thing that Javier had struggled all his life to effectively deny.

She'd rejected him because he hadn't been *good enough*. Not once, but twice, she'd looked upon him as if he hadn't been worthy to address her.

The family he didn't want or need had been allowed to get away with treating him like that.

She would not.

And before their association was over, he would make sure she took back every dismissive word, every scathing look and gesture she'd spurned him with.

CHAPTER THREE

EVEN BEFORE CARLA came fully awake, she knew he was still there. His presence was too oppressive, too hyperintense, to dismiss.

Thankfully, her headache had lessened, and, even though her broken wrist throbbed, Carla felt much better and in control of herself than she'd been a few hours ago.

So she opened her eyes, and glanced at the occupant of the armchair.

Javier was asleep.

That in itself was shocking enough to observe—the man was larger than life, a demigod who surely didn't require the rejuvenating needs of mere mortals. But it was the transformation that had overcome his face that made her eyes widen. That made her stare shamelessly.

His arms were flung over the sides of the chair, his long legs splayed in front of him. The position offered an unfettered view of the stunning landscape of his body. Powerful taut thighs tapered to lean hips and a trim waist before veering up to display a torso that would've made any athlete proud. His deep chest and broad shoulders rose and fell and his slightly relaxed jawline drew attention to the stubble that had grown in the hours he'd been here. Almost reluctantly, her gaze traced his face.

Sinfully gorgeous, Javier's features had always been a subject of acute fascination for her and this time was no exception, despite his less than formidable demeanour in repose.

Heat dragged low in her belly as she recalled what that mouth had done to her, what she'd begged him to do to her during that mad, reckless night in Miami.

He'd fulfilled her every wish, and more, with an intensity

that had sent her running for cover in a blind panic the next morning. Carla had known that Javier was bad news for her. His healthy sex life and reputation for strictly temporary liaisons with women hadn't been a secret. She'd known even before she woke up in his bed that it was only a matter of time before he notched her name on his bedpost and moved on. *Dio mio*, she'd barely kept up with him during their night of passion, her inexperience blazing through every fumbled kiss and caress that had made his sensual lips twitch with tender humour. But it was the risk to her own emotions that had finally sent her scurrying.

That had made her strike out before he'd got round to rejecting her first.

'You stare at me with such fascination, it's almost enough to make me forgot the horror on your face when you looked upon me once upon a time.'

She jumped, her mind dragging itself to the present and to the ragged contempt in his voice. She forced herself to meet Javier's gaze. 'It wasn't horror. At least not at you.'

One sleek eyebrow lifted. 'Is that supposed to make me feel better, *pequeña*? That you were horrified with yourself for choosing me to be the man you lost your innocence to?'

'Is there anything I can say that will make you stop condemning me for what I said the next morning?'

The gleam in his eyes slowly hardened to merciless chips. Still splayed out in indolent abandon, he linked his fingers over his washboard stomach. 'You told me sleeping with me was the worst mistake of your life. Of course with the benefit of hindsight I see that I was being used all along. But even if I hadn't believed you then or found a way to excuse that insult, your behaviour since has proven your words to be true. Why should I believe that anything you say now isn't just to save face?'

'Save face?' she said, confused.

'Angelis is engaged to another woman, is he not? He's

made his choice and it wasn't you. It's natural you wouldn't want the world to know how you truly feel about him.'

'I'm not in love with him. I'm really not,' she stressed when mocking disbelief draped his face.

'Then why were you seen kissing him at your charity event in Tuscany last month?'

'Would you believe me if I told you it was a mistake?'

He surged to his feet in one smooth bound, a volatile emotion bristling from his large frame. 'No. The fact is your obsession with him continues, and you don't seem to be interested in the small matter of him being committed to another. You just want what you want, don't you, Carla, and to hell with the consequences?'

'No, of course I don't. I'd never do that—'

'But you did.' He strolled closer, a predator stalking his prey, until he stood over her. 'The evidence speaks for itself.'

She shook her head, unable to believe she was having this conversation with Javier. 'It's obvious you've made up your mind about me. I said I'd return to New York with you. So why are you still here? I'm not exactly in the position to make a run for it.'

A dark frown clamped his brows. He shoved his hands in his pockets and shrugged. 'You fell asleep before I got your word that you'll stay away from Angelis from now on.'

Carla sat up gingerly and swung her legs over the side. The wave of dizziness that washed over her was blessedly brief. 'He's my agent. Avoiding him will be impossible. And counter-productive, don't you think?'

'You can and you will. Angelis has enough executives to ensure he has no personal dealings with you from now on. I'll contact him myself to make sure the request is understood.'

'Are you going to forbid me from letting him become my trainer too, which was his suggestion?' She shook her head. 'If I didn't know better, I'd think you were jealous. And you don't wear it particularly well.'

Deep, unamused laughter erupted from his throat, mocking her every word. 'Don't delude yourself. Scandal may sell newspapers, but my company has remained free of it up till now and I intend to ensure it stays that way. As for training you, we've agreed that it would be better if someone else assumes that role.'

Her unhurt hand gripped the side of the bed. 'You've been discussing me with Draco behind my back?'

'I've been trying to minimise the impact of what's happened—what are you doing? You shouldn't be on your feet.'

Carla swayed for a moment before she managed to steady herself. 'I should if I want to use the bathroom. Or are you going to forbid that too?'

A faint wash of colour highlighted his sculpted cheekbones and his lips pursed for a moment. 'Don't be ridiculous.'

She wanted to protest the ridiculousness of the whole situation. But she was too busy wincing as she placed her weight on her left foot. Too late, she remembered she'd landed hard on her hip. A second later, she was swung off her feet.

The shock of the sudden action halted her breath for a second before she regained her senses. 'What are you doing? Put me down!'

'No. You're in no fit state to be walking anywhere.'

He hoisted her up, his steps sure and confident as he strode into the adjoining bathroom. Painfully aware of her dishevelled state, she buried her reddening face in his chest. And was immediately bombarded with the unique, undeniably male scent of him. The urge to take greedy gulps of him assailed her, forcing her to do the opposite and hold her breath as he slowly lowered her to her feet.

Unable to stop herself, she risked a glance at him, to find his burnished bronze gaze on her.

'Umm…you can let me go now,' she ventured, her senses screaming at the electrifying grip he had on her arms.

He frowned. 'Will you be okay?' he asked brusquely. 'I'll go and get the nurse—'

'There's no need. I'll be fine.'

He stared at her for a few more seconds. Then he carefully stepped back. 'Don't lock the door,' he instructed.

Carla resisted the urge to perform an uncharacteristic eye roll. 'I'm not made of glass, Javier. I've suffered more falls in my career than most people will in a lifetime.'

If anything her answer drew an even deeper frown from him. 'Is that supposed to reassure me?'

'I wasn't aware that you needed my reassurance. Just my acquiescence to your every demand.'

His eyes darkened. 'You laid down the rules of our relationship, *querida*. Don't complain now that I'm playing by your standards.'

Carla was puzzling over that cryptic remark when he shut the door and left her in peace for the first time since waking up in hospital. She didn't doubt that she'd invited some degree of the hell Javier seemed intent on visiting upon her. But overall his actions pointed to a deeper reaction to what she'd done to warrant his almost volatile anger. Had she really bruised his ego that much? How could she have, when he'd been associated with some of the most captivatingly beautiful women in the world, both before and after their unfortunate one-night stand?

To complete her ablutions, she limped to the sink, washed up, and lifted her gaze to the mirror. With growing horror, she examined the bags under her eyes and the unkempt nest of her thick hair. She almost giggled hysterically at the thought of her father seeing her this way. For as long as she could remember, Olivio had demanded perfection in everything she did. She'd granted it. Because to do otherwise would've incurred his wrath. Besides, it'd been easier playing the perfect princess. It provided the flawless façade to hide behind. Seeking and attaining perfection meant she didn't have to acknowledge the flawed individual behind the mask.

Carla stared into the mirror, her heart thumping hard as she acknowledged that the shell had well and truly cracked. Her eyes looked bruised and haunted. But then what was new? Pain and betrayal were effective tools in eroding any chance of finding peace even while doing what one loved—

'Carla?'

The harsh rap of her name brought her up short. Quickly running her fingers through her hair, she took a deep breath. She would deal with her father and their acrimonious relationship once she got out of here.

First she needed to deal with the man intent on making her pay dearly for her one monumental mistake.

The moment the doctor gave her the all-clear to leave later that afternoon, Javier swung into action.

'Your father is having your things brought over. We'll stay at my hotel tonight and fly out in the morning.'

She smoothed her hand over the dark orange dress and matching shoes she'd found in her hospital closet. With the help of the nurse, she'd taken a quick shower and pulled her hair into its customary bun. The effort to make herself presentable had been worth it when she'd emerged from the hospital to find a crowd of fans cheering at her apparent recovery. As always, she'd been silently awed and a little intimidated at being the object of such intense scrutiny. Although she hadn't been willing to admit it at the time, she'd been grateful for Javier's solid presence beside her. Especially when she'd caught a glimpse of the latest newspaper headline.

'Don't I have to deal with the police, seeing as Tyson Blackwell is to be charged?'

'We'll deal with it this afternoon, if you're feeling up to it. If not, we'll handle it later. I've spoken to the authorities. They don't really need your statement to charge him.'

'They don't?'

He shook his head. 'Angelis had a member of your father's staff watching over you. Blackwell was filmed on video pushing you into making that dangerous jump.' His jaw tightened, his features cast in shadow as the car moved through traffic. 'Why did you do it?'

Her breath emerged shakily as memory slashed across her mind. Her father had finally confessed, after condemning her for wanting to sever their professional relationship, that he'd gambled all her money away. Their only asset— albeit a heavily mortgaged one—was the estate in Tuscany.

'I had a lot on my mind that morning. I wasn't thinking clearly. And before you think me completely foolish, I'd done the jump successfully over a dozen times in the days before.'

'Was your lack of concentration to do with Angelis? Or the chaos your father has made of your finances?'

She gasped. 'You know about that?'

'Your father has been pursuing this deal for the better part of a year, each time asking for more money. You didn't think I'd do my homework on why he was so eager to sign you away?'

Her insides chilled. 'So you know—'

'I know everything, *querida*. And I have you in the proverbial palm of my hand. I can ruin you with the snap of my fingers.'

That debilitating state of ennui that had assailed her on and off over the past few weeks wove over her again. The urge to give up, walk away from it all, *now*, rather than later as she'd tried to discuss with her father, was so strong it caught her breath.

'Did you hear me, Carla?'

'Loud and clear. You can ruin me. You can breathe fire. You can command the very heavens to crush me into a speck of dust. I acknowledge your almighty power over me. But please excuse me if I don't genuflect. I'm battered and bruised enough as it is.'

A dark look entered his eyes. 'What's wrong with you? And I don't mean physically. Your apathy is unbecoming in an athlete of your calibre. You haven't risen to number one by being cowed by a few challenges.'

She laughed, the sound scratching her throat. 'So you not only expect me to jump when you say how high, but I should have an attitude when I do it?'

'I'm saying representing my company with such a defeatist demeanour will not work.'

'I'll work on practising my positive mental attitude before I step in front of the camera. Is that enough for you?'

'This isn't a joke, Carla.'

'Trust me, I'm well aware of that.

She felt his probing stare for several minutes. But thankfully, he didn't press her further before they drew up to the five-star hotel in the heart of Rome.

The hotel was renowned for its ultra-private accessibility to celebrities and she breathed a sigh of relief when they were ushered through a discreet entrance and into the private lift that serviced the penthouse.

Carla walked into the sumptuously decorated room and halted when she saw her father. Beside him, several familiar-looking suitcases were stacked neatly on a caddy, which a butler was in the process of wheeling away.

The ragged notion that she was once again being managed, herded where Olivio Nardozzi wanted her to be, tore through her.

'I have a few phone calls to make,' Javier announced once he'd acknowledged her father's greeting. 'I'll leave you two to catch up. Carla, dinner will be served at eight. Make sure you rest before then.'

Before she could respond, he strode off down the hallway. She told herself his abrupt absence didn't affect her as much as the mild hollowing of her stomach indicated.

She stiffened as her father placed the crystal tumbler

he'd been drinking from on a nearby antique cabinet and crossed the room.

'*Mia figlia*, it's good to see you on your feet again. I wanted to be there when you were released, but I was assured that everything was in hand. How are you feeling?'

She didn't react as he leaned forward and kissed her cheeks. When he stepped back, she glimpsed the tight, haggard look on his face.

'I'm fine,' she replied, desperately squashing any heartache she felt over the state of their relationship. Her father had long driven home to her that he abhorred any show of emotion, especially that of weakness. In all things she was expected to be poised, controlled. Emotionless. It was the reason their ongoing rows writhed like a live wire between them.

'I hope your time in hospital has brought you to your senses?' he murmured in Italian.

Anguish ripped through her. 'If by my senses you mean I've given up my bid to lead an independent life, then I'm sorry to disappoint you but my wishes remain the same,' she whispered fiercely. 'I'm still taking a break from ice skating, and no, I haven't made up my mind how long that break will be. When I decide, I'll let you know.'

'Does Santino know about this ludicrous decision of yours? I don't believe that he does, or your contract would be in serious jeopardy by now and we'd be on our way to court.'

She bit her lip. Her contract with Javier's company didn't specifically state that she couldn't make the decision she intended to take, but she doubted he would be pleased to learn she might lose her number-one-ranking status before she'd fulfilled the full terms of her sponsorship deal.

'Contracts can be renegotiated. Nothing is set in stone yet. I'll tell him when I'm ready. And I'd thank you to stay out of that decision.'

Her father's espresso-coloured eyes hardened. 'You forget yourself, girl. You wouldn't be where you are today without me.'

'Without your punishing strive for perfection and the strict rules that ensured I had no life outside figure skating, you mean?' she sniped, the ennui rushing away to be replaced by the haunting reality of what she'd let her life become. And she couldn't even fully blame her father for that.

'I moulded you and ensured your iconic place in the history books!'

'Through fear and intimidation. At each turn you threatened to abandon me just like—' She pulled herself up short, sucking in a deep breath.

'Go on, say it. Just like your *mamma* left you?'

Her hurt escalated until her whole body was engulfed in pain. 'And we both know why she left, don't we?'

He slashed an angry hand through the air. 'I refuse to indulge you in this childish need to revisit the past. Your *mamma* is gone, and you dishonour her memory with this petty squabble you insist upon.'

'How dare you accuse me of dishonouring her memory? When you didn't even tell me she was dead until the *morning* of her funeral?'

Olivio's frame tensed, his five-foot-nine stature rigid with banked fury. 'You had a competition to win. I didn't think the news would do anything but throw you off your game.'

Her blood turned cold. 'Every time I think there's a shred of humanity in you, Papà, you prove me wrong.'

His face tightened into a hard, implacable mask. 'I don't know what has got into you these past few weeks. Whatever it is, I suggest you take the time in New York to reassess your priorities. This deal with Santino will be the making of us, if you don't mess it up. In the beginning, I was against him staggering the payments on the basis of your performance, but now I see it's a good thing. It might not be enough to save us from the bank's red letters, but if it helps keep you in line—'

'You forget I'm no longer a child. Your threats of abandonment don't frighten me any more!'

'And I haven't come this far for you to suddenly develop whimsical delusions. Only has-beens and losers scurry away with the excuse to *find* themselves. You're number one and you'll remain number one—'

'Or you'll what? Drive me to another convent like you did when I was ten years old and threaten to leave me there unless I behaved? I'm not ten any more.'

'No, you're not. But you signed a contract to keep me as your manager until you're twenty-five, and I won't be got rid of that easily. I'll take you to court if I have to.'

A vice squeezed in her chest. 'You'd do that? To your own daughter?'

'The daughter you were six weeks ago wouldn't have made these ridiculous demands. I'm not sure what happened after the charity gala—'

'Don't plead innocence, Papà. I found out that you'd tried to bribe Draco's fiancée into leaving him so you could marry me off to him! Do you know how it made me feel to hear that from Maria?' she rasped.

'I was only acting in your best interests. You were infatuated with him once. It seemed the sensible option to secure your future with his.'

She curled her fingers into fists, and winced when her broken wrist protested. 'This isn't the Middle Ages! My future is mine and mine alone to secure as I please.'

His lips pursed. 'That's where you're wrong. If you think I'm going to stand by and—'

'I think it's time for you to leave your daughter to rest, Olivio,' Javier intoned from the entrance to the hallway.

Carla started. It was a testament to his predatory stealth that neither she nor her father had heard him return to the living room. Studying his face, she tried to gauge how much he'd overheard. A flick of his gaze to hers told her he'd heard and understood enough.

And had once again acted as judge, jury and executioner.

Fed up to the back teeth of being embroiled in manipulative parents and male egos, she glared at him. 'Please stay out of this.'

Javier ignored her, his laser gaze on her father. 'I'll let you be the judge of whether you think this is the right time to be airing your…questionable family laundry.'

The statement was aimed at the heart of Olivio's pride. And he responded predictably. '*Sì*, you're right. This isn't the time or place. I will join you in New York, *cara*, when you're better recovered.'

The pecks on her cheeks were cold and emotionless, and she wondered why he'd even bothered. Yes, of course. Appearances.

She stood frozen as he shook hands with Javier, and left.

Slowly, Javier sauntered to where she stood.

'Do you intend to stand there all day?' he mocked.

'I intend to do my very best to avoid being in the same room with you as much as possible,' she snapped.

His nostrils flared. 'Watch it, Principessa. There are only so many insults I'm prepared to take until something gives.'

Carla forced herself to exhale calmly. 'You feel the same way, Javier. Don't pretend otherwise.'

'Don't presume to know what I'm feeling.'

'Fine. Whatever. Please tell me where my suitcases have been taken. I'd like to get changed.'

He regarded her for several tense seconds, then turned away. She followed him down the hallway till they reached two sets of double doors. Javier swung open the right set and walked into the room.

As with every inch of the penthouse, the suite was decorated from top to bottom with classic luxury that drew the eye to the blend of contemporary and antique pieces around the room. The ceiling had retained its lofty rococo design and rich parted drapes offered early evening views of Rome and the Vatican in the far distance.

But it was the bed that drew her eye. It was queen-sized and mounted on a double dais; the silk coverlet alone made her want to lie down and let its decadent luxury relax all her troubles away. Or was it something else entirely that drew her attention to that particular piece of furniture?

Heat rushed through her as she remembered another time. Another bed. An uninhibited period in time that had haunted her ever since.

'If you need anything, there's an intercom next to the bed that summons the butler.'

His tone was gravel rough enough to pry her attention from her dangerous memories. Her eyes met his, and, far from the cool regard of moments ago, his gaze contained a banked fire that stopped her breath.

'Okay…thank you.'

He jerked out a nod. Expecting him to leave, she waited. And felt a renewed surge of heat when his eyes conducted a slow, thorough appraisal of her. She wanted to tell him to stop, to truly leave her be. But the words stuck in her throat as the sinful attraction she couldn't seem to suppress around him engulfed her once more.

A rough sound ripped through the room. It could've come from her.

They moved at the same time—she sideways, striking for the bed. Javier lunged in her direction, then veered sharply towards the door.

'Wait.'

He froze. Turned.

'I… I wish I didn't have to ask, but…'

He frowned. 'Spit it out, Carla.'

'My zipper.' She held up her immobilised wrist. 'I won't be able to reach it with this. Could you help me, please?'

He executed a smooth return to where she stood. 'Are you sure you want my help? After all, it would involve me touching you. And I know how you feel about that,' he jeered.

She lifted her chin. 'Fine. I'll get your butler to help me.'

Before the words were fully out, her waist was grasped in a firm hold. 'Take one more step towards that door and I'll make you regret it,' he growled.

With a mere foot separating them, his warm breath washed over her face as he exhaled.

'Seriously, stop tossing out threats like confetti. It's getting old.'

One corner of his mouth quirked as he placed a finger beneath her chin and lifted her gaze to his. 'You've got a little spark back. My investment may not be in danger, after all. Turn around,' he rasped.

She held his gaze a second longer, suddenly unsure if this was such a good idea. Surely, staying in her clothes around him was better than what she was about to subject herself to? But changing her mind now was out of the question.

Swallowing, she presented her back to him. The air thickened, wrapping them up in a sultry heat as the seconds ticked by. His breath tickled her exposed nape, her body responding to that ephemeral contact by firing up her nerve endings.

His knuckles brushed her spine and Carla squeezed her eyes shut. The rasp of the zipper was amplified in the heavy silence, every inch of exposure making her heart race faster. The silk and lace teddy she wore beneath provided shockingly inadequate cover, her skin on fire from Javier's gaze.

An eternity later, his hands dropped. 'It is done.' His voice was rough, barely civil.

He was gone before she'd exhaled the air trapped in her lungs. She stumbled to the bed and sank down, her chest rising and falling with an urgency that had nothing to do with her diminished health.

Limbs trembling, she kicked off her shoes, released her hair from its knot, tugged back the covers and slid into bed, grateful for the momentary peace to gather her thoughts.

All her life she'd been caught between a rock and a hard place—please her father or bear his wrath, achieve excellence at all costs or have a life. The feeling that she was once again caught in a pincer-like situation drew a ragged sob from her throat.

Mildly shocked at the tears once again filling her eyes, she dashed them away, but they fell faster, thicker. She firmed her lips. No way was she crying over her lot in life. She would heal. She would find a way out of the situation with her father. Most of all, she would discover once and for all what had happened to her mother.

Because she didn't think she could live with the thickening shadow that she'd had anything to do with it.

CHAPTER FOUR

CARLA SURFACED FROM sleep to the sound of knocking. Momentarily disoriented, she tried to sit up, and winced as horrendous pain shot up her arm. Belatedly recalling her broken wrist, she adjusted herself and cradled her sore limb.

Another round of hard knocking shook the doors of the suite, before they swung open. Javier stood in the doorway, minus his jacket. With his sleeves rolled up, his arms were exposed in all their bronze, muscled glory.

She pried her gaze away from his arms and looked up as he approached. 'By all means, come in,' she muttered.

His features locked in a frown. 'I've been knocking for several minutes. You didn't answer.'

She hadn't planned on sleeping, had lain in bed for almost an hour, lost in her thoughts before sleep had finally claimed her. She slid her hands through her hair, noting that, although her dreams had been troubled, she felt even stronger than before.

About to respond, she jerked back as Javier took her chin in a firm hold.

'You've been crying. Why?'

She gave a bitter laugh. 'Why do you care?'

'Answer me.'

She shrugged. 'I have no idea.'

His grip tightened just a touch. 'Try again.'

'It's true. I'm not a crier. Probably not since I was ten years old. But I guess there's a second time for everything.'

'I doubt that I have the power to reduce you to tears, so this has something to do with your father and your ongoing partnership, *si*?'

She glared at him. 'Will you let it be if I say it's none of your business?'

An unfathomable emotion hardened in his eyes. 'Not if you've been lying here feeling sorry for yourself because of it.'

She wrenched herself from his grasp, partly annoyed with herself because that was exactly how she'd been feeling. She'd also realised that for the first time in her life she didn't have a punishing schedule to take her mind off the bleakness of her life. Hiding the abject hollowness the thought brought, she pushed a swathe of hair off her face. 'Did you want something in particular, or did you interrupt my me time just for the hell of it?'

His sumptuous mouth tightened before he strolled to the dressing room. Returning with a silk robe-like gown in rich, vibrant colours, he held it out to her. 'Dinner will be served in twenty minutes. You don't need to get dressed if you intend to return here straight afterwards for more of your *me time*.'

Shock gaped her mouth as she took the robe from him.

'You look surprised. You forget that I want you healthy as quickly as possible. There's only so long I can put launches on hold before schedules become impossible to handle.'

She gave a false smile. 'And here I thought you were doing this out of the goodness of your heart.'

He returned her smile with an equally false one. 'You'll soon learn that goodness and heart aren't terms most people apply to me, *querida*. But I do draw the line at decimating the sick and weak.' He jerked his chin at the robe. 'Do you need help putting that on?'

She noticed she was crushing the soft material in her fist and quickly smoothed it out. 'No. Thanks.'

He left as abruptly as he'd entered, leaving the space he'd occupied significantly less vibrant than it'd been before. Realising she was staring into thin air, she shook out the robe. The kimono-style arms offered no restriction for her bound wrist and she wondered if that was why Javier had chosen it. Then she caught sight of the discreet hotel label and realised she was affording him more courtesy than he was worth.

The scent of rich pasta and aromatic sauces hit her nostrils the moment she entered the hallway. Her stomach growled, whether to remind her that she hadn't eaten a proper meal for days or that the meal she was heading for would fall outside her regime, she didn't know. But she followed her nose to the dining room to find Javier approaching from the terrace.

He cradled a glass of red wine from which he sipped slowly without taking his eyes off her. She watched him savour the drink for several moments before he swallowed. 'You've lost weight.'

She dragged her gaze from the thick masculine column of his throat. 'Being in hospital for a few days will do that to you.'

He walked to where she'd stopped at the place setting on the dining table. 'You were already too thin when I saw you in New York a month ago,' he countered. 'Now you look even worse.'

Stung by his words, she focused on the silverware. 'What a delightful start to our dinner, you hurling insults at me.'

'I'm not hurling insults, merely stating a fact.'

'In case you need me to spell it out to you, I need to maintain a certain weight for my career.'

She was unprepared for the slide of his hand at her temple, the soft caress of her jaw before he tucked a strand of hair behind her ear. Her breath locked in her throat as he murmured, 'You forget, *cara*, that I'm intimately familiar with your body. I've availed myself of every inch of it. It may have been three years, but I remember each curve and hollow vividly. Now you have fewer curves and more hollows. I don't like it.'

Carla shivered at the low, sizzling delivery. 'Javier—'

'Whatever it is you're pining for, it's time to put it out of your mind,' he sliced at her as if she hadn't tried to respond.

'Nothing and *no one* is worth what you're putting yourself through,' he finished, his eyes narrowed and laser-focused.

She bristled. 'You think I can get over whatever it is I'm feeling just by snapping my fingers?' she demanded, incredulous.

'I believe the only person standing in your way of achieving your goals is you. Your destiny is yours to mould or throw away by the choices you make. Or by dwelling on what you can't have.' He pulled out her chair and motioned her into it.

Carla sat down, fascinated against her will and more than a little bewildered by the words falling from his mouth. 'And how has that wisdom served you?'

He spread his arms and displayed himself with shameless arrogance. 'According to the world's most successful magazine, I'm the perfect embodiment of personal and professional success. I encapsulate the very essence of work/life balance. I'm therefore the envy of every red-blooded male on the planet. Who am I to argue with that pronouncement?' he asked drolly.

'I see that you're not letting the accolade go to your head or anything.'

His lips twitched as he reached over to pour her a glass of water. But the gaze he sent her was anything but amused. 'I demand perfection. You're currently several degrees below par. You know this as well as I do. It's time to change that. You can start by eating a decent meal.'

Before she could blink, her plate was heaped with pasta and a thick, creamy sauce. Freshly baked focaccia bread spread with garlic butter was presented on a platter, along with Parmesan cheese, which Javier held out with a pointed look.

He was testing her.

Her stomach growled.

With a purse of her lips, she gave in.

The first taste had her groaning. She would hate herself

in the morning. Or congratulate herself for taking the first step in claiming her life back. Whatever. She was determined to enjoy this meal in its entirety. Which was just as well because she had no recollection of finishing her portion, only of Javier heaping another serving onto her plate and presenting her with the bread again.

She took it slower the second time, her gaze drawn repeatedly to his elegant hands as he swirled his wine.

'I'm not used to having free time on my hands. I'll go crazy sitting in one place for two weeks,' she said, striving for something to dwell on beside his hands.

'I figured as much. When we get to New York, depending on your recuperation progress, you can start familiarising yourself with the products you'll be working with.'

She frowned. 'Am I allowed to know what they are now? The contract didn't specify.'

'For confidentiality reasons.' He shrugged. 'I see no harm in telling you now. The first one will be the new line of JS1 speedboats. They're set to launch in two months' time, right before the summer.'

She broke a piece of bread and soaked up the sauce on her plate. 'I know nothing about speedboats.' But she could learn, especially if she had the time off from ice skating that she was planning. She glanced at him, debating whether this was the right time to tell him of her future plan.

'It's a good thing I have total belief in your superb acting skills, then,' he replied.

The atmosphere changed, the air clogging with silent, deadly waves of recrimination. It effectively killed any attempt to inform him of her decision, the bite of bread turning sour so she struggled just to chew and swallow it.

'We won't be able to work well together if you insist on bringing up the past every time I say something you don't like,' she pointed out.

'And that bothers you?'

She glanced up from her plate, bemused that he would

ask so obvious a question. 'Of course it does. We had a one-night stand that ended badly. I admit I was at fault—'

'How magnanimous of you,' he drawled with an edge that set her nerves jangling.

'I didn't really know what I was doing, okay?' she blurted, exasperation and shame duelling within her. 'I was younger and less wise than I am now. I was also rebelling against...' She stopped and took a breath.

'Against?' he pressed.

'I wanted to be a normal twenty-one-year-old. I wanted to experience *life*. My every experience before that night... before Miami had been punishingly regimented. The pressure was just piling on, and I wanted a little...reprieve.'

'So you used me, then made sure I knew I'd been used and discarded?' he condemned icily.

'My reaction the next morning wasn't great. I know that.' She cringed in remembrance. 'But I didn't deliberately set out to sleep with you.'

His features froze in a granite mask. 'Are you saying I somehow forced you into bed with me?'

'No, of course not! But being with you was...an extremely intense experience, Javier. I was completely out of my depth,' she confessed.

Silence descended on the table. It was a good thing she was full because Carla didn't think she could take another bite without choking. Javier's expression remained shuttered, his gaze downcast as he stared into his wine glass.

'I came on strong because you gave me every indication that you wanted me just as badly as I wanted you. I don't mind admitting that the greedy hunger in your eyes when you looked at me coupled with the ingénue air about you turned me on.' He gave a low, self-deprecating laugh. 'You had me so fooled, I nearly punched my own friend's lights out, remember? Little did I know that I was playing directly into your hands.'

The shame that had been crawling along her skin thickened. She tried to block out the memory, but it raged full and large and unavoidable.

Newly turned twenty-one, she'd negotiated a two-week break after winning another world championship and managed to wangle an invitation to spend the time off in New York with her best friend Maria and Draco. Revelling in nothing but new delights like shopping, attending her first nightclub and even sneaking in her first taste of champagne, she'd never wanted the vacation to end. She especially hadn't wanted to return to Tuscany to a father who had turned increasingly demanding and unreasonable in the weeks leading up to her twenty-first birthday. In a desperate bid to find common ground, and simply because they hadn't spoken in several months, Carla had called her mother and pleaded with her to intervene with her father.

Hoping the brief conversation would yield the results she wanted, she'd naïvely thrown herself into her last weekend of freedom by accompanying Draco and Maria to Miami. Little had she known that she'd set in motion a chain reaction of events that would haunt her for the rest of her life. Her father's phone call branding her a disappointment and a traitor had come an hour into the party hosted by Javier Santino.

The strange, tingling feeling she'd experienced when she'd met the enigmatic, devastatingly handsome Spanish man had only been superseded by her father's decimating condemnation. Years-long feelings of oppression had exploded, leading to a desperate and blind search for oblivion. With Maria nowhere to be found, she'd indulged in one too many tequila slammers, until Draco's tough-love dressing-down had sent her fleeing to the bathroom. She'd emerged to find Draco and Javier engaged in a heated argument, and, unwilling to face any more censure from Draco, she'd readily accepted Javier's invitation to go for a walk. Truth be told, she hadn't needed another excuse to be with Javier, his breathtaking looks and clear interest much more than she'd ever been used to.

Draco's displeasure with her decision had been clear, as had Javier's irritation with him. Only after numerous reassurances that she'd be fine had Draco backed down.

She'd let Javier take her hand, his formidable possessiveness a new and exciting danger she'd yearned for. Besides being with a man who made her every breath quiver, being firmly entrenched in the present had meant there was no room to think about her father. Or her mother. Or what her attempt to find her own sense of worth and happiness would mean.

The ride in his open-top sports car to the 'best coffee place in town' had ended with an incandescent, mind-blowing kiss hours later on a secluded pier, and quickly progressed back to the now empty beachfront mansion.

'Are you sure you want this?' he'd asked her several times in between tugging off her shoes, disposing of her handbag, pulling the diamond-studded clip from her hair and showering compliments as he kissed every inch of exposed skin.

A bold hand cupped him, his girth momentarily stopping her breath. 'I want to experience everything you have to give, Javier. Please don't make me wait.'

His groan echoed through her entire being. 'Say things like that to me and I'll have to take you right here on the stairs.'

'Tell me the right words to say. Teach me what pleases you.'

'*Madre di Dios.* Either you've done this enough to know that it's guaranteed to drive any man crazy,' he growled, 'or...'

'Or what?'

Golden brown eyes bore into hers. 'Or you're a sexually potent creature who doesn't even know her own power.'

'I'm...neither. I've never done...this before.'

Shock. Surprise. Blazing possessiveness coupled with something so primitive, every cell leapt with sizzling excitement. Then a bold cupping of her nape. 'Say that again, *mi corazón*. Explain it to me explicitly so there's no mistaking what you're saying to me.'

'I've never slept with anyone, Javier. I'm a virgin.' Shaky words, spoken with dread that her confession would end the most transcendent experience of her life.

'I'm to be your first?' Disbelief and a touch of reverence in his words.

'Y…yes. If you want to be.' She squeezed her eyes shut and reframed the words. 'I want you to be the first. Please don't refuse me.'

'Refuse you? Do you have any idea what the thought of you saying this…or asking another guy to be your first, does to me?'

Breath punched from her lungs, refilling an instant later with cautious hope. 'No…?'

'Let me show you.'

Scorching kisses branded her, leaving her gasping for breath, her fingers clenched in his hair as he swung her into his arms and strode for the nearest flat surface, which happened to be the first-floor hallway wall. Her silver sequinned dress seemed to melt off her body, along with the white bra and thong set, which particularly aroused a torrent of guttural Spanish words. His exploration of her was thorough, his fierce and expert attention eliciting an uninhibited response from her.

'Do you feel this, *querida*? Do you feel how much I want you?'

His erection, thick and heavy between her thighs, brought flames to her cheeks and a fire low in her belly. 'Yes.'

The involuntary twitch of her hips earned her a heart-stopping smile.

'You're a natural sensualist, but I'm going to enjoy teaching you so much more.'

'Yes.'

She was lost in delirium, the sound of the condom opening barely breaching her consciousness. Exploring him as thoroughly as he explored her became a need she couldn't... didn't want to deny. Swift, hesitant kisses grew longer, bolder, her teeth and tongue coming into play when harsh, throaty encouragement fell from his lips. A pinch of his flat nipple brought a deep shudder, making her freeze in alarm.

One strong hand captured both of hers an instant later. 'As much as I love that, you've shoved me to breaking point very quickly, Carla *mia.*' A kiss on her swollen lips, before he dropped to his knees before her. A firm grip on her thigh parted her legs. 'I need to redress the balance a little.'

The brazen possession of her sex with his mouth brought a scream that echoed through the hallway. The descent into lustful madness was instantaneous and comprehensive as pleasure imploded through her. The onslaught of her first orgasm was a stunningly unique experience that suspended time itself.

The sensation of being thrown over one broad shoulder and carried to his vast, palatial bedroom remained a delicious haze, very soon after replaced by the vivid reality of Javier, gorgeous, powerful and intensely aroused, his face stamped with carnal intent as he loomed over her.

Dark eyes locked onto hers. 'I can't wait to make you mine, *tesoro mio.*'

'*Sì*...please.'

'Wrap your legs around my waist. Tighter.'

The broad head of his erection nudged her opening. Nerves pinched at her excitement. The lower lip she bit in agitation was kissed free, his tongue probing her mouth to fan the flames of desire engulfing her.

Sweet languidness stole through her. Javier thrust swift and deep, then grimaced at her sharp scream.

'*Lo siento, querida.* Forgive me, it couldn't be helped.' Sure hands caressed her cheeks and throat, kisses planted on her lips until the hurt subsided.

Decadent fire soon replaced the ache, the residual discomfort trailing away to leave a sensation so unique and incredible, her mouth dropped open in wonder when he pulled back and slowly thrust again.

'Javier,' she breathed.

'*Sí*, I know,' he groaned, a deep shudder moving through him as he repeated the move. 'I wondered whether this chemistry was only in my imagination,' he confessed, the look in his eyes almost bashful. 'You have no idea how much it pleases me that it is not.'

Delight at her part in this indescribable union brought a sultry smile. 'I think I have *some* idea.'

His deep, low laugh, almost as captivating as what was happening to her, stopped her breath. The inkling that something totally out of her control was taking place in this bed, in this room, skittered over her skin.

It evaporated a second later when he moved again. Then she was hanging on for dear life, every emotion she'd ever experienced paling into insignificance in the face of the raw, unadulterated pleasure spinning her into oblivion.

The oblivion continued deep into the night, each experience unbelievably better than the last.

And then morning arrived.

A glance at the man she'd given her innocence to sent her emotions into freefall. She'd read somewhere that you never forgot your first. Javier Santino had attained unforgettable status even before they'd shared their first kiss.

As she lay there, Carla let herself wonder what it would be like if her life were different…if Javier were a permanent fixture and not a painfully temporary one…if the quick Internet search she'd done in the bathroom last night hadn't compared his affairs to high-octane roller-coaster rides— blood-pumping, exhilarating, but over in a blink of an eye.

'*Buenos dias, cariño.*'

Carla would never know whether it was the deep, sexy greeting or the firm tug of demanding hands she never wanted to let her go that had done it.

But the fear that she was already addicted to this...to Javier...had been real and immediate and frightening, and yet another dimension to a complicated life she couldn't afford.

Pushing him away, she leapt out of bed, keeping her back to him so her bewildered feelings wouldn't show. 'I have to go.'

'What's the hurry? It's Sunday. Let me feed you breakfast, then we can spend the day however you want. Personally, I'd prefer we stay in bed, but—'

'No! What happened last night...it's not going to happen again,' she forced out.

Tense silence finally made her glance over her shoulder. She glimpsed the stony, puzzled expression on his face. And fled.

He caught up with her in the hallway where she was busy tugging on her dress. 'What the hell's going on, Carla?'

Several avenues of explanation opened up before her, most of which revolved around newly emerging *feelings*. None of which she could voice.

So she shrugged. 'Draco will be wondering where I am. I need to get back to him.'

Nostrils flared with displeasure. 'Or you could use that incredible invention called the phone and let him know you're with me,' he rebutted.

The temptation to do that lanced her, terrifying her with its brutal insistence. What on earth was wrong with her? 'I'd much rather leave.'

Urgent hands grabbed her. 'Do you regret what we did last night?'

She opened her mouth to deny his words. To tell him that last night had been the most extraordinary night of her life. But he was giving her the perfect out, a way to retreat with her new, terrifying feelings intact.

'Yes, it was a mistake. I wish it hadn't happened.' Because now it had, she knew, bone-deep, that no other man, no other relationship would compare. And he wasn't in it for the long run.

Javier paled. 'What?'

She tried to move, but he held on. 'Javier, let me go.'

'Explain yourself first, Carla. Did I hurt you?' he whispered raggedly.

'No, you didn't.'

'Then why?'

At her stubborn silence, he cupped her chin and drew her face up. She watched myriad emotions transition over his face until a cold gleam slowly lit his eyes. 'You used me to divest yourself of your virginity, is that it?'

'I—what?' she returned, stunned.

'What's the matter? Angelis doesn't like virgins, so you thought you'd use me to take care of your little problem and now you're running back to him?'

Her mouth dropped open, shock rendering her speechless. Then, realising once again that he was handing her the perfect excuse, she raised her chin higher. 'Yes. I want to go back to Draco, if you don't mind.'

She was still reeling from the wrong turn of events when he dragged her down the stairs, flinging her shoes and handbag at her on the way. 'Get the hell out of my sight.' He wrenched the front door open. 'And, Carla?'

He waited until she turned, her insides shaking at the fury in his face.

'S-sì?'

'Pray that we never meet again. Because every single nightmare you've ever had will pale in comparison to what I'll do to you.'

'Was it worth it?' a hard, cold voice demanded.

Carla was yanked from the depths of vivid memories. She blinked hard and tightened her muscles when she realised her whole body was shaking with the force of her residual feelings.

'Was what worth it?' she asked obliquely, struggling to bring her mind back to the present.

'Sacrificing yourself in my bed to get Angelis's attention and make him jealous.'

She clenched her jaw. 'I don't know how many times I need to say it before you believe me. Draco had nothing to do with what happened between us. You made assumptions… and I just took advantage of the excuse.'

'And yet you were dating your *excuse* a month later,' he snarled.

'My mother died. He came to the funeral in England. He took me out a few times to try and distract me, that's all. Afterwards, when his sister was hurt, I spent some time with *both* of them, helping her get through it. That was all that happened.'

His lips curled. 'I may have been an outsider with a vivid imagination conjuring scenarios out of thin air. But didn't your own father try to forge a more permanent deal between you and Angelis only a few weeks ago?'

She couldn't hide from the truth. 'That doesn't mean it was what *I* wanted. And why does it upset you so much, anyway?' she threw at him.

Dark brown eyes turned to icy chips. 'No one likes to be used and tossed away like rubbish.'

She bit her lip, knowing whatever she said would come out wrong. But she couldn't stand the tension. 'We need to get past this.'

His eyes turned colder. 'Do we? What about the sound bite you gave the reporter who interviewed you after your championship win three years ago? Correct me if I'm wrong but wasn't it along the lines of, "Javier is a playboy. I don't date playboys"? Oh, and I believe someone from your *camp* followed that a few weeks later with another quote, calling me "an individual with low morals and a questionable pedigree"? Do we need to get past *those* too?'

Ice drenched her soul. From her fingertips to her toes, she lost all feeling in her limbs as she stared at him.

The events of the morning after their one-night stand had been bad enough, but this… Carla swallowed. Now she truly understood Javier's cold fury.

Understood that she appeared to have dealt a far deeper, much more personal injury to his pride.

CHAPTER FIVE

JAVIER WATCHED HER grow paler by the second, her green eyes pools of deep shock as she stared at him.

'What are you talking about? I-I didn't say anything about your pedigree…or the low morals thing,' she stammered.

'But you admit the playboy *thing*?' he drawled.

'I was just…there were rumours about us after your party. I was just trying to—'

'Distance yourself from the man who could ruin your "innocent princess" image?'

He watched her jaw tighten. 'No, I wanted to kill the rumours once and for all. Besides, I didn't think you'd welcome the association with me.'

'So you threw me under the bus to save me? How ingenuous—or should I say *ingenious*—of you.'

She swiped a shaky hand across her forehead. 'I'm sorry! The reporter caught me off-guard. As for the other thing, I know nothing about it. Even if I did, I'd never say anything like that,' she implored.

He'd investigated the source of those rumours, knew it was someone in her management team who'd made that damaging statement when questioned about Javier's association with her. Watching her try to wriggle herself off the hook, he wondered how he could think straight with the fury pounding through his blood.

'It's easy to be remorseful after the event, isn't it? And, *sí*, Principessa, my parentage *is* questionable. I'm the bastard son of an aristocrat. It's a circumstance I accepted long ago. But that didn't give you the right to go digging for it, then airing it in public for your own petty amusement.'

Her mouth worked, no doubt searching for more lies to excuse her behaviour. He waited for it, detachedly interested to see how she extricated herself from this latest stain on her character. He'd meant the words he'd thrown at her when he'd kicked her out of his house in Miami. At the time, a part of him had reeled at how desperately he'd wanted their one-night stand to continue. She should've been forgettable, the decision to create an immediate distance between them the morning after *his* to make.

Instead he'd kept up with any news on her career and personal life. And reeled even further at her heartless slurs on his reputation.

She cleared her throat. 'Javier…please—'

He stopped her meaningless words with a dismissive wave. 'Save it. What puzzles me is how can you be so exceptionally talented in one discipline of your life and yet fail so abysmally in every other aspect?'

She flinched. But slowly her head rose, her eyes meeting his boldly. Hell, she even had the gall to raise one perfect eyebrow at him.

'So…here we are, Javier. What happens next?'

He took his time swallowing the last of his wine, wishing it were something stronger, more bracing with a numbing after-effect. 'Don't worry, *querida*. The lessons I intend to teach you will be delivered in good time.'

Her swift inhalation allayed a little of his fury. She would never know how damaging the revelation about his parentage had been. It'd handed his father the perfect excuse to deny him the only thing he'd ever asked of him. The one thing he'd promised his mother on her deathbed—a proper burial with the family who'd rejected her because of her affair with his father, who had been a married man.

Bitterness stained the fury, charging through him with renewed vigour.

Unable to sit still, he surged to his feet. Her head snapped up to meet his gaze, an imploration he had no intention of succumbing to gleaming from the green depths.

When she struggled to her feet and faced him head-on,

he almost felt sorry for her. 'I didn't say those things about your parentage, Javier.'

'But the anonymous tip came from *your* management. Therefore the responsibility and the fault is yours. I have every intention of making sure you own up to it.'

She stumbled back a step. He was reaching out for her protectively with his free hand before he'd fully grasped his own instinctive action. Clenching his traitorous fist, he slammed his glass down, and shoved both hands in his pockets.

Her frailty was an illusion. She didn't need or want his help. She had a backbone of steel when it came to going after what she wanted.

'It's obvious something else is going on here other than you're letting on. Tell me the consequences so I can try and make it right,' she pleaded.

He froze. Part of him reeled that she would finally acknowledge her actions so openly. But then he remembered it was part of her usual machinations, her ability to disarm him with her words.

'It's too late to right the wrongs. All that's left to do is make the reparations.'

'And let me guess, I'll find out what those *reparations* are when you're ready?'

He smiled a mirthless smile. 'See, *chiquita*, you're already learning.'

And because he couldn't stand to watch her treacherous, offensively delectable mouth tremble for another second, he walked out of the living room, out of the suite, and out into the brisk Rome night.

Carla didn't see Javier again until the limo ferrying her to the airport the next morning came to a stop next to a stunning private jet. She'd flown in her share of chartered planes—a perk her father had deemed necessary for her image—but the Santino jet screamed a different class, even from the outside.

Tequila-gold, with thin platinum lines running from nose to fin, the aircraft was as visually masterful as its owner, who currently stood framed in the doorway at the top of the short flight of steps, arms folded and his bespoke-suited body projecting an aura of banked impatience.

She alighted, conscious of the brooding gaze on her, and smiled at the doctor who'd turned up at the hotel suite this morning with instructions to check her over. He'd pronounced her fit to travel, then accompanied her to the airport, his reassurance that her further health needs had been taken care of by Signor Santino, in the form of private medical personnel on board the plane, barely registering with Carla.

After Javier had walked out last night, she'd staggered back to her suite in a state of shock. It didn't take a genius to work out who had made those disparaging comments to the press about Javier's parentage.

Her father had been livid when the rumours of her association with Javier had surfaced in the months after her mother's death. Steeped in grief, she'd barely paid attention to the tabloids, had stuck to saying *no comment* after the initial disastrous interview with the journalist the day of her championship win.

She'd made sure after that never to be drawn on a personal subject, not knowing the damage that was being done behind her back. That Javier had been dealt a much heavier blow than to be called a playboy.

She looked up at him now as she mounted the steps, and her stomach fell. Every accusation he'd hurled at her last night was still etched on his face. The light of day hadn't brought an iota of mercy.

Whatever her father's actions had wrought had to be monumental—

'If you dawdle any longer, we'll miss our take-off slot,' he ground out.

She hoisted her handbag onto her shoulder with her un-

hurt hand and mounted the last step. It brought her within
touching distance of his sleek, silently seething perfection.
She brought up her immobilised hand and tried to squeeze
past him when he made no attempt to move out of her way.

He stopped her with a hand on her waist, his gaze burning
into her. 'You're favouring your wrist. Did you aggravate it?'

'No. But I slept badly last night. I'm certain that didn't
help,' she murmured.

He looked from her face to her wrist as if examining the
cast would determine the truth of her statement. 'Did the
doctor give you anything for it?' he snapped.

'I didn't ask.' Her mind had been on something else. Him.

Exasperation piled onto the myriad volatile emotions
swirling over his face. Firming his hold, he guided her inside the aircraft, bypassing grouped armchairs and a conference setting to a sitting area complete with a plush double
sofa and recliner. Relieving her of her handbag, he placed
it on a nearby table and motioned her onto the recliner. He
murmured in Spanish to a middle-aged woman in a neat
skirt suit before turning back to her. He leaned forward to
secure her seat belt and Carla's breath fractured.

He straightened as the woman approached. 'This is
Selma. She's part of my company's medical team. She'll
give you something for the pain.'

He waited until she'd taken the painkillers and the plane
was moving before he started to walk away.

'Javier?' His revelations last night would continue to
haunt her unless she did something about it. She cleared
her throat when he paused. 'Can we talk, please?'

'There will be enough time for that, if you insist. Right
now, I have work to do. And you need to rest.'

She gritted her teeth as he walked away, silently cursing
the guilt raking through her. If she'd been as duplicitous
and unfeeling as Javier believed she was, she could've shut
her eyes and pretended all this didn't affect her. Instead she
fidgeted in her seat as the plane took off and they raced east.

Eventually, the medication kicked in. At some point she woke to find a blanket tucked around her and the lights in the sitting area dimmed. A glass of water stood on the table next to her and she drank before once again succumbing to sleep.

She was awoken by Selma, who smiled and informed her that they'd landed and that Javier had already left the plane to head to his office.

Carla told herself the disappointment she felt was because she'd been denied the opportunity to set the record straight. And she kept telling herself that all through the next two weeks of barely seeing Javier. Of Selma, though, she saw a lot, the doctor almost frustratingly efficient in ensuring Carla was fed, watered and medicated within the four walls of Javier's ultra-luxurious Upper East Side penthouse.

Emerging from her assigned bedroom on the morning after being given the all-clear to pursue light work, Carla caught sight of herself in the large gilt mirror gracing the wide hallway, and paused in surprise.

Her skin looked healthy and vibrant and her cheeks had lost the sickly pallor and gaunt hollowness. Her newly shampooed hair, which she'd worn in a tight bun for as long as she could remember, fell in waves around her shoulders, the distinct caramel highlights catching the sunlight.

'Admiring your new and improved self?'

She jumped and turned to find Javier striding towards her. Dressed in an open-necked casual shirt and black jeans, he was the epitome of sophisticated chic, and arresting enough to make her gape for several embarrassing seconds before she regained her focus. 'There was nothing wrong with my old self,' she snapped after recovering from the shock of suddenly seeing him, larger than life and in the flesh.

'That is a subject of much debate,' he returned.

Carla moved away from the mirror. 'What are you doing here?'

Black eyebrows rose. 'At my last recollection, I lived here.'

Heat suffused her face. 'I didn't mean that. I meant, it's Friday. I thought you'd be gone by now.'

'Sorry to disappoint, but if I want to keep my famous work/life balance title I need to take the occasional day off,' he drawled.

'Is that what you're doing? Taking the day off?'

Powerful shoulders hefted a shrug. 'That depends on how well you do with your first assignment.'

She stopped in her tracks. 'Me?'

'Selma tells me you're fit enough to attend a creative meeting or two as long as your wrist is taken care of. She also tells me you're going stir-crazy. Was she wrong?'

'She wasn't,' she hurriedly replied. She looked down at the short tunic she'd thrown on after her shower because it'd been the easiest thing to hand. 'I'll go and change.'

After a swift perusal of her attire, he shook his head. 'You don't need to. The creative director will be here after breakfast. We'll work from here today.'

He headed for the dining room. She followed him into the large, sunlit room. Before now, breakfast had been a solitary affair, eaten with almost absent enjoyment while her mind worried over what Javier had meant by reparation and just how he would exact it from her.

Now as she walked towards the place set for her, she couldn't help recall how the last meal they'd shared had ended.

But looking at him, she could see little trace of the capricious emotion that had leapt from him then. She didn't fool herself into believing it was far from the surface. Javier had bided his time for three years. She didn't doubt that he would be perfectly content to toy with her a while longer yet.

Suddenly reluctant to touch on the subject she'd spent far too many hours dwelling on, she helped herself to a bagel, smothered it with cream cheese, and took a bite. Swallowing it down with a sip of coffee, she risked a glance and found him staring at her over his coffee cup. 'I'm not sure exactly what a creative director does.'

'We'll discuss the preliminary designs I have in mind for you to work with and then decide how best to go about it.'

'Don't I need to be on your speedboat to get the best visuals?'

'The speedboat shoot has been put on hold until you're no longer wearing that cast. My new premium tequila brand launches in six weeks. I've been struggling to find the right person to front it. You'll be the face of it.'

Her hand shook as she set her cup down. 'What?'

'You're not deaf, *querida.*'

'I'd rather not do that, if you don't mind.'

'But I do mind. You drink the stuff, if I remember correctly. In fact you virtually drowned in it at my birthday party three years ago. I fail to see what the problem is.'

'In light of what happened afterwards, do you really think I'm the right candidate to promote your tequila?'

His mouth twisted cruelly. 'Since you insist on convincing me the circumstances of your getting drunk that night no longer exist, it shouldn't be a problem. Besides, you won't be required to drink it, just pretend it's the best thing that's happened to you since the first time you put your ice skates on. That was the single most incredible moment of your life, was it not?'

She drew in a deep, sustaining breath, before she gave in to temptation and slapped his face. 'You obviously mean to torture me at every opportunity. If that's how you get your kicks, then so be it. But if you want our collaboration to have any hope of working, can I suggest we resolve this sooner rather than later?' When one mocking eyebrow started to lift, she ploughed on. 'So I called you a playboy. Where was the lie in that? Were you not a playboy, then? Are you not now? You date as frequently as you change your socks. In fact, I don't think the paparazzi has snapped you with the same woman twice!'

An arrogant smile twitched his lips. 'Have you been keeping tabs on me, *querida*?'

'Hardly. But it's very difficult to avoid seeing a man who flaunts himself as often as you do. If you choose to practise that work/life balance you're so proud of in public, don't complain when people take an interest.'

'Some aspects of my life may be public. You made it your business to dig up private parts about my parentage that were none of your business, and make them public.'

Her breath shuddered out. 'It wasn't me, Javier. It was my father. The only thing I'm culpable of is guilt by association.'

He regarded her for several tense seconds. 'It's not the only thing you're guilty of, *querida*, but we'll leave that for now. As for the tequila shoot, your role in it stands. You're good at *faking* things.' The discreet sound of the concierge's buzzer echoed through the room. Javier rose and rounded the table to where she sat. Bending low, he placed a kiss at her temple. 'You'll excel in this role. I insist on it. Nothing less than perfection will do.'

She still sat frozen in place when he returned a few minutes later with a casually dressed man in tow. Darren O'Hare wore boxy spectacles, behind which his grey eyes twinkled with friendliness.

'Welcome on board. We've had a hell of a time placing the right person for this launch. I was excited when Javier told me we'd landed you. I'm a huge fan,' he said, a faint Irish brogue curling his words.

Careful not to glance at Javier in case the tension between them exploded onto their unsuspecting visitor, she smiled and shook Darren's hand. 'Thank you. I'll do my best to make it work.'

Darren grinned and set down his leather portfolio. 'I've watched a few of your performances online, for research purposes, of course. Outstanding doesn't begin to describe them. Dedication like that translates into everything. You'll knock this shoot out of the park. Then hopefully I can score myself tickets to your next performance. Tickets for the last one sold out within minutes—'

'Perhaps we can get on with discussing what we need Carla to do? That is, of course, if you've finished with your shameless idol-worshipping?'

Darren froze at the bite in his boss's tone. Clearing his throat, he nodded. 'Sure...of course.'

'Great, let's take the meeting in my office.'

He led the way out, his strides swift and purposeful. Grabbing his case, Darren sent her a puzzled glance. Her smile felt as false as her insides felt brittle.

They entered the room to find Javier poised at the head of an oval table, arms folded. In silence, Darren produced poster-sized glossy shots from his case and spread them out on the table.

Carla stared down at the pictures, the attention to detail and the sheer magnificence of the graphics robbing her of breath. It was quite evident that a lot of time and effort had gone into creating the perfect outer package for La Pasión, the signature drink fronted by J Santino Inc.

She read the tag at the bottom of the first graphic.

La Pasión.
Taste The Edge.
Live The Edge.

'That's our slogan for the tequila. My department is working on the script for you and Pavlov.'

'Pavlov Krychek?' she asked, surprised that the Russian ice-skating supremo was on board with the project. His penchant for throwing diva tantrums was well known. He also had the insufferable egotistical delusion that every woman he came across would fall at his feet.

Darren smiled wryly. 'Yes, he was a pain to sign up but—'

'Sadly he'll no longer be part of this campaign,' Javier finished.

Darren blinked in surprise. 'Since when?'

'Since I fired him this morning. He made one demand too many.' His gaze shifted to her, and Carla's breath stalled. 'I don't tolerate divas, male or female. So you'll be on your own for this one. It'll be just you, the bottle and your ice skates.'

Her eyes widened. 'My skates?'

'It's your signature accessory, the essence of who you are. Otherwise you'll be any other dime-a-dozen celebrity with an eye-catching face.'

Darren nodded slowly, clearly still reeling from the shift in proceedings, but catching up quickly. 'I think that could work…'

'It *will* work, much better than the advertising department's initial idea. Perhaps someone should've brainstormed that before resources were wasted trying to land Krychek?'

A bewildered frown creased Darren's brow, as if he had no idea what he was being scolded for. Again his gaze swung to her, and Carla almost felt sorry for him. Javier Santino in this mood meant hell for everyone.

'So when is all this happening?'

Darren's glance slid to her cast. 'The idea was to shoot the ad on a real ice rink. CGI would work, but the real thing would give it much more depth.'

'Once we finalise your costume and script, we'll start with the nightclub shoots. We'll shoot the ice-skating scenes last when you're completely healed,' Javier added. 'In the meantime, Darren will supply you with some in-depth information of the product to read up on.'

'Isn't the script going to suffice?' she asked.

A terse smile curved his lips. 'You train three times a day to be the best at what you do. It's no different for me. I believe in arming myself with as much information as possible in every situation. Since you're part of this project that applies to you too. Knowledge is power. Don't you agree?'

She knew they were talking about something completely different. That he was taunting her—again. 'Yes. Of course.'

'Good.'

'Is there anything else?' he asked his creative director, who'd been watching their interaction with blatant curiosity.

Darren shook his head. 'That's it for now. All the info you need is in the packet including the schedule we hope to achieve. I'm the location scout for the shoot as well so I'll be in touch to arrange a visit to the rink we intend to use. If you have any questions, Carla, my business card is on the first page...' He trailed off when Javier's mouth suddenly flattened. 'Or I'm sure Mr Santino can help you out.'

Carla swallowed, the thought of returning to the ice suddenly chilling her skin.

'Carla?'

She looked up and caught Javier's shrewd glance. 'Yes?'

'What's wrong?'

She glanced away. 'Nothing. I'm fine.'

But she wasn't. The slight trembling that had taken hold when Javier mentioned returning to the ice rink had intensified in the time since. Much as it had every time she'd thought about it since leaving hospital. Unwilling to show her uncontrolled reaction, she turned away from the table.

'That'll be all for now, Darren,' Javier said. 'We'll touch base in the office on Monday.'

'Sure. Uh...great to meet you, Carla.'

She summoned a fuller, warmer smile, then walked to the leather sofa situated to one side of the room. Their low voices registered on the edge of her consciousness as they left the office. She sank into the seat, massaging her temples as she took deep breaths.

Javier hadn't believed nothing was wrong. She wondered why she'd even bothered trying to fob him off. Because he was back seconds later, striding straight over to crouch in front of her.

'Tell me what's going on with you. Now.'

CHAPTER SIX

JAVIER'S TEETH GRITTED as she shook her head. He didn't want to believe it was a refusal to answer him. That would mean he still wasn't getting through to her. That she didn't think he was serious about every last ounce of reparation he intended to extract from her. His gut clenched hard.

'Are you feeling unwell again?'

That would be the only reason he would accept for her behaviour. 'I told you, I'm fine.'

She tried to release herself. He refused to let her go. Holding her still this close would focus her attention on him instead of on other things. Or other men.

His jaw clenched harder, a sliver of self-disgust rising at the way he'd felt when she'd turned her stunning eyes on O'Hare. Bestowed that beautiful but rare smile on him.

Jealous. He'd been consumed with jealousy.

Which was unacceptable.

'Explain to me then why you looked as if you'd fallen into a trance just now.'

She met his gaze for one bold moment, then looked away with a shrug. 'I'm sorry you don't like the way I look when I'm thinking—'

'Don't insult my—*madre de Dios*, look at me when I'm talking to you!'

Her chin angled up. Almond-shaped pools of green glared at him. Instead of raising his annoyance level, it eased a restriction in his chest. 'I'm looking at you. Satisfied?'

'I will be, marginally, when you tell me what's wrong. And for the sake of my sanity, and yours, don't say nothing.'

Her nostrils quivered delicately with the sustaining breath she took. 'Fine. I don't want to return to the ice.'

Javier frowned. 'Not while your wrist is still in a cast,

no. That part of the ad will only be shot once the binding comes off.'

She shook her head, once more inducing a tightening in his gut. 'Can we not just use CGI like Darren suggested?'

'Explain to me why you don't want to use the ice.'

She shifted, her skin sliding against the silk tunic. Memories of how smooth and warm that skin was slashed across his brain, driving heat into his groin. 'Another fall if I'm not careful could set me back even more months. Why risk another injury for the sake of an ad campaign?'

'Because that campaign is paying you millions in sponsorship funds. Funds that could go away very easily if you don't adhere to your part of the agreement. Surely you're not so obtuse as to overlook that?'

'But we have an alternative!'

Javier sensed something else going on. Had the trauma of Blackwell's training left her with something more than just a bodily injury? Would she even tell him if that were the case? Frustrated anger rose to mingle with the irritations pulsing within him. He refused to add hurt to the equation. Because being upset that he was on the outside of something so important to her shouldn't be an issue for him. She was contractually obligated to give him whatever he wanted.

His mind veered to other things that he wanted. Things that had made him stay away from his own penthouse for two weeks because he didn't want to admit to the need hammering beneath his skin.

'The alternative doesn't work for me. So unless you want to tell me the real reason why you're making the request, the original plan stands.'

He waited. And waited some more. Her eyes shadowed, but her defiant chin stayed up, her mouth firming with whatever emotions were surging through her.

'I told you why. Obviously, you disagree. Are we done now? I'd like to get out of here, get some fresh air.'

'Carla—'

'Oh, God, please don't tell me I'm a prisoner too?'

He caught the hand she'd brought up to push him away, the knowledge that she didn't intend to share what was upsetting her hardening into a knot. He set the notion to one side for the moment. 'You're not a prisoner. But you can't go out on your own either. It's not safe.'

She stilled. 'What do you mean?'

'I mean a group of your fans—I believe they call themselves *The Nardozzians*?—are camped downstairs. If you go out on your own, you'll be mobbed.'

She paled. 'I… I didn't know. They weren't here when I went out for a walk yesterday morning.' The hand in his chest balled into a fist, pressed deeper into his flesh, and Javier got the impression she didn't know how clearly her agitation was showing. 'How long have they been here?'

'They arrived last night. Obviously word has leaked that you're in town.'

She closed her eyes for a split second. When she opened them again, her gaze lingered on his jaw. 'Damn, so I can't go out?'

Catching hold of her chin, he tilted her face. Breathed easier when her eyes connected with his. And then, because he couldn't help himself, he brushed his finger down her cheek. 'You can go out, as long as you're accompanied.'

'And who…?' She exhaled. 'You?'

'Me. Especially since I know that one of those fans has been brazen enough to propose to you several times. I believe he's even gone a few steps further and sent you some risqué pictures of himself?'

Her eyes widened. 'How do you know this?'

'When are you going to get it through your head that I know everything that is relevant to know about you?'

A shadow fleeted through her eyes. 'At least you're not purporting to know absolutely everything.'

'Sadly, *carina*, if we knew everything about each other, we wouldn't be here now, would we?'

The shadows deepened. When she tried to turn her head away, he held her still.

'Has he done anything beyond the pictures and the placards?'

Distaste showed on her face. 'He sent a few horrible letters when he was banned from going on my fan webpage.'

The surge of protectiveness took him by surprise. 'I'll make sure he gets the message about keeping clear boundaries.'

Her soft breath feathered over his hand. Despite his every instinct warning him against it, he drew her closer, the mingled scent of her perfume and shampoo washing over his senses.

'He makes me uncomfortable but I think he's harmless.'

'If he makes you uncomfortable then he's already overstepped his mark.'

Her eyes met his, surprise mingling with another emotion he couldn't read. 'Careful, Javier, or I'll confuse you with someone who actually cares one iota about me.'

His fingers slipped around her nape and tightened in her hair. The action lifted her head up further, exposing the flawless, sleek line of her neck. His senses pounded with the need to taste. He barely managed to restrain himself. 'Your confusion would be unfortunate. I'm merely protecting my investment.'

He ignored the hurt that blinked through her eyes. He couldn't lose sight of the repercussions of her and her father's previous actions. Because of them, his beloved mother's last resting place was among strangers, and each day Javier was unable to right that particular wrong was a day too long.

Sliding his fingers from her hair, he stood and shoved his fist in his pocket. 'You want to go out, be ready in half an hour. I have a video conference later.'

'I thought you were taking the day off?' she replied.

'Sadly I'm addicted to the urge to hammer down the next seemingly impossible deal.'

'You mean, the temptation to torture another human being until they buckle under your will?'

His smile felt as if it could crack ice. 'Same difference. So unless you want to be the recipient of my torture tactics, you'll do as I say.'

She muttered under her breath in Italian, the very unladylike statement bringing a reluctant smile to his lips as she hurried out of the room.

A second later, he frowned, dragging his mind from the sylph-like form of the woman whose presence in his life was anything but a laughing matter, to the reason he'd taken a rare day off.

Any trace of mirth evaporated as he contemplated the reason for his videoconference. As usual, his father hadn't given him advance warning nor any assurance that the call Javier had requested would actually take place. The banked rage that resided just beneath his skin every time he thought of the man whose blood ran through his veins threatened to resurge. The knowledge that it was because of Carla that he continued to have to deal with Fernando made him curse inwardly as he paced to the window.

Looking out to the street below, he caught sight of the clutch of Carla's fans across the street, and another form of rage took hold. She might have downplayed the seriousness of her fan's actions, but Javier knew the side-effects of hero worship and the unfortunate decisions that could unfold because of it.

He was a product of such a misstep.

Had his own mother not been blinded by stars in her eyes, she wouldn't have been taken advantage of by an unscrupulous man who saw no harm in ruining an innocent. She wouldn't have wasted her life pining for and chasing a dream that had been unattainable from the start.

Juliana Santino had died long before her time. The official cause had been cancer, but Javier knew sadness and bitter disappointment had played a huge part in his mother's demise. And the man responsible for those debilitating emotions still had a form of power over Javier because of a woman who commanded more power than was permitted over him.

He needed to end it once and for all.

'I'm ready.'

He whirled, disturbed that he'd been so lost in contemplation he'd been unaware of her return. His gaze raked over her and his senses leaped.

Her white skinny jeans moulded her hips and thighs, heeled boots and a white oversized top that insisted on falling off one shoulder drawing attention to her body. With her newly regained weight and better health had come a vibrancy to her skin.

Something hot and urgent jerked within him.

She looked a perfect picture of innocence, but it was deceptive innocence, he reminded himself.

He forced his gaze up from her endless legs. 'Why are you wearing your hair up?' he demanded before he could think the question through.

She held up her cast-encased hand and wriggled her half concealed fingers with a hint of triumph. 'I can move my fingers without it hurting too much now. The brushing took longer than I wanted and the knot isn't the tidiest, but I'm sure it'll stay up.'

He didn't want it to. He wanted her hair flowing over her shoulders, catching the light and making him guess what colour it really was, not scraped up into a careless bun, making her eyes seem huger and her flawless bone structure fracturing his ability to think coherently.

Dios, he was losing it. He growled under his breath.

Casting a searching glance on his desk, he caught up his car keys. 'Let's go.'

She grimaced at the keys. 'We're driving? I thought we were going for a walk?'

'You thought wrong.'

Her eyes sparked green fire. 'I'd much rather walk—'

'Your mob has increased threefold in the last hour. There's no way I'm subjecting you to that. So it's the car or the penthouse. Your choice.'

He knew his tone didn't indicate it was much of one, but he didn't care.

'Can we walk? Once we're away from here, I mean?' she asked.

He clenched his fist around the metal keys, knowing that if he gritted his teeth any harder his jaw would snap, and headed for the door. 'I'll think about it.'

Her mouth pursed, but she didn't protest further. They rode the lift in silence. As they passed the front desk, she greeted the concierge by name and smiled at the hapless fool, who melted into a puddle of adoration. Javier turned away from the nauseating scene, his mood darkening further when he glanced out into the morning sunshine.

She sighed as he handed his keys to the valet to have his car brought up. 'I'd rather brave it outside on my own if you're going to be this grouchy.'

He despised the bolt of alarm that went through him. 'You'd rather contend with that than be with me?' He jerked his thumb at the mob.

She tilted her head to see past him. He watched her eyes widen. The placards had grown bolder since yesterday. One in particular, from her avid fan, made Javier's skin crawl.

'"*Essere il mio, anima e corpo*,"' she muttered the words in her mother tongue. 'Wow, it seems like everyone wants something from me. It doesn't matter that I don't wish to give it. Or that I want something else for myself.'

'It that a dig at me?'

A small, sad smile curved her lips and he couldn't look away from her expression. 'It's an inescapable truth,' she murmured.

'Don't worry, *querida*, I've no intention of letting you be

owned by anyone else, either *in body or in soul*,' he para-
phrased the words on the placard.

He expected a quick comeback or at least a demand for
him to keep his possessive threats to himself. But a glance
showed the shadows were back again. The eyes that met his
were subdued, her mouth pinched.

'Por el amor de Dios,' he grated. 'If you need fresh air
that badly, come on.'

Sliding his hand around her waist, he guided her through
the double doors leading to the underground garage. The
valet accepted the tip eagerly, but his gaze stayed on Carla,
another victim of her charms.

He hurried her into the sports car, marginally appeased
when she came to life, pulling her seat belt across her body
to secure it. He shut her door and was rounding the hood
when his phone pinged.

Activating the app, Javier read the message once, then
again. The piercing disappointment that lanced him was
unwelcome evidence that he'd allowed himself to hope his
father would talk to him this time. Controlling the need to
smash his fist through the nearest wall, he yanked open his
door and slid behind the wheel, acknowledging that perhaps the drive had come at an opportune time. He revved
the engine mercilessly and earned a furtive glance from
his passenger.

'Can I ask if something's wrong without getting my head
bitten off?'

'Besides the unexpected and unwanted gift of having my
afternoon freer than I wished it to be, no, I don't wish to
discuss what's wrong.' He aimed the car at the exit. For his
own peace of mind, he didn't glance at the screaming fans
who surged for the car as soon as they spotted their idol.
Luckily the mid-morning traffic was clear and he breathed
a sigh of relief when the lights turned green. As he put miles
between them and his apartment, she relaxed.

'Was the video conference important?' she asked after a few minutes.

His laugh was abrasive. 'Since it's one I've been waiting five long years to have, you could say that.' He changed lanes, the abrupt move jerking her body against his. Her shoulder bumped his and her scent filled his nostrils. Hunger he didn't want or completely understand tore through him. His grip tightened on the wheel.

'Can't you reschedule it?'

As a touchy subject, it was singularly effective in dousing a little bit of his hunger. 'When it comes to my father, I find myself in the unique position of being on the back foot.'

He cursed himself the moment the words spilled out.

'Your father?' she echoed, wariness flaring in her eyes. 'He's the one you were supposed to conference with?'

'Until he cancelled on me for the fourth time this month.'

He sped through an amber light and onto Madison Avenue.

'Speaking from personal experience, you don't strike me as the type to sit back and let events unfold the way they want to. I'm assuming you know where your father is?' she asked.

Exhaling, he nodded. 'Yes, I do. But before you make the obvious suggestion, perhaps you should know that the last time my father and I were in the same room, we nearly came to blows.'

She gasped. 'What?'

'Sí, querida. He's the only person, besides you, who arouses distinctly *primitive* feelings in me.'

Her lips parted, a look of bewilderment crossing her face before she looked out of her window. 'I won't take that as a compliment.'

'My blood rarely gets this fired up so perhaps you should.'

'Not if it incites violent feelings within you.'

'Fired up doesn't necessarily mean violent. I can think of a few ways to express my more nascent emotions.'

Colour flared into her cheeks. 'I don't see how express-ing yourself that way helps with anything.'

'Spare me the false naiveté, Carla.'

She shook her head, and the careless knot of her hair wob-bled. He resisted the urge to hasten its demise and parked on a leafy street.

'I only meant that the problems wouldn't disappear sim-ply because you…indulged yourself in another way.'

'But if I can regress to my baser instincts and make love not war, wouldn't that put me in a better frame of mind?'

'You don't truly believe that, or I wouldn't be here.'

A rare chuckle ripped free. 'Touché.' He flung his door open and went round to help her out. Turning from him, she gazed up at the three-storey brownstone, one of many on the street.

'Where are we?'

He shrugged. 'Somewhere you're guaranteed privacy. Come on.' He walked round the side to a high, wrought-iron gate and entered the security code. The lock sprang open, and he led her through an ivy-laced trellised arch.

For a split second, Javier asked himself why he'd brought her here. There were many quiet parks he could've taken her to. Hell, with his afternoon suddenly free, he could've driven her to Connecticut or the Hamptons for her precious walk.

Her loud, pleased gasp pulled him from his short rumi-nation.

'Wow, this place is stunning!'

He turned and watched her reaction to the place his mother had loved, albeit never wholeheartedly, her deep attachment to her homeland overshadowing any other place on earth.

The smile Carla had so far only bestowed on others shone his way before she rushed past him to the large fountain and waterfall that trickled into an oval pond that still held fat koi. Miniature bonsai trees that his mother had loved to prune were dotted in pots around the garden and almost every type of rose bush budded, ready for the springtime bloom.

Still puzzling why he'd brought her here, he crossed his arms. 'What's the big deal about fresh air, anyway? Air is air. Fresh air is overrated.' He was well aware he sounded like a grumpy ape.

She didn't answer for a full minute, and Javier was sure she hadn't heard his question since she'd stopped at a white rose bush and bent low to inhale the heady scent. Hell, she even took her time to *caress* a flower. As if she had all the time in the world to stop and smell the roses. He dragged his eyes from her delectable backside as she straightened.

'I used to go for long walks with my mother when I was a child. Sometimes we'd be gone for hours. We'd compete to see who could name the most flowers. I secretly knew she was letting me win more often than not.' The memory brought a sad smile.

It sounded idyllic. The ideal pastime for a perfect princess. Bitterness dredged up his gut. Something must've shown on his face because she swallowed, and let go of the delicate bud.

'So, who does this garden belong to?'

'My mother.'

She stared wide-eyed at him for several heartbeats before her gaze swung to the brownstone. 'Is she here?'

'No. She died five years ago.'

Her green eyes clouded as they returned to him. *'Mi dispiace. Le mie condoglianze.'* Realising she'd spoken her condolences on his loss in her native tongue, she quickly amended. 'I meant—'

'Va bene, dolce principessa, I know what you meant. *Grazie.'*

'Why do you call me that? I'm not a princess.'

'Are you not?'

Her mouth pursed. 'Please don't spoil the moment, Javier.'

He wanted to point out that they weren't having a moment. That he'd chosen this place because it'd been the better alternative to her being spotted in a public park.

The words remained locked in his throat.

Instead he watched her stroll from flower to tree, bench to climbing plant, her shoulders visibly relaxing as she watched a butterfly flit from one petal to the other. He followed her down the stairs to the lower level of the garden, then leaned against an old oak tree as she continued her gentle inspection. She finally sat down at a bench and turned her almost regal face up to the sun. The rays caressed her features, bathing her skin in adoring light. A sight he couldn't pull his gaze from.

'Thank you for bringing me here.'

She didn't see his shrug because her eyes had drifted shut, the delicate lids fluttering. He knew because he was suddenly seated next to her, having had no recollection of moving from the tree.

Sí, he was really losing it.

'*De nada,*' he murmured, absurdly reluctant to spoil the moment with talk.

Seconds ticked by. His restlessness and bitter frustration abated a touch.

When she smiled, he found his own lips curving in response.

'Your mother must have loved it here. Complete peace in the middle of such a full-on, vibrant city is a rare gift.'

His smile evaporated. 'She…tolerated it. Anywhere that wasn't her home wasn't ever good enough.'

She opened her eyes and glanced at him. Wisps of silkily caramel hair caressed her cheek, and he fought the drive to add his touch to her skin. 'It wasn't enough that *you* were here?' she enquired.

Having asked himself the same question a few disturbingly low times, he should've been prepared for the muffled ache in his chest that had never quite gone away. But hearing the query from her lips sharpened the sting of knowing that he hadn't quite been enough. Nothing and no one had come close to the draw of his mother's dilapidated Northern Spanish home.

He shrugged the pain away, more than a little bewildered at how the conversation had ended up here. How *they* had ended up here. 'She cared for me, in her own way.'

Keen eyes probed. 'But?'

'Anywhere that wasn't Menor Compostela wouldn't have done for her.' Because of one man. And his dangerous influence. An influence that meant his mother hadn't been able to rest in peace even in death.

'Is that where your father is? Menor Compostela?'

'You don't already know this from your little jaunt through my private life?'

Her face clouded. 'I told you, I wasn't the one who dug through your life. My father's my manager. He heard the rumours about our…night together, and probably thought it would be prudent to know—'

'On whom his precious princess had sullied her pristine image?' he finished, renewed bitterness surging high.

'Is that notion so alien to you? Haven't you dug with equal tenacity through my life?'

'Whatever I unearthed hasn't been disclosed to the public, so yes, *chiquita*, I believe I'm above reproach in this instance.' He rose, the illusionary sense of tranquillity gone.

He curbed the bite of regret, more than a little annoyed with himself for the unsettling sensations ricocheting through him.

This day off had been an idiotic idea. Leaving her in his mother's garden, he strode up the steps and entered the empty house.

Javier wasn't sure what he hoped to find inside, but no answers came to him as he walked through rooms with sheet-draped furniture. Everything in here had been new once upon a time, a naïve conviction that granting his mother a fresh start would be what she needed to make a clean break from an unhealthy past.

Nothing he'd done had worked. Bitterness twisted his mouth. Clearly he was extremely ill-equipped to handle or even understand the female psyche.

He would be better off sticking to what he knew best— cut-throat deals and emotionless liaisons.

Except he didn't feel emotionless about one liaison in particular.

Turning away from an expensive entertainment centre his mother had never used to his knowledge, he retraced his steps to the garden.

The sound of her voice stopped him before he rounded a tall rose bush.

'No, I don't want you to come to New York, not if you're going to keep badgering me about this. My mind is made up.' She paused, and Javier heard a muffled voice. Then her breath caught. 'That's all you care about, isn't it? Would it kill you to ask how *I* am?'

Javier's fists curled, the primeval protective instincts that had floored him in the condo returning, stronger than before. About to stride into her presence, he froze as she continued, 'No, Papà, nothing has changed. I'm still taking a break from figure skating. Yes…*indefinitely.*'

The deadly ice in his veins threatened to turn him into a statue. He still managed to move. He must have because she came into view, her eyes growing wide as she tucked her phone into her pocket and drew her arms around her midriff in self-protection. She took a few guarded steps away from him.

Javier was obliquely amused by the useless action. As if anything could save her now. He'd been ready to believe there was some sort of subliminal reason for bringing her to the place he'd built for his mother. Probably because she'd also lost her mother and he'd been seeking some nonexistent connection?

Dios mío. Even the suggestion was unacceptable. He sliced his fingers through his hair. Clearly, he'd been out of his mind.

'Javier?' Her voice held the tiniest wobble.

'Answer me yes or no, Carla. Did you sign our contract knowing you planned to take an indefinite break from ice skating?'

All colour drained from her face, leaving pools of shocked, bottomless moss green. In the deadly stillness, even the insects didn't dare to move. Her lips slowly parted.

Javier braced himself. For what, he wasn't completely sure.

She swallowed hard, the movement echoing through her whole body. Or perhaps she trembled? He didn't care. All he wanted was deliverance from the vacuum of confusion taking hold of him.

'Answer me!'

A short, jerked nod, followed by a simple, 'Yes.'

Absurdly, as he turned away and left his mother's garden, Javier wished she'd lied and answered no.

CHAPTER SEVEN

'SAY SOMETHING. *PER FAVORE,*' Carla whispered. 'Anything. I can't stand the silence.'

They'd left the charming, tranquil garden, and any notion that she was getting to know a much less steel-hearted Javier, far behind. She would never dream of calling him gentle, but the glimpses of the man she'd seen in his mother's garden had touched her heart in a way that had nothing to do with the sexual tension that resided beneath the surface of all their interactions.

That man, if he had existed beyond her imagination, was nowhere to be seen now. The man who grabbed the steering wheel with barely restrained force, whose face was set in a granite mask as he wove through traffic, struck naked apprehension in her heart.

'Javier, please...'

'You weren't planning on telling me until you had your hands on the first quarter's payment.' His voice was conversational, save for the toxic ice that dripped from it. 'I'm guessing the signing bonus wasn't quite enough for you to disappear into the sunset with?'

'No... I mean yes—' She stopped and massaged her temples. 'No, I wasn't planning on disappearing, not without speaking to you first. Not that I was planning to disappear... *Dio, questo è folle.*'

His grating laugh sliced across her every nerve. '*You* think this is insane? Why did you bother even signing a contract with me? With a face and body like yours, you could've landed a number of gullible rich men who would've been only too happy to tolerate a little absence of integrity for a chance to taste what you have to offer.'

His words were a slap that left her reeling, the depth of

her hurt unbelievably deep. 'How dare you? You're being extremely offensive without just cause—'

'*Just cause?* Every interaction I've had with you so far has contained an element of deception on your part.'

'That's not true!'

'Then by all means, Principessa, enlighten me as to where I've misstepped.'

The shivers that had started in the garden rolled over her once more. 'I'd planned to take a break from ice skating, yes, but I hadn't decided exactly when or for how long.'

'And you didn't see fit to inform me of this before you signed on the dotted line? Can you honestly tell me that your decision to keep your plans a secret didn't revolve around the state of your finances?'

'The contract did. Wasn't that the whole point? You told me three years ago you never wanted to see me again. Then all of a sudden you're entertaining an endorsement contract with me? I'm not stupid, Javier. I knew there was a chance this wouldn't be just business—'

'But you entered into the contract anyway?' His lips curled on the words.

'I...hoped you'd moved on. And I planned on fulfilling my part of the deal,' she retorted. 'Because of my wrist I won't be able to compete in two months' time but there are no major championships until next year, so for the sake of your campaign I'll still be number one. I don't know why you're upset with me. Nothing has changed—'

'The insane decision to trust you, professionally, despite your abysmal private life should've been testament to the fact that this deal should never have happened. More fool me, I guess,' he bit out.

They arrived at his Upper East Side building. Far from dissipating, the crowd had only increased in the time they'd been away. Javier's fury congealed as he gunned the car into the garage.

She followed him into the lift, the confined space condensing with nerve-shredding savagery. Unable to keep silent as she was hurled up to what she assumed was her doom, she licked her lips. 'There's something else, Javier.'

Dark brows clamped tight. 'Yes?'

'My father's signed up to write a series of articles for *Vita Italia* magazine.'

'And?' he demanded.

'Technically, it shouldn't have anything to do with my career, but…things haven't been going well between us lately.'

'So he could retaliate against you in the tabloids?'

More miserable than she'd ever thought it was possible to feel, Carla nodded. 'It's worth half a million euros. He won't let it go easily.'

He regarded her for several tense seconds. The lift pinged open and still he stared at her. 'What a tangled mess you've weaved yourself into, Principessa,' he finally mused.

Exiting, he strode for the double doors leading to the penthouse.

She reached him just as he threw the door open. Desperate, she grabbed his arm. 'Javier—'

In an agile move she wouldn't have attributed to a powerfully built man such as him, he slammed the door shut and pinned her against it. His hands circled her arms, his body caging hers with predatory precision. 'Even if I chose to believe that you coming clean now isn't a clever plot to save yourself from being sued for breach of contract, it doesn't excuse you from keeping your plans from me,' he sliced at her.

This close, she could see the gold flecks overlaid on the mahogany of his eyes, harshly beautiful and completely captivating. She stared up at him, until his accusation dripped into her mind. 'You plucked me from hospital and brought me here, then left me to my own devices for two weeks. Even if I'd come to any concrete decision—which I haven't—today would've been my first chance to tell you.'

The hands shackling her arms skated over her shoulders and up the sides of her neck to rest at her nape. Heat dragged through her at the electrifying skin contact. She rejected the melting sensation racing through her body as his thumbs rested over her twin pulses.

'You play the aggrieved damsel so well,' he murmured, his breath washing over her face. 'But if you'd thought about anyone but yourself you'd have made sure that you and I weren't once again in this position.'

'And what position would that be? Me, once again appealing to your better nature and you determined to believe the absolute worst of me? Let me guess, you're going to fire me now?'

He stepped closer, bringing his body a scant inch from hers. The lethal power whipping through him and her own body's brazen excitement robbed her of breath.

'You would love that, wouldn't you? Another salacious piece of gossip for your fans to scavenge over? Is this how we're destined to interact? You inviting trouble my way every time?'

'I don't mean to,' she murmured back, her attention absorbed by the unique bruised-rose shade of his lips. The insane urge to trace the shape with her fingers was so strong she couldn't suppress the moan that rose from her soul.

His eyes darkened, his breath hissing out at the revealing sound.

'You don't mean to. And yet here we are.'

'End this, then. Fire me,' she urged.

'No.' His head descended a fraction. 'If I fire you, you'll no longer be mine to command. You'll be free to wreak your havoc on someone else.'

'So you're doing mankind a favour?'

'*Sì*, that is exactly right.'

Another inch closer and she felt the full impact of his body. Right down to the unmistakeable arousal imprinted against her belly. The vivid memory of his power inside her scorched her senses. Her nipples peaked, the sensitive buds demanding shockingly immediate appeasement.

She squirmed, her body's uncontrollable craving almost overpowering her. He moved with her, a subtle roll of his hips, a teasing slide of one broad thumb across her lower lip.

Her limbs weakened. 'Javier.' Her voice was a husky plea, either to end the torture or to satisfy it.

'You want me,' he stated, his voice deep and sure with masculine confidence.

Heat rushed into her face, ramping her temperature even higher. She wanted to look away, to deny the taunting words. But she couldn't pull her gaze from the hunger and sensual promise in his eyes.

'Do you want me to kiss you, Carla *mia*? Are you hoping perhaps that your body can achieve what your character has failed to do so far and pull me into your web?'

A part of her mourned that he would never see past the desperate misunderstanding of three years ago. But the greater part of her just wanted to experience the hot, erotic skill of his kiss.

Senses clamouring, she threw caution to the wind, her head moving in a nod before she'd fully computed her actions and the inevitable repercussions. 'Yes, I want you to kiss me.'

A muffled sound that could've been a curse or a prayer ripped from his lips. In the next breath, his mouth slanted over hers. The last vestiges of sanity ripped free, her senses plunging into free fall as pure sensation took over. Flames licked at each point of contact, which was pretty much everywhere from their fused lips to the masculine thighs tangling with hers. But the sensation of his tongue sliding against hers was what had her gasping in delight, the concentrated pleasure arrowing straight between her legs to the place only he had ever owned.

She whimpered, her bound hand sliding around his waist, holding on for dear life as he explored her with a thoroughness that seared her deeper than she'd ever been touched. Her other hand wandered up his tight body, over hard contours and heated flesh to the silky waves of his hair. A wicked memory impinged, and she fisted the luxurious strands. Javier jerked against her, a growl erupting between their lips as his erection jumped against her belly.

One hand cupped her breast, catching the stiff peak between his fingers for a delicious pull that made her groan. His other hand gripped her waist tight and lifted her off the floor. 'Put your legs around me,' he commanded.

Complying brought her most sensitive part flush against him. Striding sure and swift as if she weighed nothing, he entered the living room and laid her down on the sofa.

Slow, lingering kisses trailed from her jaw, along her collarbone to her shoulder. She tried to caress him in turn and was confronted with one immobilised hand. Frustration clawed through her...at the overabundance of clothes between them, the slow pace of his attention. With the hand still in his hair, she attempted to draw him closer, deepen the kiss. He let her have the lead, until the need for air forced her to break away.

He laughed at the rapid rise and fall of her chest.

'So needy, Principessa. Was your last boyfriend not up to the task of satisfying you? Don't worry. When I make you mine again, that memory will fade away for ever.' He started to curl his hand around her thigh.

She froze in degrees, her head battling hard with her senses as the reality of what was happening dawned on her.

When I make you mine.

There would be no charm offensive involved this time round, no drive in his sports car and laughter on a beach underpinning the sexual intent in each glance and each word.

Unlike Miami three years ago, what would happen here would be a vengeful taking, fuelled by Javier's belief that she had wronged him. Again. Desire still wove like a lingering drug in her bloodstream, but Carla unclenched her fist from his hair, ignoring her screaming senses. She couldn't let this go any further. Her vulnerability when it came to

Javier was shamefully evident in the way she was sprawled beneath him with only the clothes on her body barring her need from him.

'Don't tell me the *principessa* has remembered that she's once again cavorting with someone beneath her regard?'

She met his gaze, forcing herself to see past the mockery and acid-dipped words to the hurt and pain beneath.

'What did it do, Javier?' she ventured, hoping for a straight answer this time.

Dark-lashed eyes narrowed. *'Perdón?'*

'That statement about your parentage. What exactly was the damage from it?'

He tensed, his face tautening into an implacable mask. 'If you're trying to get on my good side, this isn't the way to go about it.'

'Please. I'm just trying to understand why you hate me so much.'

He vaulted off her, his breath escaping in harsh exhalations. Locks of hair hung in unruly waves, but even that dishevelled look lent him a rakish air that threatened to re-ignite her thawing senses.

Sitting up, she swung her legs to the floor and kept them firmly, unwillingly closed. She watched him stride to the drinks cabinet and pour himself a stiff drink. Tossing it back, he poured a glass of water and returned to set it down on the table next to her.

All without speaking.

She sighed. 'Clearly something happened to make all this torturing of me necessary. The least you can do is tell me the reason for my suffering.'

A harsh bark of laughter cracked across the room. 'You think *you're* suffering?'

She caught his meaning when her gaze dropped below his belt. Her blush was furnace-hot and deeply embarrassing. 'You know what I mean.'

He sliced his hand through his hair, unsettling the strands

even more. 'And you think understanding where I'm coming from will free you to give yourself permission to accept
my touch?' he snarled.

'Why do you act as if I've treated you like a leper?'

His smile was terse and cruel. 'You were singularly mem-
orable in your urgency to get away from me the morning
after we had sex, *querida*.'

She shook her head. 'I can tell you until I'm hoarse that
I slept with you because I wanted to. I just didn't deal very
well with the aftermath. And you're changing the subject.'
She firmed her voice, meeting his blazing gaze without
flinching.

Slowly he sauntered towards her. Instead of taking the
seat next to her, he sat down on the large teak coffee table
that complemented the rest of the earth-toned, conceptually
stunning décor. His thighs braced on either side of hers, he
leaned forward on his elbows, another hard smile showcas-
ing his impressive cheekbones. 'You want to know what
havoc your father's little digging expedition wreaked?'

She held firm and nodded.

'Muy bien,' he grunted. 'My mother was seventeen and
on her way to church one day when she caught the eye of a
rich man in his fancy car. To most people that sounds like
the beginning of a fairy tale. From my mother, it was the
beginning of the end, only she didn't know it at the time.
She'd led a strict, sheltered life and had no idea she'd caught
the eye of the son of the baron from the neighbouring town.
A *married* son of a baron twice her age. He seduced her,
alienated her from her family, who eventually disowned her,
and set her up in a run-down house on the edge of his estate.
That was where I was born six years later. I was delivered
by a retired midwife because my father didn't want anyone
to know he'd fathered a bastard, which was a standing joke
because everyone knew, of course.'

Carla's chest tightened at the pain etched on his face.

'There were complications with my birth. My mother

survived, but she was never completely whole. She should have been in a hospital with medical professionals not in a shack with an old woman to birth me.' The hands dangling between his legs tightened into hard fists. 'I grew up knowing he was the man who had wilfully sacrificed my mother's health on the altar of his reputation. Unfortunately, that wasn't the only unsavoury trait he possessed. He strung my mother along with the usual empty promise to leave his baroness for her, even while *she* supplied him with heirs and spares on a regular basis.'

'So you have half-brothers and sisters?'

One masculine eyebrow cocked. 'Of course not. I don't exist, remember?'

She flinched, and barely resisted the urge to touch him. 'You exist. If to no one else you must have done to your mother.'

'She home schooled me at his insistence—private school was never on the cards on account of his many children needing his every euro. I was only allowed to play in the garden of the house. While boys my age were bonding over football, I wasn't even allowed to climb a tree in case I hurt myself and I had to suffer the presence of the village doctor.'

Tears stung her eyes. She blinked them away quickly before he spotted the helpless empathy that blazed in her heart for him. Just for something to do, she picked up her water glass and took a sip, her heart tripping frantically as he continued.

'The upside of all that cloistered existence was that I excelled academically. If nothing else, she was quietly proud of me for not letting her down the way my father had.'

'Did she ever leave him?'

A haunted smile touched his lips, as if he was caught in a despondent memory. 'I bought her several homes around the world, had the best horticulturists recreate her beloved garden in each home. She didn't stay in any property for more than a few weeks, a month at most. It was almost as if

she couldn't physically stand to be away from that godfor-
saken ramshackle house, waiting for that bastard to spare
her a crumb of his time.' His voice was an edgy sneer, his
jaw clenched tight.

'Did you two ever interact?'

'I didn't actually *see* him up close until I was nine years
old. I broke my boundaries and snuck off to the big castle
on the hill—it was surprisingly easy. I hid in the bushes and
watched him playing tennis with one of his other children. I
wanted to walk up to him, announce who I was and spit in
his face for making my mother cry late at night when she
thought I was asleep.'

A light shudder quivered through him and she knew he
was caught up in memory. This time, she ventured a light
touch.

The moment her fingers grazed his knuckles, he jerked
away. Springing to his feet, he paced to the window. Carla
curled her fingers, berating herself for being hurt by his rejection when all the hurt in this situation belonged to him.

'I managed to get myself a scholarship to university a year
early. He turned up the day before I left, mistakenly thinking the coast was clear. I finally got a chance to give him
a big piece of my mind. The next time we met was when I
returned to Menor Compostela after my mother died.' His
mouth tightened for several tense seconds. 'Her last wish
was to be buried within her family crypt. I guess in death
she wanted to belong somewhere. But they refused. My father has the power to overrule their decision.'

'But to do that he has to publicly acknowledge his association with her?'

'*Sí,*' he breathed unevenly. 'He refused to help. Until three
years ago.'

Dread liquidised her insides. 'What happened?'

'His grapes were wiped out by freak weather a week before the harvest. He lost millions of euros' worth of stock
overnight. His Rioja had been producing mediocre wine

due to bad management for years anyway, and he was on the verge of bankruptcy. Had it been left to me, I would've happily watched him sink into the mud he valued over my mother's life,' he grated icily.

'But you stepped in?'

'On condition he did the right thing by my mother.'

Foreboding gripped Carla's nape. The bleak landscape he'd painted required no maps as to how the story ended. She wanted to tell him to stop, to forgive her guilt by association. But Javier was ruthlessly laying out the full picture. Helplessly she stared at him, bearing the full brunt of his complete condemnation.

'The tabloid quote about my bastard parentage was printed three days after I saved his precious estate. It's one thing to have your secrets whispered behind your back. As long as no one dared to confront him with the truth, he could pretend he was a pillar of society. The potential for outing a dirty little secret prompted other journalists to dig even deeper. My mother, finally accepting he would never do right by her, had got her own back by listing him as the father of her child once she knew she was dying. Someone got hold of my birth certificate and it was suddenly all over the news. He refused to take my calls for two years.'

She flicked her tongue over suddenly dry lips. 'Javier, I'm so very sorry.'

He strode back to where she sat. One falsely indolent hand tucked a wisp of hair behind her ear before his flat eyes scoured her from forehead to chin and back again.

'You probably are, *querida*. But the reality is my mother is still buried in that back yard I detested all my life because that is where she *settled* for when she knew she couldn't be with her family. I watched her *settle* for less than she was worth all her life. I have no room in my life now for forgiveness. Not until I make things right for her.' His eyes slowly narrowed. 'And you throwing obstacles in my way hasn't helped my disposition one little bit.'

Her breath shuddered out. She opened her mouth, to say what, she didn't know.

He rose abruptly, strangling any response she might have thought of. When she realised he was heading for the front door, she regained her power of speech.

'Where are you going?'

He flicked the keys he'd plucked up from a nearby console. 'This day off has turned out to be a terrible idea.'

'You're going into the office?'

'Yes. For one thing, I need to deal with the fire your father started.'

A wave of relief swept through her. 'You're stopping the *Vita Italia* articles?'

'Unless he's prepared to prove to me that there's nothing damaging to you in them, they will never see the light of day. Not unless he relishes opposing me in court. I hope he doesn't. My tolerance levels are stretched thin as it is.'

'What about your father?'

'His grapes are failing again. I just need to bide my time.'

He gripped the door handle and turned before she summoned her voice once more. 'And what about me, Javier?'

He turned with a lithe grace that was sublime to watch. Dark eyes raked her from head to toe, returning to hers far more intense than they'd been a few minutes ago. 'Patience, Principessa,' he murmured. 'I'll get round to dealing with you sooner than you think.'

He was gone before she'd exhaled her next breath. Like a deflated balloon, she sagged onto the sofa. When she managed to get her reeling senses under control, she pulled her legs to her chest and replayed everything Javier had said to her.

Cradling her chin on her knees, she closed her eyes in despair.

No wonder he'd been furious with her. It didn't matter that the major fault was her father's. Between the two of them, they'd denied Javier the one thing he craved most—peace for his mother.

She couldn't do anything about it now, the harm was done. But she could see to it that her father got the message about her life being her own from now on, once and for all. Heading to her suite, she located her phone and dialled his number. She let it go to voicemail three times before she finally left a message. Her father would answer her summons, or face the lawyers she intended to hire on Monday.

As for Javier, she prayed that, when the time came, whatever punishment he chose to dole out would be tempered with the same consideration that had prompted him to take her to his mother's secluded garden.

CHAPTER EIGHT

SHE SAW JAVIER for fleeting periods over the weekend, the last being an abrupt greeting and goodbye at the door on Sunday night when he told her he had a meeting in Los Angeles the next morning and would be gone for two days.

Slotting the mild bereft ache in her chest under the firm heading of listlessness during his absence, she gathered the product information Darren had provided and parked herself in the window seat of the living room. A glance down to the street showed the crowd that had been thinning over the weekend had finally dispersed.

Breathing easier, she made plans to go for a walk after lunch, and opened the pack.

The full-page, colour headshot of Javier stopped her breath. He was staring straight into the camera, the cobalt blue of his open-necked shirt making his eyes reflect a lighter bronze shade than their normal mahogany. His captivating mouth was trapped in the beginnings of a smile that promised charm and sin, his stubbled jaw and strong throat completing a heart-stopping package that absorbed her attention for much longer than she deemed wise. It was only when she realised her lungs were burning from holding in her breath that she impatiently roused herself from her lust-drenched stupor.

He was just a man.

A complex, dynamic man who it turned out was just as prone to human vulnerabilities as the next person.

But it doesn't make him less fascinating to you. Quite the opposite.

She flipped the page over, irritated with herself for her inability to stop thinking about Javier. The next page gave a brief history of J Santino Inc. Javier had started out as a corporate investor barely out of college. But his love for the finer things in life and a keen eye for design had seen him branch out into luxury-goods marketing by the time he was twenty-five. He'd added a late design degree and started the J Santino product range. Carla knew that the overnight success most people attributed to people like Javier was the product of hard, relentless work. But for a man like Javier, the burning desire to succeed had been born from the circumstances of his life. He'd wanted to rise above the label placed on him in his mother's womb.

Her heart squeezed and she fought the urge to turn back the page and glance at his picture once more. Instead she moved on, familiarising herself with the fascinating history behind Javier's latest launch.

He hadn't been joking when he'd referred to her tequila excess that night three years ago. What he didn't know was that she'd overheard him talking to Draco about his love for the liquor, and, feeling bold and rebellious, had decided to try it for herself. She'd been fascinated with the smoothness of the spirit and the heat that burned through her, just as she'd been fascinated with the man who'd instigated a similar heat inside her.

The rest had been history...

Or not.

She finished reading and checked her phone and email, her heart squeezing with dread and disappointment to see nothing from her father. This was rougher, uncharted territory for them, one she didn't think would get easier seeing as her father obviously didn't want to take the amicable route.

Restless and angsty, she tugged on her ankle boots. She didn't exactly feel cooped up in the apartment, but, with Felipe the butler also off for the day, the continued silence was beginning to get to her. Plus she couldn't walk past the sofa without reliving the heated moments she'd shared with

Javier, and that was wrecking her concentration. Another glance down to the street showed it was still clear.

Going to her room, she pulled a cashmere jumper over her top and brushed out her hair before pulling a stylish cap over it. Locating her sunglasses, she slipped them on and grabbed her handbag. In the foyer, she smiled at Johnny, the concierge manager, then froze as her way was blocked by a giant of a man with a crew cut and a muscle-bound body straining in a three-piece suit.

'Morning, Miss Nardozzi,' the giant greeted her.

Her smile slipped a notch. 'Morning. Umm, I'm sorry, do I know you?'

'No. We haven't been introduced yet. I'm Antonio, your minder. Mr Santino asked me to ensure you aren't disturbed if you decide to leave the building.'

Carla wasn't sure which emotion surged higher— irritation at Javier's blithe domination of her life, or the un- wanted gladdening of her heart that he was looking out for her.

Or perhaps she was deluding herself entirely by assum- ing the latter scenario. Javier had left her with little doubt that he intended to keep pursuing reparations for the wrong done to him. He didn't trust her. Antonio's presence was a bracing reminder of that. Perhaps he expected her to run away while he was in LA.

Her smile melting off her face, she glanced at the body- guard. 'I'm going for a walk. I have no idea how long I'll be.'

'Not a problem. You won't even know I'm there.'

Resisting the very unladylike urge to snort her disbelief, she exited into the sunshine, digging out her phone as she hit the sidewalk.

I don't need a bodyguard, grazie. I'm perfectly capable of ensuring my own safety so you can call him off now.

The reply came within seconds.

Since you've met him, I'm assuming you're no longer in the penthouse. He stays. And don't think about sending him away. He answers to only me.

She gritted her teeth.

This is unacceptable.

Your safety is non-negotiable. He stays. And, Principessa…

I told you not to call me that!

Any stunts you attempt to pull will be answered with equal punishment.

You're thousands of miles away. What's the worst you can do?

Try me.

Eye-roll.

Attempt that when I'm standing in front of you.

Double eye-roll.

Your fearlessness is commendable. If extremely foolhardy. Eat something, Principessa. You'll need your strength to repeat this feat of daring you're suddenly brazen enough to attempt.

Bring it.

Carla realised she was grinning as she stopped at a crossing. Curious glances from strangers had her straightening her features as she crossed the street onto Fifth Avenue. The sights and sounds of New York City buffeted her as she walked in the spring sunshine. On impulse, she stepped into an exclusive boutique of a designer whose work she was familiar with. She browsed until Antonio's solid presence outside the door began to draw attention. Smiling at the attendants, she quickly exited only to stop outside when her phone rang.

Her heart performed a crazy somersault, but the number displayed on her screen wasn't familiar. Or the one she'd texted Javier with minutes ago.

'Hello?'

'Hi, Carla, it's Darren.'

Her stomach dipped. Swallowing what she refused to acknowledge was disappointment, she injected lightness into her tone. *'Ciao*, how can I help you?'

'I know Javier is out of town, but I'll be scouting the three nightclubs we shortlisted for the shoot tonight, and wondered whether you'd like to come along. The earlier we nail it down, the quicker we can move things along.'

Carla opened her mouth, an automatic refusal rising out of habit. Socialising for anything but her career had been struck off her list after her one and only life-changing time in Miami. But slowly, she closed her mouth. The idea of spending another evening alone in the penthouse drew a grimace. Besides, this wasn't really socialising. It was work-related.

'Uh… Carla?'

'*Sì*, I'm here. I don't know much about nightclubs, but I'd like to come along.'

'Great! I'll swing by and pick you up at seven? We can get something to eat beforehand if you want?'

Eat something, Principessa.

'I want. I'll see you at seven.'

She hung up with a different smile on her face. The break for independence was a tiny one, but it felt good. She glanced at her phone again, her smile dimming at the thought of her father.

Pressing the buttons, she dialled.

He answered after several long rings. 'What do you want?'

A cloud floated past the sun, echoing her mood as her chest tightened. 'You know what this is about. I've left you several messages.'

'You can't summon me like a lapdog. You forget who is the father and who is the child here.'

'I just want to talk, Papà. Find a way to resolve this.'

He laughed, an overloud, slurred rumble that made her frown. 'Are you drunk?'

'Watch yourself, *ragazza*. You may think you suddenly hold all the cards, but I'm not averse to bringing you down a peg or two.'

'What's that supposed to mean?'

'It means call off Santino and whatever plans he has of sticking his nose in where it doesn't belong, or...'

Her stomach hollowed. 'Or, what?'

'Or I'll give a different kind of interview. One he won't have the power to stop. You want to know how your mother died? I've tried to spare you the gory details, for your own sake, but if you really want to know, I'll tell you when I'm ready. Or you can find out about it at some point in the future. Either way, I hope you're as strong enough to take the truth as you insist you are.'

'What? Papà—' Her words echoed down a disconnected line. Chills rippled over her. She didn't realise she'd stumbled to a halt on the sidewalk until Antonio cleared his throat.

'Miss, is everything okay?'

She forced life into her feet, her steps growing faster as she spotted Javier's apartment building. She crossed the foyer without looking up and was shaking by the time she let herself back into the penthouse. Her ringing phone a second later made her jump.

Hands trembling, she answered it.

'What's wrong?' Javier demanded.

'What…how do you know—?'

'Tell me,' Javier commanded.

'My father… I just spoke to him…' She shook her head to clear it, to find a way to attribute the conversation with her father to anything other than a clear threat. A threat not born in her wildest imagination.

'And?'

She clamped her mouth shut, the thick cord of guilt she'd never been able to loosen from her heart tightening even further.

'Carla.' Javier growled a warning.

'Please… I'm fine…'

A thick curse ripped through her senses. 'What did he say to you?'

'Did you stop the articles in *Vita Italia*?' she countered.

'Yes. I told you I was going to. I wasn't satisfied with some of the subject matters.'

Dread raked her stomach. 'I need you to lay off my father, Javier. Please. Until I talk to him again.'

'No. Tell me what he's up to and I'll deal with it.'

'No, questo è il mio problema. Io ne occupo io, non tu.'

'I find it adorable that you slip into Italian when you're fired up, Principessa, but you're wrong. This is not just your problem. I hate to break it to you if you haven't already worked it out, but your father is operating from a place of pure greed, just like my father when it suits him. And I guarantee that every misguided decision he makes from now on will impact both of us.'

'So you're helping me to fight him?'

'In this case, protecting you from him also protects my brand, so yes. Now, tell me what he said to you,' he insisted for the third time.

'He said something, about…my mother. H-how she died.'

'How did she die?'

Debilitating pain deadened her limbs. She stumbled to the sofa and dropped into it. 'That's just it. I don't know. I wasn't there, and he won't tell me. But I know whatever happened, it had something to do with me.'

'How is that possible?' he demanded.

'It sounds absurd, I know, but, whatever it is, I can't find out any other way, Javier. Please. Give me time to deal with him my way.'

A harsh exhalation. 'Sorry, *querida*, I can make no promises.'

'Javier!'

For the second time in the space of half an hour, Carla was confronted with a disconnected line.

Rushing to her room, she located her laptop and opened up her email. Typing without the full use of all her fingers was frustrating in the extreme.

My full and final offer—thirty percent of the endorsement proceeds, and the Tuscany villa, in return for the truth about Mamma, and no press involvement. Also, you will no longer be my manager.

She and her father would never have a proper familial relationship. She was better off accepting it now and walking away, no matter much her heart shredded at the thought. Shaking, she pressed send to her father's private email address, finally accepting that this was her only option if she wanted to draw a line under the acrimony they'd been living with for years.

She held her breath until she received notification that he'd opened it.

His response came within minutes. It reeked with a smugness that made her stomach turn.

Agreed. But I need the first payment within the next fourteen days.

Fine.

She closed her laptop, a wave of despair gripping her. She'd just negotiated her way out of her father's life. She blinked away the tears that formed and straightened her spine. For years she'd yearned for a father who loved her. Today, she needed to accept that would never happen. For some reason, he was incapable of it.

She paced the penthouse for a full hour trying to come up with a cogent solution. She'd bought herself some time, but the next endorsement payment wouldn't be for another two months.

Her heart broke as she settled on her next-best option. A quick call later and her mother's beloved cottage was listed with the estate agent. Praying it was only a stopgap measure she wouldn't need to use, Carla undressed and went into the bathroom to shower. Careful to keep her cast out of the spray, she shampooed her hair one-handed, the arduous task taking her mind off her turbulent thoughts.

It worked until she turned off the shower, then the memories from three years ago flooded back.

The training for the championship that had taken her away from Tuscany for several weeks. Her row with her father when she'd asked for some time off before the championship. Her appeal to her mother to intervene. Her time in Miami. Her father unexpectedly absenting himself from the tournament afterwards. His equally sudden return for the ceremony of her being crowned champion. His cold announcement that her mother was dead. And his unequivocal refusal to discuss how she'd died.

Carla shuddered, her skin clammy in the vast room where she stood in only a towel. Despite what the death certificate had said, she'd never managed to rid herself of the suspicion that there was more to her mother's death than she'd been made privy to.

Her father's thinly veiled comments over the years had only fed that suspicion.

The idea that he would make public whatever secret surrounded her mother's death threatened to rip her in two. Javier had intimated that she was feeding the monster by giving in to her father. But the alternative was worse. She couldn't let her mother's memory be dragged through the mires of social media for the sake of financial gain. The knowledge that it was her own father making that threat wounded her deep and long, but she would suffer it. For the sake of the mother who had loved her for as long as she could.

Firm-jawed, she dried herself and went into her closet. Vast amounts of white dominated her wardrobe.

Deliberately bypassing the white, she reached into the corner of her closet and dragged out a pair of black leather pants, a gold-threaded black top she'd never worn because the cut had been too risqué and studded black boots. She pulled the top on, her face flaming slightly at the thought of going out without a bra. Catching her hair up, she secured it with a diamond pin that had belonged to her mother. Then she went to town with her make-up.

Where she'd only worn the very lightest shades and gloss, she brushed on smoky eye shadow, cheekbone-enhancing blush, and dark red gloss over her lips.

The end result was dramatic enough to stop her breath. Before the tiny speck of doubt could take hold and ruin her night out, she snatched up her gold lamé clutch and transferred her phone and personal items into it.

The sound of the buzzer brought the relief and shameless inevitability she needed. Answering it, she finished her ensemble with a leather jacket and left the penthouse.

Darren's double take once she exited the lift buoyed her confidence and she smiled as she crossed the foyer.

'Wow, you look amazing!'

'*Grazie,*' she murmured. 'You don't look so bad yourself.'

'What, this?' He indicated his dark grey button-down shirt, black chinos, and the black jacket he wore over it. 'It's okay, but hardly the cutting edge of fashion. Not that you're not worth going cutting edge for,' he quickly amended. 'I meant, I prefer to dazzle a woman with my wit, not my attire.'

She laughed, a little of her churning emotions subsiding under the easy banter. He escorted her outside, then glanced over his shoulder. 'Umm...will that BFG be accompanying us everywhere tonight?'

Carla grimaced. 'He's harmless... I think. And barely noticeable once you get used to him.' She looked over her shoulder and smiled at Antonio. He cracked a return smile.

'Right. O...kay,' Darren responded, his tone a little bewildered. 'I'm cool with it if you are. The restaurant is a couple of blocks away.' He glanced at her heeled boots. 'You don't mind walking, do you?'

'Not at all.' She smiled and received a quick, appreciative one back. They fell into an easy stride, the conversation light and casual. It continued through a delicious meal at an Irish-themed bar and restaurant then out onto an even busier Manhattan street. 'The first club is Downtown. I have VIP passes.' He hailed a cab and helped her into it. Antonio took residence in the front seat, his burly presence making the cab driver blink hard before shrugging in defeat. Darren raised his eyebrows at her, and Carla couldn't help but giggle.

Outside the exclusive Cuban nightclub, limos competed with flashy sports cars for attention. They were shown to a VIP section with plush gold velvet sofas and an unlimited supply of complimentary drinks. Vowing to stick to a two-drink threshold, Carla sipped her first drink slowly. Their easy conversation continued with Darren regaling her with stories of his childhood in Dublin. When the club owner came over to speak to him, she took off her jacket and went down to the edge of the dance floor. She smiled noncommittally at a few interested glances, resolutely ignored the more pointed ones, then sighed in relief when Darren joined her a few minutes later.

'So what do you think?' He gestured to the club's interior and dance floor.

The rich, slightly ethnic theme was sensual enough to evoke the spirit of Javier's brand, while contemporary enough to appeal to the sophisticated urbanite.

She smiled. 'I like the music, and I think the space will work well.' During dinner, he'd expanded on the brief of *work hard, play harder* theme of the shoot, with the primary shoot being on the ice rink and the secondary at the nightclub.

Darren's hand slid around her waist. 'Want to try it out?' He grinned.

Shrugging, she nodded. 'Why not?'

They descended into the crowd to the tune of throbbing Cuban drums.

Laughing, she entered the fray, throwing her arms above her head partly to keep her wrist from being accidentally reinjured. Darren, a more than adequate partner, stayed close, his appreciative gaze dancing over her body every now and then. After two songs, the tempo changed to a slower, sexier beat. Darren danced closer, but still kept a respectable distance. Catching her forearms, he gently placed them on his shoulders, a small smile playing at his lips as he swayed in time with her.

'You really are stunningly beautiful, you know that?' he confessed in her ear.

She blushed, wishing away the sudden embarrassment and the slight discomfiting realisation that perhaps he was more interested in her than he'd let on. 'Umm…*grazie*,' she murmured.

He laughed, the careful hands he'd placed on her waist drawing her closer. 'I love your accent. In fact I don't think there's a single thing about you that I don't find—' He froze suddenly, his eyes bulging as he swallowed hard. 'Oh, hell,' he muttered.

She blinked in surprise. 'What's wrong?'

'Carla.'

Her head whipped round at the barely repressed violence in the deep, low voice that curled over her shoulder.

Javier stood three scant feet away, his nostrils flared in volcanic fury as he stared at them. His chest rose and fell in rapid rhythm, his fists clenched at his sides. The emotions vibrating off him lent him an impossibly overwhelming aura, a fact that transmitted to the nearest clubbers, who'd stopped dancing and were openly staring.

Alarmed at his unexpected presence, she went to step away and stumbled. Darren's hold tightened on her.

The growl that rose over the music had several people stepping away, more than a few of them making room and nudging each other as the threat of a salacious confrontation thickened in the air.

'What are you doing here?' she croaked.

He didn't answer. His gaze remained fixed with naked intensity on where Darren's hands rested on her waist. 'If you value the use of your limbs, O'Hare, I suggest you remove your hands from her body. Right now.'

Darren released her with comic swiftness. 'Mr Santino—'

'Leave. Now.'

Outrage sparked within her. 'Javier! You can't do that—'

'Take *your* hands off the man, Carla, so he can leave, or I won't be responsible for what happens next,' he snarled with a guttural tone that was barely coherent.

But she got the message.

She took her time, though, despite the quaking unfolding alongside the outrage, because she refused to be intimidated. Darren stepped away, his apprehension escalating as he swallowed hard again. He attempted to cast her an apologetic glance. Javier took a single step towards him and he changed his mind, turning in the opposite direction to disappear through the seething crowd.

Javier turned his bristling frame to her. 'You have two minutes,' he bit out.

She raised one brow, unwilling to admit the blood strumming urgently through her veins was in any way to do with his sudden dramatic appearance. That would hand him too much power over her. 'Two minutes for what?'

'To retrieve whatever you came here with. Or we leave without it.'

'What makes you think I'm going anywhere with you?' she challenged.

His eyes gleamed. 'Principessa, for once in your life, do what is best for you. You do not want to test me right now. I can guarantee you that. You certainly don't want to do it here, in full view of your captive audience.'

A quick glance around showed they'd drawn even more interested glances now Darren had scurried away. Thankfully, the club had a 'no photography' policy, but that didn't mean their every move wasn't being recorded by security cameras.

'They're not staring at me. You're the one making a spectacle of yourself.'

Once again he didn't respond. She got the distinct impression he was holding onto his control by the thinnest thread. The staring contest lasted a full minute.

Then, blood roaring in her ears—with embarrassment only, she was sure—Carla walked off the dance floor and climbed the steps to the VIP area. Antonio handed over her clutch and jacket, then stepped forward to make room as they left the club.

Supremely conscious of Javier's seething presence behind her, she could barely walk and was thankful when they emerged into fresh air.

She immediately struck out for the busy intersection three blocks away. Less than a handful of steps later, Javier stepped firmly into her path. 'Where the hell do you think you're going?' His voice was a razor-sharp blade, lethal and unmistakeable in the semi-darkness.

'I told you I'm not going anywhere with you.'

'Think again.'

'Do me a favour, Javier, and leave me the hell alone!' She whirled round and tore blindly down a side street.

She noticed two things mere seconds into her flight. One, the alley was smoky and dark with a single yellow bulb strung high above their heads. Two, it terminated in a dead-end a few hundred feet away. She heard Javier snarl a *do not disturb* instruction to Antonio before his sure, measured footsteps echoed between her frantic ones. A dozen feet from the sheer wall soaring high in front of her, she turned and stood her ground.

He stalked closer, his dark clothes lending him an air of unbridled masculinity and danger.

Despite herself, she shivered. 'You don't frighten me, Santino.'

He laughed. 'I know I don't. But we both know why you're running. Rest easy, *chiquita*, you're in luck. I'm in the mood to give you exactly what you want.'

CHAPTER NINE

JAVIER'S EYES NARROWED on her, his senses still grappling with the changes in the woman standing in front of him. Perhaps it was the rage boiling his blood that had him so unbalanced. Or the flaying alarm that had gripped him when he'd returned to the penthouse and found her gone. Either way, he straddled the very edge of control as he watched her sassy mouth tighten.

'As usual, I have no idea what you're talking about. I don't care for whatever it is you think I'm in the mood for.'

'What the hell are you wearing?' he sliced at her, his gaze taking in the dramatic beauty of her face, the shiny leather hugging her hips and thighs, and the top that was slashed in too many provocative places to require a bra. The transformation from innocent to sultry siren was playing holy havoc with a libido he'd spent the last forty-eight hours battling. And failing.

'They're called clothes, Javier,' she threw back at him.

He stalked closer. She retreated. Her back touched the damp wall and she froze.

He consciously unclenched his fingers and sucked in a sustaining breath. 'I returned home to find you gone. No note. No phone call. Had it not been for Antonio, I wouldn't have had a clue where you were. And when I find you, you give me *attitude*?'

Her eyes sparked in the dim light. 'You hung up on me mid-conversation. What did you expect, that I would be curled up in a ball of misery, crying my eyes out?'

'I was in the middle of a meeting when we talked. I rearranged my schedule and took the rest of the meeting on my flight back from LA. If you'd bothered to answer me when

I called you back once my meeting ended, we could've finished our conversation.'

She frowned. 'I got no call from you.'

'I landed three hours ago. Check your phone.'

Rebellion blazed for a second before she dug through her tiny bag. She activated it, her eyes widening a touch. 'I was in the nightclub. I didn't hear it.'

'Clearly. You were too busy on the dance floor, running away from your problems by rubbing yourself against the first available guy. I'm flattened by the overwhelming sense of déjà vu.'

'I wasn't rubbing myself against Darren! We were working on your precious campaign. And even if we weren't, what's it to you? So what if maybe I wanted to spread my wings a little? Does it state in my contract that I have to remain celibate while performing my duties to the almighty Javier Santino? No, it doesn't.'

He stiffened, pure hellfire rushing through him. 'You were planning on *sleeping with him*?'

Heat stormed into her face. 'That's none of your business. But of course that doesn't matter to you, does it? You just had to step in and ruin my fun.'

He closed the gap between them, physically unable to stop himself from reaching for her. '*Fun?* Is that what you were looking for? You want to spread your wings sexually? Is that it?' he muttered, each word he spoke lancing him hard and merciless. The idea that she would do this in his absence, invite another man's hands on her body, ripped a path of insanity through his brain.

'N…no, not exactly.'

Javier didn't hear her. His attention was wholly absorbed by the delectable gleam of her red-glossed lips, the memory of their taste as intoxicating to his senses as the most potent spirit. His hands slid from her shoulders down her torso, his fingers easily spanning her trim waist. He jerked her to him, and slanted his mouth over hers before he had time to think.

His kiss was hard, a merciless punishment for every frame of what he'd seen when he walked into the nightclub, every moment he'd wasted thinking of her, reliving her desperate pain after her father's phone call, and the helplessness he'd experienced from three thousand miles away. Hell, he'd even gone so far as to wonder if he'd overblown the events of the morning after their night together in Miami and she hadn't actually acted that badly.

And all the while she'd been dancing her troubles away!

She shuddered, her mouth resisting his for a second.

Then she opened for him. Soft. Warm. Drugging in the extreme. His hands trailed over her hips to cup her behind, the pliant leather almost non-existent as he moulded her to him. With a soft moan, she twined her arms around his neck, her shapely body plastering itself against his.

Dios, but she incensed his every cell. He'd returned with a plan, a strictly professional one he'd intended to present to her. Seeing her with O'Hare, their heads close together, on the verge of *dirty dancing*, had firmly altered the landscape of his clearly nonsensical misgivings.

Far from the distraught creature he'd thought he'd encounter on his return, he'd been confronted with a sensual being intent on driving every red-blooded male in the nightclub into a sexual frenzy.

Spreading her wings...

Clearly he'd imagined her earlier distress.

She moved against him, sleek and sinuous. His blood pounded thicker, his heart pistoning hard against his ribs. Javier widened his stance, pinned her against the wall and brought one hand between them.

Lifting the hem of her top, he dragged his nails across her abdomen. It was the lightest of touches and yet she shivered as if caught in an arctic storm.

Her responsiveness hadn't lessened in the time since they were last together. The gratifying thought spurred him on. A quick, deft fumble, a lowering of her zipper, and his fingers were sliding over her silky skin, beneath lace made hot by her arousal.

Her shocked gasp singed his mouth as he found his mark. His free hand clasped her nape, and he broke the kiss. 'Is this what you want, Principessa? Is this the type of *fun* you're looking for?' He thrummed the wet, nerve-engorged bud. Her tiny scream barely echoed through the alley, the greedy roll of her hips already seeking more.

He gave her a little more, grimly gratified when her fingers bit into his neck. 'Javier! *Dio mio...per favore...*'

He drew back a touch, stared down at her enraptured face and knew he had to have her. All logical reasons why not be damned. 'You'll get your chance to spread your wings. But you do it with me. And only me. *Comprende?*'

Eyes clamped shut as she chased her elusive pleasure, she whispered, *'Tu sei pazzo!'*

'I'm far from crazy. Since you're so keen to embrace a whole new you, go right ahead. But if you think I'm going to sit back and watch you throw yourself at every idiot who smiles at you, think again. Consider our contract renegotiated. From now on, *I* will be the one to give you pleasure.'

Her head dropped against the wall, her breath coming in aggrieved pants. *'Santa Maria,* I'm *not* having this conversation right now.'

He teased her saturated opening, earning a frustrated whimper.

'Open your eyes, *querida,*' he commanded silkily. 'Closing your eyes and wishing your troubles away only work in fairy tales.'

Eyes heavy with arousal, frustration, and eternally enthralling, met his. Keeping their gazes locked, he leaned forward and licked her lower lip. He nipped at the soft flesh, then pressed one finger inside her. 'Mine. You will be mine, *exclusively,* until I say otherwise,' he breathed.

Another shudder rippled through her, followed by several more as he increased the friction. He drew back again, his senses leaping with the need to witness her surrender.

'*Per favore*…please,' she groaned, her head falling forward onto his shoulder.

He slid his finger deep into her tight, silky heat, then growled as she found her release seconds later.

A horn sounded nearby, followed by shouts of revelry tearing through the night air. Javier wondered dazedly how he'd kept upright as the sweet sounds of her climax echoed for his ears alone.

One minute passed, then two. Stepping back, he righted her clothes.

'Can you walk?' he demanded thickly.

Another tiny shudder, then she nodded. '*Sì.*'

He pressed a kiss to her temple, then slung his arm over her shoulders, gratified when she burrowed into him.

His limo idled on the kerb, the back door guarded by Antonio. Javier helped her into it, and shut the door behind them. When she went to move away, he stayed her. She collapsed against him, but remained silent as the car crawled through traffic. Although her breathing steadied, he knew she hadn't fallen asleep from the furtive glances she cast at him.

'We can discuss this now, or we can discuss it in the morning. Either way, my conditions remain the same.'

She pulled away, and this time he let her have a little distance. She would be back where she belonged soon, anyway.

'Why?' she queried.

'Why what?'

'Why do you want me?'

A bitter laugh scraped his throat. 'If I could explain the mysteries of sexual chemistry, I would be a far richer man.' He slid his fingers into her hair. 'But I want you. Badly. And you want me.'

'You can't hold me to a new, *sexual* contract. That's deplorable,' she disputed hotly, but he didn't miss her lingering glance at his mouth, and the unsteady breath she took when her eyes met his.

She wanted him. Almost as badly as he wanted her, despite having come apart in his arms mere minutes ago.

The memory lit fresh flames in his groin.

'No, but I did talk to your father again. He believes you are on the verge of reaching a new agreement with me. So let's hear it.'

Alarm chased over her face, followed by a touch of uncertainty. A swallow moved her throat. 'I was going to ask for an amendment to our agreement.'

'One that benefits your father?'

'One that buys me a little time. An early release of the second quarter payment to him and a percentage of my future earnings will end our business relationship. And I get to find out what happened with my mother.'

Javier allowed the wave of sympathy that surged at her words. He'd been caught between a rock and a hard place where his mother was concerned. Having no immediate solution to the problem of his father wasn't an issue he'd relished. But *that* would all be over soon. He scoured her face, took in the change. An instant later the memory of another man's hands on her eroded his sympathy.

'You can have your amendment tomorrow. If you give me what I want.' Still holding her captive, he traced his finger over her passion-bruised bottom lip, the urge to kiss her again firing up inside him. 'And before you revert to the tired line of not wanting me, remember that I could've taken you in that alley, completely and as many times as I wanted, and you would've begged me for more. This way we put our cards on the table. There will be no illusions or misapprehension on either of our parts. And you can't get on your high horse afterwards and claim you weren't thinking straight.'

Perfect eyelashes swept down. 'And if I don't agree?'

'Your father pursues his imprudent financial schemes until such time as the fallout adversely affects me and my company. Then I take steps to hold you both accountable and you lose what little assets you have.'

She opened her mouth to speak as the car stopped in front of his penthouse building.

He stopped her by pressing his lips against hers, hot and hard, then pulled away before temptation got out of hand. 'Take the night, think about it and give me your answer in the morning. I know you'll choose wisely.'

'You're so certain you know what I'll decide?'

He shrugged. 'Besides the pleasure you'll receive in my bed, there's the added benefit that once your father knows you're mine, truly mine, he'll think twice about threatening you again.'

'So those are my two choices? Choose you or choose him?'

'The writing's been on the wall for a while, Principessa. This way you know you're backing the right horse.'

He flung the door open and grabbed her hand. In the bright light of the foyer, he caught a clearer glimpse of her outfit and cursed himself for giving her the night to agree to his demands. The ache in his groin alone threatened to fracture his mind.

Although his every instinct screamed at him to go after her when she muttered goodnight and made a beeline for her bedroom, Javier stayed put.

Morning would come soon enough.

Carla Nardozzi would be his.

She would most certainly *not* be his.

Not in the cold, calculated way he'd spelt out in the darkness of his car. There had to be another way. She toyed with getting Draco to negotiate on her behalf, but her agent had done his part. This renegotiation of the contract was private, between her and Javier. Besides, based on the current strained relationship between the two men, she didn't think

Javier would welcome her turning to the man he thought she was trying to make jealous three years ago.

She tossed in the pre-dawn light and a different dilemma flared again. The shameful knowledge that Javier had been right, that she would've given herself to him in that alley, couldn't be erased. The release she'd received at his hand had been gratifying, but it'd barely dented the depth of her hunger. She could continue to deny it, continue to keep him at arm's length with her words alone. But they would be lies.

That didn't mean she had to give in.

The bed linen twisted around her heated body as she fidgeted. The simple truth was, had their circumstances been different, had they been meeting again after three years as casual acquaintances reconnecting again, Carla knew she would've given in to her body's clamouring. The pull between them would've been too great to deny herself a chance to explore it. Especially having already experienced the intensity of it.

But all that aside, she knew there was no way she could walk away from the chance to find out what happened to her mother, the opportunity to finally lay her ghost to rest. Hadn't she only yesterday vowed to do everything she could to get to the truth?

Just as Javier had brought himself to do the unthinkable and tolerate the father who'd rejected him at every turn all his life, for the sake of his mother, didn't she owe her mother the same? Was the body she'd already given willingly to Javier, and couldn't deny she would give again were their circumstances different, suddenly too high a price to pay?

She didn't deny the irony of finding common ground with the very man who was threatening that ground, but as the sun crested the horizon Carla rubbed her eyes and faced the decision head-on.

In a few short hours, she would agree to become Javier Santino's mistress.

Exactly why that sent a terrible little thrill through her, she shut her eyes firmly against examining.

'Ah, there you are. *Buenos días*, Carla. I was beginning to think I would be subjected to a lonely breakfast by myself.'

Carla refrained from pointing out the many breakfasts she'd had on her own since arriving in New York. Nor did she imagine for an instant that Javier's easy tone was in any way a barometer for his mood. What really spelled out his mood were the narrowed, piercing eyes that tracked her from the dining-room door to her seat. Silently, she accepted as she sat down that she might have contributed to that look by oversleeping past her usual first light waking.

With indolent grace, he scoured her face, now devoid of last night's make-up, before leaning forward to tuck a strand of her hair behind her ear. The action, so poignantly gentle, and yet so ruthlessly calculated, sent a tremor through her.

'Javier, I've come to a decision,' she started, wanting to get this over and done with as quickly as humanly possible.

'Let us eat first, *chiquita*. That way neither of us risks a spoilt appetite if the news delivered and whatever reaction it produces isn't agreeable to our digestive systems.'

He nodded to Felipe, who hovered discreetly nearby. Sterling silver domed dishes were unveiled and her plate heaped with all her favourite foods. Managing a stiff smile at the butler, she attempted to make a dent in the poached egg, toast and slices of ham before her. Fresh fruit appeared on another platter. Before she could shake her head, Javier picked up a large chunk of pineapple and sliced it into smaller pieces.

Forking a square, he presented it to her. His eyes were still narrowed, gauging her stance on a subject he suddenly seemed reluctant to discuss.

For a moment, Carla wondered if he was nervous about her decision. Although it seemed impossible to imagine it now, she'd witnessed his pain and misery when he'd talked about his childhood. His vulnerability had shown then, and she wondered if it was there now, hidden beneath his brusque and intense demeanour.

She took the offered fruit and watched him feed himself a piece. In silence, he shared the pineapple between them until it was finished. Then he sat back and finished his coffee.

When she set her own empty cup down he rose. 'Now we've had our fill, let's talk.'

He walked out of the dining room, the white shirtsleeves rolled up his forearms and the dark grey trousers lending him a casual air she knew was false. Thinking they would conduct their business in the taciturn surroundings of his study, she was taken aback when he led her out onto the vast, wraparound terrace. Sunlight framed his lithe form, bathing his hair and body in a vibrant glow as he strolled over to the high terrace wall, and observed the iconic view for a full minute before he faced her.

'Tell me your decision,' he said abruptly.

Carla started to lace her fingers, then grimaced when her cast got in the way. She walked forward, stopping several feet away when the immutable force of his aura threatened to swallow her whole. 'I agree to your conditions.' Clearing her throat so her voice emerged stronger, she continued, 'I'll be your...whatever term you want to place on this association of ours.'

His eyes turned dark and stormy. 'The term is *mine, querida*. You'll be mine.'

Her breath shuddered out. '*Sì*. I'll be yours,' she whispered.

She wasn't sure what she expected. A triumphant fist pump? A battle cry of victory? No, those weren't quite Javier's style.

'Come here, Carla,' he commanded after a full minute of stomach-churning silence, his voice steeped in quiet authority.

She went. She was long past the point of equivocating

and had accepted that this would be her fate. At least for the short term.

Strong, corded arms banded her waist, bringing her flush against his hard, hot male body. From chest to knees, she was plastered against him, barely able to breathe for the strength and power of him, for the electricity zapping crazily through her body. Breath growing shallower by the second, Carla waited to be swept off her feet. For what had started in the dark, smoky alley last night to progress to its turbulent conclusion.

And yet, now she was in his arms, Javier didn't seem in a hurry to speak, to take what belonged to him. One hand left her waist and trailed upward, the single tie securing her hair pulled away and disposed of before he slid his fingers through the strands to cradle the back of her head. The massage was as unexpected as it was alarmingly soothing. And even more disconcerting were the feelings that surfaced when he tucked her head into his chest, his chin lightly resting on her crown.

Safe and secure.

Both emotions absurd, of course, considering she was fully aware of why he'd demanded this sacrifice from her. The evidence of it was a hot and rigid presence against her belly, a reminder that whatever was going to happen between them would be purely physical.

But Carla stood still, allowed herself to breathe in his scent, let his arms draw her even closer into his body, and, just for the hell of it, brought her arms to rest against his chest.

'Eres mio,' he murmured throatily after an eternity.

Although she didn't understand the words, there was a profound sense of claiming within them, and for a single instant Carla let herself wonder...*what if...?* The judder through her heart warned her she was risking being badly burnt by fire; warned her to end this bizarre lull.

Javier beat her to it.

Releasing her, he took a casual step back and extracted his phone. 'My lawyers will have the financial amendments to the contract drawn up and delivered for you to sign by lunchtime. Felipe will witness it,' he stated matter-of-factly. 'I'm assuming you don't want the usual cooling-off period to apply?' He raised one eyebrow at her.

To counter the bereft feeling spiking through her, she crossed her arms. 'No, I don't. I believe in getting the inevitable over with.'

'I'll assume you're talking about your father, and not us. If you're referring to us, then please accept that there will be no *getting it over with* any time soon.'

Her insides jerked in alarm. 'Are you sure? Your attention span when it comes to your women hasn't changed, has it? So if I'm lucky, I'll only need to amuse you for two weeks, maybe three at the most?'

He sauntered towards her, his fingers tapping out numbers on the flat screen of his phone. He lifted it to his ear as he reached her, his free hand capturing her chin, his thumb conducting a lazy, fiery sweep over her bottom lip. 'I've waited three years to have you again, *dulce* Carla. If you think there will be a swift conclusion to what is about to happen between us, you have my advance sympathy.'

Before she could speak past the bolt of consternation that lanced her, he was turning away, speaking clear instructions into the phone. The buzzing in her ears prevented her from hearing what was being said, and, in a way, Carla was thankful. At some point in the night, she'd convinced herself this would be short-term thing, a way for Javier to satisfy his need for vengeance before he finally set her free. The idea that he didn't intend to do just that was scary enough, without listening to him spell out his full ownership of her to faceless lawyers over the phone.

She jumped when his hand arrived at her nape. A swathe of hair was pushed out of the way as his other arm reclaimed her waist, this time bringing her back to his front. His mouth found her heated skin, and trailed lazily over it, before drifting to her ear. 'I have to head to the office now. If you need any clarification on the contract, feel free to call me. Otherwise, Felipe has instructions to pack a suitcase for you. I'll see you at the airport tonight.'

She turned sharply, and his lips grazed the corner of her mouth. Before she lost the already fraying train of thought, she blurted, 'Airport? Where are we going?'

'We fly to Miami tonight.'

Miami. Where she'd first lost her head, and her innocence to him. 'I...why do I need to come along for a business trip?'

He tasted her with a light bite, then soothed the graze with his tongue. Carla couldn't help the desperate shiver that coursed through her.

'It's not a business trip, *amante*. I'm going to try that time-off thing again. First, to celebrate you returning to my bed. Then to celebrate my birthday in two weeks' time.'

CHAPTER TEN

JAVIER'S LUXURY BEACHFRONT property was just as resplendent and opulent as she remembered it. Set over three floors with a master suite poised on a mezzanine level above the top floor, the all-white mansion was ablaze with strategically placed floodlights as Javier guided her across the large expanse of green grass that separated the helipad from the residence.

The hand at her back stayed as they entered and were greeted by the six-strong staff. Carla tuned out as Javier conversed in rapid-fire Spanish with the buxom older woman who was his housekeeper. Instead, she looked around the interior, memories flooding her brain.

The huge main salon beyond wide double doors was where she'd seen Javier the moment she'd entered the house with Maria and Draco three years ago. It'd been almost as if he'd been waiting for her, his eyes had zeroed in on her instantly, and he'd never let up the intensity of his scrutiny and attention. Not for one moment.

Not until she'd been in his bed.

Then it'd increased a hundredfold.

'Taking a trip down memory lane on your own, *querida*? You don't think it rude not to wait for me before reliving the spectacular experience of our first coming together?'

She jumped at the mocking voice. Face flaming at the thought that he'd say such a thing in front of his staff, she turned away from the colonial Spanish-themed décor, away from the sweeping staircase where he'd nearly lost control and taken her that night. But the staff were nowhere in sight, having been dismissed while she'd been lost in her lustful recollections.

Meeting his bold gaze, she fought not to blush again. He

meant to torture her at every turn. But she was a step away from learning the truth about what happened to her mother. She had to hold that thought firm and true to see her through this. Even if the anticipation of what was going to happen here tonight rushed a continuous stream of almost debilitating excitement through her blood.

'I thought it would be rude to force you to relive something you obviously still find a touchy subject,' she countered.

His lips compressed. 'But I intend to replace those unfortunate memories with better ones.'

'Is that why you brought me here? To rewrite history?'

'Trying to rewrite history is impossible. But there's no reason why you shouldn't be allowed to make a better impression this time round.'

'Has anyone told you how impossibly arrogant you are?' she launched from the depths of the trepidation shaking through her.

'Has anyone told you how utterly delicious you are when you're trying to hide your anxiety with useless bravado?'

She flicked a dismissive hand. 'You're being ridiculous… again.'

He caught her hand, used it to pull her to him, then dragged her behind him to the breathtakingly beautiful salon. He paused in the middle of the gold-carpeted room and captured her jaw in his hands. 'And you're acting like a timid little virgin.' His face hardened. 'Drop the act, Carla,' he sliced at her. 'I'm choosing not to dwell on the other lovers you've had since you were last in my bed and what they would've wanted from you, but if you think that you playing some sort of sacrificial damsel turns me on, trust me, it doesn't.'

She barely managed to suppress a gasp, and tore her gaze from his.

'You know how crazy it makes me when you don't look at me when I'm talking to you, *querida*.'

She shook her head. '*Santa Maria*, can we please just get this over and done with?' she blazed at him, still studiously avoiding his gaze.

'We will not, as you say, get this over and done with. Constanza is preparing our dinner, which we will enjoy—'

'I'm not hungry,' she interjected. 'I had a late lunch.'

'Indeed you did, but I have it on good authority you barely touched the insubstantial sandwich you had Felipe prepare for you. So perhaps you want to come clean, and tell me what's really bothering you?'

She cast around for something to say, anything that would disguise her internal chaos. But the more she dwelled on what was to come, the more her senses unravelled.

She cast a swift glance at him, but the moment their eyes connected, she couldn't look away. Her breath shook out of her lungs as she blurted, 'I'm not... I don't...'

A look crossed his face, a flash of frightening bleakness before his expression settled back into its usual haunting, arrogant beauty. 'You don't...what? Want me?' he queried icily.

Saying yes she wanted him more than her next breath was dangerous. Saying no would be a lie. She hesitated, and with each second his expression grew tauter. Knowing she was only damning herself, she licked her lips. 'Javier...please—'

He swung her into his arms before she managed to form the right words. In quick, commanding strides, he crossed to the far side of the room. The lift tucked discreetly into the corner of the room blended effortlessly with the décor. A thumb print scan granted them access. Javier entered and the doors slid shut, sealing them inside.

Carla tried to wriggle free, but he held her tight, a warning growl emitting from his throat as the lift shot upward. She was still grappling with her words when it stopped and the doors slid open.

She hadn't forgotten the sheer magnificence of the master suite in Javier's mansion. But three years ago she'd been too intoxicated with his presence to take in the smaller details. This time she forced herself to look around, tried to find anything that would ground the runaway emotional freight train inside her. The retractable roof that displayed the spectacular skylight at night was still above her head, half opened to catch glimpses of a few bright stars set against a velvet backdrop. Unlike the priceless works of art that decorated his house, his bedroom only boasted four pieces. A bust of some god-like icon, two Renaissance paintings she knew without looking too closely were masterpieces, and, in the space between his bedroom and private living room, a white baby grand piano on top of which stood a simple wooden-framed picture.

Carla hadn't had the chance to get a closer look at the photo, but she thought it was of his mother.

She wasn't granted a chance now as he swung sharply towards the bed.

'You insist on denying what's between us when we both know it's a useless lie. You want me to force you to admit you want me, is that it? So that when you close your eyes to sleep you can pretend every whisper and moan was coerced from you?'

'No, Javier—'

'Well, think again.' His voice was soft and deadly. 'Before we're done tonight you will beg me to take you. And you will beg for it each time after that.'

She gasped as he caught the hem of her long-sleeved, cowl-neck dress and pulled it over her head. It landed at her feet without ceremony, leaving her in the platform heels and the matching peach bra and panty set she'd donned before they left New York.

The bite of hunger on his face was undeniable, but his mouth still twisted as he stared down at her. 'At least you didn't wear white. That would've taken things a step too far, *si*?'

She shivered at his raw, intense scrutiny, her nipples peaking with harsh demand as his gaze dropped and lingered at where the lace cupped her breasts. Heat lanced her, the ferocious fever roaring through her veins just from the look in his eyes.

With the grace of a magnificent predator, he circled her, eliciting decadent goosebumps on her flesh as he trailed sultry air over her with his movements. He stopped for an interminable age behind her, until every nerve in her body screamed for relief.

'Exquisite,' he rasped.

Finally, she felt him reach out and slowly untie her hair from its customary knot. The tresses fell heavily onto her shoulders. His fingers sank into them, much as they had this morning on his terrace in New York.

'I don't like your hair all caught up. I want it free to run my hands through whenever I feel like it. You will not wear it up again while we're here. Understood?' he rasped in her ear.

Another shudder rolled over her. Her throat clogged, she could barely answer. 'Yes.'

'Good.' Sliding his hands from her hair, he grasped her shoulders and turned her round. For an instant a naked, bewildered look was on his face, then it disappeared just as quickly. 'Kiss me, Carla,' he demanded.

Her heart faltered, then banged with renewed vigour against her ribs. Swallowing, she closed the gap between them, her heels lending her a fleeting confidence as she lifted herself the last few inches to press her lips against his. A snapped-off growl punched between them. Head swimming, she opened her lips and tasted him. Hot and virile, he was like a drug she couldn't stay away from. Feeling bolder, she deepened the kiss, her arms lifting to slide around his neck, then glided her tongue along his lower lip.

Firm hands grasped her waist, plastering her to him before his hands slid down to cup her pert behind. In a move that was shockingly erotic, he rolled her against his raging erection, the blatant intent behind the move arrowing need straight between her thighs. Unable to help herself, she pressed even closer.

A harsh exhalation burned her lips before he took over the kiss. Commanding, potently male, he devoured her mouth with ruthless vigour. Just when she didn't think she could stand the flames of desire, he picked her up and laid her on the bed.

Heart racing even faster, she watched, dazed as he ripped his buttons free and tugged off his shirt. Dry-mouthed, Carla stared at the sleek beauty of him. Smooth and toned without a spare ounce of flesh, Javier was truly breathtaking. Her awe at his amazing body tripled when he unbuckled his belt and kicked away his trousers and boxers.

Dio mio, he was impressive. Far more than she'd allowed herself to remember during those secret nights when she'd been unable to stem the memories. Her breath stalled as he prowled to the bed. Slowly, he tugged her shoes off, swiftly followed by her bra and panties. From the bedside drawer, he extracted a condom, which he tossed on the bed.

Then he wrapped his hands around her ankles and drew her legs apart. From head to toe she was exposed before him. And she was incapable of hiding. Her limbs were his to command as he pleased. He arranged her legs around him, then he bent his impressive body over her.

He kissed the silken space between her breasts, taking his time to cup each mound, mould her flesh in his big hands and roll her turgid nipples between his fingers.

Her back arched off the bed as sensation snaked through her like a live wire. Each moan was answered with a deeper caress, a harder nip until her head was thrashing on the pillow. Catching one nipple in his mouth, he rolled the tight peak over his tongue before he sucked deep.

'Ah, *Dio*,' she gasped as harsher sensations arrowed between her legs.

She was burning up. Every caress drew her closer to the

peak she'd only experienced at this man's hands. Her hips twisted, need wild and untamed clamouring through her. His lips finally left her breasts, trailing lower down her body, bestowing hotter, more fervent kisses over her skin.

He reached the juncture of her thighs and she stopped breathing. Intent fierce and clear on his face, he lowered his head. At the first bold kiss, her eyes rolled shut.

He pulled away and froze.

'Eyes open, Carla. Tell me you want this. There will be no more hiding,' he instructed hoarsely. 'No more pretending this isn't happening.'

She forced herself to stare into his molten gaze and not drown in the torrential storm raging over her senses. 'I want this. Please…'

His nails raked lightly over her lower belly. Then again, harder. Pleasure like never before exploded beneath her skin. 'Again,' he demanded fiercely.

'I want you, Javier,' she murmured his name, needing to ground herself. Another drag of his nails.

With a deep groan, he rolled his tongue over her, expertly finding that most sensitive bud that sent her wild. His exploration was brazen, his determination to wring every ounce of response from her a purpose that raged from his every pore. From one heartbeat to the next, she was cresting that blissful peak, her senses in free fall as ecstasy slammed into her.

The sound of foil ripping was the precursor to the deeper, longer, more decadent pleasure she knew awaited her when she surfaced from the depths of her blinding release.

Javier reared over her, taking hold of her injured hand to rest it on the pillow above her head. Then he planted himself between her thighs, his full weight supported on his elbows as he stared down at her.

'Who do you belong to?'

'You. I'm yours. Please,' she gasped.

A hard, possessive kiss on her lips, followed by a deep

exploration with his tongue, then he surged into her with one deep, true thrust.

The pace was steady, his gaze fierce on her face as he took complete possession of her. Carla wanted to look away, suddenly afraid of what he would see in her eyes, especially since she wasn't sure what her raw emotions betrayed. But the dark depths of his gaze held her prisoner, each gleam mesmerising, his open hunger almost as absorbing as what his body was doing to hers. Uncontrollable shudders rolled through her as pressure mounted. Her moans mingled with his deep groans until they melded into one erotic litany that swirled around them.

'Carla,' he whispered her name as he plunged his fingers into her hair and ramped up the tempo of his thrusts.

The sound of her name on his lips, like this, shattered something inside her. As much as she wanted to convince herself this was an emotionless coupling, she knew it wasn't.

Not when she was floating out of herself, her heart unfurling like a flower towards the sun.

A touch of panic seized her. 'Javier, *non posso…* I… please…'

Javier felt a deep shudder reel through him, the last vestiges of doubt washing away beneath the pleasure overtaking him. He'd pondered whether he'd done the right thing by acting this way, by bringing her here, to the place where she'd scored a direct hit to his pride. Right in the moment, he knew nothing could persuade him otherwise. She was exactly where he wanted her to be, in his bed, beneath him, his name on her lips and ecstasy stamped in her gorgeous eyes. He trailed a hand down her side, felt her very skin strain towards him, and he wanted to roar his triumph.

For far too long, he'd wanted her. Had wondered whether he'd dreamed their potent chemistry and was savagely delighted that he hadn't.

She made another fractured sound, a twist between a sob and a moan. *That* singular sound that spelled how close she was imploded every useless thought. Her hips twisted up to meet his, her slick channel a hot fist around his manhood.

The roar that punched from him was as alien as the peak he crested a minute later. Both far surpassed the norm and threw him headlong into a kaleidoscopic unknown. Breathing ragged and desperate, he buried his face in her neck and deliberately emptied his mind of thought.

He couldn't deal with the unknown at the moment. Hell, he felt as if he were skating the very edge of sound reasoning from the moment he'd taken her call yesterday afternoon. Among those absurd feelings, the need to cherish and protect were ones he couldn't comprehend. He had no intention of comprehending them. At long last, she was back in his bed. That would be the extent of his personal dealings with Carla.

He raised himself up and stared down into her face. Lust-glazed eyes met his and he exhaled when they didn't immediately slide away. Leaning down, he tasted her kiss-swollen lips, groaning when they clung briefly to his. He indulged them both for a minute, before reluctantly pulling away to dispose of the condom.

On his return he saw that she had rolled onto her side, away from him. Javier tried not to let the sight disturb him. She would not be going far this time. Nor would any attempt to reject him ring true. Her responses had been genuine. And borderline innocent, just like the first time. Almost as though she hadn't taken any other lover since him.

He frowned. The urge to probe the extent of her sexual history hovered on his tongue, but he curbed it. Simply because that didn't matter in the here and now. And not because the idea that she might have been with someone else messed with his head.

Sliding into bed, he gathered her close, releasing a trapped breath when she came willingly, melted against him. She laid her injured hand on his chest and he found himself reaching for it, smoothing a kiss over the cast before curling his fingers over it.

She raised her head and her eyes met his. The quiet fire he'd missed seeing in them was back. But so was the bewildering feeling powering through his own body. Leaning down, he kissed her one more time. When her lids drooped, he settled her firmly against his body.

'Sleep now, if you want to, *querida*. You've passed the first test with flying colours.'

He tried not to read too much into her response when she murmured, 'I'm so glad,' then promptly drifted off to sleep. But he was wide awake several hours later, staring up at the stars, his mind abuzz with unsettling thoughts. When one thought kept recurring—that he was dreading the approach of morning in case history repeated itself with a vengeance—he grunted and kicked away the tangled sheets, a wicked thread of satisfaction spiking through him when Carla opened her eyes. He was donning protection and sliding into her before she was fully awake. After that, he encouraged her to join him in raiding the fridge.

Then, sated, he dragged her back to bed.

Carla awoke splayed out on top of Javier. She knew he was awake because his fingers teased through her hair in long, lazy movements. Her heart kicked hard as the events of last night flooded her mind. But as much as the euphoria made itself felt, it was the bright sunlight filtering in through the curtains that made her stomach dip in alarm.

Her last experience of the morning after had been abysmal. And she didn't doubt that the memory would be in the forefront of Javier's mind too.

'I'm willing to forget our previous experience if you are.'

Her head jerked up. Polished mahogany flecked with gold regarded her steadily, but she saw the steady tic in his cheek as his fingers continued to play with her hair.

With every cell in her body, she wanted to say yes, to brush the unfortunate incident under the carpet and forget it'd ever happened. But she owed him an explanation. 'No, I don't want to forget it. I want to explain.'

His eyes darkened but he nodded. 'Very well. Go on.'

She bit her lip. 'That week we met was the first time I'd ever been given any form of freedom or time off since I was twelve years old. The day I was accepted into the international figure-skating programme, my life stopped being my own.'

Javier frowned. 'I thought you loved it.'

'I did. I do,' she replied, but Carla knew the ambivalence she'd been feeling lately bled into her voice. 'It's the only thing I excel at, but it's hard to love something when you know without it you're nothing.'

His frown deepened. 'Nothing? What are you talking about?'

'If I wasn't a figure skater what would I be?'

'Whatever you want to be. You're the only one who can set limitations on yourself.'

She shook her head. 'That's just it. I don't want to be anything else, but I was never given a choice of what I *could* be. Does that make sense?'

His fingers trapped in her hair. '*Sí*, it makes sense. But I don't understand what this has to do with what happened three years ago.'

A flicker of shame singed her. 'My father was against me coming to New York with Maria and Draco. He wanted me to return to Tuscany with him for the two-week break, like always. We…fought badly, but I refused to back down. But every minute I was away I was terrified of what he'd do.'

'What do you mean? Did he physically hurt you?'

'No, but he…had his ways when I disobeyed him.'

Javier flipped their positions and reared over her. 'What ways?'

'He would have my trainer double my training, or my favourite horse would suddenly be lent to a neighbour's daughter for the summer.'

His jaw tightened. 'He wanted to show you he was in control.'

'*Sì*. But three years ago, I turned twenty-one. And I challenged his authority by taking my two-week break without him. But that wasn't all I did. I called my mother and begged her to intercede with him on my behalf over his controlling behaviour.' Her voice broke, the emotions she'd held in check for so long bubbling to the surface.

A firm hand cupped her jaw, his thumb trailing over her cheek. 'What did he do?'

'He called me…during your party. He told me he was disappointed in me. That I shouldn't have got my mother involved in our lives again.'

'Again?' he queried.

Carla swallowed. 'She left when I was ten. I won the regional skating championship when I was nine, and had been scouted for the nationals. My mother thought I was too young for the intensity of the training. My father disagreed. They fought for a solid year and, towards the end, their arguments got more intense. My father never physically abused her, but I could tell he was close to it.' She shuddered in remembrance of the latent violence that had lingered in those confrontations. 'The week before she left, she cried every night. When she told me she was leaving, I was shattered, but I was also relieved.'

Javier's eyes darkened with quiet fury. 'She never contemplated taking you with her?'

'My father would never have allowed her to do that. He worked in a factory when I was a child. The moment he realised my potential, he gave up his job. I was his ticket to a dream life and he wasn't about to let it go.' Bitterness and sorrow duelled for supremacy within her. Javier saw it, leaned down and placed a gentle kiss on her lips.

Tears prickled her eyes but she blinked them away.

'So you reached out to her when you turned twenty-one…?'

'My father had planned out my life for the next five years, and I was suffocating.'

'You could've walked away, started afresh with a new management team.'

She shook her head. 'We're locked into a management agreement that ends when I'm twenty-five. Or at least we were. Once this new deal goes through, I'll be free of him.'

He swore under his breath. 'So your mother was your only option?'

Her heart shuddered, regret biting deep. 'She agreed to talk to him. She was on her way to Tuscany when I came to Miami. He called me during your party, and I'd never heard him so angry. Something in his voice scared me, but I convinced myself it was nothing.'

'That's why you got drunk?'

She gave a shaky nod. 'I wanted to drown him out… to drown everything out.' She risked a glance at him and found his steady, intense gaze on her. 'I didn't regret what happened to us, but…'

'But?' he bit out.

'But, I would've done things differently if I'd had another chance.'

'How differently?'

'I would've started the evening sober, for a start.'

'*Sí*, but you weren't drunk by the end of it.'

Unable to resist, she grazed her fingers over his morning stubble. 'That's because *you* made sure I wasn't. Can you imagine if it'd been someone else less honourable than you?'

He tensed. 'Did we agree not to mention other people while you're in my bed?'

'I didn't mean…that was a hypothetical question, Javier,' she admonished.

He gave a stiff, arrogant shrug. 'Spare yourself my hypothetical wrath and stick to your story, *querida*,' he suggested.

'I woke up the next morning hating myself for hiding behind my mother and not facing my father. I hated the circumstances that brought us together and I didn't handle it well.'

'So you deliberately let me believe you were going from my bed to Angelis's?'

Heat crawled up her face. *'Mi dispiace molto.'*

'And the dates in London? The kiss in Tuscany?'

'All completely platonic. I'm not in love with Draco, Javier. I swear. I never have been.'

He stared at her in silence for a full minute, before he nodded. *'Bene,'* he replied gruffly, then took her mouth in another heart-stopping kiss.

After several minutes, he raised his head. 'We seem to have come full circle, Carla. Give me your word that you're mine and I'll let this matter rest.'

'I'm yours,' she affirmed.

He kissed her again, then nodded for her to continue.

'For years I'd been promising myself that when I could I would walk away from my father. But in the end I wanted everything. My career, my father, my mother, everything in harmony. A stupid wish, of course.'

His mouth twisted. 'The day we stop dreaming and striving for the unachievable is the day we die. Don't beat yourself up about it.'

'But don't you see? I wanted too much. Because she died.'

He stiffened. 'But you said you don't know how she died. How do you know it's because of what you asked of her?'

The thorns that had never quite melted away from her heart pierced her unbearably. 'Because if I hadn't got her involved she would still be alive. I begged her to intercede with my father, and she died because of it.'

CHAPTER ELEVEN

JAVIER SLOWLY PULLED back from her. The absence of his warmth struck her almost as deeply as the pain ravaging her insides. He sat with his back against the massive headboard, his features inscrutable. In the next instant, he pulled her up against him, one strong arm around her shoulders as he leaned her back against him.

'You believe your father did something to her or you wouldn't be torturing yourself this way,' he stated, cutting right to the heart of the matter.

Her breath caught. 'I don't want to think that…but I can't help myself.'

'Tell me what you know.'

'Not much. All I know is she went to Tuscany to talk to him. She didn't leave there alive. I found out she was dead a week after I left you, after I'd completed my three-day competition in Switzerland.'

'*Dios mio.* He didn't tell you?'

'He didn't want the news to affect my performance. The first I knew of her death was on the way to the funeral home. He said it was an accident, that he was sorry, but I needed to put it behind me as soon as possible.'

Carla didn't realise she was crying until his thumb brushed the moisture from her cheeks. Then, as if the floodgates of her grief had been ripped open, thick sobs exploded from her heart. Javier held her closer, both arms folding her into his body as she purged her grief. Selfishly, she clung to him, knowing deep down that it was unwise, but unable to stop herself from soaking up his support.

Gentle words spoken in Spanish floated over her. Long moments later, her hiccups the only sound in the room, Carla attempted to pull away.

He held her still. 'Stay.'

'No, I shouldn't—'

'Reliving the past was bound to resurrect bad memories for you. Don't be distressed for needing a shoulder to lean on sometimes. We both know you're strong when you need to be.'

Her laughter was harsh and one hundred per cent self-deprecating. This time when she pulled away, he let her. Rising on her knees, she brushed away the last of her tears and faced him. 'Strong? If I was I wouldn't have left it another three years after her death to finally seek answers. I wouldn't be giving in to my father's demands for a *bribe* just so I find out how my own mother died. That doesn't make me strong!'

A muscle ticced in his jaw. 'We try to find answers the best way we can.'

She spiked her fingers through her hair, bewilderment raging high. 'I don't know why you're trying to make me feel better, Javier. If it hadn't been for me, your mother would be resting in peace by now.'

One corner of his mouth lifted in a grim smile. 'That was your father's doing, not yours. I was hacked off when I lumped you in with him. You can't be held accountable for his failures. For my part, trying to afford my mother some peace now doesn't alter the fact that I left her with Fernando for years, distanced myself as far away as I could.'

'You left because you wanted to make a better life for both of you,' she countered.

'*Sí*, but also because a part of me was disappointed that she wanted so very little for herself. That she was too weak to break away from his poisonous presence. No matter where she was in the world, she pined for him. It was a weakness I didn't understand. So in the end, I left her to it. And she died alone.'

Tears she'd thought were long spent clogged her throat

again. 'So you're saying we deserve this anguish we're both going through?'

A heavy shrug. 'We can accept our part in the theatre of our lives, even flog ourselves daily for it. But you can't lose yourself because of it.' His smile turned grimmer. 'Or let those rightly responsible get away with it.'

A cold shiver went through her. She might have fooled herself into believing she'd found common ground with Javier. That the shoulder he'd lent her had come without strings. As she watched him reach for her, she knew how wrong she'd been.

He might understand her plight, might even empathise on some level, but he still held her responsible for a large degree of his unresolved issues with his father.

And for that, she would continue to pay with her body.

Heart slamming hard in her lungs, and desperate not to let him see how his final words had affected her, she slid her arms around his neck as he rose from the bed and headed to the large, marble-floored bathroom.

'So…what now?'

'We take a shower and then I take you for an early lunch.'

Javier couldn't get to the bottom of his fury long enough to gain proper control of it. Hell, he could barely see past the red haze that crossed his vision each time he thought of what Olivio Nardozzi had, and continued to, put his daughter through.

He'd made love to Carla in the shower with an edge of rage he knew she'd felt. She'd been with him every step of the way, but he'd glimpsed the shaken look in her eyes afterwards as they'd dressed.

He'd known the other man was as self-centred and avaricious as they came, perhaps even more so than his own father—which was saying something—but he'd never imagined Olivio would put his own child through such raw turmoil.

As he navigated his sports car along the highway towards South Beach, he suppressed a crude curse. He'd spent the night mostly awake and had hated himself for it because he'd dreaded the morning would bring a repeat of Carla's rejection three years ago. What he hadn't expected was a wild swing in the opposite direction, a dropping of her guard and a complete baring of her soul that had left a previously unknown part of him touched and reeling. A part he didn't want to examine, much as he didn't want to examine the real reason he'd instigated this whole thing with Carla in the first place.

He glanced over at her, satisfaction pulsing through him that the subject of her and Angelis had finally been put to rest. Truth be told, now jealousy was no longer blinding him, he could see that Angelis had only ever been looking out for her. And three years ago, Carla hadn't actually come right out and confessed that she was in love with her agent, had she? Looking back, he realised it was the deeper effect of her father's actions that had fuelled his need for vengeance.

And even that need was dissipating.

She returned his gaze and he lost his train of thought as his eyes drifted over her.

Her stretchy cream dress ended a good few inches above her thighs, showing off her slim legs in a mouth-watering expanse of light golden flesh. The material skimmed her curves in a way that made his palms itch to follow each thread of cotton, and Javier was ridiculously jealous of the seat belt that rested between her breasts. As he watched, she twitched beneath his scrutiny, her hand lifting to tuck back the hair shifting in the breeze of his open-top car.

A different sort of turbulence attacked him, this time much lower in his body but equally insistent. And equally unsettling. Carla hadn't been far off in her accusation that his sexual liaisons were fleeting at worst and a step above short term at best. He certainly didn't crave any woman he dated after having her as many times as he'd had Carla in the last twelve hours. Yet, his body's continual reaction to her threatened to reduce him to hormonal teenager status.

'Are you going to spend the entire journey in silence?' she asked, her voice a touch shaky, he knew, from the thick, aggressive vibes he was throwing out.

He opened his mouth to respond in a way that would ease her agitation—another first for him—but then his gaze touched on her bound wrist. 'Your lawyers have been in touch about Blackwell's trial?' It wasn't really a question that required an answer. He'd kept up to date on what was happening with the ex-trainer in Italy.

She nodded. 'It's happening in three weeks. Draco says I don't need to be there. The video testimony is enough.'

He squashed the residual jealousy that lingered at the mention of her agent. 'When did you speak to him?'

'Yesterday.' A bold but wary glance flicked his way, her green eyes turning a shade darker. 'Javier?'

'Sí?' he responded, more than a little perturbed at how much pleasure his name on her lips brought him.

'You two used to be good friends, yes?'

His jaw tightened. 'What's your point?'

'You know what my point is.'

He shrugged. 'And I'm trying to be the bigger man here, but you kissed him at your charity event, did you not?'

She gasped. 'Surely you can't still be jealous about that? He's crazy about his fiancée!'

Javier's hands tightened on the steering wheel as he wondered why he couldn't get control of yet another irrational emotion. 'You can assess for yourself how I feel when we see Angelis at my party.'

Her eyes widened with surprise, then a touch of pleasure that made him grit his teeth. 'They're coming here?'

'Should I be put out that you've already forgotten about my birthday celebration?'

'I didn't think… I thought it would be just us.'

He captured her hand and brought it to his lips, his pulse

spiking at the touch of her silky skin. 'As much as I want to keep you all to myself, I need to uphold my *party hard* reputation. Angelis and his fiancée have already accepted my invitation. You want us to be friends again, make me forget that kiss and I'll give it a shot,' he half teased. 'You see? I can be progressive after all.'

Despite his words, Carla sensed his tension as they pulled up in front of a silver, futuristic-looking building opposite an inner city park. After helping her out, he handed his keys to a hovering valet and pulled her to his side.

A quick kiss at her temple turned into a trailing caress that ended at the corner of her mouth. Carla's pulse was dancing wildly by the time he straightened.

'Forgive me for the quick pit stop. I won't be long.'

Carla looked around the foyer with interest. Young executives buzzed around, their casual yet frenetic appearance indicating a creative atmosphere. 'What is this place?' she asked.

'My production design crew are based here. They have the altered specs for the tequila bottle ready for me to inspect.'

'I thought the design was finalised.'

A quizzical smile teased his sensual mouth. 'As did I. But inspiration struck and I went with it.'

Intrigued and more than a little surprised that he would bring her to inspect what was obviously a special project for him, Carla followed him into the lift. He positioned her in front of him, then proceeded to plant hot, shockingly erotic kisses on her neck.

When the lift pinged to a stop, he groaned. 'Perhaps I should've postponed this meeting. The timing of this wasn't the best idea.'

'Perhaps you should have,' she teased. 'Although I doubt it would've happened.'

He turned her around in his arms, his eyes narrowed as he scrutinised her face. 'You trying to make a point, *querida*?'

She shrugged, her heart doing a funny little dance at the predatory light in his eyes as his gaze dropped to her mouth. 'You keep threatening to take a day off, but I've yet to see you actually take one.'

The hands gripping her waist tightened a fraction before he set her free. 'I need intense stimulation otherwise I get bored. You think you're up to the task of providing me with such stimulation?' he rasped.

Heat flowed up her neck and completely engulfed her cheeks. 'There's only one way to find out…*caro*,' she countered bravely, unwilling to let on just how out of her element she really felt.

Dark, mesmeric eyes glinted with a feral light that strangled her breath. The hand that curled around hers was implacable, possessive. The urgent strides that had her trotting to keep up announced that her gauntlet had been accepted.

Carla was reeling from just what she'd let herself in for when Javier led them through double glass doors into a large room. The circular seating area contained an inner carpeted area with a raised platform. In the middle of it stood a tall object draped with black silk.

Three executives rose as they entered. All young, all eager to make an impression as they greeted Javier.

'Mr Santino. It's good to see you again.' The closest man shook hands with him.

Javier nodded to the other two, and, without letting go of her hand, walked to the middle of the room. 'I need to be elsewhere, gentlemen. I'd appreciate us getting on with it?' The statement was couched as a question, but the order was clear.

'Of course. The specs are just what you asked for.' The oldest in the group, clearly their leader, pulled back the silk cloth with a flourish.

What little oxygen remained in Carla's lungs after glimpsing the raw, predatory hunger in Javier's eyes evaporated as she stared at the redesigned tequila bottle. Much of the original design had remained the same, but where the neck had been a sleek line tapering to the rounded base, it now flowed in a distinct, unmistakably feminine shape. A shape that grew intimately familiar the more she stared at it.

Blushing to the roots of her hair, she tried to disentangle her fingers from Javier's. He held on tight, his eyes riveted to the life-size bottle as he rasped, 'Thank you for your hard work, gentlemen. Now if you'd be so kind as to leave us.'

The moment they were alone, she let out a stunned breath. 'You can't!'

He turned sizzling eyes to her. 'I can't what, *querida*?' he enquired silkily.

She gestured frantically at the bottle. 'You can't do…this.'

Circling behind her, he caught her around the waist and frogmarched her to the bottle. 'You belong to me. Give me one good reason why I cannot immortalise you however I wish to.'

She could think of one. *Dio*, she could think of several, the paramount of them being she only belonged to him on a temporary basis. None of what was happening between them would last beyond the next few weeks. But all her objections—and the peculiar pang that lanced her heart—vanished as she stared at the stunningly beautiful bottle.

His hands slipped from her waist, down to capture her hands. Linking her fingers with his, he brought them up to the neck of the bottle to grip the glass. Cool and smooth, the glass quickly warmed beneath her fingers. Or perhaps it was her imagination, and her fevered hormones alone were responsible for heating the bottle. He drew their hands down to rest on the upper curve, his head aligned with hers. She didn't need to turn her head to know he was staring at their joined hands on his creation.

'Now every time I touch this piece, I'll think of you,' he murmured in her ear.

Carla gave a single shake of her head, unable to comprehend the enormity of his testament. He might no longer hate her as much as she'd imagined he once did, but this…

She swallowed. 'Javier…'

'I wish I'd had this brought to the house. Now I need to get myself under control before we can leave.'

Another blush fired up her cheeks as she caught his meaning. She groaned as he pulled her back against him, the rigid line of his manhood searing into her behind for one charged moment before he set her free.

When she stumbled a few steps away, he didn't stop her. His gaze was once more on the bottle, his scrutiny blessedly clinical as he examined it fully. After a few minutes, he nodded with satisfaction and walked towards her.

The designers hovered outside and Javier invited them back in. Questions were fired out in rapid succession, most of which flew over her head as her gaze continually strayed to the bottle.

You belong to me…

The unyielding possession in those words should've frightened her, made her want to strike out for the independence she was desperately seeking in her life. But they reached into the heart of her, claiming a hitherto unknown part of her she hadn't realised was waiting for such a claiming. A claiming she was ready—

'Carla?'

She jumped. 'Yes?'

Javier smiled with the barest touch of mockery. 'It's time to go,' he intoned.

She blinked and realised the executives had left. Rising and casting one last glance at the bottle, she slipped a hand into the one he held out.

Javier led her out into the early afternoon sunshine. Thinking they were about to drive somewhere else, she followed him when he led her across the street and into the park.

'What are we doing here?'

'We're having lunch.'

Seeing no restaurant or anything resembling an impromptu picnic, she glanced back at him.

With a grin, he led her towards a food truck blaring out salsa music. The ruddy-faced chef greeted them in loud, rambling Spanish.

Javier responded, his graceful hand movements drawing her attention to his strong arms and the ripped body currently clothed in dark jeans and a sea-green rugby shirt. She watched him give an order she had no hope of following before leading her to the small table set for two at the side of the truck. Pulling out a chair for her, he went back to the truck and returned with two wrapped packages, paper plates, and two bottles of water.

She opened her package to a mouth-watering barrage of flavours. Aware that Javier was watching her, she took her first bite. And groaned.

'Dio mio.'

His grin widened. 'Very few things beat a well-prepared Cuban sandwich.' He passed her a bottle, then unwrapped his before taking a sizeable bite.

She took another bite. 'It's incredible.'

He nodded. 'It may be Cuban but it reminds me of a dish my mother used to prepare.' A slight frown wrinkled his brow, as if the memory was an unexpected one, but it was gone in a flash.

They'd delved far deeper into each other's histories than she knew he normally allowed. But she couldn't stop herself from probing deeper. 'Is that why you prefer to live here? Because it reminds you of home?'

His jaw clenched. 'I never had a home.'

'You know what I mean—'

He raised dark, intense eyes to her. 'Do I? I think we've got our lines crossed somewhere along the line. You had a home, albeit a brief one until your mother left. I had the equivalent of a prison, where each knock on the door either made my mother jump in fright or sick with inevitably thwarted anticipation. Neither of those two things made for anything resembling a *home*.'

'But despite all that, you had a parent who loved you. Does that not count for something?'

He chewed for a long time before he swallowed and pushed the remaining sandwich away. 'Not when you live in constant fear of being abandoned the moment the long-given promise showed signs of being fulfilled. And my father played his cards just so by keeping my mother from never giving up that her dreams would eventually come true. The end result being that I was always on tenterhooks that the only parent I had could be taken from me in the blink of an eye.'

She caught his hand in hers before she processed the action. 'I'm sorry.'

For a stark moment, he seemed perturbed by her sympathy. Then his lashes swept down. With a nod, he linked his fingers with hers, and grabbed his water bottle with his other hand. 'Finish your meal, *querida*. You have an afternoon of stimulating me to be getting on with.'

His low, deep laugh at her blush fired up her already scorching arousal. He didn't let up the sweltering possessive looks as he led her back to his car and slid behind the wheel. Nor did he make any bones about giving his staff the afternoon off once they returned home.

The moment the staff vacated the premises, he slid her dress over her head. Then he finally took her on the sweeping staircase, the way he'd threatened to three years ago.

The rest of the week continued in the same vein, with the exception of Javier working less and less each day. It was almost as if once he got into the rhythm of having time off, he threw himself into it with the same ruthless vigour he pursued every other area of his life. By the end of their first weekend, he'd introduced her to a high-speed trip on his latest speedboat—the JS1—a food tour of Little Havana, and sunbathing in the nude on his private beach. He'd swayed her through sensual salsa moves at an exclusive nightclub, which had abruptly ended when he'd dragged her off the dance floor and into his limo. They hadn't made it home and Carla had experienced her first, sizzling lovemaking session in the back of a car.

The only hiccup had arrived when Javier had proclaimed the nightclub to be the ideal venue for the tequila shoot and introduced her to his new, female, creative director. Her guarded query as to Darren's whereabouts had earned her a hard stare, followed by a terse, 'He's been promoted to head up a fascinating new project. In Alaska.'

Her wince hadn't gone unnoticed. Luckily, he'd let the moment pass.

By the middle of their second week, sensing his restlessness, Carla proposed a tentative start to the shoot. Jemma, the creative director, had hinted they could start with some strategic publicity shots that wouldn't show her cast.

They arrived at the nightclub just after lunch. The lights were dimmed but, with no customers around, the hexagonal seats and the glittering gold chandeliers lent the place an even more special feel. The crew of ten bustled about setting up the stage, and for the first time in a long time Carla felt a buzz.

The six costumes comprising three designer gowns and three cocktail dresses chosen for the shoot were sublimely beautiful, and when she took her place on the marker for the photographer, she couldn't stop the smile that curved her lips.

Javier came up behind her as she stood on the railing of the balcony that fed two wide, sweeping staircases. 'You seem pleased, *querida*.'

Her smile stretched, just as her heart had begun to expand with joy each time he used that endearment. 'I didn't think I'd enjoy this, but now that it's happening, I like it.'

'Why did you think you wouldn't enjoy it? You've done other sponsored shoots before.'

She shrugged, her gaze taking in the tiny platinum lights that glittered the dance floor. 'Yes, but wearing a watch or the latest ski jacket is different than this. This is a whole new experience.' An experience heightened by the man who stood so close, she could feel his warmth all around her; smell his powerfully unique scent. Both made her want to turn around, burrow into him and drown in that sensation.

She kept her ground, barely, as his arms rested on the railing on either side of her hips. 'In that case, enjoy it to the max. But don't lose sight of the depth of your talent. I've seen you skate. You may not have chosen that career for yourself, but you excel at it because it comes from your soul. Take a break if you need to—we'll work something out—but never forget the gift you've been given.'

Long after he'd walked away and the photos had been taken, his words lingered. And later that night, when the cadence of his lovemaking changed, his hitherto masterful possession gentling into a much more poignant claiming, she was left shaken, unable to separate reality from what her heart suddenly seemed to be yearning for—a sign that Javier saw this cluster of situations that had brought them together in a more meaningful light. But how could he?

He'd shaped his project after her—literally—but he was a man who collected trophies, who had homes around the world and more expensive toys than any one man could ever enjoy in a lifetime.

And you're just one bauble for him to possess briefly until he grows bored...

The harsh bruising to her heart was so immediate and terrifying, she gasped.

Javier's head jerked up from where he'd been trailing

post-coital kisses on her shoulder. 'What's wrong?' he demanded.

Sucking in a breath, she shook her head quickly and raised herself up onto her elbows. 'Nothing.' She kissed him, seeking shameful refuge in the melting that filmed the pain. 'Nothing at all.'

CHAPTER TWELVE

NOTHING AT ALL.

She continued to recite those three words to herself throughout the frenzy of party preparations over the next three days. Relieved to see that Javier didn't mind her getting involved, she pulled on hostessing skills learned from an early age after her mother's departure. Back when her father had wanted to rub shoulders with the well-to-do without incurring the expense of it. Then later it'd been another way to tie her to his side, to control her, while basking in the limelight of her success.

He'd called them a *team*, and she'd convinced herself that meant *something*. Until it'd been far too late.

She strode out of the dressing room, where she'd been putting finishing touches to her make-up before the party, to the bedside table. Before she picked up her phone she knew there would be no message from her father.

The promise of funds had been well-received. Not so much the hold Javier had initially placed on the transmission of the money—with her approval—until her father had delivered on his promise to tell her about her mother. Her father's grim silence was meant to prolong her anguish. In the end, Carla had requested that Javier just release the money to him, but her father still hadn't called.

And the tension was succeeding in getting to her—

'Is there a reason you're staring at your phone when I need you downstairs with me?' came a semi-brusque query.

Setting her phone down, she turned. One of the things she'd quickly learned to accept was that Javier wanting what he wanted *when* he wanted wasn't something she could change any time soon. Another thing she couldn't change was her heart's crazy leap whenever her eyes connected with his. The ferocious intensity of his gaze seemed to have acquired an even pithier depth lately, as if he saw beneath her skin, to every unsettling emotion she didn't want him to glean. Carla wanted to believe she was succeeding in hiding her feelings, but a steady voice inside mocked her feeble attempts.

He reached her and captured her hands. 'Our guests are arriving.'

The collective statement caused yet another shifting of her emotional foundation. Watching him, she silently despaired at how effectively his every word and look battered at her defences; how her heart seemed to live for just such a moment, when he looked at her as if she really mattered to him.

'I'm ready,' she finally managed when she could speak past the trepidation clogging her throat.

His answer was to lift her hands away from her body, his appreciative scrutiny flooding her with idiotic pleasure. '*Sí*, you are. The gown is perfect on you,' he stated with pure, male satisfaction.

'*Grazie,*' she murmured.

The sleeveless red gown fitted her like a dream, a sleek confection of criss-crossed chiffon and silk that hugged her torso and hips and fell to her ankles in a gentle flare. She'd fallen in love with it the moment Javier had presented her with it this afternoon, despite the unease that had lanced through her at the thought that his claiming of her was attaining *absolute* proportions. His drawled observation that she hadn't packed for the party and didn't have time to go shopping had been meant to appease, except she'd glimpsed the barely concealed look of triumph on his face as he'd walked away after her acceptance of the gown. But even that hadn't been enough to dim her enjoyment of the garment.

The thought that she was escaping an oppressive prison for a gilded one made her heart lurch, until she reminded herself of the transient nature of her current situation. Pinning a smile on her face, she met his narrowing eyes. 'Shall we go?'

'Not just yet.'

Her eyes widened as he reached into his dinner jacket and pulled out a large, flat box. Before he opened it, she stepped back.

'Javier, no.'

A trace of displeasure gleamed in his eyes. 'It's my birthday, *mi amante*, you're not supposed to refuse me.' He opened the box to reveal a heart-meltingly gorgeous platinum chain from which a large teardrop diamond hung.

'And you're supposed to receive presents, not give them!' For reasons she couldn't fathom, the sight of the necklace seemed to compound her roiling emotions. 'This isn't necessary, Javier.'

'I don't do it out of necessity,' he drawled. 'Merely because it complements your dress. Feel free to return it at the end of the evening if you feel that strongly about it.' He plucked the chain from the velvet and waited expectantly.

With no choice but to argue, and keep their guests waiting, or give in gracefully, Carla turned around and lifted the newly styled fall of her hair. He secured the necklace, the cool stone resting between her breasts, then he stepped back. 'Oh, one thing I neglected to mention.'

She turned. 'Yes?'

He shrugged. 'Sadly, now that you've worn it, it's non-returnable. It's not the vendor's policy, of course, but my own. So you're stuck with it.'

Speechless, she stared at him, watched a dark, wicked smile break over his face. It heated her blood and singed her insides as he tucked her arms into his and led her from the room. She was searching for an adequate comeback when they reached the double doors of the great room.

A different sort of trepidation hit her as she heard familiar voices. But that all changed when an additional voice sent her rushing in.

'Maria!'

The whine of the electrical wheelchair sounded over the soft background music as her friend turned at the sound of her name.

'There you are. We were thinking of sending out a search party for you.' Dark of complexion and as strikingly beautiful as her brother was handsome, Maria Angelis scrutinised Carla's face with wide and shrewd eyes as she rolled forward.

'You're a little early. Not that I mind at all.' Carla leaned down and hugged her friend, striving not to show the heartache that lingered at the edges of her interactions with Maria.

Maria, once a talented figure skater, had suffered a crippling fall as a result of being pushed past her training capabilities by Tyson Blackwell. Unlike Carla, Maria hadn't escaped with a simple broken wrist and a concussion. She'd severely damaged her vertebrae, resulting in permanent disability. It was the reason Draco Angelis had fought so strenuously to have Tyson Blackwell brought to justice.

Her gaze lifted past her friend's shoulder to see Javier shaking hands with Draco. The gesture was a touch tense, but Draco's fiancée, Rebel Daniels, made a comment that had both men chuckling.

Breathing slightly easier, Carla concentrated on her friend. 'How are you?'

'Much better now that bastard is on the brink of a long jail term.' Maria's voice held satisfaction and the same ironhard will that had seen her through intense rehabilitation and eventual acceptance of her situation. It was the same will that had bolstered Carla when she'd been met with resistance from her father and Tyson Blackwell. 'Thank you for agreeing to press charges,' her friend added.

Carla shook her head. 'No, thank you for standing by me when I needed you.'

Maria quirked an eyebrow in a move acutely reminiscent of her brother's. 'Not sure about the standing part, but you're welcome.'

Shocked laughter barked out of Carla, and she leaned down and pressed a kiss to her friend's cheek. Before she could straighten, Maria added, 'Besides, if I could walk I'd be fighting you for your Spanish hottie. And that just wouldn't be fair.'

Unable to stem the blush that rose in her face, she stammered, 'I'm not…he's not—'

She clamped her lips shut as the trio approached. Rebel Daniels smiled and enfolded her in a big hug, easing the constriction that had clamped Carla's heart on seeing her.

'Rebel, I owe you an apology,' she started.

A hand sporting a huge diamond waved her words away. 'Bygones. For everything.' She cast an eye at Draco, then Javier. 'I know the fuller story about your father and Blackwell now, and I'm only sorry we didn't nail the bastard before he did that to you.' She nodded at Carla's wrist. 'But if you insist, I know how you can make it up to me.'

'Oh?'

She exchanged a bliss-filled look with Draco. 'Come to our wedding. Draco tells me you're out of commission for another few weeks. The wedding is next month. I'd love to have both you and Javier there. I kinda insist, actually.' She grinned unashamedly.

Carla's lips parted; she had every intention of making an appropriate refusal. By then she had no idea where she'd be. She would either still be with Javier, or, more likely, freshly released from her sojourn in his bed. In neither scenario could she envisage herself in a position to attend a wedding—

'We'd love to be there,' Javier replied in easy, confident tones.

Carla barely stopped her mouth from dropping open.

Rebel's breathtaking smile widened. 'Great! Now, Javier, I hear you're seriously into your tequila. Any chance of a slammer before the hordes descend on us?'

The gaze he'd levelled on Carla after his shocking response to the wedding invitation lingered for another in-finitesimal second before he nodded at Rebel. 'Of course.'

'Cut her off after one, Santino. I need her sober for the meeting in the morning with the wedding co-ordinator *she* insisted on hiring,' Draco drawled with only a hint of ex-asperation.

Rebel made a face. 'Just because you're a drill sergeant doesn't mean you get to opt out of your own wedding plan-ning. You'll sample the same amount of cake as I do, and weigh in on the china patterns.'

'Go drink your slammer now, Arabella, before I embar-rass us both by showing everyone here who's boss.'

Rebel laughed, but her cheeks flared with adorable colour as she hooked her arm though Javier's. 'Come on, Maria,' she invited her future sister-in-law.

Carla sensed Draco's presence beside her as they watched Javier lead the ladies to the far side of the room where the bar had been set up.

'Are you not interested in the tequila party?' she asked the tall, dark man.

'No. I've already had a preview of Javier's tequila. It's the best of the best, as usual. I've also seen the new bottle.' His gaze reluctantly left his fiancée's laughing figure to connect with Carla's. 'It's an…interesting change from the original design. Anything I should know about?'

She shook her head, and saw Draco's gaze swing to her new loose, layered hairstyle. His raised eyebrow caused her colour to heighten. 'I'm fine, Draco.'

He watched her for several seconds, then nodded. 'San-tino tells me the situation with your father isn't resolved yet.'

Carla felt a touch of irritation. 'You've been discussing me?'

'His interest seems genuine, and I'm not about to argue with that. So, your father?'

Pain lanced her heart. 'It's not resolved yet, but I'm han-dling it.'

'Good.'

She managed a wobbly smile before voices filled the hall-way.

Catering to the never-ending stream of guests meant Carla didn't have time to dwell on Javier or whatever his interests were where she was concerned.

She caught a brief reprieve when the DJ cranked up the music and the guests flooded to the dance floor. She skimmed the room and caught sight of Javier engaged in conversation with two guests. About to glance away, she froze when his head snapped suddenly up and his gaze captured hers. Carla wasn't sure how long she stayed in place, a prisoner to his imposing regard.

She jumped as a hand clamped on her arm. 'Jeez, you two need to get a room. Or a whole resort. Whatever. Do me a favour and make eyes at each other later, okay?' Rebel laughed. 'I need to use the ladies' room and I don't trust anyone else with my fiancé. Dance with him until I get back?'

'Um…'

'Thanks! And tune him out if he starts with the overprotective big brother thing.' She grinned at Draco's narrow-eyed stare, then disappeared in the direction of the powder room.

Carla stepped into his arms, her cast-bound hand on his shoulder as he led her around the floor. 'I promise not to tune you out again,' she stated.

'You probably won't need me for anything other than business matters from now on.' He looked down at her, his imposing frame commanding her attention. 'You've come a long way, you and Maria, and I'm proud of you. But I'm still a phone call away if you need me.' His gaze swung over her head, to the side of the room where she could feel another set of intense eyes boring into her back as she danced with Draco. 'For anything. Understand?'

Tears prickled her eyes and clogged her throat. She managed a murmured '*grazie*' before a firm hand seized her waist.

'Mind if I cut in?' came a hard voice.

Another speculative expression crossed Draco's face. 'Not at all,' he drawled before he relinquished her and struck off in search of his fiancée.

'Once again I find you dancing with a man who is *not* me,' Javier stated through gritted teeth. Dark eyes scoured her face, then his mouth flattened in a harsh line before she was jerked against him. 'And you're on the verge of tears.' His snarl held a touch of bewilderment. 'Know this now, *querida*, my *progressive* attitude has its limits.'

Carla sighed, the need to throw her hands up in surrender weighing her down. With each moment that she'd acted as his hostess, each moment his gaze had met hers across the room tonight, she'd known she was fighting a battle she was doomed to lose. Whatever feelings she was developing for Javier, they wouldn't be easily discarded once he was done with her. Which meant that even as she gloried at being in his arms right now her foundations were fracturing, the tsunami of pain gathering strength somewhere beyond her sight and reach.

'If I didn't know better, I'd think you invited him here to test me.'

His nostrils flared. 'I didn't. But those tears aren't very reassuring, and I find myself in dire need of reassurance.'

Her breath hitched. Swaying close until their torsos met, she spiked her fingers through the silky hair at his nape and gripped tight enough to get his attention. Dark eyes clashed with hers and, throwing caution to the wind, she let her naked emotion show. 'What do I need to do to prove that I want you? Only you?'

His pupils dilated, his chest rising in a shuddering breath. 'I'm sure you can think of something.'

In the end there was only one way to prove herself, one language they both understood. In the early hours of the morning, when every last guest had been wined and dined and sent on their way, she kissed her way down Javier's lean, powerful body and revelled in the shudders that shook his frame.

Mounting him, she took him deep inside her, watched him fight his control for an age before he finally roared his release. Catching her to him, he murmured thick, incoherent words in Spanish. And she...barely stopped herself from saying words that had no place in what was happening between them. Clasping her arms around him, she held him tight till he drifted off to sleep.

Only then did she reach for her phone to read the message she'd returned upstairs to find waiting for her.

Funds received. If you want to know what happened to your mother come home. But come alone.

Javier told himself it was tiredness casting the shadows in Carla's eyes. He even managed to believe it for the better part of a week. She smiled when he walked into the room, engaged him fully and attentively in conversation, and lost herself completely in his arms each time desire whipped sharp and urgent between them.

But something was wrong. Her laughter wasn't quite as carefree and a fleeting expression of panic crossed her face when she thought he wasn't looking. Most telling of all, she'd begun to catch her hair up in that blasted knot again. Javier was certain she wasn't aware she was doing it. Each time he'd reached out to free it, she'd looked surprised. And a touch alarmed.

He gritted his teeth and tossed his pen onto his desk. Swivelling in his chair, he stared out at the New York skyline, wondering if geography was playing a part in the general sour mood he found himself in today.

After her last X-ray her doctor had agreed to remove her cast and replace it with a tensor bandage. She'd also conditionally freed Carla to work, and she'd wholeheartedly thrown herself into the tequila shoot. The test shots strewn across his desk were already perfect. He turned back and stared at the photos.

Dios, she was breathtaking. The pale gold skater leotard and gold-hued tights gave the illusion of her being nude, with the exception of the gold ice skates adoring her feet. Stunning green eyes, made up to deliver a sultry look, stared straight into the camera…into him…her legs parted wide enough to frame the life-size bottle as her fingers gripped its neck.

The results surpassed his every expectation. She was sexy, provocative enough to guarantee a mega-successful launch. The creative director had proclaimed herself happy with her so far and had progressed to the ice-skate shoot. In another forty-eight hours, the shoot would be over.

She would be back in New York with him. With her eyes still shadowed with emotions she was determined to hide from him.

Snarling a curse, he reached for the phone.

She answered on the second ring, with the same breathy excitement she'd met him with when he'd flown back to Miami at the end of each working day. Each time he'd hoped the shadows would be gone. Each time he'd looked deeper and found they'd grown.

'*Ciao*, Javier.'

'I have your test photos on my desk,' he said as a starter, because he didn't want to be met with a patently false *nothing* when he asked what was wrong.

'And?' she asked, a thin thread of dread lacing her voice.

'They're good.'

Her laughter held a tinge of relief. 'Just good? Jemma must have been exaggerating then when she said you loved them?'

He relaxed in his seat, a knot of tension unravelling from

his shoulders. 'Fine. They're great. How did the practice shoot go?'

'I'll let you be the judge of it. I detest watching myself on video. And there wasn't much actual skating involved. Just a lot of simulated moves and posing.'

Javier refrained from mentioning he had a copy of it awaiting his review on his laptop. He wasn't exactly sure why he hadn't been able to bring himself to watch it yet. 'You'll get my verdict soon enough,' he prevaricated.

'Are you on your way homc?'

He heard the careful anticipation laced with the tiny trepidation and his fingers tightened around the phone. The urge to batter her defences, demand to know what she was hiding, powered through him. But he couldn't fight this battle. Not just yet.

'No. Not tonight.'

'What…umm…why?'

'My father got in touch. I guess the waiting game is over. I'm flying to Spain tonight.'

Silence punctuated by her soft breathing flowed over him. Javier wanted to demand her every thought, her every need. But he kept silent.

'How long will you be away?' she finally asked.

'Two days, three at the most. He has no bargaining chips remaining.' And he intended to drive that message home should his father decide to indulge in another useless ego trip.

'I hope you're successful,' she murmured.

All of a sudden, he'd had enough. Enough of dancing around their issues. Enough of the distance yawning between them. 'Come with me,' he suggested.

She gave a soft gasp that reached into him and settled around his heart. 'I can't. I would be sabotaging your project if I left now.'

'I don't care.'

'I do, and so should you.'

'Are you berating me?' he growled.

'I wouldn't dream of it,' she flung back.

'Are you at the ice rink?'

'*Sì*...yes.' The trepidation in her voice grew. 'I'm laced up and ready to go.'

'*Querida?*'

Her voice caught. 'Yes?'

'You're perfect. You'll be fine.'

A tiny broken sound escaped her. '*Grazie*. I... I needed that.' Voices murmured in the background. 'I have to go, Javier.'

The knot returned to his shoulder. Larger. Tighter. A similar one settled on his chest. 'I'll call you tonight.' He paused. 'Tell me you'll miss me,' he ordered softly.

A tiny sigh echoed in his ear, followed by taut silence. '*Sì*, I will miss you.'

The click of the line came far too soon. He wanted to call her back immediately. Wanted to hear her voice again.

Javier realised in the moment before he jumped to his feet and scooped up his laptop that he wanted a whole raft of things when it came to Carla Nardozzi. Things he had no right to demand but was going to anyway. As soon as he put his mother's ethereal and corporeal remains to rest.

Halfway across the Atlantic, he finally clicked on the link.

Her short, gold-spangled dress hugged her hips then flared out mid-thigh. Her hair flowed freely, just the way he liked it. Among the extras hired for the shoot, she shone bright and vibrant. She swayed to salsa music, arms outstretched to embrace life or a lover lucky enough to be allowed into her orbit.

Then, staring straight into the camera, she spoke the words. 'La Pasión. Taste the Edge. Live the Edge.'

He shut down the video, and the laptop, and swallowed hard as every ragged, unravelled sensation he'd felt around her finally made intense, mind-bending sense.

For three long years, she'd ruled his thoughts, peppered his every fleeting relationship. Not just because she had struck to the heart of his masculine pride. *Sí*, there had been that. He couldn't deny it. But more than that, Carla had struck something deeper, more substantial. Only he'd failed to see it till now.

His hand jerked towards the phone. But he pulled back. What he needed to say to her couldn't be done over the phone. He had to be there, in front of her, staring into her eyes.

He exhaled. A few days. A week, tops. Then this insanity would end.

Ten days later, Javier landed on the lawn of his Miami home and sprinted towards the house. The self-imposed radio silence from the moment he'd arrived in Menor Compostela had been hell itself, but he'd needed it to deal with the chaos he'd suddenly found himself embroiled in.

Vaulting up the shallow steps where the garden ended and the terrace began, he threw open the double doors and startled an advancing Constanza.

'Where is she?' he demanded as he crossed the room. His calls en route to the airport in Spain hadn't been answered. Neither had the ones he'd made on his plane heading home.

'*Señor?*'

'Carla. Is she upstairs?' he threw over his shoulder as he trotted into the hallway. He slowed as his housekeeper shook her head.

'*Lo siento, señor*, but the *señorita*, she's gone.'

His foot froze on the bottom step. 'What do you mean, *gone*?' Ice rolled down his spine even as he said the words. Because hadn't a part of him known? Hadn't a part of him suspected this would happen?

Futile anger congealed in his stomach as Constanza's gaze turned to pity. 'She left four days ago, *señor*.'

His breath punched through his throat. 'She's been gone

for over half a week and—?' And what? He'd given no explanation to his staff as to her presence in his life. As far as his employees were concerned, she was just the woman who'd been working for him by day and warming his bed at night. They'd afforded her respect because she'd been with him, but beyond that Carla might as well have been a treasured painting hung on a wall and admired but nothing else.

He slashed his fingers through his hair, his feet pounding the hallway as he paced back and forth. Belatedly, he realised his housekeeper was trying to get his attention.

'Yes?'

She reached into her pocket, warily extracted the folded envelope and held it out. Puzzled, Javier glanced at it. 'What's that?'

'Señorita Carla, she left it for you.'

CHAPTER THIRTEEN

'I NOW PRONOUNCE you husband and wife.'

Why did I come?

Why did he?

Her letter had been clear. More than clear. And his silence in the weeks after had all but shouted his acceptance of her need for no contact. So why was Javier sitting behind her in the church pew, his eyes glued to her back? She knew she wasn't deluding herself about the potency of his stare. He'd arrived ten minutes after the ceremony had started. She knew because the murmurs his presence had drawn had made her look behind her.

One look.

One ferocious, intensely rigid stare back from him, and she'd hastily straightened.

He hadn't joined in the hymns. Or snapped a photo of the stunning bride and groom sharing their first kiss. He'd remained, statue-still behind her, his attention riveted one hundred per cent on her.

The foolish wish that she'd worn her hair down was quickly squashed beneath more desperate anguish. The realisation on the night of his birthday party that she loved him had come as no real surprise to her. Nor had the inevitable acceptance that her love was doomed to bring her nothing but pain. She'd lost her head over him in record time. Or had that love been lying dormant for three years, her heart already his to possess the moment he'd possessed her?

Carla had spent far too many hours debating the whys and wherefores. Each had brought her to the same conclusion. There had never been one single hope of a future with Javier. Her tie to him should've begun and ended on paper.

Except it hadn't…

It had begun with her body and ended up in her soul—

'Are you going to sit there all day, pretending I don't exist?' his hard voice snarled in her ear.

Carla started. A quick glance showed the last of the wedding guests straggling out of the small island chapel where Draco and Rebel had married in his native Greece. Outside the sun blazed in its oblivious glory. Inside, she shivered, her heart leaping into her throat as she finally allowed herself to look at Javier.

His neatly trimmed five o'clock shadow accentuated his hollower cheekbones, his bespoke suit draped upon his lean body with an inherent grace and elegance reserved for demigods.

Standing, she faced him properly. 'Javier—'

'No. We're not doing this here. Two people have been lucky enough to find what they want in each other. I won't ruin their day.'

'Then why did you come?'

Dark brows clouded. *'Perdón?'*

'Despite my asking, no, *pleading*, with you to give me space, here you are. You could've stayed on the opposite side of the chapel. There are over five hundred guests here. We needn't have seen each other. And yet here you are.'

His nostrils flared, as if he couldn't believe the words spilling from her lips. 'Because you owe me an explanation. And because you chose to vanish off the face of the earth for the past three weeks. *That is why!*'

Her heart slammed into her stomach. 'My letter wasn't enough?'

His hand slashed the air. 'Your letter was—' He stopped, then shook his head. 'I won't be drawn into this here with you, Carla. We will go outside and wish the happy couple well. We will stay for a glass or two of champagne. I might even bring myself to dance with you. But you and I will leave this island together. Tonight. And we will settle this once and for all.'

He whirled from her, his designer shoes clicking in perfect staccato as he headed outside.

Following him, Carla saw heads turn as he joined the wedding party. Handshakes and kisses were exchanged with the bride and groom. Then he was turning towards her once more. Icy eyes locked on hers as he held out his hand to her. But within the depths, Carla caught an edgy vulnerability, a faint light that attempted to jump-start her hopes. Carla berated herself for reading signs where there were none.

His jaw turned to granite at her hesitation.

'For heaven's sake, Carla. If you don't grab onto that and hold on with everything you've got, I damn well will.'

The exasperated whisper came from beside her. She looked down to see Maria glaring at her. 'Go, dammit.'

She went. Not because she truly believed there was something to grab onto. But because before her heart shrivelled up and deserted her for the final time, she wanted to touch Javier. Selfishly feel his vibrant skin against hers one last time.

His fingers closed over hers and her blood kicked back into her veins.

This is an illusion. This is temporary.

Everything about this is temporary.

But she took her seat next to him at the great wedding feast. Clinked glasses with him for the wedding toast. Smashed plates and applauded Draco and Rebel's first dance.

Javier didn't offer to dance with her after all. Which was just as well. Her heart had dropped to her toes by the time Rebel left to change for her honeymoon trip.

'Excuse me,' she murmured, then fled before Javier could stop her.

She found Draco momentarily alone in one corner of the many terraces that graced his multi-storeyed island villa.

'Draco.'

He turned, his smile blisteringly radiant, before he frowned. Catching her by the arm, he drew his thumb down her cheek. 'Carla, are you all right?'

She blinked back tears that had been clogged in her throat for hours. 'Please, don't worry about me. Today belongs to you. I'll find my own way to be okay. I promise.'

His frown deepened. 'Carla…'

She stood on tiptoe and hastily placed a kiss on his cheek. 'Give my love to Rebel.'

Turning, she found Javier standing six feet away. The bleakness that lanced his features tore at her. Again hope threatened to rise.

But she was tired. And battered.

She walked past him, through the ballroom overlooking sheer cliffs and a glorious sunset. She heard him behind her but didn't stop until she reached the lift. He entered after her, staying on one side of the small car, his arms folded as he stared straight ahead.

It was only as she stood beneath the pillared courtyard awaiting the buggy that would take her to the chopper reserved to fly guests back to the mainland that he spoke.

'Where have you been these past few weeks, Carla?'

She contemplated silence. Talking was dangerous. It fed an urge to reveal innermost desires that had no chance of birth, never mind growth. But this was a safe subject that had nothing to do with her breaking heart. 'My mother bought a cottage near Maidstone, on the English coast where she grew up. She left it to me. I put it on the market when my father…when I thought I'd need the funds. Three weeks ago the agents contacted me with an offer. I came down with the intention to clear it out.'

'But you decided a cottage in the middle of nowhere was the perfect hiding spot?'

'I wasn't hiding.'

The buggy arrived. He helped her into it, then took his place next to her. From shoulder to thigh, their bodies connected. Carla lost the power of speech. And Javier didn't seem inclined to continue their conversation as they were driven towards the aircraft area.

When the buggy started to slow down beside the chopper, Javier tapped the valet on the shoulder. 'Take us to the airstrip.'

'But I'm going to the mainland to catch my flight back to England.'

His mouth flattened. 'You can catch a flight with me. Or we can talk on my plane before you catch your flight. Either way, we're talking.'

'Javier, this is pointless.'

A look of actual pain crossed his face, making her want to take back her words. But short of the definitive words or the commitment from him whose twin was lodged in her heart, she knew nothing would ease her heartache. And being with him, like this, was turning out to be far worse than she'd imagined.

The buggy arrived at the steps of his plane. He got out and waited, his eyes hard and unmoving on hers.

To prolong this would be to prolong her pain. She alighted and climbed the steps into the plane.

Save a single attendant, there was no sign of Javier's crew. Which was good because she didn't want witnesses to her heartache.

The plane took off in record time. The moment the seat-belt sign flashed off, Javier surged to his feet.

He paced the space in front of her for terse minutes, before he leaned over her chair.

'What must I do to prove to you that I can be worthy of you? How can I even do that if you won't give me a chance?'

Carla's mouth dropped open. 'What are you talking about?'

Reaching into his jacket, he produced a familiar-looking sheet. 'I'm talking about this,' he snarled. 'Your *Dear John* letter.'

'You…kept it?'

Incredulity lightened his eyes. 'That's what interests you in all this? Whether or not I kept your letter?'

He slammed the sheet on the table next to her. 'Explain it, *por favor.*'

She licked lips gone dry with trepidation. 'Which part?'

'*All of it!*'

Carla stared down at the words that had killed her to write, her limbs leaden as she reached for the single, most difficult thing she'd ever had to do.

Javier,
I returned to the ice today, and you were right. I love it. It's in my blood. But I'm not in love with it. Not at the moment. Maybe it will return. Maybe it won't. I need to give it time.

There's an old saying about loving something and letting it go, right? But I allowed myself to love it again for the sake of your shoot. I hope you like the result. If you don't... I'm sorry, but I'm done. Done faking. Done pretending I don't want what I want.

I deserve better than that. We both do. I still intend to fulfil my endorsement obligations to you. But I think it would be best if I deal with your team going forward. You will most likely be angry with me, but I hope you grant me this clean break.

For all that has gone before, I'm sorry. But please, let me be.
Carla

The paper disappeared as he snatched it back up. A peculiar fire blazed in his eyes. 'You're done *faking*? Exactly which part did you fake with me? The days when you couldn't stop smiling at each new experience we shared, or the nights you came apart in my arms?' he finished, his voice a hoarse, bleak rasp.

Her breath shook out in searing recollection. She reached out, for what, she didn't know, but he turned in a tight, horribly graceless pace.

'You want what you want? How am I supposed to have a chance of offering myself up to help you achieve it when you disappear without trace?'

'I didn't think you'd want me to stay, knowing…'

He stopped. 'Knowing what?'

She shook her head. 'It doesn't matter. You said you'd be gone for a few days…that you'd call. You didn't…'

'So you took it as an excuse to bail? When will you stop running from me? From *us*?' He stared down at her, a stiff entreaty in his eyes, before he shook his head. 'Maybe I'm truly insane. I have to be, don't I, to keep throwing myself at your feet when you don't want me?'

She gasped. 'Javier—'

'You're right. You deserve better. I just haven't been self-less enough to see it.' He balled the letter and thrust it into his pocket, before he gripped his own nape in a merciless hold. 'I didn't call you because my father was in the middle of having a stroke when I arrived.'

'What?'

'He survived, but he's lost the power of speech and will most likely be wheelchair-bound for the rest of his life.'

'I… I don't know what to say.'

His mouth twisted. 'I think you've said plenty. Anyway, under his power of attorney, his eldest son has assumed his responsibilities. I was able to negotiate with him. He signed the document allowing my mother to be buried with her family.'

She stood and moved towards him. 'I'm so pleased this is over for you. That you both have closure.'

He inclined his head, but the mask of weariness and pain didn't dissipate. When his gaze lifted, his eyes held pools of deep anguish. 'What did I do that was so unforgivable, Carla? Was it forcing you to be my mistress? You didn't sleep with me against your will, I *know* that.'

She reached out and touched him, unable to abide his

pain. 'No, it wasn't that. It was never that. I left because I had to. I stayed gone because—'

'What do you mean you *had to*?'

'My father texted me on the night of your party. He was ready to tell me what happened to my mother.'

'Why didn't you tell me? I would've taken you—'

'That's just what he didn't want. He wanted me to come alone. I was terrified it meant the worst. That he'd killed her in a rage because I'd asked her to intervene with him on my behalf.'

'And did it?'

She shook her head, the relief of finally being able to put it behind her easing her heartache. 'It was an accident. Caused because they were rowing, and she was trying to get away from him, but it was an accident. She stormed out of the house and didn't watch were she was going. She slipped and hit her head going into the pool. My father had security cameras installed when he started buying expensive art. I… couldn't bring myself to watch all of it, but I saw enough to know he was telling the truth…'

'And he kept all this from you because…?'

She shrugged, although the pain of that knowledge deadened her limbs. As did the pain of her decision to walk away from her father, once and for all. Somewhere down the line, she might learn to forgive him for some of the things he'd done, but right now she was too raw to even bear the thought of him. 'It was just another way for him to control me, and he took it.'

Javier cursed, long and dark. His hand jerked out, as if to reach for her. At the last moment, it dropped to his side. 'You said you left because you had to go. What kept you from coming back?' he asked in a dead voice.

'You.'

'*Sí*, of course. The problem has always been me.'

'Yes, it has. Loving you has been a big problem for me. But living without you will be an even greater one.'

He paled. All colour left his vibrant face as he stood thirty thousand feet up in the air. 'You…' He shook his head. '*No entiendo.* I don't understand.'

She closed the distance between them and cradled his face in her hands. 'I didn't come back to you because I thought you only wanted me for the short term. I couldn't stand the thought of staying and loving you only to be cast aside sooner or later.'

Feverish eyes examined her for an age, before he shut his eyes in disbelief. 'I've loved you for three desperate years, *querida.* You ripped my heart out when you walked away from me that morning. After that I tried every means possible to get you back in my life. And now you…you…' He groaned and slanted his mouth over hers. The kiss wasn't gentle or sweet. It was three years of ravaging want and passionate need plugged full bore into their beings.

When he raised his head, they both gasped for air. Without giving her a chance to recover, he swung her into his arms and headed for the master suite at the back of the plane.

Clothes ripped in a frenzy of impatient desire. Fingers locked in her hair and pulled out pins. 'You're not allowed to wear your hair up again. Ever.' He caught her by the waist and rushed her to the bed.

Laughter, pure and joyous, ripped from her throat. 'What about when I'm competing?'

'You've decided to go back to the ice?'

'Not just yet. I want to enjoy being with you for a little bit. But I feel my love for it returning every day.'

He stretched out beside her and caught her face in his hand. 'It will be more glorious than ever, *mi amor.* And before that we will make up for every single day we've wasted thus far.'

Her back arched off the bed as he trailed his hand down her body. 'And how do you propose to do that?' she rasped in a voice heavy with desire.

'By signing you to another contract, of course.' He surged above her and parted her thighs.

'What type of contract?'

'A lifelong one, where you wear my ring and take my name. And where I get to worship you every night and love you every day,' he responded, his voice guttural with need. 'Do you accept?'

Tears filled her eyes. 'I accept. You were my first and my only, and I vow to be yours for ever.'

With pure adulation lighting his eyes, he entered her with one smooth thrust.

'*Lo ti adoro*, Javier.'

'As do I, *mi amor*. Never, ever doubt it.'

* * * * *

REVENGE AT THE ALTAR

LOUISE FULLER

To the Nell, for holding my hand on the plane
and not cutting your hair!

All my love.

CHAPTER ONE

As THE WHEELS OF her private jet hit the runway Margot Duvernay looked up from her laptop and gazed pensively out of the window, her fingers twisting at the 'Team Bride' wristband on her arm.

As CEO of the legendary House of Duvernay champagne business, she worked hard. The last five years had been particularly challenging, both emotionally and financially—so much so that, incredibly, Gisele's bachelorette week in Monte Carlo was the first time off she'd had in months.

But her father Emile's unexpected message had abruptly cut short her stay.

Walking purposefully across the T tarmac, she climbed into the waiting air-conditioned limousine and pulled out her phone. She replayed his message, frowning at the giggling and the Bossa Nova music she could hear in the background. If only she had picked it up sooner, she thought regretfully, her soft brown eyes creasing. Emile was just so unreliable, and so easily distracted...

But on the plus side he had definitely mentioned *selling* his shares, and that was a first.

Leaning back against the seat, she watched as the beautiful mansard-roofed headquarters of her family's two-hundred-and-fifty-year-old business came into view, feeling a familiar mix of pride and responsibility. She loved everything about the building—the cool, quiet interior, the sense of history in the wood-panelled boardroom and the symmetry of the façade. To her, it was more than just bricks and plaster. It was a legacy—and also a burden.

Just like the position of CEO.

Margot breathed out slowly.

Growing up, she had never imagined being in charge of Duvernay—never once wanted the power or the responsibility. By nature, she loathed being in the spotlight, and after graduating she'd been happy to head up the company's newly created environmental department.

However, her older brother Yves's tragic death on the ski slopes of Verbier had left her with no alternative but to take over the family business. Of course, Emile would have liked the status of running a global brand. But even if he hadn't been cold-shouldered by his in-laws, he preferred topping up his tan to analyzing market trends. Her brother Louis might have been taller than her, but at just sixteen he had been far too young to step up, and her grandfather had been too old, too devastated by grief. It had been hard enough for him to deal with his daughter's accidental drug overdose, but the shock of losing his grandson too had caused a series of strokes from which he had still not fully recovered.

And so it had been left to Margot to do what she had always done—pick up the pieces—and that was why she was hurrying back to Epernay this morning.

Inside the brightly lit foyer, the reassuring familiarity of everything calmed her slightly, but as she stepped into the lift her phone began to vibrate in her hand and she felt her composure wobble. Glancing down at the screen, she drew in a quick, shaky breath and her heart began to pound with a mixture of hope and relief.

Thank goodness! Finally it was her father.

'Emile. I was just about to call you—'

'Really? I thought you might be sulking.'

Gritting her teeth, Margot felt a spasm of irritation. Honestly, her father was so exasperating, and so monumentally thoughtless sometimes. When he hadn't returned her messages she had started to panic, to worry that maybe he'd changed his mind. Clearly, though, he'd just been playing hard to get.

But now she could hear the elation in his voice and suddenly she didn't care about his stupid games. What mattered was that she knew he'd been telling the truth. Finally he was ready to sell the shares.

Her heart began to beat faster.

The timing couldn't be better.

Not only would it mean that the business would be whole again in time for her brother Louis's wedding, it would also give her grandfather a much-needed boost. Since his last stroke he hadn't been himself, but this would be the perfect tonic. For this wedding was more than just a romantic ceremony—it was about continuing the family name and ensuring the future of Duvernay.

She felt her chest tighten. And, of course, for her, buying back her father's shares would have an additional and thankfully undisclosed benefit of sending a strong message to the bank.

'Oh, Papa.' Her father was such a child, but today of all days she was prepared to indulge him, and so, despite her annoyance, she spoke placatingly. 'You know I've been trying to get hold of you. I must have rung you at least a dozen times.'

She felt a rush of excitement as she played back her father's rambling message inside her head. He'd mentioned something about flying up to Reims, but that had been hours ago. She glanced at her watch. Surely he must be here by now?

Her mouth was suddenly almost too dry to get words out. 'Where are you staying? I can come to you, or I can send a car to pick you up.'

Her pulse accelerated. She couldn't believe it. Finally it was happening. The moment she'd been waiting for almost her whole life.

Buying back the 'lost' shares, as her grandfather referred to them, was a goal that had preoccupied her since she'd taken over the reins of the business. In doing so, she would not only make Duvernay whole again, she would also bring closure to the whole sorry complex mess of her parents' marriage and the repercussions that had followed her mother's tragic death.

She felt her pulse tremble.

Her father and her grandparents had always had a fraught relationship. Emile might look like a film star, but to them he was just a horse trainer—eloping with their nineteen-year-old daughter had not endeared him to her straitlaced and image-conscious family. His decision to live off Colette's trust fund had merely deepened the rift.

But after her death, it had been his refusal to turn over her shares to his children that had turned a difficult relationship into a bitter stand-off.

Emile had always claimed it was an act of self-preservation. Her grandparents had seen it as an act of spite. Either way, the facts were undeniable. Her father had threatened to take her and her brothers to Switzerland if he wasn't allowed to hold on to the shares, and her grandfather had agreed to his demands on two conditions: that he give up custody of his children to his in-laws and that they keep their mother's name.

Margot shivered. Once she had thought that grief might

bring the two sides of her family closer. In fact the reverse had happened. There was still such bad blood between Emile and his in-laws that even now they both took every opportunity to point-score.

But maybe now that might finally change.

The thought made her heart leap upwards. It would just be so wonderful to put all of this behind them before Louis's wedding. Her first task, though, was to pin Emile down...

'Papa?' she repeated, trying to sound casual. 'Just tell me where you'd like to meet.'

'That's why I'm calling—'

His voice had changed. He sounded a little uneasy—defiant, almost—and briefly she wondered why. But before she had a chance to give it any more thought he started talking again.

'I did try, so you can't blame me— Not now, *chérie*, put it over there. I waited as long as I could...'

Hearing a soft but unmistakably feminine murmur, Margot frowned. Even now her father couldn't manage to give her his full and undivided attention. Her mouth thinned. No doubt he was already celebrating the upcoming sale of his shares with his current batch of hangers-on.

And then her heartbeat froze, and she felt her fingers tighten involuntarily around the phone as his words bumped into one another inside her head like dodgems at the funfair. 'Blame you for what?'

'I waited as long as I could, *poussin*, but it was such a good offer—'

His use of her childhood nickname as much as his wheedling tone sent a ripple of alarm over her skin. Her father only ever called her *poussin*—little chick—when he wanted something or when he wanted to be forgiven.

'What offer?' she said slowly.

The lift doors opened and she stepped out into the glass-ceilinged atrium. Straight ahead, she noticed her PA hovering nervously in front of her office door, and her heart gave a sickening thump.

'What have you done, Papa?'

'I've done what I should have done a long time ago.' The wheedling tone had shifted, become defensive. 'So I hope you're not going to make a fuss, Margot. I mean, it's what you've been telling me to do for years—sell my shares. And now I have. And I have to say I got a damn good price for them too.'

It was as if a bomb had exploded inside her head. Blood was roaring in her ears and the floor seemed to ripple beneath her feet.

'You said that if you were going to sell your shares you'd come to me first.' Margot felt panic, hot and slippery, run down her spine.

'And I did.' There was a burst of laughter in the background and she felt her father's attention shift and divert away from her. 'But you didn't pick up.'

'I couldn't. I was having a massage.' She let out a breath. 'Look, Papa, we can sort this out. Just don't sign anything, okay? Just stay where you are and I will come to you.'

'It's too late now. I signed the paperwork first thing this morning. And I *mean* first thing. He got me out of bed,' he grumbled. 'Anyway, there's no point in getting out of shape with me—just talk to *him*. He should be there by now.'

'Who—?' she began, but even without the tell-tale clink of ice against glass she could tell her father was no longer listening.

She heard the click of his lighter, then the slow expulsion of smoke. 'Apparently that's why it all had to be done so early. He wanted to get up to Epernay…take a look around headquarters.'

Margot gazed dazedly across the honey-coloured parquet floor. No wonder her staff were looking so confused. Clearly the newest Duvernay shareholder was already on site. But who was he—and what had he told them?

Her pulse stuttered in time with her footsteps. There were already enough rumours circulating around the company as it was—and what would the bank think if they heard that Emile had suddenly decided to sell his shares?

Silently she cursed herself for not picking up her messages—and her father for being so utterly, irredeemably selfish.

'It'll be fine,' Emile was saying briskly.

Now that the worst was over he was clearly itching to be gone.

'You're so rational and practical, *poussin.*'

She could almost see him shuddering even at the concept of such qualities.

'Just talk to him. Maybe you can persuade him to sell them back to you.'

He was desperate to be off. If Margot had been the sort to scream or hurl abuse she would have unleashed the tide of invective churning in her throat. But she wasn't. A lifetime of watching the soap opera that had been her parents' marriage had cured her of any desire for a scene. For a moment, though, she considered telling Emile in the most *ir*rational, *im*practical terms exactly what she thought of him.

Only, really, what was the point? Her father's 'me first' morality was precisely why he'd kept the shares in the first place.

'Although somehow I doubt it…'

Her father exhaled again, and she pictured him stubbing out his cigarette with the same careless force with which he had upended her dreams of taking back control of Duvernay.

'He seemed absolutely set on having them. But, truthfully, I think I might have done you a favour. I mean, he *is* the man of the moment, right?'

The man of the moment.

Margot blinked. Her brain was whirling, her thoughts flying in a hundred directions. She had read that headline. Not the article, for that would have been too painful. But, walking through the centre of Paris last month, she had found it impossible to tear her gaze away from the newsstands. Or more particularly the head-and-shoulders shot that had accompanied the article, and those eyes—one blue, one green—staring down the Champs-Élysées as if he owned it.

'Man of the moment?'

Her voice sounded blurred, shapeless—like a candle flame that had burnt the whole wick and was floundering in wax.

'Yeah—Max Montigny. They say he can turn water into wine, so I guess he'll give those stuffy vignerons a run for their money— Yeah, I'll be right there.'

Margot tried to speak, but her breath was thick and tangled in her throat. 'Papa—' she began, but it was too late. He was talking over her.

'Look, call me later—well, maybe not later, but whenever. I love you, but I have to go—'

The phone went dead.

But not as dead as she felt.

Max Montigny.

It had been almost ten years since she'd last seen him. Ten years of trying to pretend their relationship, his lies, her heartbreak, that none of it had happened. And she'd done a pretty good job, she thought dully.

Of course it had helped that only Yves had ever known the full story. To everyone else Max had been at first a trusted employee, and later a favoured friend of the family.

To her, though, he had been a fantasy made flesh. With smooth dark hair, a profile so pure it looked as though it had been cut with a knife, and a lean, muscular body that hummed with energy, he had been like a dark star that seemed to tug at all her five senses whenever she was within his orbit.

Only as far as he was concerned Margot had been invisible. No, maybe not invisible. He *had* noticed her, but only in the same jokey way that her own brother had— smiling at her off-handedly as he joined the family for dinner, or casually offering to drive her into town when it was raining.

And then one day, instead of looking through her, he had stared at her so intently she had forgotten to breathe, forgotten to look away.

Remembering that moment, the impossibility of not holding his gaze, her cheeks felt suddenly as though they were on fire.

She had been captivated by him, enthralled and enchanted. She would have followed him blindly into darkness, and in a way she had—for she had gone into his arms and to his bed, given herself to him willingly, eagerly.

From then on he had been everything to her. Her man of the moment. Her man for ever.

Until the day he'd broken her heart and walked out of her life without so much as a flicker of remorse in those haunting eyes.

Afterwards, the pain had been unbearable. Feigning illness, she'd stayed in bed for days, curled up small and still beneath her duvet, chest aching with anguish, throat tight with tears she hadn't allowed herself to weep for fear that her grandfather would notice.

But now was not the time for tears either and, swallowing the hard shard of misery in her throat, Margot greeted her PA with what she hoped was a reasonable approximation of her usual composure.

'Good morning, Simone.'

'Good morning, *madame*.' Simone hesitated. Colour was creeping over her cheekbones and she seemed flustered. 'I'm sorry, I didn't know you were coming in today. But he—Mr Montigny, I mean—he said you were expecting him.'

Smiling, Margot nodded. So it was true. Just for a moment she had hoped—wanted to believe that she had somehow misunderstood Emile. But this was confirmation. Max was here.

'I hope that's okay…?'

Her PA's voice trailed off and Margot felt her own cheekbones start to ache with the effort of smiling. Poor Simone! Her normally poised PA looked flushed and jumpy. But then no doubt she'd been a recent recipient of the famous but sadly superficial Montigny charm.

'Yes, it's fine, Simone. And it's my fault—I should have called ahead. Is he in my office?'

She felt a stab of anger. Max had only been back in her life for a matter of minutes and already she was lying for him.

Simone shook her head, her confusion giving way to obvious relief. 'No, he said that he would like to see the boardroom. I didn't think it would be a problem…'

Margot kept smiling but she felt a sudden savage urge to cry, to rage against the injustice and cruelty of it all. If only she could be like any other normal young woman, like Gisele and her friends, drinking cocktails and flirting with waiters.

But crying and raging was not the Duvernay way—or at least, not in public—and instead she merely nodded again. 'It's not. In fact, I'll go and give him the full guided tour myself.'

Straight out the door and out of my life, she thought savagely.

Turning, she walked towards the boardroom, her eyes fixed on the polished brass door handle. If only she could just keep on walking. Only what would be the point? Max Montigny wasn't here by chance. Nor was he just going to give up and disappear. Like it or not, the only way she was going to turn him back into being nothing more than a painful memory was by confronting him.

And, lifting her chin, she turned the door handle and stepped into the boardroom.

She saw him immediately, and although she had expected to feel *something*, nothing could have prepared her for the rush of despair and regret that swept over her.

It was nearly ten years since he had walked out of her life. Ten years was a long time, and everyone said that time was a great healer. But if that was true why, then, was her body trembling? And why did her heart feel like a lead weight?

Surely he shouldn't matter to her any more? But, seeing him again, she felt the same reaction she had that first time, aged just nineteen. That he couldn't be real. That no actual living man could be so unutterably beautiful. It wasn't possible or fair.

He was facing away from her, slumped in one of the leather armchairs that were arranged around the long oval table, his long legs sprawled negligently in front of him, seemingly admiring the view from the window.

Her heart was racing, but her legs and arms seemed to have stopped working. Gazing at the back of his head, at the smooth dark hair that she had so loved to caress, she thought she might throw up.

How could this be happening? she thought dully. But that was the wrong question. What she needed to ask— *and answer*—was how could she *stop* it happening? How could she get him out of her boardroom and out of her life?

Letting out a breath, she closed the door and watched, mesmerised, as slowly he swung round in the chair to face her. She stared at him in silence. This was the man who had not only broken her heart, but shattered her pride and her romantic ideals. Once she had loved him. And afterwards she had hated him.

Only clearly her feelings weren't that simple—or maybe she had just forgotten how effortlessly Max could throw her off balance. For although heat was rising up inside her, she knew that it wasn't the arid heat of loathing but something that felt a lot like desire.

Her mouth was suddenly dry, and her heart was beating so fast and so loud that it sounded like a drumroll— as though Max was the winner in some game show. She breathed in sharply. But what was his prize?

Gazing into his eyes—those incredible heterochromatic eyes—she saw herself reflected in the blue and green, no longer nineteen, but still dazzled and dazed.

All those years ago he had been model-handsome, turning heads as easily as he now turned grapes into wine and wine into profit. His straight, patrician jaw and high cheekbones had hinted at a breathtaking adult beauty to come, and that promise had been more than met. A shiver ran through her body. Met, and enhanced by a dark grey suit that seemed purposely designed to draw her gaze to the spectacular body that she knew lay beneath.

Her breath caught in her chest and, petrified that the expression on her face might reveal her thoughts, she pushed aside the unsettling image of a naked Max and forced herself to meet his gaze.

He smiled, and the line of his mouth arrowed through her skin.

'Margot…it's been a long time.'

As he spoke she felt a tingling shock. His voice hadn't changed, and that wasn't fair, for—like his eyes—it was utterly distinctive, and made even the dullest of words sound like spring water. It was just so soft, sexy…

And utterly untrustworthy, she reminded herself irritably. Having been on the receiving end of it, she knew from first-hand experience that the softness was like spun sugar—a clever trick designed to seduce, and to gift-wrap the parcel of lies that came out of his mouth.

'Not long enough,' she said coolly.

Ignoring the heat snaking over her skin, she stalked to the opposite end of the room and dropped her bag on the table. 'Why don't you give it another decade—or two, even?'

He seemed unmoved by her rudeness—or maybe, judging by the slight up-curve to his mouth, a little amused. 'I'm sorry you feel like that. Given the change in our relationship—'

'We don't *have* a relationship,' she snapped.

They never had. It was one of the facts that she'd forced herself to accept over the years—that, no matter how physically close they'd been, Max was a cipher to her. In love, and blindsided by how beautiful, how alive he'd made her feel in bed, she hadn't noticed that there had been none of the prerequisites for a happy, healthy relationship—honesty, openness, trust…

The truth was that she'd never really known him at all.

He, though, had clearly found *her* embarrassingly easy to read. Unsurprisingly! She'd been that most clichéd of adolescents: a clueless teenager infatuated with her brother's best friend. And, of course, her family was not just famous but *in*famous.

Even now, the thought of her being so transparently smitten made her cringe.

'We don't have a relationship,' she repeated. 'And a signature on a piece of paper isn't about to change that.'

His gaze held hers, and a mocking smile tugged at his mouth as he rotated the chair back and forth.

'Really?' He spoke mildly, as though they were discussing the possibility of rain. 'Why don't we call my lawyer? Or yours? See if they agree with that statement.'

Her head snapped up. It was a bonus that Max hadn't spoken to Pierre yet, but the very fact that he was hinting at the possibility of doing so made her throat tighten.

'That won't be necessary. This matter is between you and me.'

'But I thought you said we didn't have any relationship?'

She glared at him, hearing and hating the goading note in his voice.

'We don't. And we won't. I meant that this matter is private, and I intend to keep it that way.'

Max stared coldly across the table. Did she *really* think that he was going to let that happen? That she was in control of this situation.

Nearly a decade ago he had been, if not happy, then willing to keep their relationship under wraps. She had told him she needed time. That she needed to find the right moment to tell her family the truth. And he had let her beauty and her desirability blind him to the real truth— that he was a secret she would never be willing to share.

But he wasn't about to let history repeat itself.

'Are you sure about that? I mean, you know what they say about good intentions, Margot,' he said softly. 'Do you really want to head down that particular road?'

There was a taut, quivering silence, and Margot felt her face drain of colour, felt her body, her heart, shrinking away from his threat.

There's no need! she wanted to shout into his handsome face. *You've already cast me out of heaven and into a hell of your making.*

But she wasn't going to give him the satisfaction of knowing how raw her wounds still were and how much he had mattered to her.

She returned his gaze coldly. 'Are you threatening me?'

Watching the flush of colour spread over her collarbone, Max tilted his head backwards, savouring her fury. He had never seen her angry before—in fact he'd never seen her express any strong emotion.

At least not outside the bedroom.

His pulse twitched and a memory stole into his head of that first time in his room—how the directness of her gaze had held him captive as she had pressed her body against his, her fingers cutting into his back, her breath warm against his mouth.

Margot might have been serious and serene on the surface, but the first time he had kissed her properly had been a revelation. She'd been so passionate and unfettered. In fact, it had been not so much a revelation as a revolution— all heat and hunger and urgency.

Suddenly he was vibrating with a hunger of his own, and he felt heat break out on his skin. Slowly, he slid his hands over the armrests of the chair to stop himself from reaching out and pulling her against him. The muscles in his jaw tensed and he gritted his teeth.

'Only the weak and the incompetent resort to threats.

I'm merely making conversation.' He looked straight into her flushed face. 'You remember conversation, don't you, Margot? It's the thing you used to interrupt by dragging me to bed.'

Margot stared at him, her body pulsing with equal parts longing and loathing. If only she could throw his words back in his face. But it was true. Her desire for him had been frantic and inexorable.

She lifted her chin. So what if it had? Enjoying sex wasn't a crime. And it certainly wasn't sneaky or dishonest—like, say, deliberately setting out to seduce someone for their money.

Eyes narrowing, she yanked out one of the chairs with uncharacteristic roughness and sat down on it. Pulling her bag closer, she reached inside.

Max watched in silence as she pulled out a fountain pen and a leather-bound case. Ignoring him, she flipped it open and began writing with swift, sure strokes. Then, laying the pen down, she tore the paper she'd been writing on free and pushed it across the table towards him.

It was a cheque.

A cheque!

His breathing jerked and his jaw felt suddenly as though it was hewn from basalt. He didn't move, didn't even lower his gaze, just kept his eyes locked on her face as with effort he held on to the fast-fraying threads of his temper.

'What's that?' he asked softly.

Her mouth thinned. 'I don't know how your mind works, Max, and I don't want to, but I know why you're here. It's the same reason you were here ten years ago. *Money.*' Margot gestured towards the cheque. 'So why don't you just take it and go?'

He was watching her thoughtfully, his expression somewhere between incredulous and mocking. But there was a tension in him that hadn't been there before.

'That's amazing,' he said finally. 'I didn't know people actually did this kind of thing in real life. I thought it was just in films—'

'If only this was a film,' she said coldly. 'Then I could just leave you on the cutting room floor.'

Max gazed across the room, anger shrinking his focus so that all he could see was the small rectangular piece of paper lying on the tabletop. Of course it would come down to money. That was all their relationship had ever been about. Or, more precisely, his complete and utter lack of it.

Margot was a Duvernay, and Duvernays didn't marry poor outsiders. His breath seemed to harden in his lungs. Not even when they had claimed them as family, welcomed them into their home and their lives.

Briefly he let the pain and anger of his memories seep through his veins. Officially he might have been just on the payroll, but for nearly three years he had been treated like a member of the clan—and, stupid idiot that he was, he had actually come to believe in the fiction that although blood made you related, it was loyalty that made you family.

Later, when his perception hadn't been blunted by desire and emotion, it had been easy to see that any invitation into the inner sanctum had been on their terms, and it had never extended to marrying the daughter of the house.

Only by then he had lost his job, his home and his pride. He had been left penniless and powerless.

But times had changed. Leaning back, he smiled coldly. 'It's not enough.'

Margot clenched her jaw, her brown eyes glowing with anger like peat on a fire. 'Oh, believe me, it is.'

Even if she had written a row of zeros it would be more

than he deserved. He had already cost her enough—no, too much—in pain and regret.

'So take it and go.'

He shifted in his seat, and she felt another stab of anger that he should be able to do this to her. That after everything he'd already taken he could just swan back into her life, into her boardroom, and demand more.

Controlling her emotions, she closed her chequebook with exaggerated care and looked up at him. 'Why are you here, Max?'

He shrugged. 'Isn't that obvious? I'm a shareholder and a director now, so I thought we should talk.'

'You could have just telephoned,' she snapped.

'What?' His mouth curved up at one corner. 'And miss all the fun.' He let his eyes home in on the pulse beating at the base of her throat. 'Besides, I wanted to choose my office.'

She watched almost hypnotised as he gestured lazily around the room. 'Pick out a desk…wallpaper maybe…'

Folding her arms to stop her hands shaking, she glowered at him. The shock of everything—her father's phone message, Max buying the shares, his sudden and unwelcome reappearance in her life—was suddenly too much to endure a moment longer.

'Just stop it, okay? *Stop it*. This is insane. You can't seriously expect to work here. Or want to.'

He raised an eyebrow. 'Is there a problem?'

She looked at him in disbelief. 'Yes, of course there's a problem. You and me…our history—'

Breaking off, she fought to control the sudden jab of pain at the memory of just how cruelly one-sided that history had been.

'I don't care how many shares you buy, you are not stepping foot in this boardroom again. So how much is it?' She forced a business-like tone into her voice. 'How much do you want?'

She waited for his reply but it didn't come. And then, as the silence seemed to stretch beyond all normal limits, she felt her spine stiffen with horror as slowly he shook his head.

'I don't want and I certainly don't need your money.'

Watching the doubt and confusion in her eyes, he felt suddenly immensely satisfied. Buying the shares had been an act of insanity on so many levels, but now, having Margot in front of him, knowing that his mere presence had dragged her here, it all felt worth it.

Colour was spreading slowly over her cheeks.

'Take the cheque or don't—I don't care.' She lifted her chin. 'But either way this conversation is over. And now I suggest you leave before I have you removed—'

'That's not going to happen.' His voice sounded normal—pleasant, even—but she felt a shiver of apprehension, for there was a strand of steel running through every syllable that matched the combative glint in his eyes.

'I'm not just the hired help now, baby. I'm CEO of a global wine business. More importantly, as of today, I'm a bona fide director of this company.'

He paused, and she felt as if the air was being sucked out of the room as he let his gaze linger on her face. Pulse racing, she realised that only a very foolish woman would underestimate a man like Max Montigny.

'*Your* company.'

He lounged back, and suddenly her heart was thumping against her ribs.

'Although that may be about to change.'

'What do you mean?' Her voice was like a whisper. She cleared her throat. 'What are you talking about?'

He shrugged. 'Right now you might live in the big chateau, have a private jet and a chauffeur-driven limousine, but I've seen your accounts.'

She frowned, started to object, but he simply smiled and she fell silent, for there was something knowing in the gaze that was making her skin start to prickle with fear and apprehension.

'Your father showed them to me. And they make pretty bleak reading. Desperate, in fact. Oh, it all looks good on the outside, but you're haemorrhaging money.'

Margot could feel the colour draining from her face. His words were detonating inside her head like grenades. Suddenly she was deaf, dazed, reeling blindly through the dust and rubble of the mess she had sought so hard to contain, struggling to breathe.

'That's not true,' she said hoarsely. Her lungs felt as though they were being squeezed in a vice. 'We've just had a difficult few months—

'More like five years.' He stared at her for a long moment, his gaze impassive. 'You asked me why I'm here. Well, that's it. That's why. Your family is about to be ruined and I want to be here to see it.'

He stared at her steadily, his eyes straight and unblinking, and Margot stared back at him, stilled, almost mesmerised by his words. 'What are you talking about?'

'I'm talking about retribution. You and your family ruined my life, and now I get to watch your world implode.'

Margot shook her head. Stiffening her shoulders, she forced herself to look him in the eye. 'No, you seduced me, and then you asked me to marry you just so you could get your hands on my money.'

For a moment he didn't reply, then he shrugged, and it was that offhand gesture—the casual dismissal of the way he'd broken her heart—that told her more clearly than any words that he was being serious.

Watching the light fade from Margot's eyes, Max told himself he didn't care. She deserved everything that was coming. They all did.

'And I paid for that. You and your family made sure I lost everything. I couldn't even get a reference. No vineyard would touch me.'

Remembering the shock and helplessness he'd felt in the hours and days following Margot's rejection, he bit down hard, using the pain of the past to block out her pale, stunned face.

'Now it's your turn.'

He leaned back against the leather upholstery, his eyes never leaving hers.

'I only bought shares in your company to get a ringside seat.'

CHAPTER TWO

MARGOT SAT FROZEN, mute with shock, her heart lurching inside her chest like a ship at sea in a storm.

'How dare you?' Blood was drumming in her ears, and her body vibrated with anger and disbelief. 'How dare you stand here in my boardroom and—?'

'Easily.'

She watched in mute horror as Max stood up and, raising his arms above his head, stretched his shoulders and neck. His apparent serenity only exacerbated the anxiety that was hammering against her ribcage.

'And I'll find it easier still to stand in your office and watch the administrators repossess that beautiful custom-made Parnian desk of yours.'

He was walking towards her now, and suddenly her breath was coming thick and fast.

'That won't happen.' She stood up hastily, her gaze locking on his, trying to ignore both the intense maleness of his lean, muscular body and the way her pulse was jumping like a stranded fish in response to it.

'Oh, it will.'

He stopped in front of her, his eyes—those beautiful hypnotic eyes—pinning her to the floor even as her head spun faster.

'Your business is in a mess, baby—a bloated, unstable, debt-ridden mess. House of Duvernay?' His eyes narrowed. 'More like house of straw!'

'And you're the wolf, are you? Come to huff and puff?' she sneered, her gaze colliding with his.

It was the wrong thing to say—not least because there was more than a hint of the wolf about his intense, hostile focus and the restrained power of body. For a moment, she held her breath. But then he smiled—only it felt more as if he was baring his teeth.

'I won't need to.' He studied her face. 'I won't need to do anything except sit back and watch while everything you love and care about slips through your fingers.'

The air was vibrating between them. 'You're a monster,' she whispered, inching backwards. 'A cold-blooded barbarian. What kind of man would say something like that?'

He shrugged, his expression somewhere between a challenge and a taunt. 'The kind that believes in karma.'

Margot was struggling to speak. She wanted to deny his claims. Prove him wrong. But the trouble was that she knew that he was right.

The business *was* a mess.

Her brother Yves might have resented his glamorous parents, but he had been more like Colette and Emile than he'd cared to admit, and five years after his death she was still trying to clear up the consequences of his impulsive and imprudent management style. Only nothing she did seemed to work.

Her heart began to beat faster. How could it? She didn't have her great-grandfather's vision, or her grandfather's ruthless determination and drive. Nor was she full of Yves's flamboyant self-assurance. In fact, if anything, the opposite was true. She'd found the responsibility of ensuring that the family legacy stayed intact increasingly overwhelming and as her self-doubts grew the profits continued to shrink. Finally—reluctantly—she'd decided to put up the chateau as security.

Her pulse began to beat faster.

Even just thinking about it made her feel physically sick. Not only had the chateau belonged to her family for sixteen generations, in less than two months it was supposed to be the setting for her brother Louis's wedding.

It had been a last-ditch attempt to reassure the bank. Only it hadn't worked. Max was right. The business was failing.

She shivered.

Or rather *she* had failed, and soon the whole world would know the truth that she had so desperately tried to hide.

Watching her in silence, Max breathed out slowly.

He'd waited nearly ten years for this. Ten long years of working so hard that he would often fall asleep eating his evening meal. Unlike Margot, he'd had to start at the bottom. His jaw tightened. His job at Duvernay should have opened doors to him throughout the industry but, thanks to her family, that ladder had become a snake with a venomous bite.

After being more or less banished from France, it had taken him years to claw back his reputation. Years spent working punishingly long hours at vineyards in Hungary, and studying at night school until finally he had got a break and a job on an estate in California.

But every backbreaking second had been worth it for this, and although the shares had been expensive he would have paid double for this moment of reckoning.

His chest tightened. Finally he'd proved the Duvernays wrong!

He was their equal—for he was here, in their precious

boardroom, not as some low-paid employee but as a share-holder.

He wanted to savour it. But although Margot looked suitably stunned—crushed, in fact, by his words—strangely, he was finding it not nearly as satisfying as he'd imagined he would.

Confused, and unprepared for this unexpected development, he stared at her in silence. And then immediately wished he hadn't, for with the light behind her, the delicate fabric of her white dress was almost transparent, and the silhouetted outline of her figure was clearly visible. It was almost as if she was naked.

A beat of desire pulsed through his veins.

Not that he needed a reminder. Margot's body was imprinted in his brain. He could picture her now, as he'd seen her so many times in those snatched afternoons spent in the tiny bedroom of his estate cottage. Lying in his arms, the curve of her belly and breasts gleaming in the shafts of fading sunlight, a pulse beating frantically at the base of her throat. Each time, he'd felt as though he was dreaming. He'd been completely in her thrall—overwhelmed not just by desire but by an emotion he had, until meeting her, always dismissed as at best illusory and at worst treacherous.

At first he'd tried to deny his feelings, had avoided her, and then, when avoiding her had become untenable, had been offhand almost to the point of being brusque, willing her to brand him rude and unapproachable if it meant hanging on to some small remnant of self-control.

But it had been so hard, for his body had been on fire, his brain in turmoil, all five senses on permanent high alert. He'd wanted her so badly, and for a time he'd believed that she wanted him in the same way. Insistently. Relentlessly.

Unconditionally.

And so he'd proposed—wanting, needing to make permanent that passion, that sense of belonging to someone, and of her belonging to him. He'd had no words for how he'd felt. It had defied description. All he had known was that he had a place in her life, her world. He had believed that unquestioningly. Only of course he'd been wrong.

Margot had wanted him, but her desire had been rooted in the transitory and finite nature of an affair—and more specifically in the illicit thrill of 'dating' her older brother's employee.

He felt anger spark inside him, and his eyes cut across the room to the line of portraits of Duvernays past and present.

Of course proposing to her had been his second mistake. His first had been to believe that his rapport with Yves was real, that it meant something. He had been lured not so much by the family's wealth and glamour, but by their sense of *contra mundum*, and the chance to be admitted into their world had been irresistibly potent to someone with his past.

With hindsight, though, he could see that his presence had always been subject to the grace and favour of the Duvernay family. They might have tolerated him, but he had never really belonged—just as Margot had never really belonged to *him*.

He felt his heart start to beat faster.

As a suitor, he'd always known that he was an underdog, a wild card—but, stupid and naive fool that he'd been, he'd actually respected her for seeing beyond his bank account and his background. Admired her for choosing him, for taking that risk. Now, though, he knew that the risk had been all his.

His hands trembled and he felt a rush of irritation at his naivety. No wonder he wasn't really *feeling* this moment.

He might have created a business to rival theirs, but what had haunted him—and what still rankled and had made every relationship since Margot a short-lived and deliberately one-sided affair—was the fact that, just like his mother, he hadn't been good enough to marry.

The Duvernays might have welcomed him into their home, but ultimately they had never considered him worthy of permanently joining their inner circle. Not even Margot. *Especially not Margot.*

His head was suddenly pounding.

For nearly a decade he'd told himself that watching the House of Duvernay implode would be enough. Enough to erase the sting of humiliation and the pain of being so summarily cast out and ostracised. Only now, here, standing in this boardroom, it was clear to him that there was another, more satisfying revenge to be had: namely, seizing control of the business from Margot.

It was the only possible way to exorcise this lingering hold she had on him. To punish her as she deserved to be punished. For she had wronged him the most. Her betrayal was the most personal and the deepest.

His pulse twitched as for the first time he noticed the band on her wrist, his brain swiftly and efficiently deciphering the cursive writing. He felt warmth spread across his skin. And it just so happened that he knew the perfect way to make his revenge exquisitely and fittingly personal.

Exhilaration hit him like a shot of pure alcohol and, resting his gaze on her profile, he steadied himself. 'I know how you must be feeling...'

Her head jerked towards him, her long pale blonde hair catching the light as it flicked sideways.

'I doubt that.' Dark brown eyes wide with anger and outrage locked on to his. 'Having feelings would make you human, and you clearly don't have an ounce of humanity.'

Staring at the pulse beating in the base of her throat, Max gritted his teeth. He had plenty of feelings for Margot, unfortunately most of them seemed to be occurring somewhere in the region of his groin.

Fighting off the frustration that was circling like a caged dog inside his head, Max took a step towards her. 'I *do* know. You might not have thought I had much to lose, but thanks to your brother I lost the little I had,' he said coolly.

Margot blinked. At the mention of her brother's name anger surged up inside her like a hot spring. 'Yves was protecting me.'

'Yes, by destroying me.'

She reeled back from the controlled fury in his voice. 'That wasn't his intention.'

'You think?'

She glared at him, not knowing what she hated more: the coolness in his eyes or the mockery distorting his beautiful mouth. 'Yes, I do. He just did what any brother would do. I wouldn't expect you to understand that. I wouldn't expect you to understand feelings like loyalty and lo—

She broke off, appalled at what she had so nearly spoken out loud—not just the fact that she had loved him but loved him rapturously, with her body, heart and soul. Only her love had been unreciprocated—humiliatingly unilateral. Worse, it had blinded her to what he was really thinking.

A sudden sharp spasm of pain twisted her stomach, and the words he'd spoken to her so long ago suddenly echoed inside her head.

'It was all about the money. You and me. That's why I proposed. I just wanted your money.'

She felt his clear-eyed gaze probing her face, and more than anything she wanted to raise her hands and shield her eyes, conceal the emotions that were rising up inside her. But she wasn't about to give him the satisfaction of knowing how badly he'd hurt her. Or that the pain of his betrayal felt as fresh today as it had ten years ago.

Ignoring the thudding of her heart, she glared at him. 'Just because you don't care about anything but money—'

'You mean the money that you don't currently have?' he said softly. 'Remind me, Margot. What is Duvernay's net to EBITDA ratio these days?'

Their eyes clashed, and she flinched inwardly at the anger and resentment taking shape in the no-man's land between them.

Forcing herself to stand her ground, she wrapped her fingers around her elbows. 'Why do you care? Or do you just want to gloat about that too?'

His face was still, but his eyes were glittering in a way that made the air thump out of her lungs. For a moment they stared at one another in silence, and then finally he shrugged. 'I wasn't gloating,' he said simply.

The mildness of his tone caught her off guard, for it was so at odds with the adversarial tension swirling around the room and inside her chest.

'I just like to be in full command of the facts. That's how I run my business.'

His eyes were fixed on hers, calm, appraising, unnerving, and she felt her breathing jerk, saw the muted colours of the walls slamming into focus.

'Well, luckily for me, whatever you might like to believe, Duvernay isn't your business,' she said, lifting her chin and returning his gaze, her brown eyes sparking with resentment.

How dare he do this? Saunter back into her life with his newly acquired shares and his careless gaze, unlocking the past and upending the present.

For a second there was total silence, and then his mouth

curved slowly upwards. Despite herself, she felt her pulse flutter, for his smile was still so difficult to resist, and even though she wanted to deny its power she could feel a trembling heat starting to creep over her skin.

And he hadn't even touched her, she thought, her heart lurching against her ribcage.

'Well, *luckily for you*—' he paused, his eyes resting calmly on her face '—that could all be about to change.'

Abruptly his smile was forgotten, and she stared up at him in confusion, her skin tingling, mouth drying with fear and anticipation, trying and failing to make sense of his casual statement.

'All you need to do is say yes.'

His words hung in the air between them and she felt panic spread through her. Suddenly she was having to work hard to breathe. Her pulse gave a leap of warning. Something was happening—something undefined but important.

'Yes to what?' She was aiming for the same tone of neutral formality, but instead her voice sounded oddly hollow and strained.

Max held her gaze. He wanted to see her reaction. To watch the moment of impact. 'To marrying me.'

Margot gazed at him, rooted to the spot, her stomach clenching with shock. She knew her face had drained of colour, but she was too busy trying to quiet the chaos inside her head to care.

'Marry you!' Shaking her head, she gave a small, disbelieving laugh. 'You're crazy. Why would I want to marry *you*?'

'Is that a no?'

His face was closed, expressionless, but she could feel the anger rippling beneath his skin. Only she didn't care. Right now all she wanted to do was hurt him in the same way that he'd hurt her—was still hurting her. Or maybe not in the *same* way, for that would mean Max had a heart, and she knew from bitter, personal experience that wasn't the case.

But she could certainly puncture the beating core of Max Montigny—his masculine pride.

'A no? Of course not.' She glared at him, her own rage shocking her. 'Who could possibly resist a man like you, Max? I mean, it's every woman's dream to marry a lying, scheming hustler!'

Sarcasm did not come naturally to her any more than anger did, but coming so soon after her father's betrayal and the shock of seeing Max again his proposal was just too cruel, too painful.

Once, marrying Max had been her dream. When he and Yves had turned up for supper one evening she had looked up from her plate and just like that she had fallen in love. Actually, not fallen—it had been more like plummeting…like a star falling to earth.

His presence in her life had felt miraculous. The thrill of seeing him, talking to him, had been a new kind of bliss—both pleasure and pain—for he had been so smart and sexy, bewitchingly beautiful and impossibly laid back, and yet so unattainable. She had been desperate, hopeful, smitten—and then, unbelievably, it had happened.

Only she had never suspected why. Stupid, naive and crazily in love for the first time, she had never imagined the truth until that terrible afternoon when Yves had discovered them.

'Feeling better? Or do you want to start throwing punches as well as insults?'

Max's voice was as cold and toxic as nerve gas. Lifting her head, she cleared her throat, straightening her back, feeling the zip of her dress tingling against her spine.

'Sorry,' she said, without a hint of remorse. 'But I just can't imagine under what circumstances you think I'd ever, *ever*, even consider marrying *you*.'

His gaze didn't flicker. 'How about circumstances in which I agree to save your business?'

She stared at him, the sheer unexpectedness of his words making the edges of her vision watery. 'Save my business…?' she repeated slowly.

He nodded. 'If you agree to become my wife.' He paused, studying her face. 'It's up to you, of course.'

He was speaking with a mock courtesy that made her want to hurl her bag at his head.

'I can just leave. The choice is yours.'

Her skin was prickling and her heart was beating so loudly that it was getting in the way of her thoughts. 'That's not a choice,' she said hoarsely. 'That's blackmail.'

For what felt like a lifetime he stared at her thoughtfully, and then finally he gave a casual shrug.

'Yes, I suppose it is. But on some levels all business is blackmail.' His face was impassive, his eyes steady on hers. 'And that's what this is, Margot. It's just business.'

The truth, of course, was that he wanted to prove her and her family wrong. To demonstrate irrefutably that he *was* good enough to marry her. That his name was equal to hers. But his instincts warned him against revealing the truth, for surely it would show weakness to admit that their low opinion—*her* low opinion—still tormented him?

Besides, there was no need to reveal anything. Not when he already had a ready-made reason at his fingertips. Widening his stance, he focused his attention on the woman in front of him.

'Unlike yourself, I'm not in the habit of throwing good money after bad, and your father's shares are useless to me if Duvernay goes bankrupt.'

She took a breath, bracing herself as though for a blow. 'What has that got to do with marrying me?' she asked stiffly.

Tuning out the apprehension in her voice, he let her words echo around the room. 'Isn't it obvious? I'll marry you, and in return you'll give me your shares. That will make me the majority stakeholder in Duvernay and allow me to run the business as I see fit.' His mouth curled into a goading smile. 'By that I mean profitably.'

Her eyes narrowed. 'You're so arrogant.' Seething inwardly, Margot watched him gaze dismissively around the boardroom.

'It shouldn't be too hard. Frankly, I could turn this company around in a heartbeat.'

She gave a short, mirthless laugh. 'Wouldn't that require you to have a *heart*, though, Max?' she said sweetly.

He smiled. 'Oh, I have a heart, Margot—and more importantly, unlike your brother, I also have a head for business.'

Her brown eyes narrowed. 'I don't want to know what you think about my brother any more than I want your money,' she spat.

He gazed down at her, unperturbed by her outburst. 'No, I'm sure you don't,' he conceded.

His eyes gleamed, the centres darkening so that suddenly it felt as though she was being dragged bodily into his pupils.

'But whether you want my money or not is largely irrelevant. The fact is, you need it.'

'I don't—' she began.

He waved her words away as though they were some kind of irritating insect. 'You do. And, frankly, the sooner the better. I'll give you free rein with the wedding arrangements...' he was watching her lazily, as though her consent was a foregone conclusion '…although I draw the line at wearing any kind of patterned waistcoat. So marry me, give me control over our destinies, and I'll make all your problems go away.'

'I doubt that. From where I'm standing, *you* are the biggest problem. You're conceited and selfish and utterly lacking in sensitivity.'

His smile widened. 'Presumably that's why I now own a quarter share of your business?'

Stifling an impulse to slap his smug, handsome face, Margot fixed her gaze on the gardens outside. How long was he going to carry on with this game? For surely that was all this talk of marriage was to him. A game designed to humiliate her further.

So stop playing it, then, she told herself irritably. *You're the CEO of a global business, not some dopey nineteen-year-old student.*

With a strength that surprised her, she turned and met his gaze head-on. 'I'm not going to give you my shares, Max,' she said flatly. 'And I'm definitely not going to marry you.'

His expression didn't change, but somehow she found that less reassuring rather than more, and moments later she realised why. She might have thought she was simply stating the obvious, but Max clearly thought she was calling his bluff.

'Is that right?'

She glared at him, her skin prickling with resentment—not just at his arrogance but at the beat of desire pulsing through her veins, and the knowledge that only Max had ever done this to her. Got under her skin and made her feel so off-balance. And the fact that he could still make her feel this way, that he still had this power over her, threatened her as much as his words.

She took a step back. 'Yes, it is,' she said quickly. 'You

and I were a mistake I'm not planning on repeating. We're certainly not marriage material.'

'Why not? I'm a man…you're a woman. There are no obstacles preventing us from tying the knot.'

Jamming her hands into the pockets of her dress, she looked up at him, disbelief giving way to exasperation, then fury. 'Aside from mutual loathing, you mean?'

Glancing around the boardroom, he shook his head slowly. 'You see? This is why your business is struggling, baby. You're just too resistant to change, to new ideas.'

Her eyes narrowed. 'Oh, I'm sorry. I didn't realise blackmail was so on-trend!'

He laughed, and before she could stop herself—before she even knew she was doing it—she was laughing too. How could she not when his mouth curled up so temptingly at the corners, wiping the mockery from his face so that he looked heartbreakingly like his younger self?

And, fool that she was, she felt her pulse lose speed, felt a sudden overwhelming urge to reach out and touch the curve of his lips, to feel again the hard, masculine pressure of his body against hers.

Heat burned in her cheeks and she breathed in sharply. Her reaction had been instinctive, involuntary, but she was already regretting it. How could she *laugh* with him after everything he'd done to her? And how could she let herself feel anything other than hatred and contempt for this man who was backing her into a corner, demanding something that was impossible for her to give?

She felt his gaze on the side of her face.

'What was that you were saying about mutual loathing?' he asked.

The mocking note was back, and she looked up defiantly, her whole body stiffening into fight mode. 'Just because you can make me laugh *once*, it doesn't mean anything.'

Dragging her gaze away from the indecently lush mouth, she stared past him.

Except that it did.

She winced inwardly. It was all there in her voice—everything that she didn't want him to hear or to know about how she was feeling—and that was why this conversation had to stop now.

'You might have a head for business, Max, but you have zero understanding of human nature. If—*if*—we were to get married, we wouldn't just be talking in the boardroom.' She felt a sudden prickle of ice run down her spine. 'We'd have to live together. Share a home.'

Share a bed, she thought silently, her face suddenly hot as his eyes narrowed on hers and something moved across the irises that made her breathing quicken.

Cheeks burning, she began speaking again. 'Share our lives. And how are we going to do that? We can't even be in the same room together without—'

But she never finished her sentence. Instead she made the mistake of looking up at him, and instantly the words stalled in her throat.

She felt her body tense, almost painfully, and then her legs started to shake just as they had the first time she had ever seen him. Dressed in faded jeans, a T-shirt that hugged the muscles of his arms, and wearing dark glasses, he had looked like a cocktail of one part glamour to two parts cool. And then he'd taken his glasses off, and it had been like a thunderclap bursting inside her head.

Over time she had, of course, grown used to how he looked. But at least once a day it had caught her off guard, and now apparently nothing had changed. The seemingly random arrangement of mouth, nose, cheekbones still had the same power to rob her of even basic impulses, such as breathing and speaking.

'Without what?'

Her stomach tightened with awareness. The air felt suddenly charged with a different kind of tension, and his voice had grown softer. Too soft.

She could feel it slipping over her skin like a caress, so warm and tempting and—

Deceptive! Had she really learned nothing from what happened between them?

Ignoring his eyes, she crossed her arms in front of her body, shielding herself from the pull of the past. 'It doesn't matter.'

'Oh, but it does. You see, I need an answer,' he said, and the smoothness of his voice in no way diluted his uncompromising statement.

'Well, tough!' Her eyes widened. 'You can't seriously expect me to give you one here and now?'

For a moment he didn't reply, just continued to stare at her thoughtfully, as though he was working out something inside his head.

'Actually, I can—and I am.'

Her pulse shifted up a gear as he glanced at the surprisingly understated watch on his wrist.

'Deals have deadlines, and this one runs out when I walk back out through that door.'

She took a breath, fear drumming through her chest. 'But that's not fair. I need time—'

'And *I* need an answer.'

The commanding note in his voice whipped at her senses so that suddenly her head was buzzing and the glare of the sunlight hurt her eyes.

'And, to be fair, you have had ten years.'

Margot blinked. 'You can't compare what happened

then with this.' She felt suddenly sick. Surely he didn't think that this 'proposal' somehow picked up where they'd left off?

'This is nothing like before,' she said shakily.

'I agree. This is far better.'

She gaped at him speechlessly, uncertain of how to interpret his words, and then suddenly she shook her head, her eyes snapping upwards. 'Better! What are you talking about?'

Her voice was too loud. So loud that someone in the corridor would be able to hear her. But for the first time in her life she didn't care what other people might think.

'How is this better? How could this ever be better?'

'It's simpler. More transparent.' His gaze dropped to her throat, then lowered to the V of her dress. 'What you see is what you get. And, despite all your talk of mutual loathing, I think we can agree that we both like what we see.'

Margot felt something dislodge inside her. His closeness was making her unravel. She wanted to disagree. To throw his remark back in his face. Only she didn't trust herself to speak—not just to form the words inside her head but to say them out loud.

Her pulse hiccupped with panic, and his gaze cut to hers. Surely though he couldn't sense the way he made her feel?

But of course he could—he always had. And, as though reading her mind, he reached out and gently stroked her long blonde hair, his touch pulling her not just closer, but back to a past that she had never quite relinquished.

'I can't give you time, Margot, but I can give you a reason to marry me.'

His gaze rested on her face, his eyes drawing her in, and she felt her nerves quiver helplessly in response to the message in the darkening irises.

'You have given me a reason, Max,' she said shakily. 'It's called blackmail.'

There was a moment of silence, and then his gaze shifted from her eyes, dropping and pressing onto her mouth. Suddenly her skin felt too hot and too tight, and she had a slip-sliding sense of *déjà-vu* as he took another step closer, the intensity of his eyes tangling her breathing.

'Actually, I have a better reason.'

For perhaps a fraction of a second her brain was screaming at her to turn, to move, to run. And then his lips closed on hers and heat surged through her body as his arm curved around her waist. Her hands rose instinctively, palms pressing into the rigid muscles of his chest—but not to push him away. Instead her fingers curled into the front of his shirt and she was pulling him closer, even as his hand curled around her wrist.

The touch of his mouth, his hands, his body, was so familiar, so intoxicating, that she would have had to be inhuman not to respond. He was warm and solid and real—more real than anything else in the room, in the world.

It was impossible to deny, and he was impossible to resist…like drowning. The pain and the misery of the last ten years was fading into a pleasure that she had never expected to feel again, a pleasure she had only ever felt in Max's arms.

Something stirred in her head and she felt a kick of resistance.

Only it was all a lie, a cold-blooded seduction. He hadn't felt anything. Not then, and definitely not now.

And just like that the spell was broken. Heart still racing, she jerked her mouth free and pushed him away.

Resurfacing into the cool, sedate daylight of the boardroom, she felt heat burning her face. Only now it was the heat of humiliation. How had she let that happen? Why had she given herself to this man? A man who felt nothing for her and used her feelings as a weapon against herself.

Oh, he *wanted* her—but certainly not because he was powerless to do otherwise...

Skin burning, she took a step back and pressed her hand against her mouth, trying to blot out the imprint of his lips, wishing there was a way she could erase him as quickly and permanently from her life and her memory.

But the truth was that even when she'd had every reason to do so she hadn't managed to wipe Max from her mind. And now she actually had a reason for him to be in her life.

Her pulse fluttered and she felt a momentary swirling panic rise up inside her chest like storm water. And then just as swiftly it drained away. This was not a time for feelings to get in the way of facts. And the facts were bleak.

The business was not just failing, it was heading for bankruptcy. And it wasn't just Duvernay the business that was facing ruin. If—no, *when* the business collapsed, her family would be thrown into the spotlight, humbled and humiliated. Worse, they would be homeless.

She didn't want to marry Max, but without his money her life and that of her family—the life they all took for granted—would not just be difficult, it would cease to exist. And how would she—how would *they*?—cope living like ordinary people?

Her heart contracted. They wouldn't. And she couldn't expect them to do so.

Briefly, she felt the weight of her responsibilities. For if this was to work then once again she would have to put her family before herself. To lie and keep secrets. But what choice did she have?

Right now, Max was her only option. Without him all would be lost.

Heat burned in her cheeks. But wasn't there just a tiny part of herself that was relieved to have Max there, going into battle alongside her? And, really, was marriage such a big sacrifice to make for the sake of your family and a two hundred year legacy?

She stilled her breathing, like a diver preparing to jump, and then, before she could change her mind, she said quickly, 'Okay, I'll marry you. But it has to look and feel real, like a traditional wedding. We'll need to talk about it properly.'

As an attempt to reassert her power it was pretty meaningless. She was in no position to demand anything—she knew it, and he knew it too—and yet she also knew instinctively that she couldn't allow herself to be a push-over.

She'd half expected him to rise to her challenge. Only he didn't. Instead he merely nodded, as though she'd asked him to email her an invoice rather than discuss the conditions of their marriage of convenience.

'Of course. I'll be in touch.'

And with that he turned, and suddenly she was alone.

She stared after him, her heart beating out of time, her limbs shaking with relief and a strange kind of excitement.

Finally he was gone—but of course she would see him again soon. Only that wasn't the reason why her heart was fluttering to the ground like a wounded bird. It was because the next time she saw him it would be as his fiancée.

CHAPTER THREE

STRIDING BACK INTO his Parisian hotel suite an hour later, Max tossed his phone carelessly onto one of the large velvet-covered sofas in the main living area.

He didn't know whether to feel elated or stunned.

Or just plain furious!

He should be on his way to Longchamp. He was due there to present a trophy to the winner of the big race, and normally he loved going to the races—whatever happened at the bookies, fast horses and beautiful woman were a winning combination.

But after leaving the Duvernay headquarters he'd got his PA to cancel. He'd had no choice. Margot had not only got under his skin, she was resonating inside his head. Her every word, every gesture, was running on a continuous loop like a live news feed from which it was impossible to turn away.

But why? He'd got what he wanted, hadn't he?

His mouth thinned. It should have all been so straightforward. A part of him had been planning some sort of revenge against the Duvernays for nearly a decade, painstakingly working towards the moment when finally he would prove to Margot, her brother, her whole damn family that they had been wrong about him.

And everything had been on schedule—right up until

the moment she'd walked into the boardroom. His mind scrolled back to when he'd turned around and seen her in that dress—a dress that despite its couture credentials had somehow managed to conjure up memories of carefree summers, feel-good songs playing on car radios and the smell of hot bare skin.

Margot's hot bare skin.

He blinked. No wonder he'd been driven to act like that. Proposing marriage and then kissing her. His brain had been like bubble gum.

Frowning, he slid his hand under his tie and tugged it loose, before pulling it over his head and tossing it in the same direction as his phone. He felt tired, and the tension in his neck was making his back ache.

Infuriated by the devastating impact Margot had wrought on his mood and on his body, he slowly scanned the exquisite room, as though the opulent *fin de siècle* furnishings and huge gold-framed mirrors might offer up some kind of antidote. When that failed, he turned and stalked across the gleaming wood floor to the open French windows, stepping outside onto the roof terrace that adjoined his suite.

Directly opposite, the Eiffel Tower rose above the Paris skyline. Normally he found the sight of the city's most iconic monument inspirational for, like him, it too had initially struggled to be accepted before finally finding national and global fame.

Now, though, as he looked across at the familiar iron structure, it seemed oddly insubstantial.

His jaw tightened. A bit like the 'logic' that had driven his most recent actions.

He felt a rush of irritation, his shoulders tensing so that a spasm of pain nipped his spine. For 'logic' read 'libido'.

Barely registering the incredible three-hundred-and-sixty-degree views of the city, he gripped the balustrade, breathing out slowly as for maybe the hundredth time he ran through the morning's events, trying to disentangle the motives behind his behaviour.

Buying Emile's shares had been a luxury—overpriced and self-indulgent. Buying them, though, had served a purpose, for it had taken him to the Duvernay boardroom and a showdown with Margot.

A showdown that should have ended there.

And it would have ended there if he hadn't asked her to marry him.

Tilting his head back, he closed his eyes. At the time, marrying her and taking possession of her shares had seemed like a perfectly reasonable next step. The best and the only way to satisfy the hunger for revenge that had driven him back to France after nearly a decade.

Now, though, he could see that, whatever chain of events he had triggered in that boardroom, the truth was that his actions had been driven not just by a desire to possess Duvernay, but by a desire to possess Margot herself.

It had been if not a moment of madness then an act of impulse—an instinctive urge both to let go and move on from the past and at the same time continue that tantalising *pas-de-deux* with the only woman who had left an imprint on his soul. A woman who had burned him so badly that he had spent the intervening years running from the hurt, afraid to slow down and face his feelings, afraid to feel full-stop.

But for some reason, as he'd come face to face with her in that picture-lined room, he had decided not only to stop running but to re-stake his claim.

To what? he mocked. *Certainly not her heart.*

She might have accused him of being cold-blooded, but Margot's heart lay buried beneath a layer of permafrost.

Opening his eyes, he gazed irritably across the skyline. None of this would have happened if he'd just stuck to the plan—only he'd had to go and let things get personal.

But of course he had. Because it was personal. Deeply and guttingly personal.

Margot had mattered to him like no other woman ever had. But then, she'd been like no other woman he'd ever known—and it hadn't just been about the sex. Before he'd met her he'd been so messed up—hungry for respect and respectability and yet resentful that he had to keep on earning it, asking for it, pushing for it.

She had been his serenity. His salvation.

His mouth thinned. Or so he'd believed until that evening when she'd tossed his proposal back in his face like a glass of wine. Ever since then he'd been carrying his pain and resentment like a dark storm cloud.

A storm cloud that had burst with a clap of thunder in that boardroom today.

But was it really that surprising? He might have bought the shares and engineered the meeting, but seeing her again had still been a shock.

Before she'd arrived he'd told himself she wasn't going to be as beautiful as he remembered, or as desirable. That kind of loveliness didn't last. But he'd been wrong—actually, more like deluded!

His body had responded to hers with a swiftness and an intensity that he'd never experienced around any woman except her. And as for her looks—

Well, he'd been wrong about that too.

Aged nineteen, she had possessed a beauty that had already been straining at the leash. With a pure clean-cut profile, pensive light brown eyes and almost ludicrously long legs, she'd been a mesmerising mix of coltish hesitation and a seriousness not common in one so young.

Today, though, she would not have looked out of place sashaying down the catwalk at Paris Fashion Week—or, better still, circling the paddock at Longchamp with all the other thoroughbreds. For she had outgrown or maybe grown into her long limbs, and there was no trace of that youthful hesitation. Only the soft half-pout and simply styled long, pale blonde hair still hinted at the girl he'd proposed to all those years ago.

He felt his pulse dart. Or it would have done if that girl had ever been real. But he knew now that she had only ever existed inside his head.

So who, then, was he marrying? And, perhaps more importantly, why was he prepared to go ahead with such an impulsive and ill-thought-out decision?

Breathing out slowly, his mind took him back to that first and last summer they'd spent together. A summer of love—secret, snatched love.

Margot had told him she needed to find the right moment to tell her family and, smitten with feelings that were powerful and compelling in their unfamiliarity, it had been an easy decision for him to go along with her wishes.

Cocooned together in the bedroom of the cottage that had come with his job, nothing had ever felt so good, so right—not even the first time he'd stepped foot in a vineyard.

It had been so new to him…so precious. He'd thought going public would end his bubble of happiness instantly. There would be no more just the two of them. Everything would change irrevocably.

His mouth curved downwards. Of course he hadn't anticipated quite how catastrophic that change would be— although maybe he'd always suspected the truth. That her secrecy and hesitation stemmed not from a desire to prolong the perfect private bliss of their affair, but from a belief that he was only good enough for sex, and that one day she would discard him like pomace—the unusable skins, pulp, seeds and stems from the wine grapes.

He was suddenly working to breathe.

This time, though, it would be different. This time there would be no sneaking around, no secrecy, no hiding him away.

If it had just been about recouping his money then, yes, he would have sat back and waited for her business to fail before stepping forward to scoop up the spoils. But why wait? Marrying her would have the same outcome, only it would be immediate—and it would be much more pleasurable.

Not only would he be in the driving seat at Duvernay, but Margot Duvernay—heiress and aristocrat of the wine world—would be his wife. His lawfully and very *publicly* wedded wife.

Gazing down at the city, he smiled happily, back no longer aching, suddenly immensely gratified with how the morning had played out.

Switching off the shower, Margot smoothed the water away from her face and silently breathed in the scented steam.

The camellia and jasmine body wash had promised to soothe her body and mind, but judging by the way her heart was still racing it clearly wasn't powerful enough to soothe away the aftershocks caused by the morning's events.

To be fair, though, she couldn't really blame the shower gel. Short of industrial quantities of alcohol. or maybe concussion, she wasn't sure that *anything* could counteract a close encounter with Max Montigny.

Chewing her lip, she wrapped a towel around her damp

body, grateful for the comforting warmth and softness of its embrace.

Had anyone else bought her father's shares it would have been an awkward but bearable meeting, with a discussion followed perhaps by coffee. But instead it had been more like a gladiatorial battle, and there had been only one proposal on the agenda—Max's.

A proposal she had accepted.

Her pulse accelerated, and the saliva dried in her mouth as panic and fear at what she'd consented to do spiralled up inside her like a swarm of bees.

However, panicking wasn't going to change the facts—and they were simple. Not only had she agreed to transfer her shares to Max, she had also agreed to become his wife.

After he'd left she had briefly considered calling her lawyer. Only what would have been the point? She knew without even bothering to check that the contract he'd signed with Emile would be watertight.

Besides, right now, taking Max's money was the only way she could save her business *and* her family. And if that meant giving him her shares and marrying him, then that was what she would do.

She felt her stomach lurch, and some of her bravado began to ooze away. That was easy to say, but she couldn't pretend even to herself that the reality was going to be anything but challenging.

Glancing down at her wrist, she shivered. She could still feel his handprint on her skin, could remember the way their bodies had fitted together as they'd kissed, and the helpless, sightless oblivion of her passion.

Her hands fluttered involuntarily in her lap. Closing her eyes, she clutched the towel more tightly.

Her response to him wasn't that surprising, she thought defensively. And, given their history, surely she could forgive herself? The physical attraction between them had always been so overpowering and relentless that kiss had been inevitable. But, while her craving for Max might be understandable, even forgivable, giving in to it would only complicate things.

For the sake of her sanity and her pride it was clear that this deal would only work if she kept her feelings out of it. Viewed that way, she might just be able to believe that their marriage was simply another business transaction—a civilised, functional, mutually beneficial agreement between two consenting adults.

She felt her breath clog in her throat. All she needed to do now was believe her own sales pitch.

Opening her eyes, she stared slowly around her bedroom.

If only she had somebody she could confide in. It wasn't that she didn't have friends. She did. But friends were for fun—for nights out and playing tennis, going shopping. Telling them the truth about her life was just not an option. After so many years of keeping so much of the Duvernay drama under wraps, what would she say? Where would she start?

Nor could she share her fears and anxieties with her family, for they relied on her to be strong and steady and solicitous.

If only there was someone she could trust with her burden.

Her mouth twisted. *Like a husband.*

But, although her feelings for Max might be complicated and confusing, she knew with absolute certainty that she didn't trust him. Or at least that she only trusted him to hurt her.

Her pulse twitched and she felt a sudden urgency to move, to escape the loop of her thoughts. Stalking into the dressing room, she snatched a pair of faded blue jeans, a V-neck T-shirt and a pale grey ballet-style wrap.

If only she could just disappear. Get into her car and keep driving. Leave France, Europe—or better still become an astronaut...

She tugged the wrap around her waist and knotted it savagely. And do what?

She might escape Max, and the mess-in-waiting that was her business, but she would never escape her feelings. Even if she was floating hundreds of miles above the earth in a space station she would still be worrying about her family and trying to manage the chaos they produced.

That was what she did. What she'd always done since childhood, during the many evenings and weekends when her parents' volatile relationship had spilled over into a merry-go-round of accusations and denials.

When finally one of them—usually Colette—had stormed off in tears, it had been down to Margot to act as a go-between. And then, after they had inevitably retreated to the bedroom, it had been down to her to make up some story for the maids about how that vase had got broken, or why her father's clothes were scattered over the lawn. Yves, of course, was long gone, hiding out at a friend's house, and Louis had been a baby.

For a moment she stared silently at her reflection in the full-length mirror, seeing not herself but the dutiful little girl who had always done the right thing. Sorting out her parents' messes even if that had meant lying and keeping secrets.

And now she would be lying and keeping secrets for the rest of her life.

It would be easy simply to blame Max. *Marry me, or watch your business fail and your family end up homeless* was hardly much of a choice. But it wasn't that simple.

No one had made her go into the boardroom and face him. She could have got back into the lift, and sent in the lawyers. But some part of her had *wanted* to see him— and not just see him, she thought, her cheeks flaming as she remembered that kiss.

And Max hadn't come simply to gloat, or to pick out an office. He could have scheduled the meeting some- where public, like a restaurant, but he had wanted to be alone with her too.

Looking down, she saw that her hands were shaking again. Theoretically, she knew that she should loathe him. But clearly her body hadn't received the memo about how it was supposed to behave when she met the man who had crushed her dreams and broken her heart.

It might make no sense, and even just thinking it made her feel helpless and angry, but although she might have to lie to everyone else she wasn't going to lie to herself. And the truth was that in spite of everything that had hap- pened between them, and the fact that they no longer liked or trusted or respected one another, they still wanted each other with an intensity and desperation that overrode all logic and history.

Tipping her head back, she let out a long, slow breath. Perhaps, though, it was just the shock of seeing him again, she thought hopefully. Maybe when she saw him next time she would be immune to his charms.

She sighed. It didn't seem likely, but at least she wouldn't have long to find out.

The thought of seeing him again was making her heart pound so loudly that it took her some seconds to register that her phone was ringing.

She felt her muscles tense, her body pulling up sharply, like a horse refusing to jump a fence, and suddenly the air was humming around her.

Was it Max?

Instantly her heart gave a great leap, and as she walked swiftly back into her bedroom she gazed nervously down at the phone, oscillating from side to side on the polished surface of her dressing table.

But it was just Louis, calling from his week-long bachelor party in Marrakech.

Her heartbeat started to slow and she stared down at the screen, unnerved by the sharp sting of disappointment she felt at reading her brother's name. Usually she loved talking to her younger brother.

Louis had been too young to really register his parents' turbulent marriage so, unlike his older siblings, he had no memories of the past to colour his present. Instead he had inherited his parents' best qualities. Handsome and charming, like his father, he also had his mother's spontaneity. He was loved by everyone, and in return for this universal gift of love he wanted everyone around him to be happy. Particularly Margot.

The thought drove her back a step.

It was starting already. The lies and the secrecy. Only she wasn't ready. She wasn't ready to lie to Louis yet, she thought, panic blooming in her throat as her brain finally registered the tiny camera icon on the screen. And definitely not to his face.

But she was going to have to. For how could she suddenly just announce that she was going to marry a man she had never so much as mentioned before?

Louis would be stunned, devastated and hurt. Just picturing the lines of his face made her heart contract painfully and she felt a flicker of despair. Would it never end? Would she ever be free to just live?

Her pulse accelerated.

She could almost picture Max's handsome face. Could hear his soft, goading voice daring her to make a choice.

Her hand hovered over the phone and then, cursing softly, she took a quick, sharp breath and picked it up, swiping her fingers across the screen.

'Louis! How lovely to hear from you!'

Her breath ached in her chest as she smiled down at her brother's face.

'How's Marrakech?'

'It's amazing. I feel like I'm on a movie set.'

She smiled. His face was so unguarded, so flushed with happiness, and she felt some of the tension inside of her loosen.

'Well, I got the photos you sent and it looks beautiful,' she said truthfully. 'Are you having fun?'

'Of course. You know, I can't believe you haven't been out here.'

Louis sounded genuinely confused, and Margot experienced the sensation that she often did when speaking to her brother—a kind of shock that she was related to such a normal, well-balanced person. To him, Marrakech was just a beautiful, glamorous destination. The perfect backdrop for a week of hedonism. The fact that his family owned a former palace in the old city was just a bonus and a happy coincidence.

To her, though, the Palais du Bergé would always be the place where her parents had fled after their many rows— only Louis didn't need to know that.

And that was the other reason she'd agreed to marry Max. Louis needed protecting from the truth, and Max's money and her silence would make sure that continued to happen.

When the time was right she would give him an expurgated version of the last few days. But right now she was just grateful for the chance to think about something other than Max's life-changing reappearance in her life.

She cleared her throat. 'Oh, you know—I've just never really got round to it. Too busy at work. But let's not talk about that now. Tell me what you've been up to.'

'I'm not ringing to talk about me, Margot.'

Louis looked and sounded so uncharacteristically stern that she found herself smiling. 'So who *do* you want to talk about?'

'I want to talk about you, and why you're in France when you're supposed to be in Monaco. Is this your way of telling me that you still don't approve of me getting married?'

Margot grimaced, guilt digging her beneath the ribs. With all the drama with Max, she had completely forgotten about Gisele and Monte Carlo.

'No, of course not,' she said quickly. 'And I never didn't approve. I was just worried—you're both so young.'

She had been worried at first, but although both Gisele and Louis were impulsive and indulged, they lacked the self-absorption and wilfulness of her parents—and, more importantly, their relationship was not simply based on sex.

'So why did you leave?'

The petulance in her brother's voice was fading, but he was still frowning.

'Oh, Louis, I'm sorry. I really did want to stay, only something came up—'

'Something or *someone*?'

She froze, his words slamming into one another inside her head. Her body reacted instinctively, like a hare spooked by the shadow of a hawk, stilling and shrinking inwards as her legs gave way beneath her and she slid noiselessly onto the bed.

Damn Max! Had he spoken to Louis? Had he spoken to her grandfather as well? And, if so, what had he said to them?

'So? Are you going to tell me what he wanted or not?'

Louis's voice was impatient now, but she hardly registered the shift, so great was her misery at the way all the parts of her life that she'd worked so hard to keep separate were now suddenly and violently converging.

'Yes, of course.' The smile on her face was starting to hurt, and it was an effort to force herself to speak. 'I just didn't want to bother you while you were away. I thought it would just be easier if I handled it—him—on my own.'

She heard her brother sigh. 'He knows how to pick his moments, doesn't he? I mean, he makes no effort to have any sort of relationship with me, and then when I'm not even in the country he just randomly leaves me a message.'

Margot blinked in confusion. 'What message?'

Louis frowned. 'Exactly! *What* message? It was just him drinking and talking rubbish. Except for the part when he said that he didn't really want to talk to me. That he was just trying to get hold of you and he couldn't.' There was a moment's silence. 'So what was it then? What was so incredibly urgent that the great Emile Lehmann actually deigned to call *me*?'

For a moment she couldn't speak. Her whole body felt weak, buffeted by a fast, wild, rushing relief, and she badly wanted to laugh. Only suddenly it felt horribly close to wanting to cry—for what if she'd actually blurted everything out?

Tightening her grip around the phone, she took a breath and said as casually as she could manage, 'He just wanted to talk about a business venture.'

'You mean he wanted money? Seriously, Margot. Did he know where you were, or what you were doing there?'

He shook his head, exasperation in his voice. 'No, of course not. I mean, why would he know anything about my life? I'm only his son.'

She bit her lip, for now there was more than exasperation, there was pain too.

After she and her brothers had gone to live with her grandparents, Yves had refused to see Emile any more. He had always distanced himself from their parents' behaviour, so maybe he'd thought distancing himself from a father he considered weak and embarrassing was the next logical step.

Her grandparents had seemed to think so too, and had done nothing to dissuade him. Nor had they encouraged Louis to stay in contact with his father. In fact it had been Margot alone who had kept in touch with Emile.

She breathed out softly. She knew her father should have done more. But her grandparents had made it so difficult for him that inevitably he'd given up. It was all so stupid and senseless—but that didn't mean that Louis wasn't hurt by the fact that their father only ever talked to her.

'It wasn't just business,' she said quickly. 'He wanted to get you and Gisele a wedding present.'

The lie was so swift and slick that for a moment she almost believed it herself. And, of course, by the time the wedding happened she would have chosen a gift, coaxed Emile into sending it, and then it wouldn't be a lie any more.

'I think he felt awkward.'

She felt suddenly tired. How had she become this person? Not only was she able to lie to her own brother without flinching, she already knew the arguments she would use against herself later to rationalise her behaviour.

'He said that?' Louis looked at her uncertainly, but he

sounded somewhat appeased. 'I'm surprised he even remembered I'm getting married.' He paused. 'But why did that mean you had to leave Monte Carlo?'

She didn't blink. Instead she stared across her bedroom at the Renoir lithograph of a young woman that had been a gift from her grandfather for her twenty-first birthday. It had always been one or her favourite pictures, and now she found the girl's calm expression particularly comforting.

'There was a problem at work,' she said quickly. 'Me coming back had nothing to do with Emile. It was just a coincidence.' She hesitated. 'Did Gisele mind?'

'A little. But she didn't actually think you would go at all, so—'

'I wanted to go,' she protested. 'And I would have stayed. I was having fun.'

'Liar!' Louis burst out laughing. 'You hate themed parties.'

She started to laugh too, and for a moment it was just the two of them, and life was simple and sunny again. 'True, but I'm only human—and there's something strangely irresistible about a lace body stocking and fingerless gloves.'

She'd wanted to hear her brother laugh again, and listening to his whoop of delight she felt a rush of pure, uncomplicated love for him.

'Please tell me there are photos.'

She smiled. 'Maybe! But what happens on bachelorette week stays on bachelorette week.'

'So, did you sort it out?'

The shift in topic caught her off guard, and it took a moment for her to understand the question. Without even meaning to do so Louis had introduced Max into the conversation, and just like that she was back in the boardroom, her body just inches from his, the pull between them like a living, pulsing force of nature...

Quickly pushing the image aside, she cleared her throat. 'Yes—it's all sorted.'

Her heart began to pound. *Was it?* Did agreeing to marry a man you loathed simply to save your family from public humiliation count as sorted?

Yes, she thought fiercely. It did. It might not be the future she'd pictured, but it would be far better than any she could produce without Max's investment.

'My sister the big-shot boss.'

Louis sounded gleeful. He had no interest in the business, but his admiration of Margot was partisan and unquestioning, and she felt another rush of love for him.

'You are *so* going to give this new *terroiriste* a run for his money. Have you met him yet?'

Margot frowned. The term wasn't new to her. There was a growing movement among wine-growers around the world that wines should be a unique expression of soil and climate—not a result of artificial intervention from chemical pesticides and fertilisers. She had been trying for years to push Duvernay to become more biodynamic, but change had been slower than she would have liked, because change required money that she simply didn't have.

Her pulse twitched, and she realised that her thought process was inching dangerously back towards Max and that conversation in the boardroom. With another effort of will she dragged her mind back to Louis's impatient, handsome face.

'Have I met who? What are you talking about?'

'You know—this Max Montigny. Guillaume had a chat with him at the country club and he told him that he's looking to move into the region. Apparently he's already got his eye on one of the big champagne estates.'

For a moment Margot couldn't speak. The shock of hearing Louis say Max's name out loud was just so deep and sudden. Only not as much of a shock as learning that Max's intentions were a matter for public discussion. Somehow that made everything feel a little sharper, more in focus. More urgent.

She pressed a fingertip against the side of her head, pushing down on the pain that had begun pulsing there. 'What did Guillaume think?'

Guillaume was Gisele's father, a genial industrialist who had made a fortune in telecommunications and was now looking to move into politics.

'What? About Montigny? Oh, he liked him—but he said he couldn't figure him out. That he looked like a film star but sounded like a banker. Until he started talking about wine. And then he sounded like a revolutionary.' Louis paused, as though he couldn't figure Max out either. 'But I don't think you need to worry about him, Comtesse du Duvernay.'

She smiled automatically. It was a childhood nickname. Yves and Louis had used to call her that whenever they'd thought she was being too bossy. Only now it felt like a cruel joke—an empty title for a woman who had traded herself like a chattel, marrying not for love but money.

'Is that right?' she said quickly, forcing a lightness into her voice that she didn't feel.

Louis grinned, the tiny screen barely diminishing the infectious power of his smile. 'Damn right, it is. If anyone can handle him it'll be you.'

After she'd hung up Margot blow dried her hair, and applied her make-up with careful precision. Glancing in the mirror, she felt her stomach clench. She might be CEO of one of the biggest champagne producers in the world, but this was her real skill. Presenting an image of serenity and control to the world while inside chaos reigned.

With an effort, she tried to arrange her thoughts to

match her outward composure, but Louis's words kept stubbornly weaving through her head like the subtitles to a movie she didn't want to watch.

Film star. Banker. Revolutionary.

Blackmailer.

She gritted her teeth. It sounded like a warped child's nursery rhyme, but in fact it was just another reminder of how little she knew Max. And, despite her brother's faith in her, of how ill-prepared she was to manage him.

Her throat tightened. But then she wasn't just *managing* Max, was she? She was marrying him.

CHAPTER FOUR

'Would you like sparkling or still water?'

Glancing up from the bread roll she had spent far too long buttering, Margot smiled politely at the waiter. 'Still, please.'

She glanced across the table to where Max was discussing the wine with the hotel's sommelier. They were having lunch in his hotel suite. He had texted her an hour earlier, telling her what time to arrive, and although she was irritated by the no doubt deliberate short notice she was grateful not to have to prolong the agony, and relieved that he'd suggested lunch and not dinner.

Although now she was here she couldn't help feeling on edge, for being summoned to his rooms had made her feel like some kind of concubine.

Carefully, she laid her knife across her side plate. He had also—and this time she had no doubt that he'd done it deliberately—omitted to tell her where he was staying.

Of course he hadn't been hard to find. Judging by the amount of column inches given over to his presence in Paris, Max Montigny's whereabouts were not just a key piece of information to her, but a matter of fascination to most of the French public.

Her heartbeat twitched.

His casual, arrogant assumption that she'd have no

choice but to track him down made her want to reach over and slap his beautiful face. But what did it matter, really? In the wider scheme of things it was just another hoop for her to jump through—a nudge to remind her that he was in charge. Not that she really needed the balance of power in their relationship to be pointed out. Every humbling second of yesterday's meeting was seared onto her brain.

But, although it been painful and humiliating to have to accept his proposal, of the many emotions she was feeling the one that was overriding all others was not anger, nor even misery, but oddly relief. Since Max had offered to marry her and turn her business around, for the first time in the longest time some of the crushing burden of responsibility she'd been carrying around seemed to have lifted from her shoulders.

Finally there would be somebody by her side. Somebody who would have her back. She shivered. If still felt strange, though, putting her life and her family's future into the hands of Max Montigny.

Her mouth felt suddenly dry.

If only the secrecy and lies surrounding their arrangement had felt equally unfamiliar. But they hadn't. Instead everything—the half-truths she had told her grandfather about where she was going, her decision to drive herself and thus not include her chauffeur in the deception—had all conspired to make time contort.

And the unsettling sensation of past and present blurring hadn't gone away when, having kept her waiting for ten minutes, Max had finally strolled into the room, dressed casually in jeans and a grey T-shirt.

His lateness had been as deliberate as his failure to tell her where they were meeting, and she had found it just as provoking, but that wasn't the reason her heart had begun beating faster.

Watching him move towards her, with a languid purpose that had made her stomach tighten painfully, she had been forced to face the truth. That her body's response to him in the boardroom had been no one-off. And that, even while she loathed him, his beauty could still reduce the world around her to mere scenery.

'Good.'

Max's voice cut into her confused thoughts and, looking up, she felt her eyes bump into his. Instantly, she felt a rush of nerves, as though she was about to tackle the Cresta Run instead of merely eat lunch.

'Thanks, Jean-Luc.' His gaze never leaving her face, he dismissed the sommelier with a nod of his dark head. 'I hope you don't mind but I thought it would be easier if I selected the wine.' The corners of his mouth twitched. 'Save any arguments.'

'Of course,' she said tightly, her heart banging against her chest. 'What did you choose?'

'A Clement-Dury Montrachet to start, and then a Domaine-Corton Pinot Noir to follow.'

'I like them both,' she said truthfully. 'Especially the Montrachet. It has such a good finish.'

Max grinned suddenly, and the unguarded excitement in his eyes caught her off-balance.

'It does, doesn't it? I like the balance of flavours—and that citrus really resonates.' He picked up the wine menu and flicked through it idly. 'They've got a great list here… really strong on small producers.' His face grew mocking. 'Although, rather embarrassingly for them, the management turned me down when I was starting out.'

Margot looked at him blankly, caught off guard by his remark, for—just like the rest of his life—Max's dizzyingly rapid rise to success was a mystery to her.

'It must have been hard for you,' she said cautiously. 'It's amazing…what you've done.'

He shrugged. 'I worked hard, and it helped that we got some outstanding reviews in the wine press.'

She nodded, but she hardly took in his words. She was too distracted by the speed with which their relationship was moving. Yesterday they had been hurling the verbal equivalent of thunderbolts at one another, and yet here there were today, talking almost normally, just like any other couple having lunch.

Tearing off a piece of her roll, she slid it into her mouth and forced herself to chew. And that was what she'd wanted, wasn't it? A civilised arrangement, free from un-settling feelings and even more unsettling actions.

Her skin grew warm as once again she remembered that kiss in the boardroom, remembered pleasures buried but not forgotten, the glowing imprint of his lips and fin-gers on her skin…

The sommelier returned at that moment and, heart pounding, she waited for him to pour the wine into their glasses. When finally they were alone again she said crisply, 'Is that why you chose this place?' She made her-self look across at him. 'Or was it the allure of the black door?'

She was referring to the famous hidden entrance to the building, which allowed the hotel's A-list clientele and their overnight guests to come and go without having to face the intruding lenses of the paparazzi.

His mouth curled upwards. 'The former, I'm afraid. Sadly, I don't have anything or anyone to hide from the press.' He made a show of hesitating, his eyes glittering with amusement. 'Oh, I'm sorry. Was that the Duvernay way of telling me that you're planning on staying over?'

She glared at him, torn between fury at his arrogance and despair at the lurch of heat his words produced.

Picking up another piece of bread, she mashed butter into it savagely. 'If you seriously believe that, then you must have an awfully vivid imagination.'

He stared at her across the table. His expression was still pleasant and interested, but there was a definite tension in the air.

'I don't need an imagination to remember what it's like between us, Margot.'

Her body felt suddenly soft and boneless. She knew he was talking about what had happened in the boardroom, but she deliberately chose to misinterpret him.

'I'll have to take your word on that,' she said stiffly. 'What happened between us was such a long time ago and so brief I can barely remember it.'

'Really?'

The word slid over her skin like a caress, and he gave her a smile that made the edges of her vision start to blur. Breathing in unsteadily, she curled her fingers into her palms, feeling her skin tighten with shame at how easily she had succumbed to the pull of the past. At how even here, now, her body was responding to his with a hunger and a lack of judgement that was both undeniable and humiliating.

As though reading her thoughts, he leaned forward, his eyes resting on her face, watching the colour spread slowly over her cheeks.

'Then your memory must be *awfully* poor, indeed. Or just in need of refreshing, perhaps.'

For a second they both stared at one another, and then he picked up his wine glass. '*À ta santé.*'

The meal was perfect. The hotel's chef was renowned, and clearly he was determined to impress. Ratte potatoes topped with a mousseline of smoked haddock and Sologne caviar was followed by turbot with wild pink garlic in a brown butter zabaglione. There was an array of seasonal regional French cheeses, and to finish an iced coffee parfait with a lemongrass-infused chocolate sorbet.

Laying down her cutlery, Margot felt sudden panic squeeze her chest. Throughout lunch the constant presence of the staff had prevented any long, awkward silences, and she had been able to smile and chat quite naturally. But now the meal was coming to an end, and as the waiters quietly left the room, she felt her pulse start to accelerate.

Being alone with Max had been difficult enough when she'd been shocked and angry. Now, though, the shock had faded, and her anger was at best intermittent—like Morse Code.

Unfortunately, what hadn't faded was her susceptibility to his beauty and sexuality. Her shoulders stiffened. But even if she couldn't control her body's response to him, she certainly didn't have to act on it.

Yes, she might have agreed to become his wife, but there was a huge difference between what was legal and what was *real*. Their wedding might be legal, but it would be purely for show. No ceremony, lawful or otherwise, could stop Max being the man who was blackmailing her into marriage—in other words, her enemy.

Remembering again that near-miss kiss in the boardroom, she shivered. Except what kind of enemies kissed?

Picking up her glass, she took a sip of wine. She wasn't going to think about that now. All she wanted to do at this moment was get through this meal, discuss the terms of their agreement and then leave.

Her mouth twisted. That, at least, was different from the past.

Back then she and Max had been desperate to be alone.

To have privacy to talk, to touch, to laugh, to listen. But there had always been people around them—estate workers, guests staying at the chateau, and of course her family. Back then it had been like a kind of torture to have to remember that they were 'just friends', and that she couldn't touch him as she did in private.

Quashing the memory of just how much she had liked to touch him in private, she looked up and found Max watching her appraisingly, the blue and green of his gaze so level and steady that her heart began banging inside her throat.

Hoping that her face revealed nothing of her thoughts, and eager to be away from his scrutiny, she said stiffly, 'Shall we take coffee in the lounge?'

To her relief, he nodded, but as she walked into the large, opulent sitting room she swore silently. It was bad enough there were no armchairs, but the curtains had been drawn against the piercing afternoon sun, and there was something about the shadowy room and the sleek black velvet sofas that made her stomach flip over—some hint of a private salon, of soft breathing and damp skin...

Summoning up what she hoped was a casual smile, she sat down. Seconds later she felt him drop down beside her, as she'd known he would, and then his weight tipped her slightly sideways, and she felt her pulse stumble as his leg brushed against hers.

Instantly the hairs on her arms stood up, and it took every ounce of willpower she had not to lean into the heat and hardness of his thigh and press her body against his.

Shaken by the close contact, shocked by the explicitness of her thoughts, she turned and stared quickly across the room to the gap between the curtains.

Outside the window Paris was all pink blossom and golden sunlight. It was the most perfectly romantic of backdrops and her heart began to beat faster, for it seemed so glaringly at odds with what she and Max were agreeing to do.

'Coffee?'

She blinked, then nodded, but in truth her mind was already slipping away—back to the memory of another sunlit afternoon and another cup of coffee.

It had been a moment of rare impulsiveness. Knowing it was Max's day off, she had gone to his cottage alone. She had felt bold and reckless—in short, nothing like her normal self. But when Max had finally opened the door, shirtless, his eyes neither green nor blue but somewhere in between, her bravado had fled, her body stilling, her mind blank with panic. Because that was as far as she'd got inside her head.

Everything else had been just a fantasy.

And maybe it would have stayed a fantasy—only, incredibly, Max had asked her in and made her a cup of coffee. A cup of coffee that had sat and gone cold while her fantasy became real. Or so she'd thought at the time.

She cleared her throat. 'Just black. Thank you.'

'When did you drop the sugar?'

Drop the sugar? She stared at him blankly. Was that some kind of code or slang?

He raised an eyebrow. 'You used to take sugar.'

It was not quite a question, and his voice sounded softer, almost teasing, as though the nod to their shared past had softened his mood.

But it wasn't fair of Max to change the tone from *sotto* to *scherzando* without warning. Nor was it fair of him to smile like that, she thought helplessly, her eyes drawn inexorably to the slight fullness of his lower lip. It wasn't fair of him to remind her of the past she'd worked so hard to forget. A past that hadn't even been real.

She cleared her throat.

'Yes, I did.' She nodded. 'But I stopped putting it in my coffee a few years ago. In fact, we barely eat any sugar at home any more—extra sugar, I mean.'

Max stared at her in silence, his face showing none of the emotion that was tearing through his chest.

Watching her talk, he had forgotten just for the briefest of moments why she was there. Forgotten why 'it'—the two of them—had ended all those years ago. Instead, he could only think of the reasons it had started.

Her smile. Her laughter. Her brain. He'd loved that she was smart—not just book-smart, although she had always been that but perceptive in a way that had suggested she was far older than nineteen.

And her body.

Useless to lie. He was a man, and what normal heterosexual man wouldn't respond to that arrangement of contours and curves and clefts. His heart thumped against the roof of his mouth and an answering pulse of desire started to beat in his groin.

Ignoring the heat breaking out on his skin, he forced himself to speak. 'Any particular reason?'

Margot shrugged. She hadn't expected him to pursue the topic, and suddenly she was grappling with how much to give away. Her grandfather's poor health was not common knowledge, but to give no answer would be just as revealing.

'My grandfather had a stroke about six months ago,' she said flatly. 'Modifying his diet was something the doctors suggested we do afterwards.' She took a deep breath. 'But I'm sure you didn't invite me here to talk about my grandfather's diet.'

Glancing down at her diamond-set wristwatch, she lifted her chin.

'And I know you must be as busy as I am. So perhaps we should start discussing the terms of our arrangement?'

Max felt himself tense. If he'd needed a reminder as to why their relationship had always been a non-starter it was there in those sentences, he thought on a rush of fury and resentment. For even now, when she was here *only* at his bidding, she still couldn't stop herself drawing a line in the sand, pointedly shutting him out of anything that trespassed on Duvernay matters and bringing the conversation back to business.

Briefly he considered telling her that the deal was off. That if she wanted money that badly there was a bank two doors down from the hotel and another one on the next street. But then he felt his pulse slow.

Looked at differently, Margot had done him a favour, reminding him of what mattered to her: her business and her bloodline. Both of which had been off-limits to a nobody like Max—until now.

He let his gaze drift slowly over her face. 'From memory, it was less of an invitation and more or an instruction,' he said softly. 'Or do you still think you have some say in what's happening here?'

Her eyes flared and he felt a beat of satisfaction, watching her struggle to stay calm.

'Fine! You told me to come,' she retorted, a note of frustration sharpening her voice, 'and I'm here. So, are we going to discuss our marriage or not?'

He lounged back, the shadow of stubble on his jawline co-ordinating perfectly with the velvet nap of the sofa. 'We are,' he said finally, his eyes never leaving her face, 'but first I want to give you this.'

Reaching into his jacket, he pulled out a small, square box.

His mouth curled into a mocking smile. 'Don't get too

excited. It's from necessity, not any sort of romantic impulse on my part. You'll need to wear it. In public, at least.'

Flipping open the lid, he dropped the box carelessly into her open hand.

There was a short, spiralling silence.

Gazing down, Margot felt her stomach clamp tight, like a vacuum sealing inside her. The ring was beautiful. A huge yellow diamond flanked by two smaller white diamonds. And yet for some reason she couldn't seem to take it in. Instead she could feel herself being dragged back in time, to the moment when Max had stood in front of her, a pear-cut sapphire set in a band of gold in his outstretched hand.

It had been the most exciting moment in her life.

And the most terrible.

The picture was frozen inside her head. Max, his face expressionless, herself, silent and rigid with shock. And then Yves strolling in, his easy smile twisting, his mood turning from sweet to sour in the blink of an eye, shouting accusations and threats, teeth bared like a cornered dog.

Her brother's anger had been shocking, awful, brutal. But not as brutal as Max's admission that none of it had been real. That he'd only ever wanted her for her money.

'It's beautiful.' She knew her voice sounded stilted, fake, but it was all she could manage.

Max studied her face. It was his own fault. For years he'd wanted to believe that he'd been wrong. That she had really wanted to be his wife, and that given the opportunity—

He gritted his teeth. But of course he'd been right the first time. Yves's intervention had merely brought things to a head. Showing not a flicker of emotion, he said quietly, 'I'm glad you like it.'

Margot looked up. Something in his voice elbowed

aside the promise she'd made not to ask about his personal life. She couldn't help the sudden swirling riptide of curiosity from rising up inside her, for of course she was curious.

And so, in spite of her intention to stay silent, she found herself saying, 'It's lucky neither of us had other commitments.'

She held her breath, waiting for an answer, a sharp needle of jealousy stabbing beneath her heart.

Max felt something heavy dragging down inside of him. If only he could reach across and shake that fixed, polite smile from her mouth. Or maybe it was himself he wanted to shake—anything to shift the dark, leaden ache in his chest.

Watching her, he felt his breath tangle into knots. Luck had nothing to do with it. After Margot he'd had relationships—no-strings, sexually satisfying affairs that had helped ease the sting of her rejection. But work had been his real commitment, for there he had been able to harness his anger and resentment, and that had driven the ambition that had taken him back to France and to that meeting with Emile.

Clearing his throat, he bit down on the anger rising inside him. 'Don't you mean lucrative?' he said coolly.

Her head jerked up, and the stunned, helpless expression on her face made something claw at him inside. But he told himself he didn't care, and pretending he'd noticed nothing, he smiled casually.

'I've picked out wedding rings for both of us, so all you need to do is speak to your family,' he continued relentlessly. 'Tell them that you'll be away for a couple of days. Oh, and you'll need a dress.'

'Away where? And why do I need a dress?' She frowned suspiciously.

He raised an eyebrow. 'To get married in, of course. We leave for the Seychelles tomorrow.'

She gazed at him in wordless disbelief, a flutter of fear skittering down her spine. 'Tomorrow?'

His eyes were cool and mocking. 'What?' he asked softly, and she could hear the taunting note in his voice. 'Did you think I was going to wait another ten years?'

Her head was suddenly aching and her vison was going watery at the edges. She opened her mouth, then closed it again. Her brain seemed to have stopped functioning. 'This is a joke, right? I mean, you can't expect me to marry you *tomorrow*.'

'I don't. The paperwork won't be ready in time.' The upward curve of his mouth was like a fish hook through her heart. 'I do, however, expect you to marry me in three days.'

For a moment she could only stare at him in stunned silence. And then finally she shook her head, her blonde hair flicking from side to side like a lioness's tail. 'I don't care about what you expect,' she snapped, her eyes clashing with his. 'That isn't going to happen.'

Over the last twenty-four hours she had, if not fully adjusted to her fate, at least accepted the benefits of marrying Max. But as far as she was concerned telling her family was a long way off. She'd anticipated an engagement period of several months, during which time she would have got her grandfather and Louis used to the idea of Max as her boyfriend, then her fiancé. Now, though, the option of gently breaking her future plans to them was not just under threat, it was in pieces.

She shivered. Her stomach felt as though it was filling with ice.

For most people a wedding in an exotic location with few legalities and a minimal waiting time would probably sound spontaneous and romantic. To her, though, it sounded like an exact duplicate of her parents' hasty elopement.

But she couldn't explain that to Max. Not without revealing more about herself than she was willing to share with a man who was not only blackmailing her into marriage, but was incapable of even the most basic human empathy.

She gazed at him stonily. 'Surely you can understand that? I mean, what exactly am I supposed to tell my family? I can't just roll up and announce that I'm getting married.'

He shrugged. 'Come, come, Margot. You're a Duvernay. You can do what you like. Besides, you've had a lot of practice in lying. I imagine you'll think of something.'

The rush of fury was intoxicating. Suddenly she was on her toes like a boxer, fingers twitching, clenching and unclenching. 'You unspeakable pig—'

He cut across her, his voice razor-edged and cold as steel. 'Spare me the outrage. You lied to your family for months about our relationship last time. Now you only have to do it for three days.'

'Wasn't it lucky that I did?' she snarled. 'At least they were spared *your* lies and deceit.'

There was a charged silence. He didn't reply, just continued to sit there, his face taut, his eyes impassive. And then, just as she was about to demand a response, he abruptly stood up and with careless, unhurried ease, walked to the door and yanked it open. Stepping aside, he stared coolly back across the room, his jawline and cheekbones suddenly in shadow.

'Let me make this simple for you, Margot. Either you agree to marry me in three days or you walk through this door now and take your chances with the bank.'

His tone was pleasant, but there was no mistaking the ultimatum in his voice.

Margot gazed at him in silence, her heart skidding sideways like car on black ice. Surely he was calling her bluff. He had to be. And yet she couldn't bring herself to find out, for if she got up and walked towards the door it was just possible that she would lose everything.

She had no weapons to bring to the fight, and escalating things would only make that fact obvious to Max. All she could do was back down with as much dignity as she could manage.

'Since you put it so charmingly,' she said stiffly, ignoring the heartbeat that was telegraphing frantically inside her chest, 'I'll do it.' She lifted her chin, her brown eyes locking on to his face, staring him down. 'But on one condition.'

'Condition?'

She heard the hint of surprise in his voice, and felt a fleeting quiver of satisfaction. 'Yes, damn you.' Matching his level, assessing gaze with what she hoped was one of her own, she gave a humourless laugh. 'What did you think? That I'd just bow down to your threats and intimidation?'

Max let his eyes drift over her face, seeing both the pulse quivering at the base of her throat—that beautiful, graceful throat—and the discs of colour spreading over her cheeks. No, he hadn't thought that, and in a way he hadn't wanted it either. He would never want that from this woman who had been like a living flame in his arms.

Casually he pushed the door shut and walked across the room, stopping in front of her. 'Name it,' he demanded.

'As soon as we're married I want to tell my grandfather and brother in person—before details are released to the press.'

The marriage would be a shock to both of them, but she knew that they would accept and understand it better if she told them herself.

Max stared down at her, trying to ignore the heady scent of her perfume. It was a shock. Not her demand—which was almost laughably inconsequential—but the intensity of his relief that she hadn't got up and stormed through the door. Irrational though it sounded, it didn't matter that the marriage hadn't happened. She already felt like his wife. And, having got so far, he wasn't about to lose her now.

Letting her win this particular battle was unimportant in the scheme of things. It certainly didn't mean that he was about to give her power over anything else—like his feelings, for example. Besides, he had other, more effective ways to remind her that he was in charge.

He raised his shoulders dismissively. 'Okay. I'm happy for you to do that.' His eyes locked on to hers. 'Just as I'm sure *you're* happy to sign the prenuptial agreement I sent over.'

Turning, he picked a laminated folder up from the table behind the sofa and held it out to her.

'I take it you've read it?'

Margot nodded. Her heart began to thump against her chest.

He had emailed it over last night, and she'd gone over it twice. It contained no surprises. But it still jarred, though—stung, actually—the fact that ten years ago she had taken him at his word, whereas now he was demanding that she make no claim on his estate.

Her lips tightened. 'Yes, I've read it. There don't seem to be any problems.'

Aside from the small, incontrovertible fact that she was bartering herself to a man she had once loved without restraint, and with a hope she now found inconceivable.

Suddenly she just wanted to sign the damned thing and be gone. To be anywhere that Max wasn't.

She reached into her bag, but he was too fast for her.

'Here—use mine.'

He was holding out a black and gold fountain pen. It was identical to the one her grandfather used, and just for a moment she thought she might be sick. But, swallowing the metallic taste in her mouth, she took the pen from his fingers with what she hoped was an expression of pure indifference and, flipping through the document to the last page, carelessly scrawled her signature next to his, doing the same again seconds later on the other copy.

Misery snaked over her skin, but she wasn't about to let Max know how much she was hurting. He might hold all the cards, but there was some small satisfaction to be had from not acknowledging that fact—particularly to him.

Only suddenly that wasn't enough. Suddenly she didn't just want to hide her pain, she wanted to hurt him as he had hurt her. Laying the pen carefully on top of the paper, she looked up and deliberately fixed her gaze on his maddeningly handsome face.

'One last thing. Just so we're clear, this marriage is a business arrangement. Sex—' she punched the word towards him '—is not and is never going to be part of the deal. Whatever physical relationship we had, it happened a long time ago.'

A mocking smile tugged at his mouth. 'I wouldn't call twenty-four hours a long time.'

Mortified, she felt the air thump out of her lungs. How she regretted that kiss—or if not the kiss then the treacherous weakness of the body that had allowed it to happen.

'That was just curiosity,' she said quickly, trying to sound as if she meant it, as though only a fraction of her mind was on him.

'I just wanted a taste—you know, an *amuse bouche*. See if the menu was still worth sampling.' She was aware that her cheeks were flushed, that her voice was shaking ever so slightly, but she forced herself to hold his gaze. 'Only I guess I've grown up a lot. Had a bit more experience…tried different flavours. I know some couples go for that "sex with the ex" thing, but I'm going to pass on it.'

She could hardly believe the words that were coming out of her mouth. It felt unreal, talking that way, and to Max in particular, but she knew that she had his attention. For a moment she held her breath, waiting for his reaction, already anticipating his fury. But his face didn't change, and when finally he spoke his voice was as expressionless as his unblinking eyes.

'Of course you are—and now, unfortunately, I have another meeting scheduled. I hope you enjoyed your lunch…'

Gazing up at him, it took a moment for his words to sink in, and then, as they did, she realised with a rush of embarrassment that he was waiting politely and patiently for her to leave.

Back in her car, it took several minutes of deep breathing before her hands stopped shaking and she could start the engine. Pulling out into the late-afternoon traffic, she could feel questions pawing at her brain like a pack of dogs with a bone. Why had he acted like that? Why hadn't he thrown her remark back in her face?

Leaning back against the smooth leather seat, she rested her arm against the doorframe, and gnawed distractedly at her thumbnail.

Even at the most basic level her words would have been insulting to any man. But to Max it had been personal. So why had he deliberately chosen not to respond?

She pressed her thumb against the corner of her mouth.

It was probably just another attempt to belittle her. Or maybe he was trying to mess with her head so that she'd end up with all these unanswerable questions swamping her brain. Or—

An icy shiver slipped down her spine, and she groaned softly.

Or maybe he just hadn't believed her.

And, really, why would he? When she didn't even believe herself?

Remembering the moment when he'd pressed his mouth to hers—the all-encompassing heat of that kiss and the way her body had surrendered to his—she felt heat flare low in her pelvis...

The blast of a horn burst into her thoughts, and she watched dully as a taxi surged past her, the driver gesticulating and shouting abuse into the warm, sticky air.

Her arms felt like jelly, and with an effort she indicated left, out of the city.

She was such a fool! Instead of puncturing his pride, her stupid denial had merely drawn attention to the terrible, humiliating truth. That she still wanted him with an intensity that was beyond her conscious control. But, terrible though it was to have betrayed herself like that, what was far worse was the private but equally devastating realisation that she couldn't imagine a time when that humiliating fact would ever change.

CHAPTER FIVE

RESTING HER HANDS against the edge of the balcony adjoining her hotel bedroom, Margot gazed out across the Indian Ocean, her brown eyes narrowing against the glare of morning sunlight, the thin silk of her robe lifting in the warm breeze coming off the water.

In just over five hours she would be Mrs Max Montigny—even just thinking that sentence made her feel dizzy. Or maybe that was the adrenaline. Her muscles clamped tighter. Either way, everything had all happened with such surreal speed that none of it felt real, and the sense of unreality was only being exacerbated by her idyllic surroundings.

Her gaze drifted back inland. The view from her hotel room was pure fantasy. A castaway island of palm-tree-framed beaches fusing with a dreamy turquoise sea. But there was a wildness to its beauty too, so that it was easy to feel you were the first person ever to leave your meandering footprints in the powdery white sands.

Raising a hand to block out the sun, she squinted down the beach. Perhaps not quite the first person. A figure was moving effortlessly across the dunes, covering the distance with impressive speed.

Wearing a black vest and shorts, his tanned skin gleaming like polished wood in the sunlight, Max was returning from his morning run. He moved with a focus and steadiness that in turn steadied *her*, so that some of her tension ebbed away.

Even from a distance, and with the sun in her eyes, his body looked just as spectacular as she remembered it—lean and sculptured and powerful. Her eyes lingered greedily on the striped bands of his taut, abdominal muscles before dropping to where the V of his obliques met the sagittal line of fine dark hair in the centre of his stomach.

He was so perfect, so tempting. An intoxicating blend of strength and beauty that made her feel weak with desire. Her mouth twisted. Not that she'd given in to temptation again. But being around Max again was not just unsettling physically, it was messing with her head too—dredging up memories, making her question the life she was living, the choices she'd made.

Over the last few years boyfriends had come and gone, but none had lasted, and that was completely understandable. Running the House of Duvernay was most definitely not a nine-to-five job, so her personal life had by necessity taken a back seat to her professional one, and she'd been grateful it had, for she hadn't been ready or willing to get too involved, to get hurt again, to *feel*.

Or rather she'd been scared not of feeling something but of never feeling *as much* for anyone as she'd felt for Max.

She bit her lip. Even now she could remember it—the stunned realisation, part-fear, part-euphoria that he had chosen *her*, wanted *her*.

Her stomach clenched. No, not her. Her money.

Breathing out, she gazed at the moving figure.

If only she could go back to that time—back to when she'd believed that he wanted her for herself. Her heart gave a twitch of irritation. And do what? Let her stupid, treacherous body betray her again?

She glanced back at Max, her eyes tracking his progress. The sun was already high overhead, but he seemed immune to the heat of its rays. He was running—no, make that sprinting—effortlessly across the sand, as though he was training for some elite military unit.

And then, as though he'd crossed an imaginary finishing line, he pulled up sharply, his legs slowing to a jog, then to a walk as he glanced down at his watch.

Her pulse was racing as hard as if she too had just run the length of the beach, and then her breath stalled in her throat as she watched him reach into the pocket of his shorts and pull out his phone.

She felt her eyes narrow. Surely today of all days he might have stopped working. But it was pointless getting angry about it. After all, it wasn't as though this marriage was anything other than a business arrangement for either of them.

Although, thanks to Max's extensive and careful preparations, nobody except the two of them would ever know that it wasn't real. Not only had he organised the paperwork and arranged the venue, he had sorted out the food, the flowers, and flown out a team of stylists to oversee everything on site. And everything was spot-on.

All she'd had to think about was the dress...

A light breeze lifted her hair in front of her face and, pushing it aside, she felt her pulse dip. Given that she was only marrying Max to save her business, it really shouldn't matter what she wore. But, to her surprise, her wedding gown still felt like more than just a dress to her.

Staring up at the cloudless sky, she let the sun warm her face. Back in Paris, feeling harried by the pace of his arrangements, she had considered choosing an off-the-peg dress from one of the big department stores. It had been a childish impulse, really—another meaningless attempt to prove how little she cared about him and their phony wedding.

But in the end she hadn't been able to bring herself to do it. And it hadn't just been because of the risk that somebody might spot her browsing the rails and leak it to the media.

Lowering her head, she drew in a deep breath. She was a Duvernay, and in her family's history weddings were not just celebrations but life-impacting events, defined not just by who you married but what you wore.

Her grandmother's dress had been spectacular. A fairy tale confection with metres of tulle and millions of hand-sewn pearls. It had taken fifty seamstresses nearly three months to create.

In contrast, her mother had recycled the simple knee-length tulle-skirted dress that she'd worn for her eighteenth birthday party.

Each had known instinctively what she wanted to wear to marry the man she had chosen to be her husband. Only where did that leave her? She was marrying a man she didn't love, out of necessity. What exactly was the dress code for a marriage of convenience?

Despite the heat of the sun, Margot shivered.

It didn't help that she was being forced to do something she'd actually dreamed of doing. Ten years ago she had been happily imagining a wedding day in the future. Only Max had been more than just her groom—he'd been the air she breathed, the gravitational pull of her world.

For a second she braced herself against the pain, fingers tightening against the balustrade. But that had been then. In the present, this wedding wasn't about Max. Just like the rest of her life, it was about creating an illusion.

She needed her grandfather to accept her sudden decision to get married. Actually, she wanted him to be happy about it. Only with the speed and secrecy of the arrangements so closely mirroring his daughter's elopement, she knew that the only way to make that happen was by staging the perfect wedding.

And, no matter how little time there had been, Max Montigny's wife would *never* wear a department store dress. Her gown, just like her ring, would have to look the part. As her groom undoubtedly would.

Max was still talking on his phone, his handsome face relaxed and unguarded, and something about his expression made her heart contract—for she could still remember just how heavenly it had felt to be the object of that gaze.

Her fingers trembled against the smooth wood as she wondered what it would feel like if today was actually real, and instead of her money or her business, Max actually wanted her.

It was not the first time that thought had crossed her mind. In fact, it had been popping into her head with maddening regularity ever since she'd watched him walk out of her boardroom that first day. But thinking it could ever happen would require an almost childlike level of imagination, and she was done with building castles in the air. The only castle she cared about now was her family home.

She needed to focus on the facts—which were that Max might be in control of her business, but she was in control of everything else. And that included how she chose to respond to him. All she had to do was stay cool and detached and civil and their marriage would hopefully be civilised too.

Glancing down at Max's sweat-slicked skin, she licked her lips. That might be easier in theory than in practice. Although Max wasn't quite the barbarian she'd accused him of being, he was still the least civilised person she'd ever met, seemingly untroubled by blackmail and extortion.

However, even from the short amount of time they'd spent discussing his plans for Duvernay, she had to admit that he'd actually been modest when he'd said he had a head for business. He was smart, quick and creative—and, although he had an innate authority that reminded her of her grandfather, he was also surprisingly willing to listen to his staff. And even more surprisingly to her.

She had expected to be swept aside, but instead, at his suggestion, they would be working together as co-CEOs, his argument being that having 'two in the box' was better than one.

If only their marriage could be as equable and as close, she thought wistfully.

At that moment, almost as if he could hear her thoughts, Max turned and stared fixedly across the beach towards her balcony.

Her pulse jumped. Hot-cheeked, horrified that she had been discovered in such a blatant act of voyeurism, she turned her face away from the magnetic pull of his gaze and inched back into her room.

Her skin was prickling. *Oh, how was she going to do this?* She couldn't even face him at a distance and from the safety of her hotel room. How was she going to stand opposite him and repeat vows neither of them believed to be true?

If only there was another way...

But there wasn't.

Duvernay's problems were not going to just disappear, and that was why she was here and why she was going to go through with this marriage.

A knock on the door broke into her thoughts and, grateful for the interruption, she tightened her wrap. The time for thinking was over. Now she needed to get ready for her wedding.

Three hours later she was standing nervously in front of the mirror, gazing at her reflection. The transformation was complete.

'You look beautiful.'

Her eyes darted gratefully to Camille Feuillet, friend and premier couturier from her favourite fashion house, who had flown out from Paris late last night. She had known the older woman ever since she was a gauche teenager, struggling with shyness and a famous mother. Camille had helped her find a style, and she was the one person she'd trusted to design a dress for her wedding day.

'It's lovely,' she said slowly. 'Camille, you are so clever. I never dreamed that it would look like this—that I could look like this.'

She had expected to feel different, but this was like alchemy. The dress was exquisite—and romantic. Camille had insisted on finishing the final details herself, hand-embroidering Margot and Max's initials into the beautiful, intricate floral lace veil.

Margot felt suddenly shy. Thanks to the woman standing beside her she would not only be able to convince her family and the world's media that she was marrying the love of her life, she would be able to do so feeling good about herself—just like a real bride.

'Thank you, Camille,' she said softly.

'You are so welcome.' Camille smiled, and then her face creased and she brushed a hand against her eyes. 'I promised myself I wouldn't cry but I can't help it. You just look so lovely.'

'More like lucky!' Despite the ache in her chest, the smile she gave the other woman was genuine. Camille had made her a wedding dress of heart-stopping beauty. It wasn't her fault the wedding itself was a sham of what it might have been.

'You've given me so much help and inspiration. I couldn't have done it without you, so thank you. And thank you for coming all this way. I know how busy you are—'

'It was my pleasure.' Camille hesitated, and then, glancing over at Margot, she giggled. 'Besides, I think this might be the one time your extremely cool fiancé actually gets a little hot under the collar, and I wouldn't want to miss that for anything.'

Margot nodded. Her smile didn't falter, but she felt her pulse quiver. No doubt most grooms *did* get emotional, seeing their bride, but then most grooms hadn't blackmailed their bride down the aisle. And Max didn't *do* emotion—or at least not the romantic, helpless kind of emotion that Camille was talking about.

Instead, he was fine-tuned for winning.

Remembering the dark, calculating glitter in his eyes when he'd kissed her in the boardroom, she knew that his desire was as cold and controlled as his heart. Whatever Max was feeling and thinking right now, she would lay odds that it had more to do with his business than his forthcoming nuptials.

'Are you ready?'

Camille's voice broke into her thoughts and, steadying her breathing, she turned and nodded. Then, pinching the edges of the veil between her fingers, she lowered it carefully over her face and walked slowly towards the door and her future.

On the other side of the hotel, his dark suit a contrast to the bleached boards of the chapel, Max Montigny stared down at his phone, his fingers hovering over the keyboard.

He was standing slightly apart from the priest, and the two elderly estate workers who had been carefully chosen by his security team to act as witnesses for the wedding were waiting patiently behind him, but he was barely aware of them, or of his surroundings.

Not the sun that had drained the colour out of the sky, or the tiny open-sided chapel that was smothered in white frangipani flowers. All his concentration was fixed on his phone.

He read the message on the screen, deleted a few words, retyped them and then finally deleted them all.

Switching the phone to 'silent', he dropped it in his pocket. It had taken him nearly ten years to get to this point, and he wasn't about to tempt fate with an unnecessary and premature text. Soon enough Margot would be wearing his ring, and then the whole world would be able to see that Max Montigny was the equal of the Duvernays.

He breathed in sharply. The thought of Margot finally becoming Mrs Montigny was dizzying. Bracing his shoulders, he gazed at the ocean. If only he could steady his breathing… But it was impossible to do so, for every time he inhaled, the warm, fragrant air reminded him of the perfume Margot wore.

It was driving him crazy. Not just the fact that the scent of her seemed to be following him everywhere, but the way it conjured up the memory of her brown-eyed challenge in his hotel room.

'I just wanted a taste…you know, an amuse bouche. *See if the menu was still worth sampling. I know some couples go for that "sex with the ex" thing, but I'm going to pass.'*

He'd known she was lying, but somehow that only made her claim more maddening—and frustrating.

Ignoring the pulse beating in his groin, he straightened his cuffs and turned towards the priest and the witnesses, nodding in acknowledgement. From years of keeping his own counsel he knew that the expression on his face gave nothing away—not even a hint as to the thoughts twisting through his head—and the thought calmed him. Revealing emotion—*feeling* emotion—was an act of self-destruction, a handing over of power to the person most equipped to hurt you the most.

And that was particularly true of the woman he was about to marry.

He let out a slow, unsteady breath. What amazed him was that he'd actually got this far. Back in France when Margot had given in to his demands, he had been too busy struggling with the various emotions produced by seeing her again to register the full consequences of his proposal.

It had been an act of impulse and pride—for, much as he'd moved on with his life, a part of him had never forgotten or forgiven her for throwing his proposal back in his face, just as he himself had been thrown off the Duvernay estate.

Now, though, impulse would become legal fact—a contract only dissolvable by law. In less than an hour Margot would be his wife, and that thought blew his mind. Or it would have done if he hadn't chosen that particular moment to look up.

His heart gave a lurch and his fingers tightened involuntarily as he watched Margot step tentatively into the chapel, her wary brown gaze resting on his face as she approached him.

Behind him, he heard someone—the priest, probably—clear his throat. There was a flurry of activity and he knew that he should turn round, that he needed to turn round in order for the ceremony to start. But he couldn't look away. His eyes were beyond his control, following her hungrily, pulled by some inexorable force, like twin tides dragged by the luminous pale loveliness of a new moon.

He felt his heart slam against his ribcage, his eyes taking in every detail as she took another step towards him—

and then stopped. A hush like a held breath had fallen over the chapel, and even the ocean's waves seemed to be silent, as though their ceaseless motion had been stilled by the presence of such flawless beauty.

She looked exquisite. Beneath the veil her long blonde hair was scooped into some kind of low bun, her bare shoulders were gleaming in the sunlight, and her dress...

His gaze travelled over the delicate lace of her bodice to the gently flaring skirt. He had expected her to look lovely—what bride didn't? But Margot was more than just beautiful. She had always been more than just beautiful. She was a mystery that he'd obsessively wanted to solve, that had always been just beyond his reach.

Until now.

And so, ignoring tradition, he walked towards her and held out his hand.

The service was short and to the point. Speaking the vows, and listening to Margot repeat the familiar promises of love and loyalty in her soft, unwavering voice, he couldn't actually believe that it was happening. And yet here he was, sliding the band of diamonds set in gold onto her finger, and she was pushing a plain gold band onto his.

Lifting her veil, he watched the pupils of her eyes widen in the shade of the chapel. The certificate they would sign in a moment would be tangible evidence that finally he had proved her and her family wrong. That was why he was here, and he should be feeling relief, satisfaction, triumph... And yet he felt tense, almost restless, as though there was something more...something more important than retribution only he wasn't sure what it was.

His gaze shifted, slid upwards to her eyes, and he took a deep breath, confounded by the conflict he saw there. It reminded him of that first winter he and his mother had moved to Paris, struggling with the sudden loss of their old life and with feelings he hadn't understood.

He'd felt so young and helpless, so lost and alone, so stripped of all defences, and the thought that Margot should be feeling like that now resonated inside him, so that suddenly his stomach was churning, his breath jamming in his throat.

His hand twitched and he almost reached out, as any human would, instinctively wanting to comfort her. But to have done so would have been clumsy—inappropriate, somehow.

Quickly, he reminded himself that the only way this marriage would work would be to keep memories and emotions out of it. She had agreed to become his wife and he didn't owe her any gentleness. He could simply have sat back and watched her business collapse, but instead he had given her and her family a way out from financial ruin and public humiliation.

It might not be the marriage she wanted, to the man she wanted, but as far as he was concerned she had got more than she deserved.

'Margot and Max, you have expressed your love to one another through the commitment and promises you have made, and celebrated your union with the giving and receiving of rings.' The priest smiled.

It was just words, Margot told herself nervously.

But, hearing the priest talk about love and commitment, she felt her heart start to pound. Glancing down at her hand, Margot stared at the diamond band nestling against her engagement ring. It was breathtakingly beautiful. Elegant. Timeless. And it wasn't just the ring. Everything—the sun-soaked setting, the lush, fragrant flowers, the smiling priest, even Max himself—was so perfect it was impossible to resist.

Her pulse gave a leap like a startled deer.

Especially Max.

He was close enough that she could differentiate between the heat of his body and the warmth of the spice-warm air.

Dry-mouthed, she stared at him, her eyes fluttering helplessly over the man standing beside her, her gaze drawn to his face. Not because he was now her husband, but because he was and would always be her magnetic north, and the pull between them was beyond any kind of rational thought.

Particularly when he looked so devastating.

The dark fabric of his suit fitted him like a second skin, and the pure, brilliant whiteness of his shirt perfectly offset his compelling eyes and *café crème* colouring. In the shade of the chapel his features looked as though they might have been cast from bronze.

He was the perfect groom in every way, and just for a moment she couldn't help herself. All the promises she'd made to herself earlier that morning were overridden, and she let herself imagine what it would be like if this was a marriage of love and Max simply wanted *her*.

That thought was still uppermost in her mind as the priest looked across and, smiling again at both of them, said quietly, 'You are no longer simply partners and best friends. Today you have chosen to be joined in marriage. Therefore, it is my pleasure to pronounce you husband and wife. Max, you may now kiss your bride!'

Max felt a jolt pass through his body. So that was it. It was over—finished. Done.

Or maybe it was just beginning.

His breath seemed to tear his throat as he looked into Margot's eyes. Something was happening in them. They held an expression half-startled, half-spellbound.

And then he realised why.

He wasn't sure of how or when it had happened but he was holding her, his arm curving around her back so that she was pressed against his body.

He stared down at her, a flutter of heat sidewinding over his skin. Her lips were the same colour as rose petals, her mouth a curving pink bow that he knew tasted as good as it looked. Kissing her was part of the ceremony. But after what she'd said to him in his hotel it felt more like a dare. A chance to raise the stakes. A challenge he could not walk away from.

He wanted to prove her wrong—to show her and everyone watching that she couldn't resist him. And, lowering his head, he let his mouth brush against hers. It was more of a graze than a kiss, fleeting and feather-light. But even as he lifted his head he felt his stomach flip. She stared up at him in silence, her gaze finding something, needing something...

And, looking down into her wide, unguarded brown eyes, he felt a rush of possessive desire as swift and unstoppable as white water rapids.

Finally, she was his wife.

His.

Pulling her soft body closer, her slid a finger under her chin and tipped her head up. His heart was pounding and the air was tightening around them as he studied her face. And then he was kissing her hungrily, one hand wrapping around her waist, the other pushing through her hair, anchoring her against him.

Margot felt the ground tip beneath her feet.

Grabbing at his jacket, she clutched at the smooth fabric

as his tongue parted her lips. And then she was falling...
falling back in time...her body responding unquestioningly, willingly, to the power and heat of his mouth.

Around her the world was spinning faster and faster,
like a ride at the funfair. She felt giddy and clumsy and
boneless. All she could do was cling on tight to the one
solid object she could find. And, leaning into Max's hard,
muscular body, she closed her eyes.

And suddenly there was only Max. His mouth, his
hands, the warm density of his chest. She wanted him,
and she had no conscious thought or physical wish to hold
back, to do anything but open her body to his.

But even as the taste of him filled her mouth she felt
his body tense, and then he was breaking the kiss, and instead of his pulse beating through her veins like a metro-
nome she could hear the tranquil sound of nearby waves
washing onto the beach.

Dazedly she looked up at him, pressing her hand against
his chest to steady herself. But only for a second.

She felt her body stiffen, and a damp stickiness began
creeping over her skin. Only it had nothing to do with the
balmy subtropical heat and everything to do with the cool,
appraising look in his eyes.

Her limbs felt as if they were made of wood.

Had she learnt nothing from the past?

Ten years ago Max had used other such kisses to seduce
her, to fool her into believing his lies. This time, though,
he didn't need to fool her. It was the priest and the witnesses he needed to convince, so that they would see what
he wanted them to see. Not an act of coercion or revenge,
but two people declaring their love for one another.

And clearly it had worked.

She felt her stomach plunge as the priest stepped forward, his gentle face creased in a smile of wonder and ap-

proval. 'You have kissed many times, I'm sure. But today your kiss means so much more. It has sealed your marriage. Today, your kiss is a promise.'

Max looked over at her, his eyes glinting as they swept over the flush that she knew was colouring her cheekbones.

'Yes, it is,' he said slowly. 'One I fully intend to keep.'

They were signing the register. Margot felt as though she was sleepwalking. Posing above the heavy leather-bound book, pen in hand, she smiled for the photographer, trying her hardest to look like the radiant bride that her grandfather and brother would be expecting to see.

There was confetti, champagne and congratulations. By the time they were walking back to the hotel Margot's mouth was aching with the effort of smiling and she felt exhausted, but also relieved, for now that it was done there was no more need to agonise over whether she was doing the right thing.

She was Margot Montigny now. And she knew that her grandfather and Louis would accept her marriage. For the first time since Emile had dropped his bombshell the burden she was carrying felt lighter. Now all she wanted to do was get back to France and break the news to her family.

Stomach swooping downwards, she stepped unthinkingly into the waiting limousine. And then, as the doors closed and the sleek black car began to move forward, she felt a sharp dart of apprehension.

Frowning, she turned to Max. 'Where are we going? I thought we were eating at the hotel.'

His handsome face looked relaxed, and the colour of his eyes was indistinguishable in the cool, shaded interior of the car. 'It's a surprise,' he said softly.

Her heart thumped clumsily against her ribs. 'I don't like surprises.'

His eyes rested on her face, and something about the steady calmness of his gaze unnerved her more than his words.

'Is that right? I thought all women liked surprises.'

She glared at him. 'Flattering though it is to be compared to every other female on the planet, I would rather just stick to the plan. The plan we agreed on.'

Something flared in his eyes. 'We just got married. Can't I be just a little bit romantic?'

Ignoring the prickle of heat in her cheeks, Margot stared at him. 'Not in my experience—no. Besides, we both know this isn't about romance, so stop pretending it is and take me back to the hotel.'

His gaze was steady on her face. 'That's not going to happen.'

She shook her head. 'Oh, yes, it is. You said we would eat and then fly home.'

'I did, didn't I?'

He shifted in his seat, and something in the casual way he leaned back against the leather made a fog of panic swirl up inside of her.

'So what's changed?' She glowered at him.

He shrugged, but his eyes on hers were curiously intent. '*You* have, baby. Before you were just a woman— now you're my wife.'

Her heart contracted. 'I know I'm your wife,' she said mutinously. 'But I don't see why that means we can't eat at the hotel. Or not eat at all.' She held his gaze. 'I'd be happy to fly home now.'

'And miss our honeymoon?' he said softly. 'What would people think? And I know how much you care about what people think, Margot.'

The blood drained from her face. Something cold and clammy was inching down her spine. 'No, that's not what we agreed, Max.' Her voice was a whisper now. 'You can't do that—'

'And yet I am.' His gaze swept over her face. 'Don't worry. It's no trouble. You see, I have a house here. Just along the coast. And that's where we're going to spend the next two weeks. Just the two of us. What could be more romantic than that?'

CHAPTER SIX

THE DRIVE TO the house passed quickly and silently.

For Margot, silence was the only possible option. Pressed into the corner of the car, she was just too angry to speak. But inside her head angry accusations were whirling around like a flock of seabirds.

How dared he do this?

How dared he unilaterally change their plans? Ignore everything that they'd agreed, trample over her feelings and wishes?

She'd agreed to marry him on one condition—that she could speak to her family before rumours of their wedding became public knowledge. It was the only condition she'd set, and even though she was doing everything he'd asked he still hadn't managed to do that one thing for her.

Her jaw clenched painfully. How could she be so gullible? All that rubbish about being happy to tell her grandfather in person, letting her believe that they were going to fly back to France, when all the time he'd just been pretending so that he could do what he'd said he'd wanted to do right at the start—watch her family suffer.

She glared at him, her cheeks flushing with colour. He was selfish, thoughtless and utterly untrustworthy.

Her fingers curled into the fabric of her dress. All her life it had been the same, the people who were supposed to love her had just done what they wanted, put their needs above hers, and then expected her to put up with it.

No, not just put up with it, she thought savagely. They actually expected her to smile in public while in private they turned her world upside down.

But then selflessness was not part of her family's DNA. Or apparently her new husband's.

Beside her, Max stretched out his legs—a man without a care in the world. A man who was apparently either oblivious to or unconcerned by her silence.

She clenched her teeth. It wasn't that she'd expected him to be thoughtful. Given that he was blackmailing her into marrying him that would have been insane. But surely the whole point of this stupid arranged marriage was that there were rules...boundaries. They'd made an agreement and now Max had broken it.

Her hands tightened in her lap. It wasn't the unfairness of his actions that was so upsetting. Nor did she really care about ego. This was about her grandfather and her brother, and how they would feel when they woke up tomorrow and discovered that she'd sneaked off behind their backs to get married.

Her heart contracted. There was no way she could get in touch with her grandfather. She couldn't risk waking him with news like that—not when his health was so precarious. And while she *could* try ringing Louis... really, what would be the point? It was the last night of his holiday. He was probably out celebrating and having fun with his friends. If she spoke to him now it would ruin everything.

Her heart gave an angry thump.

If Max had done what he'd agreed they'd do, and they had flown back to France, she would have been able to make things right.

She'd had it all planned. They would go straight to the chateau and Max would wait downstairs while she took breakfast up to her grandfather. His favourite breakfast: *café au lait* and eggs benedict—a legacy of his time in America—but using a slice of *tartine* instead of muffins. Then she would sit on the chair beside his bed and take as long as was necessary to reassure him that she hadn't turned into her mother.

It wouldn't be easy, but she knew that she would make him understand. And once he was dressed and composed they would go downstairs together, and everything would be fine.

She swallowed. Now, though, Max had made that moment impossible. Now her grandfather would wake to the news headlines that his beloved and utterly reliable granddaughter had been lying to his face and had eloped.

He would be heartbroken. And there was no doubt in her mind that, whatever he'd just told her about wanting to surprise her, that had been Max's intention all along.

'I know how much you care about what people think, Margot.'

Her skin felt hot, her cheeks burning with humiliation that she should have been so stupid as to trust him. Stiff, angry words were bubbling in her throat and she turned towards him, her eyes seeking his in the cool darkness of the limo's interior.

But before she could open her mouth to unleash her fury she felt the car start to slow and realised that they had arrived at Max's house.

She watched him step out into the sunshine, and then somehow she was taking his hand. There was a small round of applause and, glancing up, she saw that they were not alone. A group of people—presumably Max's staff—all wearing white polo shirts and cream-coloured shorts were standing in two lines on either side of the stairway leading up to the house, their friendly faces beaming down at her.

But it was not their smiles or even the brightness of the sun that made her blink. It was the building behind them.

Her heart bumped against her ribs. Theoretically, she knew the extent of Max's wealth. But, gazing up at the beautiful white modernist villa, she finally understood just how hard he must have worked, and despite the fury simmering inside her she couldn't stop herself from admiring the way he had managed to create this life for himself.

Was it really so surprising, though? Even when she'd first met him it had been clear that Max was no average employee. It hadn't been just his good looks that had made him stand out from everybody else. He'd been bright, focused, creative and exceptionally determined.

Her mouth twisted.

No doubt the same ruthless determination that had made him such a successful businessman made it equally easy for him to disrespect her wishes. She needed to remember that the next time she felt like admiring him.

Inside the villa the decor was modern, almost austere, and only a subtle change in flooring from bleached wood to the palest pink marble signalled the transition between inside and out. But even if the change had been signposted with flashing neon lights she would barely have noticed the difference, for her attention was fixed on the terrace where, beside the bluest pool she had ever seen, a beautiful glass table was set for two beneath a gleaming white sail-like canopy.

Gazing past the table to the ocean beyond, Margot swallowed. She had forgotten all about eating, and she was simmering with so much suppressed rage that she'd completely lost her appetite anyway. But this was her 'wedding breakfast', and of course to accompany the meal there would be—

'Champagne, darling?'

Max stepped forward, his eyes resting on her face, the irises so startlingly blue and green that she had a sudden vivid flashback to the first time they'd met, and how it hadn't felt real. Not just the dual colours of his gaze, but the fact that he was *there*, in her kitchen, this extraordinary, arrestingly beautiful man, talking and laughing and smiling...

Her spine stiffened. And now he was smiling at her again. Only not as a dangerously handsome stranger, but as her dangerously handsome, *self-serving* husband.

'I chose it especially,' he said softly. Leaning forward, he twisted the bottle towards her so that she could see the label. 'It's the Duvernay Grand Cru from the year we first met.'

Her lips curved into a stiff smile as she took the brimming glass. 'How considerate of you,' she said tightly.

There was a pulsing silence, and then he gently tapped his glass against hers.

'You see—it's almost like your family are already here, giving us their blessing.' His mocking gaze flickered over her face. 'And, really, what better way could there be to mark the start of *our* married life than a glass of champagne from *our* estate?'

She stared past him. 'Oh, I can think of one or two scenarios.'

He laughed. 'Why do I get the feeling that all of them involve me being in some kind of mortal peril?'

Shaking his head, he lounged back against his seat.

'I meant what I said in the chapel, Margot. As of now, you're my wife. For better, for worse...for richer, for poorer.' He gave a slow smile. 'Or, given our particular agreement, maybe that should be for poorer, for richer.'

For a moment she considered throwing the contents of her glass in his face, but just then one of his staff stepped forward with a selection of canapés, and instead she took a mouthful of champagne.

It was a good year, she thought dispassionately. An almost perfect balance of citrus and cream, with a just a hint of raspberry.

Her muscles tightened. Her grandfather had always said that a great champagne was like a love potion, but it would have to be a remarkable vintage indeed for her to forget that their marriage was a business merger in everything but name. And that Max was a total snake in the grass.

Through a combination of polite, if a little stilted, conversation and carefully timed smiles, she managed to get through the meal. Then the still smiling staff started to melt away, and finally they were alone.

Instantly she pushed her untouched cup of coffee away, her fingers twitching against the table-top.

Max stared at her with a mixture of mockery and resignation. 'The monsoon season is over for this year,' he said softly, lowering his gaze so that his eyes were suddenly in shadow. 'And yet I sense a storm is brewing.'

'Damn right it is.' Instantly her bottled-up resentment rose to the surface, like the bubbles in her family's legendary champagne. 'If you think I'm staying here for two weeks with you, acting out some pantomime of a honeymoon, then you must be insane. We had a deal. I have kept my side of that deal, and I expect you to keep yours. So, unless you have a reason for changing our plans other than sheer bloody-mindedness, I suggest you get hold of your pilot and tell him that we will be leaving for France tonight.'

'Or what? Are you going to swim home?'

She glared at him. 'If it means getting away from you, then, yes.'

He didn't reply—just stared at her so intently and for so long that she wanted to scream. And then finally, in a gesture that seemed designed solely to aggravate her, he shrugged carelessly.

Margot glanced at him helplessly. She felt as though she would burst with rage. Was that the sum total of his response? Was that seriously supposed to be some kind of answer?

'What does that mean?' she snapped. She could hear her overstretched nerves vibrating in her voice, but she didn't care any more. 'You're not in some *nouvelle vague* film, Max. This is real life. My life. And I am your wife—legally, at least—so could you at least do me the courtesy of actually saying something?'

Raising an eyebrow, seemingly unperturbed by either her words or her tone, he gazed at her impassively. 'Okay—it means that any deal we made most certainly did *not* include you flouncing off to the airport to catch the first flight home after we'd exchanged our wedding vows.'

His expression didn't shift, but she felt a sudden rise in tension as she mimicked his tone. 'Well, *any deal we made* also didn't include you and me building sandcastles for two weeks.' She glared at him. 'I mean, what exactly do you think we're going to spend our honeymoon doing?'

There was a tiny quivering pause, just long enough for her to realise the full, horrifying idiocy of what she'd said, and then the air seemed to ripple around her as her words continued to echo into the sudden silence.

What she had been trying to say was that as theirs wasn't a regular kind of marriage, their honeymoon was hardly going to be all moonlight walks and long afternoons in bed.

Only it hadn't sounded the way she'd intended. In fact it couldn't have sounded any worse.

Her throat felt suddenly scratchy and dry as, leaning forward, he gave her an infuriating smile.

'Oh, I expect we could probably think of something to pass the time...'

She wanted to deny it. But the trouble was, he was right—and, no matter how much she wanted it to be otherwise, it didn't change the fact that her body still ached for the wordless, exquisite satisfaction that he alone had given her.

Rigid with mortification, her cheeks flooded with colour, she glanced past him, cursing herself, cursing him, and cursing her father for putting her in this impossible position.

If only she could just flick a switch so that she could stop feeling like this. If only it was just thinking. If only she could just separate her body from her brain. But as her mind filled with images of her and Max moving in blurred slow motion she felt her breath quicken.

Suddenly her heart was pounding, and she could almost taste the adrenalin. She felt like a gladiator, waiting outside the arena, poised and ready for combat. Only this time it was herself she was fighting. Her desire for Max was dangerous and, as she knew from experience, the kind of passion they shared came at a price. It trampled over your pride, crushed your dreams and cleaved your heart in two.

Ignoring the clamouring demands of her body, she lifted her chin. 'I know we could. But that doesn't mean that we should.' She swallowed, struggling to find the words that would stop her feeling, stop her needing. 'So if that's why you broke our agreement then I'm sorry to disappoint you, but unlike you I have principles.'

His eyes glittered and, sensing the anger unfurling beneath his apparently calm demeanour, she felt her stomach clench. But he had no right to feel angry. He hadn't been bullied and manipulated. He hadn't been made to perform like a puppet on a string.

She took a breath, desperate to divert the conversation to less dangerous territory. 'Besides, in case you've forgotten, you're supposed to be saving my business—and you can't do that if we're both here cavorting about on a beach!'

Her heartbeat scampered. Even now that Max was co-running Duvernay she still felt horribly responsible. She had already been worried about taking more time off work so soon after going to Monte Carlo, but she had been expecting to be gone for just a few days, not two weeks.

His lazy gaze didn't shift from her face, but the air felt suddenly fat with tension.

'Luckily for you, I can multitask,' he said coolly.

Max stared at her. He was good at multitasking, but right now he was struggling to hold on to his temper at the same time as trying to justify why just one kiss had overridden his meticulous and completely non-negotiable plan to return to France immediately after the wedding.

His temper wasn't improved by Margot insisting on talking about Duvernay. She was acting as if he was just some troubleshooter she'd hired to fix her damned business instead of her husband. And she had accused him of being unromantic!

He gritted his teeth. Maybe they should have gone home. Everything had been in place. His private jet had been waiting on the runway and he had personally signed off on a carefully worded statement to the press about his sudden marriage to Margot Duvernay. All that there had been left to do was make a phone call—a call he had been wanting and waiting to make for so long—and then finally he would have been able to flaunt his new wife to the world.

Only as he'd brought his mouth down on hers and she'd leaned into him everything had changed.

Holding her body, feeling her frantic, unguarded response, he had been engulfed by a raw and ferocious need that had blotted out all logical thought. There and then he'd decided that the rest of the world could wait. Finally Margot was his wife. She was his, and—for the foreseeable future, at least—he was not going to share her with anyone.

But he was not about to admit that out loud, and certainly not to Margot—particularly when all she seemed bothered about was her wretched business.

'I don't leave things to chance,' he said. 'I have people reporting back to me and everything's running smoothly.' He lounged back in his chair, letting his long legs sprawl out in front of him. 'Why are you making this into such a big deal? You wanted traditional, and a honeymoon is a wedding tradition. I'm just ticking all the boxes,' he lied.

Margot looked at him resentfully. It was true that she had wanted to keep the wedding as traditional as possible, but only for the benefit of her grandfather and Louis. And she had never so much as hinted at having a honeymoon.

A honeymoon!

Her brain stumbled, tripping on a thought of just exactly how she and Max might spend their honeymoon. Sunlit hours passing into darkness, hands splaying against warm, damp skin, bodies shuddering, surrendering to one bone-dissolving climax after another—

Her heart was pounding.

'Then I suggest you untick them,' she said curtly.

His gaze didn't so much as flicker. 'I must say I'm a

little surprised—I wasn't expecting wedding day nerves,' he said lazily. 'And there was I, thinking you were only marrying me for my money.'

She gave a humourless laugh. 'You're deluded.'

'And you're overreacting,' he said coolly.

'Overreacting?' She shook her head in disbelief. 'If you don't understand why I need to get back then you must be even more insensitive and self-serving than I thought.'

Her brown eyes narrowed.

'Perhaps you were raised by wolves. Or maybe you don't have any family,' she snarled. 'Or maybe, like every other unfortunate soul who crosses your path, they prefer to keep well clear of you. Frankly, I don't much care.'

Watching his features grow harder, she felt a quiver of unease. But so what if she'd offended him? If someone basically lied, and then lied again, why should she be nice about it?

She took a deep breath. 'But I do care about my family. You knew I wanted to tell to my grandfather in person. You knew it, and yet you completely ignored my wishes.'

He let his gaze rest on her accusing face. '*Your life. Your wishes.* You seem to be forgetting that this isn't just about you. It's about us. But then you never really got the hang of *us*, did you, Margot?'

Margot stared at him unsteadily, the air thumping out of her lungs. How was this her fault? He wasn't the one who'd been tricked and manipulated, lied to and misled.

Her body was quivering with anger and frustration. Was this how it was going to be? Every conversation filled with pitfalls and traps, like a game of snakes and ladders where a stray move or two could send them tumbling back into the past.

Suddenly her eyes felt hot, and she blinked frantically. She was not going to cry. She was not going to let him know that he could hurt her. But she also wasn't going to sit here and listen to his stupid, self-righteous accusations—not after everything he'd said and done to her.

'That's because there was no *us*, Max.' Her breathing jerked, for even as she said the words, a part of her was hoping he would deny them. But of course he didn't. He just continued to stare at her, his face expressionless, his eyes still and steady.

She cleared her throat. 'There was me, and there was you. We were different people. We wanted different things then, and we want different things now. Nothing's changed.'

His eyes lifted to hers. 'Except that now you're my wife,' he said slowly.

Mesmerised by the possessive note in his voice, she was suddenly holding her breath. And then almost immediately she felt a chill come over her body. Was she really that shallow? Surely this conversation encapsulated everything that had been wrong between them, and explained why their relationship could never be what it should. Sex acting as a substitute for tenderness and sensitivity? Aged nineteen, she hadn't really understood the difference, or maybe she'd thought it would be enough.

But now she did—and it wasn't.

'So what if I am?' she said, finally finding her voice. 'You've made it clear that I don't matter to you. You don't respect me or my feelings, or care about my opinions. And you sure as hell don't understand relationships. Or is this *really* what you think marriage is supposed to be like?'

She broke off, hating the emotion in her voice. Suddenly she couldn't bear it any more. There was no point in talking to him. Standing up, she took hold of her wedding ring and tugged it loose from her finger.

'Here—you can have this back. You see, it doesn't matter how many rings you give me, Max, or even how many bits of paper I sign, I will never truly belong to you.'

She tossed the ring onto the table and then, clutching the fabric of her skirt, she turned and walked stiffly towards the villa.

Somehow she found her way to her—their—bedroom. It was decorated in the same style as the rest of the house, all pale wood and neutral-coloured walls. Cool, contemporary, masculine.

Except the bed.

She gazed in stunned, wordless disbelief at the beautiful four-poster bed, a lump building in her throat. On the other side of the room the doors to the deck had been left open, and the canopy of muslin above the bed was quivering in the warm tropical breeze. Beneath the canopy, the white sheets and pillows were strewn with the palest pink and white petals. It was ludicrously, perfectly romantic.

Her pulse was suddenly racing, and warmth stole over her skin as, dazedly, she stepped closer to the bed. Reaching down, she let her fingers drift over the crisp white sheets. Kicking off her shoes, she felt her heart contract. Everything was such a mess.

Ten years ago this would have been everything she wanted, and she wished with an intensity that was painful that she could just forget the past and—

And what? What exactly was she supposed to do and feel now?

There were hundreds, maybe thousands of books and blogs outlining wedding etiquette, and probably even more devoted to achieving a happy marriage. But what were the rules for Max and Margot? The first time she had loved him unconditionally and he had wanted her money. Now he wanted her business and she needed his financial support.

She felt suddenly close to tears again.

Being married to Max was just so much more complex than she'd imagined it would be. In her head, she'd pictured something like her grandparents' marriage—traditional, formal. They had married young, not for love but for dynastic reasons. But despite that unpromising start they had grown to care for one another, and there had always been respect and trust. How were she and Max ever going to get to that stage?

Her body tensed, and she sensed that she was no longer alone. Somebody had come into the bedroom, and without turning she knew it was Max. She didn't have to see him. The connection between them was so intense she recognised him simply by the prickling heat creeping over her skin, and the way the compass point inside her began to quiver.

She couldn't help herself. Turning, she felt her body still as she watched him walk slowly towards her.

Don't come any closer, she thought, her breath catching in her throat.

'Why not?' he said softly, and her pulse began to race as she realised that without meaning to do so she must have spoken out loud.

'There's no reason for you to do so,' she said, flattening the emotion out of her voice. 'You've got the marriage licence and the share certificates, so you have everything you want.'

He stopped in front of her, and for one endless moment they stared at each other, wide-eyed, their bodies barely inches apart.

'Not quite everything.'

Jolted by the roughness in his voice, she tried to answer. But before she had a chance even to think about what words to use, let alone form them into a sentence, he took another step closer.

She tried to move, to put some distance between them, but her body was rooted to the floor. The air felt suddenly heavy and tangled, as though the monsoon he'd mentioned earlier was about to break inside the room. Heat was chasing over her cheeks and throat, and then her stomach flipped over as he reached out and, taking her hand, gently slid the wedding ring back on her finger.

'I came to tell you that you do matter. And I do respect you.'

She stared at him. He looked tense, serious, not at all like the teasing, self-possessed man who had dominated her life for the last few days.

'And I do care about your feelings and opinions.'

He paused, and she realised that his hand was still holding hers. It was lucky that he was, for she felt suddenly strangely unsubstantial, as though at any moment she might simply float away.

'Although, given how I've behaved, I can completely see why you would think the opposite.'

Margot stared at him, confused. There was strain in his voice—not anger...uncertainty, maybe—and although he hadn't actually said he was sorry, his words had sounded almost like an apology. Whatever she had expected Max to say, it hadn't been that, and she wasn't sure how to reply.

But the part of her brain that was still functioning prodded her to respond, and so she said the first word that came into her head. 'Okay.'

His eyes bored into hers and she felt her legs wobble, for there was no mockery or hostility in the blue and green of his irises, and no anger in her heart. With a mixture of panic and yearning, she realised that without the restraining presence of their mutual animosity he was too close, that his mouth—that beautiful, temptingly kissable mouth—was dangerously close, and that she was starting to feel dizzy.

Dizzy with...

His hand slid around her waist, and even as her fingers curled into her palms she felt the floor tilt beneath her feet. Every ounce of reason and self-preservation she possessed was telling her to move, to push him away. This—*them*—was a bad idea. She needed to stop it from going any further. Stop it while she still could.

Lifting her hand, she pressed her fists against his chest, meaning to push him away. But somehow her fingers weren't responding. Instead they seemed to be uncurling and sliding over his shoulders, and she couldn't seem to stop herself from gazing at his mouth.

She was giving out all the wrong signals, and yet they felt right—more than right. They felt inevitable and necessary.

'Okay...?' His brows drew together, the muscles in his face tightening with concentration. 'Okay, and now you want me to leave? Or okay, you want me to stay?' he asked hoarsely.

Somewhere inside the wreckage of her brain, it occurred to her that his breathing was as uneven as hers. There was a long, simmering silence. She inhaled shakily. Her body was throbbing with a desperate yearning to feel his soft mouth on hers, to give in to the teasing pleasure of his tongue—only she knew that to tell him that would be foolhardy and self-destructive.

She knew she should lie to him. But she was so sick of lying. Everything else about their relationship might just be for show, but this—this need they felt for each other—was real so why fight it?

'Margot...'

She was suddenly too scared to meet his eyes, scared that he would see the indecision and the longing in her face.

But, lifting a hand, he cupped her chin and forced her to look at him, and the dark, blazing intensity of his gaze made her breath catch.

'I want you,' he said hoarsely and, lowering his mouth, he brushed his lips momentarily against hers. 'I've wanted you ever since you walked into that boardroom. I want you so badly I can't think straight. I don't even know who I am any more. All I know is that my body burns for you...'

He hesitated, and she could sense that he was steadying himself, that he would stop if she asked him to.

'But you need to tell me what *you* want.'

She stared at him dazedly, her blood humming, an ache of desire spreading out inside her like an oil spill, and then finally she slid her fingers up into his hair and whispered, 'I want you too.'

Lifting her chin with his thumb, he stared down into her eyes for so long that she thought she would fly apart with wanting him, and then slowly he lowered his head and kissed her.

She could hardly breathe. Gently, he parted her lips, pushing his tongue into her open mouth, tasting her, his breath mingling with hers as his fingers slid over the lace of her bodice.

Her skin was growing warm, and an ache that felt both hollow and yet so heavy was spreading out inside her. His fingers were moving ceaselessly, brushing against her breasts, slipping around her waist, and then lower to the curve of her buttocks. She moaned against his mouth and instantly felt his body respond. His fingers grew more urgent, and suddenly he was pulling at the buttons down the back of her dress, and as each button came loose she felt something inside her open up too.

'Max…' she whispered, and her own fingers dropped to the waistband of his trousers and began to tug at the fabric, pressing against the hard outline of his erection.

Max breathed out unsteadily. As his fingers slipped beneath the bodice of her dress he felt his groin harden. Her skin felt impossibly smooth and, lifting his mouth from hers, he buried his lips against her neck, seeking out that pulse at the base of her throat. He felt her stir against him, blindly seeking more, and suddenly he wanted more too. More of that skin, more of her mouth, and more of that pulsing heat that he could feel beneath her dress.

Breaking free, he took a step back and yanked at the collar of his shirt. Ignoring her hands, he tugged it over his head and then, his eyes holding hers, he reached forward and released her shoulders, watching dry-mouthed as the dress slid slowly to the floor.

Underneath she was naked except for a pair of rose-coloured panties tied at the sides with ribbons. Gazing at her naked breasts, he felt his skin catch fire. She was so beautiful—more beautiful than he'd remembered—and, stepping towards her, he tugged her body against his, feeling her nipples harden as they brushed against his bare chest. Lowering his head, he sucked first one and then the other into his mouth, almost blacking out as he felt her squirm beneath his tongue. And then she was pulling at the buckle of his belt, her hands clumsy, her breath suddenly uneven as she freed him from his clothes.

'Margot, Margot—slow down,' he begged. 'Just wait.'

But she wasn't listening, or maybe she was ignoring him. Suddenly he didn't care. Pulling her against him, he lifted her and not quite steadily lowered her onto the bed. Leaning forward, he yanked the ribbons of her panties free, and then she was clutching at his shoulders, pulling him closer, guiding him inside her.

Margot gasped. Looping her arm around his neck, she gripped him tighter, her hips rising, her body opening to meet his thrusts, her hands digging into the muscles of his back. She was shaking with eagerness and relief, for there had never been anyone like him and she knew there never would be. With him, there was no need to think. Everything was pure instinct, and each knew exactly what the other wanted and needed.

As the heat building inside her fanned out like a solar flare she was arching upwards, her thighs splaying, her body gripping him inside and out, until she could hold back no more and she shuddered beneath him. She felt his hands tighten in her hair, his body tense, and then, his breath quickening, he buried his face against her shoulder and, crying out her name, thrust inside her.

CHAPTER SEVEN

IT WAS NEARLY TEN O'CLOCK. Already the quivering sun was high in the sky, and soon the pale sand would be too hot to stand on in bare feet.

Glancing down, Max frowned. As a child, he'd been to the seaside twice—once with his mother and Paul, and once with his school. But it was a long time since he'd walked barefoot anywhere, except between his bathroom and his bedroom or to and from his pool. In fact, it might even be the first time he'd ever been on a beach without shoes as an adult.

But, unusual as that was, walking barefoot couldn't really compete with some of his other more recent and less rational 'firsts'.

Staring out across the bay, to where a couple of seabirds were bobbing peacefully on the water, he ticked them off inside his head.

Obviously getting married to a woman he didn't love or trust took pole position. But a close second was buying those shares from her father. He'd never paid over the odds for anything and, looking back on it, there had been absolutely no need for him to do so. Although Emile had been maddeningly evasive and capricious, his demand had been modest in comparison to what he'd ended up offering for the shares.

Which brought him to another first—paying for a woman.

Beneath his dark glasses, his eyes narrowed. He didn't like the way it sounded but, despite what he'd said to Margot, and told himself about why he'd married her, that was in essence what he'd done.

And then, of course, last night had been the first time he'd ever chased a woman—or at least followed one.

Watching Margot turn and walk away, he had been too angry to move, his head simmering with barely contained frustration that within the space of a heartbeat she had thrown their honeymoon *and* her ring back in his face. And what had she meant by him not understanding relationships?

He gritted his teeth. He understood relationships perfectly. He should too: he'd had the ultimate learning experience, watching his mother put her life on hold, waiting, hoping—and for what?

For nothing, that was what.

He took a calming breath. No, Margot was wrong. He *did* understand relationships. It was simple, really. If you didn't ask you didn't get.

A wave broke, spilling water over his feet, and he realised that in the time he'd been walking down the beach the tide had begun to turn.

He glanced down at his wrist automatically and frowned. He'd left his watch on the bedside table.

And left Margot sleeping in his bed.

He felt his muscles tighten, heat lapping over his skin like the tide on the beach. In bed, their quarrel had been forgotten, their bodies blurring in a passionate embrace that had shaken him not just physically but emotionally— for he never had felt that close, that committed before. But of course he'd never been married before.

Margot might be sleeping now, but she hadn't slept much last night. Neither of them had. His lips curved upwards. In fact, her curiosity had almost killed them both. But as the dawn had crept into their room he had woken out of habit, and then...

Then he'd had two choices. Stay and wait for Margot to wake too, and carry on where they left off. Or get up and go.

A movement out in the bay caught his eye, and he saw that the two seabirds were squabbling over something—food...territory, maybe. Whatever it was, their battle was really not that different from his fight with Margot yesterday—every relationship was just a power struggle.

His mouth twisted. But his argument with Margot had been nothing in comparison to the conflict raging inside him when he'd woken this morning.

Stay or leave?

It had been a simple enough choice. Only for some reason he had never struggled so much to make a decision.

His pulse jumped in his throat and he felt an instant answering pulse in his groin. Obviously his body had been urging him to stay. Waking to find her legs tangled between his and her long, silken hair spilling over his chest had felt good—more than good. It had been intoxicating. And as he'd breathed in the scent of her he'd had to force himself back from an edge of almost primal, driving desire.

He stared not quite steadily down the beach, remembering how it had felt to run his urgent hands over her warm skin and feel the sweetness of her tight body gripping his. Watching her beautiful pink lips part and then melt into a half-pout of surrender, he'd lost control. She had been so responsive, so hot.

Even now the memory of the fierce directness of her

gaze as he'd moved inside her was turning him inside out. Everything—all the bitterness, the lies, the anger, all of it—had ceased to exist. There had been only Margot, and finally she had been his.

So why had he got up and left?

He drew in a deep breath. He'd thought he had it all figured out. Buy the shares—prove the Duvernays wrong. Marry Margot—prove her wrong. Sleep with Margot—prove her wrong again. Feel better.

His muscles tensed. Only it had been he who had been wrong—times four.

He should have felt sated and complete, and physically he did. Only he hadn't been able to shift a sense that something was missing, or maybe off-key.

He still felt like that now, and that irritated him, for he had no reason to feel that way. Margot was his wife and yesterday, and again and again this morning, she had become his lover, clinging to him, pulling him deep inside her body with a desperation that had matched his own.

Breathing out unsteadily, he wondered why that thought should make his chest tighten?

But it was obvious, really, he thought with relief a moment later.

Even before he'd made his first million, few women— if any—had been out of his reach, and his reputation for playing hard to get was completely justified.

Only ever since he'd walked into the House of Duvernay headquarters his self-control seemed to have gone AWOL.

Yesterday he had been like a starving man, satisfying his hunger. His need to take Margot had been shocking in its urgency, and it had understandably caught him by surprise for he was used to being the one in charge both in business and emotionally. But today, he couldn't pretend that it would be anything other than reckless to show her how much power she had over him.

And that was why he'd had to get up and leave this morning—to demonstrate some of that famed self-control.

So now they were all square. He'd proved his point. Why then was he still here, watching the wildlife and the waves? After all, this was his honeymoon.

Honeymoon—the word and all that it implied ping-ponged inside his head and, feeling his body harden, he turned towards the villa. And then he stopped. Glancing down at the outline of his erection, he breathed out slowly. Perhaps it might be a good idea to wait just a little longer…maybe cool off first. A quick swim would be the perfect way to damp down his libido and dull his senses before seeing Margot again, and it wouldn't hurt to keep her waiting and wanting more.

Without giving himself a chance to change his mind, he tugged his shirt over his head, tossed it onto the sand and began wading purposefully into the water.

Margot woke to sunlight and the sound of waves. It took her perhaps half a second before she realised that she was alone, and that the Max-sized space in the bed beside her was empty.

Rolling over, she touched the pillow. It still had the imprint of his head, and she could smell his aftershave and the scent of his skin, and for some reason she found herself smiling.

It was stupid, really, to feel so happy—probably it was asking for trouble—and yet…

She breathed out slowly.

And yet the strain of the last few days seemed to have lifted from her shoulders. She felt not just spent, but serene, for now she was free to touch Max, and to taste him, to wrap her legs around his quickening body without guilt or shame.

Now that it had happened, she could admit that it had always been just a question of when, not if. But when exactly had it started?

Maybe in the car, when Max had thrown that curveball at her. She had been so angry and hurt. But then, at the villa, his 'apology'—or at least his honesty following so quickly on the back of their row—had caught her off guard.

Her pulse twitched. Or maybe it had started before that. In the boardroom. Or perhaps when she'd walked past that newsstand in Paris and read his name.

Her name too now!

Max had left his watch on the bedside table and, glancing over at it, she frowned. It was almost midday and she wondered where he was.

Her pulse jitterbugged.

She couldn't remember falling asleep, but she could remember the way he'd curved his hand around her waist, anchoring her to him. Could remember too the way that same hand had cradled her head as his powerful body had thrust into hers.

She had never felt so wanted, so desired—and, okay, it had been just sex, but it had been *real*. Nobody could fake that kind of passion, that kind of tenderness.

And didn't that somehow change things a little between them? Perhaps they could be honest with one another on one level at least.

'You're awake.'

She blinked and, rolling over, she lifted her head and gazed up at him. Max was standing motionless on the deck outside the bedroom, wearing nothing but a pair of faded black shorts, an unbuttoned denim shirt and a pair of dark glasses. Droplets of water clung to the tanned muscular skin of his chest and legs, and his sea-drenched dark hair was moulded to the beautiful bones of his skull.

He looked cool and relaxed and impossibly sexy—like a photo shoot for a modern-day pirate—and as his eyes locked on to hers she felt something tug beneath her skin just as she remembered that she was naked. Her cheeks began to tingle and she felt suddenly shy—which was stupid, really. It wasn't as though he hadn't seen all of her already. And not just seen, she reminded herself, her heart jumping at the memory of how his hands had moved over that same naked skin he was staring at now.

As though reading her mind, he smiled slowly, the edges of his mouth curling up in a way that made her skin instantly grow warmer. Cheeks burning now, she tried to match his smile with a casual one of her own. But it was difficult to act naturally when all she could think about was what else that mouth could and was probably about to do.

Swallowing hard, she sat up and said quickly, 'I didn't hear you get up. I would have come with you.'

His gaze hovered over her flushed face, and then dropped to the tiny pulse beating at the base of her throat.

'That's okay. You needed to sleep.'

Tugging off his dark glasses, he stepped inside the room and walked slowly across the smooth wooden floor. He stopped beside the bed, and her pulse jumped in her throat as inch by inch his eyes drifted over her bare skin, slowly tracing the contours of her body.

Looking up at him, she felt as if she was floating—and then her heart began beating against her ribcage as, dropping his sunglasses on the bedside table, he leaned forward and kissed her gently on the mouth. She arched her back, her lips parting, and she felt her insides start to melt as he deepened the kiss.

'Sweet…' he murmured against her mouth, and then he was kissing her again, such tender, slow kisses, as though they had the whole of their lives before them.

Which they did, she thought dazedly a moment later, as his hand cupped her breast, his thumb teased the nipple and she felt her body shudder in response.

In an instant he had stolen her thoughts, her identity, even her breath, so that suddenly she was panting. 'Max, please…'

She reached up, blindly seeking more contact, expecting him to move, wanting him to touch her. But he didn't move closer. Instead he ran his hand over her breast and up to her shoulder and then released her.

She stared up at him, her hands balling into fists, her body so hot and tight and tense she thought it would explode.

'I thought—' she began, but her words dried up as he turned and, picking up his watch, frowned down at it.

'Baby, I need a shower and some breakfast. And besides…' His gaze burned into hers and she felt her pulse leap. 'Surely I more than satisfied your curiosity yesterday and this morning.'

Watching him unzip his shorts and push them down over his muscular thighs, Margot felt her stomach flip over. But not from desire this time. His words echoed ominously in her head, and suddenly she knew what he was getting at. It was that stupid, *stupid* remark she'd made in his hotel room, and clearly he'd been waiting for just the right moment to throw it back in her face.

She felt hot and dizzy, anger mingling with shame that she had actually thought Max had wanted her with the same desperate urgency with which she'd wanted him, when all the time it had just been about proving a point.

It might have felt real, but then Max was good at that, she thought savagely—good at making her believe what she wanted to believe. And she'd even given him some help, by listening to that tiny part of her mind that had wanted to be wrong about him, wanted to believe in the fantasy of their explosive sexual chemistry.

A rush of misery and helplessness broke over her, like one of the waves splashing against the shore outside their room. It was the same old story—a story that had started when she was a child, trying to defuse the tension between her parents, and then her father and her grandparents. She was so used to seeking out the good and ignoring the bad that it was almost second nature now for her to spin straw into gold.

Only she wasn't a child any more, and nor was she a spectator. This was her marriage. Her life. And she wasn't just going to stand by with a smile on her face while he played power games.

Her dress—her beautiful wedding dress—lay where Max had pulled it from her frantic body and, sliding out of bed, she picked it up and draped it over one of the cream-coloured armchairs that sat on either side of the doors to the deck.

Stalking into the dressing room, she yanked a pale blue embroidered sundress off the shelf. She pulled it over her head and, without even bothering to look at her reflection or brush her hair, she pushed her feet into some flip-flops and strode onto the deck.

Outside, the beach felt gloriously open and empty. Kicking off her shoes, she walked down to where the lightest imaginable surf was trickling over the sand like champagne foam.

Her mouth thinned. Actually, *not* champagne. She was sick of champagne. Sick of the whole wine-making world and everyone in it. Particularly Max.

She grimaced. Even just thinking about him and his stupid, mammoth ego made her head pound as though she'd drunk a magnum of Grand Cru.

She had thought that having sex with him would be the one true part of their marriage. Only now it seemed that it had been just as superficial and sham as the rest of their relationship—and not just in the present. The memory of what they'd once shared now felt unbearably tainted too.

And she only had herself to blame. She'd known what he was like. Or she should have. After all, what kind of a man blackmailed a woman into marriage?

Her stomach clenched. Sex might have made it feel more intimate and personal, but the truth was that this had never been anything other than a business arrangement—a merger of money and power and status. Anything else was just nonsense, concocted inside her head.

The sound of music and laughter broke into her thoughts and, glancing out to sea, she spotted a cruiser dipping through the water. On the gleaming white deck a group of men and women were dancing, their heads tipped back to the sun, swimsuit-clad bodies radiating heat and happiness.

She stared at them enviously. They seemed so at ease, so uninhibited, and in their loose-limbed freedom they reminded her of Louis and Gisele and their friends. She watched for a moment, lost in her own thoughts, and then, just as she was about to carry on walking, one of the men must have noticed her, for suddenly he was waving, and then they were all waving and calling to her.

It was impossible to hear what they were saying, but their excitement and enthusiasm was infectious, and without even realising that she was doing it she began waving back at them.

'What the hell do you think you're doing?'

A hand gripped her arm and her body was pulled round sharply. Max was standing beside her, wearing a pair of swim-shorts. Her first thought was that he had changed clothes. Her second was that he was incandescent with fury.

She shook his hand off, her own simmering anger rising swiftly to boiling point. 'I would have thought that was obvious. It's called *waving*—'

'Don't give me that.' He interrupted her. 'It's our honeymoon, and you're standing out here on your own, waving at strangers. What if that had been a boat full of photographers?'

She glared at him. 'It wasn't. And even if it was, what I do or don't do—including waving at strangers on boats—is none of your business. Now, if you're done with throwing your weight around, I'm going to go for a walk.'

Staring down into her defiant face, Max felt his body tense with frustration. It was a feeling that was becoming increasingly familiar since Margot had re-entered his life.

Earlier, returning to the villa from the beach, he had felt the barriers he had so arrogantly created inside his head all but disintegrate as he'd caught sight of her glorious body, spread out so invitingly on the rumpled sheets. Thankfully he had succeeded in hanging on to his self-control by a thread, helped by what must surely have been the coldest shower he'd ever had.

But when he'd walked back into the bedroom his hard-won composure had instantly evaporated as he'd realised that Margot had simply upped and left without so much as a word. His mood hadn't improved as he'd stalked stiffly through the villa. Not wanting to alert his staff to the fact that his wife appeared to have vanished, he'd been forced to pretend that he'd mislaid his phone.

He gritted his teeth. And now, when finally he'd tracked her down, not only was she completely unrepentant, she was clearly looking for a fight.

His eyes narrowed and, by holding his breath, he managed to hang on to his temper. 'Actually I'm far from done. You're my wife now, and if you're expecting our marriage to be civilised—'

'Civilised!' Her gaze clashed with his. 'You don't know the meaning of the word. Do you seriously think it's civilised to just take what you want and move on when you're done—?' She broke off as he started to shake his head.

'So that's what this is about? It was just a shower, Margot.'

The dishonesty of his remark made her breathing jerk in her throat. 'Don't do that, Max. Don't treat me like I'm stupid. It was not *just* a shower. It was you making a point. And I will not let you treat me like some toy you can pick up and play with and then forget about.'

He frowned. 'Are you insane? How could I forget about you? I've just spent the last thirty-five minutes looking for you.'

Her heart was trying to get out of her chest. 'Well, you wasted your time. You might be my husband legally, but our marriage is just a business agreement. It only exists when we're on show, in public—as you just proved to me.'

Max took a step towards her. A thread of fury was soaring up through his body like mercury in a thermometer. He felt breathless with anger and frustration.

'Better that than only existing in the bedroom,' he snarled, unable to hide his emotions any longer.

'What is *that* supposed to mean?' she snapped.

The air around them felt suddenly thick and dark and volatile, like a cloud of bees about to swarm.

'You know exactly what it means. It's the reason you didn't want to marry me all those years ago.'

She glared at him. 'I didn't want to marry you because you only wanted my money. Or have you forgotten telling me that was why you proposed?'

His gaze didn't flicker. 'That was after you'd already let your brother do your dirty work. But the least you could do now is have the guts to tell it like it was.'

'And what was it like, Max?'

His face hardened. 'I was good enough for sex, just not for marriage.'

There was a short, sharp pause. Margot was staring at him as though he'd suddenly started speaking in a foreign language, but he wasn't sure if it was what he'd said or the harshness with which he'd said it that had silenced her.

Margot stared at him in confusion. Her heart was thumping hard against her chest. She was shocked by his words. More shocked still by the fact that he obviously believed them.

Her mouth twisted. Or, more likely, wanted to believe them.

'That's not true—that wasn't how it was! It *wasn't*,' she repeated, as he began shaking his head dismissively.

'Really? Then why were you so worried about keeping us a secret? Oh, sorry, I forgot—' his mouth curled upwards into a sneer '—you were waiting for "the right time" to tell everyone.'

Anger flared inside her. How dared he be so self-righteous? 'Yes, I was. But what was your excuse?' she snapped. 'Because it wasn't just me who wanted to keep our relationship quiet, was it?'

Max breathed out silently. For a moment he thought about telling her the truth. That going public would have meant sharing her with her family, breaking the spell of that summer. And then he came to his senses.

'Nice try. But next to you I'm an amateur when it comes to keeping quiet.'

'What are you talking about?' she said hoarsely.

'I'm talking about when I asked you to marry me before. I gave you a ring. Do you remember what you did? What you said?' His voice was steady, but a muscle was pulsing in his cheek. 'No? Then let me remind you. You did nothing, said nothing. You basically acted like I'd embarrassed you.' His eyes burned into her. 'No, actually, like I'd embarrassed myself.'

She shivered. That wasn't how she remembered it. In her head it had been a moment of shock, drowned out almost immediately by Yves's arrival. Her brother had been white-lipped with rage at what he'd clearly thought was personal betrayal by a man he'd liked and trusted. He'd been angrier, though, with himself, for not protecting her, and so he'd been cruel and unfair. She should have stopped him, only…

'I wasn't embarrassed,' she said slowly. 'I was in shock.'

His mouth thinned. 'Why?' he demanded. 'We'd talked about getting married—'

'Yes, in the *future*.' She stared at him, her pulse stop-starting like a stalled car. 'But not right then. I was nineteen, Max. I was still at university. No, hear me out.' She held up her hands as he started to interrupt. 'You have to understand. I had no idea you were going to ask me. It wasn't in my head. I wasn't ready. I was young and…' She hesitated.

They were heading into dangerous territory, and the

thought of confronting what lay ahead made her want to crawl into a darkened room and roll up in a ball. But, looking up at the tense, set expression on his face, she knew that retreating was not an option.

She drew in a breath. 'And I was scared.'

Max stared at her in silence. She was telling the truth. He could hear it in her voice, feel it stinging his skin.

'Why would you be scared?' He'd sounded harsher than he'd intended and she looked over at him. Hearing her breathe out unsteadily, he felt his stomach clench, for he could see that she was still scared now. 'You were scared of *me*?' The thought horrified him so much that he actually couldn't speak any more.

'Of *you*?' She shook her head, eyes widening with horror. 'No, of course not. I was scared of making a mistake, of doing what—'

As she looked up into his eyes he saw her face stiffen, as though she was doing some complicated arithmetic in her head, and then she bit her lip.

'Oh, what's the point? You wouldn't understand.'

For a moment he thought about his own past, and his own private fears. And then he stopped thinking.

Reaching out, he took her hands. 'I might,' he said gently.

He felt her body go rigid, and for a moment he thought she was going to pull away from him, but finally she sighed.

'Okay… This is going to sound crazy, and you probably won't believe me, but when you proposed I wasn't even thinking about us or the ring you'd given me. I was thinking about my mother's engagement ring.'

Hearing the taut note in her voice, Max frowned. It did sound crazy, but for some reason he still believed her.

'I know you probably don't have much interest in celebrity gossip, but you might have heard about my parents?'

He nodded. He could remember his mother following the story in the newspapers, only he'd been too young to care. 'Just the basics. They eloped, and later on your mum accidentally overdosed.' He spoke gently, wanting to ease the impact of his words.

Her face stilled. 'They eloped when she was nineteen. It was a massive scandal. Everyone was looking for them. They ended up hiding in Marrakech, in the house where Louis is staying.'

She smiled bleakly, and he felt something heavy settle on his shoulders at the flash of hurt.

'They were so young and so beautiful, and everyone thought it was incredibly romantic. But it devastated my grandparents, and the reality wasn't romantic at all.'

He felt her fingers tighten around his, and her smile faded.

'They might have looked like the perfect couple from the outside, but honestly, though, their whole relationship started and ended with sex. It wasn't happy or healthy— just compulsive…like an addiction.'

She looked up at him defiantly, only somehow her expression seemed to accentuate her vulnerability.

'And that's what you thought we'd be like?' he asked.

Margot blinked, the directness of his question momentarily silencing her. 'I didn't think anything,' she said finally. 'I just panicked.'

For a moment she considered telling him the *whole* truth. That she'd loved him, and that he was still the only man she'd ever loved. But she'd laid enough of herself bare. Telling the truth now wouldn't alter the facts. Max hadn't loved her then, and he didn't love her now.

Looking back to that devastating moment when his

world had imploded, Max felt his chest tighten painfully as for the first time he contemplated a different version of events. And a new and unsettling realisation that he might not only have misjudged Margot all those years ago, but completely overreacted.

'Why didn't you tell me about your parents before?'

She shrugged, and the resignation in that simple gesture made his breath catch in his throat.

Looking down at her feet, she began digging her bare toes into the sand. 'I suppose I didn't know if I could trust you.'

He frowned. 'Is that why you kept us a secret?'

She didn't answer for a moment, and then slowly she shook her head. 'Maybe at first. But not later. Then I wanted it to be just you and me. I love my family, but they can be so demanding.'

'You mean your father?'

Margot stared at him. For a moment she'd actually forgotten that Max had met Emile. She gave him a weak smile. 'I hear you woke him up.'

Max grimaced. 'I paid for those shares in ways you'll never know.'

He was attempting a joke, trying to lighten the mood, but she couldn't shift the memory of his accusation.

She bit her lip. 'You were wrong, Max. I was never ashamed of you. I just knew that if I told my family they would complicate things. It's what they do.'

He stared down at her, his eyes glittering strangely. 'And what do *you* do?'

'Me? I'm a fixer-upper.'

That was an understatement. She seemed to have spent most of life problem-solving for her family, and with a tiny wrench of doubt she wondered what would happen if she just stopped. Was that why they loved her? For what she could do for them, not who she was.

Swallowing the lump of misery in her throat, and fearing she had given too much away, she shrugged. 'I make it all look perfect—which with my family is practically a full-time job. They might look flawless from the outside, but my father is living proof that appearances can be deceptive.'

Max hesitated. For a moment he stared at her in silence, as though working something out in his head, and then, taking a step closer, he pulled her into his arms.

'True,' he said slowly. 'But sometimes things are what they appear to be. Like the chemistry between us. That's real. You can't fake it, or pretend it doesn't exist.' Gently he reached up and stroked her hair. 'You were right about this morning. I was trying to prove a point. Only unfortunately I've just ended up proving what an idiot I am.'

He stared down at her, trying to make sense of everything that was going on inside his head. Coming down to the beach, his anger had been hot and righteous, but now her honesty, and the courage it had taken for her to be so honest, made him feel angry with himself. Margot was not the person he had thought she was. She was not selfish or self-absorbed. On the contrary, she seemed to have spent most of her life sacrificing herself to the demands of her family.

Breathing out softly, he slid his hand under her chin and tilted her face upwards. 'Why do you think I changed my mind about going back to France?'

Margot stared at his face in silence, not understanding why he was asking her that question now, and wondering where the conversation was heading.

His grip tightened. 'Because I want you as much as you want me, Margot. More than I've ever wanted any woman. I didn't want a honeymoon just because of what people might say if we didn't have one.' He smiled faintly. 'I think you know me well enough to believe that I can hold my own in the world.'

She nodded mutely, her heart hammering in her chest as his smile twisted.

'But clearly I haven't given you reason enough to believe that changing my mind was not an act of complete thoughtlessness. So let me make it clear now. Changing our plans wasn't supposed to upset you or your family. But I know now that it did, and I'm sorry. For not talking to you about it first. And for being a jerk this morning.'

Lifting her hand to his mouth, he kissed it lightly.

'I know I haven't covered myself in glory these last few days, but I'm not a monster.' He stared down into her eyes. 'It's not too late to fly back. If that's what you want, then tell me and I'll make it happen.'

Margot bit her lip. It was an olive branch, or maybe an attempt at reparation...

'You'd do that? For me?'

His fingers closed more firmly around hers. 'Of course. You're my wife. I'm not in the habit of making empty promises. I made vows, and I meant them.'

She wondered what he meant by empty promises, but something in his expression warned her that now was not the time to ask him.

It's not too late to fly back. I made vows, and I meant them.

Gazing up at him, his words echoing inside her head, Margot was torn. Part of her wanted to make things right with her grandfather. But Max had apologised, and he'd admitted that he wanted her. That the attraction between them was special. For a moment she was in a daze, but as she caught sight of her wedding ring she made up her mind.

'I want to stay. But I'd like us to talk to my grandfather and Louis.'

His expression didn't change, but he wrapped his arms around her, pulled her closer, and she felt his heart beating unsteadily.

'Then that's what I want too,' he said softly.

CHAPTER EIGHT

ROLLING ONTO HER FRONT, Margot closed her eyes and let the book she'd been failing to read slip from her fingers.

After a night in Max's arms she was feeling drowsy and sybaritic, so she had decided to spend an hour by the pool. The sun felt wonderful on her bare skin, and she was feeling wonderful too, the tranquillity of her mind complementing the languor of her body.

It wasn't just the heat that was making her feel so relaxed. Today felt almost like a new beginning, for finally she had told her family about her marriage.

She had spoken first to her grandfather and then to Louis, and even now she couldn't quite believe how well it had gone. It had been so much easier than she'd expected—mainly thanks to Max.

He had been with her the whole time, literally holding her hand. Remembering his quiet but easy self-assurance, she felt her pulse jump. She doubted there were many people who had the charisma and confidence to manage a man of her grandfather's status and gravitas. But, hearing Max talk, she had known that nobody would question the validity of their marriage. He had seemed utterly unfazed, and his certainty had been irresistible.

But then everything about Max was irresistible. His

looks, his resoluteness and his power were an aphrodisiac that made her ache to feel his hands on her body again.

Pushing aside an image of what those hands could do, she wondered how and when he'd learned to behave with such poise. He might be her husband, but his background was still as much of a mystery to her as it had been nearly ten years ago.

Stretching her arms out, she shifted against the cushion of the sun lounger and thought back to their argument on the beach, and the confession that had spilled out of her afterwards. Their anger had been so intense it had felt like a storm cloud breaking. Only somehow, out of her fury and his, they had come to a better understanding.

Her skin began to prickle. Or rather *he* now understood *her*, for the sharing of information had been entirely on her side.

She hadn't meant to confide in him about her parents' relationship, but between the endless blue of the ocean and the relentless blue and green of his gaze there had been nowhere to hide.

And, even though she had never put it into words before, it had been easy to tell him the truth—maybe because he had listened to her in a way that no one else had ever done. Her staff hung on her every word at work, and her family were always asking for advice, but Max had really *listened* to her, as if she mattered to him. And it had been his concentration and persistence which had finally broken down the barriers she'd built to stop the prying gaze of the world.

Remembering his remark about empty promises, she wondered what he'd meant. She would have liked to ask him, only his manner had not exactly encouraged further discussion. And it had been no different in the past. If ever she had tried to ask him about himself he had simply batted her questions away and changed the subject.

Aged nineteen, she'd thought it didn't matter that she hardly knew anything about him. In truth, she'd been too in love, and too astonished that he was no longer treating her just as Yves's younger sister but as a woman, to do anything but bask in his attention.

There had been other reasons, too, why she had purposely not cross-examined him. As someone who valued her own privacy, she was sympathetic to other people's reticence, and so she'd been if not happy then understanding of his silence.

But now...?

She sighed. They might have reached a kind of truce, but no matter how much she would have liked to peek into the complexities of Max's mind she wasn't feeling nearly brave enough to question him about his background or his private life.

Or, worse, his feelings.

And maybe she didn't need to, for when her body was pressed against his, and she could feel his heart beating in time to hers, she felt as if she knew everything there was to know about him.

She felt a pang of remorse as she remembered how she'd accused him of being insensitive and self-serving.

He wasn't. She knew that now. He was capable of compassion and, unlike a lot of people with money and power, capable and willing to apologise.

Realising how much he had upset her, he had offered to return to France, and even though she had agreed to stay at the villa she knew that he had meant what he'd said. And, athough she had wanted to tell her family in person, she didn't regret her decision. On the contrary, right now she could think of nowhere she'd rather be—so much so that she was struggling to remember why she had ever thought that having a honeymoon was such a bad idea.

She felt a warm, tingling feeling in the pit of her stomach. After they'd called her grandfather Max had led her back to the bedroom and stripped both of them naked, his mouth urgently seeking hers, kissing her so deeply that she was breathless and dizzy. And, curling her legs around him, her hands shaking with eagerness as they'd spread over the muscles of his back, she had guided him inside her restless, aching body.

Lifting her head, she turned her face away from the sun. But it wasn't just about the sex. Max was great company too. He was well-read, and interested in what she'd read—they had talked about everything from tax reform to the rise in popularity of Peruvian food. And he made her laugh—*really* laugh—in a way she had almost forgotten she could.

It was easy to see why her teenage self had fallen under his spell. And here in the sunshine, far away from the relentless, unforgiving demands of real life, it would be as easy to feel the same way about him now.

Her stomach clenched. Easy, but terrifying at the same time.

For despite knowing that she was letting herself get swept away by the romantic setting and the new openness between them, the truth was that a part of her had always wanted to believe in him—to reimagine their history with a happy ending.

And, even though it was stupid and pointless and crazy, even dangerous to think that way, with every hour that passed she just couldn't seem to stop herself wanting to believe that their intimacy and mutual hunger for one another was more than just physical attraction.

A pair of warm hands slid over her back and her pulse darted forward like a startled fish.

'Hey, sleepyhead.'

Max nuzzled her neck, and she felt heat rush to the spot where his lips were caressing her bare skin. Tipping her head back slightly, she let her cheek graze his, breathing in the mix of coffee and cologne and some undefined but potent essence of maleness that made her heat rush through her body.

Rolling over onto her back, she opened her eyes and gazed up at him, wondering if she would ever get used to how gorgeous he was. Stomach flipping, she reached out and curled her hands around his biceps, her thumbs pressing into the hard muscles.

'I'm not sleeping, I'm worshipping the sun,' she protested, a beat of blood starting to drum inside her head. 'Why don't you join me?'

Gently cupping her face in his hand, he lowered his mouth, brushing his lips against hers. 'I'd much rather worship you,' he whispered.

He raised his head, and the intent in his beautiful eyes made her body feel suddenly boneless.

'But, as I'm very devout, and it may take me some time, I think we should go somewhere a little more comfortable,' he said softly. And, pulling her to her feet, he led her back to their bedroom.

They made slow, passionate love all morning, stopping only for Max to crawl out of bed and bring back some lunch, which they ate with their fingers.

Later, they walked along the shoreline, happy just to hold hands and pick up shells and pieces of driftwood, until finally it became too hot and they retreated to the villa and to bed again.

'Are you okay?'

Margot glanced up at Max. She was lying in his arms, her body damp and feverish, still trying to catch her breath. 'I am—are you?'

His eyes were dark and lazy as they rested on her face.

'Yes, but...' He paused, his hand caressing the curve of her hip in a way that made her body start to shake inside.

'But what?' she asked quickly, knowing that if she waited too long to reply her skin would grow warm and she would rapidly lose the power of both thought and speech.

He sounded casual, but in contrast his expression was tense, expectant. 'I need to make a phone call.'

What? Now? Can't someone else do it?

Her disappointment was instant, and clearly it must have showed on her face for, grimacing, he shook his head and answered her unspoken questions. 'I can't delegate this one, but it won't take long.' His gleaming eyes drifted hungrily over her naked body. 'I promise.'

Kissing her lightly on the lips, he slid out of bed and tugged on a pair of linen trousers.

Staring at him, she frowned. 'Where are you going?'

'I'm going to use the study. I have to,' he said as she started to protest. 'There's no way I can concentrate with you here like—'

His words faltered as she leaned back against the pillow and moistened her lips. 'Like what?' she asked innocently.

He groaned. 'Margot, please don't make this any harder than it already is,' he said hoarsely.

Tilting her head to one side, she smiled. 'Make *what* harder, Max?'

'Very funny.'

His eyes narrowed, and the slow, hot glance he gave her made her heart ping-pong inside her chest. 'Do not leave this bed. I'll be ten minutes, tops, and then you and I are going to...'

She held his gaze, and there was a moment of pure, pulsing silence.

And then, his jaw tightening, he swore forcefully. 'Ten minutes,' he said softly, and before she had a chance to reply he turned and walked swiftly out of the room.

Watching him leave, Margot rolled over and pulled his pillow against her stomach, wanting to capture the last traces of warmth from his body.

It was silly, really, given that it was only lust, but the fact that he clearly wanted her so badly made her feel ludicrously happy, even though the space in the room where he'd been made her feel empty inside.

It was annoying that work had intruded, but in a way she was pleased that he was so committed to making good on his promise to turn her business around. He'd made at least one call a day since they'd arrived at the villa, usually while she was in the pool or taking a shower. But they were always short, and afterwards he was doubly attentive.

Clutching the pillow tighter, she wrapped the still-warm sheet around her naked body and, listening to the calming rhythm of the sea, imagined his return...

She must have dozed off. Waking, and aware of a shift in the light, she reached over to the bedside table and picked up her phone. Glancing at the screen, she frowned. Max had said ten minutes, but he'd been gone more like twenty-five.

She bit her lip, uncertain of whether to stay in bed or go and find him. Reluctant to move, she fell back against the pillow. He would probably be back soon, she told herself.

But after another five minutes she couldn't bear it any longer. Sliding out of bed, she picked up the shirt that he'd discarded the night before and pulled it over her head.

As usual, aside from the sound of the surf, the villa was still and quiet. The staff were not just discreet, they were virtually invisible—since that first day, she had only seen Aurelie, the housekeeper, once.

In the hallway, she headed towards the study, but as she reached the half-open door she hesitated as she heard Max's voice. If he'd been talking to a member of his staff then she would have walked right in, and had he sounded angry she would probably have sneaked away. But he wasn't angry, and he definitely wasn't talking to his PA or his accountants or his lawyer.

Her pulse stumbled.

She couldn't hear exactly what he was saying, but there was a warmth and ease to his voice—a tenderness that made her hands start to shake. It was the kind of shared tenderness that only two people in a long and close relationship would have, and she knew instinctively that he was talking to a woman.

And not just any woman—a woman he loved very much.

For a moment she couldn't move. Her legs seemed to have turned to ice. And then, breathing out unsteadily, she took hold of the handle and slowly pushed the door open.

Max had his back to her. He was gazing out of the window, his phone pressed against the side of his head, and suddenly the blood was roaring in her ears—for this was almost exactly how she'd found him in the boardroom. Only then he'd been sitting down, wearing a suit, and now he was standing bare-chested, shifting restlessly, the hard, primed muscles of his beautiful athlete's body rippling as he talked.

'Look, I have to go now.'

The gentleness in his voice made her feel hollowed out with misery.

'I know. I wish you were here with me too. But I'll speak to you tomorrow, I promise.'

He rang off, and she watched his fingers curl around the phone, her pulse staggering, her chest so tight she thought it would burst. And then he turned and saw her. And, however bad she had felt moments before, she knew that nothing in her life would ever hurt as much as seeing his face and the truth in his eyes.

'How long?' she whispered. Her throat was so constricted that it hurt to speak, but the pain was nothing to the pain in her chest. 'How long?' she repeated, more loudly this time. 'How long have you been seeing her?'

He stared at her blank-eyed. 'I think you must be a little confused—' he began.

But she cut across him, for there was no way she could listen to any more of his lies.

'No, actually, I think I was a *lot* confused. So confused, in fact, that I'd actually started to believe that you wanted to make this work.' Her mouth curved with contempt. 'What was it you said? *"I'm not in the habit of making empty promises."*' Clenching her teeth, fighting the desolation and despair clogging her throat, she shook her head. 'I'm such an idiot. I really thought you were talking about me, when all the time you were talking about your mistress!'

'Mistress!'

His face hardened, and before she had a chance to register the flash of white-hot anger in his eyes he had crossed the room in three strides.

'You clearly are confused if you think I'd ever make any woman my mistress.'

'Don't lie to me, Max,' she exploded, his denial lighting the fuse of her shock and anger. 'I heard you. I heard you talking to her—'

'No, you didn't, Margot.' His mouth twisted, and she could see the muscles in his arms and chest straining. 'You heard me talking to my mother.'

There was a dull, heavy silence. She stared at him, almost floating with shock, her anger swept aside by his words. Up until that moment she'd never heard him refer to any kind of relative, even in passing. In fact, she'd thought that maybe he didn't actually have any family, and that was why it had been easy for him to be so blasé and dismissive about hers.

'Your mother?'

'Yes. My mother.'

There was a different tone to his voice now—a roughness that wrenched at something inside her, made her want to reach out to him. As if he sensed that, he turned abruptly and walked towards the window.

Staring after him, Margot swallowed. His back was towards her, and she could see the effort with which he was holding himself still, holding in the emotion which had split his voice.

'Max—' She took a step forward and then stopped, her pulse skipping a beat. She knew his anger—knew that it could be ice-cold or like a fire beneath his skin. But this was different. If it was anger, then it was a desperate and stricken kind that she had never seen before.

His shoulders tensed, and his breathing was ragged. 'Just go, Margot.'

He couldn't bear to look at her, to have to see what she was feeling.

'No. I'm not going anywhere.'

She spoke softly, as if she was unsure as to how or even if he would respond, but even without seeing her face he could sense that she meant what she was saying.

Turning slowly, he stared at her in silence.

Mistress.

How could one word cause so much pain? But was it that surprising, given that it embodied both his mother's crushed hopes and his own sense of helplessness? A helplessness he couldn't let Margot see.

Only there was no way out, for she was standing just inside the room, her body blocking the doorway.

'This is not your problem,' he said flatly.

Shaking her head, she took a step closer. 'Yes, it is. You see, I made promises too.'

'Yes—under duress.'

He had made her do it so that he could right an alleged wrong. Or that was what he'd told himself. But marrying Margot had never really been about getting his money's worth for her father's shares, or punishing her for not wanting him ten years ago. The truth was both simple and more complex. Only he'd never discussed his mother with anyone—never so much as hinted at the turmoil of his past—and he didn't know what to say or even how to start now.

Brown eyes flaring, she held his gaze. 'That's not true. I had choices, and I walked into that chapel willingly.'

She hesitated, and before he had a chance to react she had taken two quick steps forward and taken his hand.

'And I'm here willingly too.' She hesitated again. 'Are you okay?'

He could hear that she was worried about him, see by the slight tremble of her mouth that she cared, and that in itself made his head spin. But it was her touch, gentle but firm, that convinced him to tell her the truth. For she was standing in front of him not as some bargaining chip or sacrifice but as an equal. And as for telling a difficult truth—hadn't she done that herself, yesterday?

He nodded. 'She worries about me if I don't ring when

I say I'm going to ring. That's why I couldn't stay with you earlier.'

Margot nodded. He was keeping his promises. Her head was filled with a blur of questions and conjecture but, glancing up at him, she knew there was only one question she needed to ask right now.

'Is everything all right?'

His face tightened. 'She misses me. But I've talked to her and she's okay now.'

Margot nodded. More than anything she wanted to stay on the island with Max but, remembering his reaction when she'd got upset about her grandfather, she didn't hesitate. 'Do you need to go back?'

He shook his head slowly. 'She has people with her. They're good—not just professional, but kind. She trusts them.'

A pulse was throbbing in the side of her head. 'Is your dad not around?'

She gazed at him uncertainly. Even as she had spoken she'd wondered why she didn't already know the answer to such a basic question. And why it felt as if his answer would be the key to unlocking this complex, compelling man who had dominated her life since she was a teenager.

Slowly he shook his head again. 'He's never been around. The relationship was over before she even found out she was pregnant. She told him, but—' Catching sight of her face, he shrugged. 'It's fine. You can't miss what you don't know.'

Thinking about her own childhood, and how much she'd longed for her life to be simple and stable, Margot wasn't sure if she agreed with him. But she was too scared to say so for fear of disturbing the thread of his thoughts and derailing this uncharacteristic openness on his part.

'I suppose not. But it must have been hard for her by herself.'

She felt his fingers tense, and then tighten around hers.

'She managed okay.' His eyes were intent on her face. 'And she wasn't always by herself. When I was about eleven she met this guy called Paul. She was working as a receptionist at a law firm, and he was one of the clients.'

'What was he like?'

He turned towards her, the hazy sunlight floating into the room making his eyes glitter like gemstones.

'I was eleven. I don't think I knew what he was like.' He gave her a crooked smile. 'He ran a logistics company. But as far as I was concerned he had three cars—two of them convertibles—and he supported the same football team as me, so I thought he was cool.'

His face softened.

'And he made my mum happy. She always used to worry so much about money, and work, and me, but after she met Paul she seemed to relax. I guess it was good for her to have someone around she could rely on.'

Margot nodded. She knew exactly how Max's mother must have felt. The relief of not being alone, of not always having to be the person in charge.

'We moved into a new house, and Paul more or less moved in with us. He was away on business a lot, but it didn't matter. By then I'd worked out that he wasn't that interested in me. But that didn't matter either, because he took us on holiday and he bought me new football boots.'

He paused.

'Only it was different for my mum. I knew she really wanted to marry him. I asked him about it once, but he said it was too soon and that he needed to get his business established. He gave her a necklace instead of a ring, and then I went to boarding school and I suppose I just forgot about it.'

Something in his voice pulled her chest tight, but she made herself say lightly, 'Did you like school?'

He shrugged. 'It was fine. I was good at most things, and I was in the football and rugby squads, so I was always training or playing matches. I didn't really have time to get homesick.'

She felt it again—this time in her throat. A tightening, almost a nervousness, and then her heart began to beat a little faster. 'But you did go home?'

His shoulders were so rigid now it looked as though they would snap. 'Only Saturday afternoons, after the match. Except this one time.'

The muscles in his arms shifted and tensed.

'Why? What happened?' Holding her breath, she waited for him to answer.

'I'd been away at school about a year. It was the end of November and the school boiler broke. We got sent home, only some of us decided not to go home. We went into Paris instead. And that's when I saw him.'

She saw that Max was staring out of the window, except a moment later she realised he was actually staring at their reflection.

'We were walking past a restaurant and he was inside, sitting at a table with this woman and three children—a boy and two girls. And that's when I realised. It wasn't that he didn't want to marry my mum. He couldn't. Because he was already married.'

Margot felt her stomach coil in on itself.

'That's awful. Did you tell her?'

For a moment he didn't reply, and the silence seemed to stretch out of the room and across the ocean to the blurred line of the horizon.

'I didn't have to,' he said finally. 'She already knew. She'd known for years and she'd just been waiting and hoping.' He shook his head. 'I got mad—*really* mad with her. I told her she had to have it out with Paul and give him an ultimatum.' He smiled tightly. 'You know how I love an ultimatum.'

He was attempting to make a joke, but the weariness in his voice made the breath catch in her throat.

'And then what happened?'

'She confronted him. And he told her that even if he hadn't already been married, she wasn't "wife material". That women like her were only good for sex.'

She groped for something to say but she couldn't speak. In part she was stunned by the brutality of Paul's remarks, but what had left her speechless was the fragment of memory rising to the surface of her thoughts. Max's accusation on the beach that he had been *"good enough for sex, just not for marriage".*

At the time she'd thought he was just throwing out insults. Now, though, she saw that his choice of words had been deliberate. And now she knew why. Ten years ago, when she had been too stunned to speak in his defence, he had thought—understandably—that history was repeating itself, that she was judging him as Paul had judged his mother.

Her heart contracted and she felt a sudden overwhelming urge to cry—for she could see now that her silence had been as cruel as Paul's words. Not only had she hurt him, she had reinforced his deep-rooted fear that he wasn't good enough. No wonder he had wanted her father's shares so badly. He had wanted to prove himself—prove her wrong.

Max breathed out unsteadily. He had never talked so much, or so openly. He felt drained but, looking at Margot's face, he could see only concern, and that gave him the strength to continue.

'I don't think he liked being made to feel like the bad guy, so that was it. He broke up with her. Stopped paying the rent and my school fees. My mum had a kind of breakdown. She couldn't leave the house, let alone work. She still can't. That's why she didn't come to the wedding. She couldn't have—not even if it had been in France.' He threw her a small, stiff smile. 'In the end, we got this apartment in Saint-Denis. You might have heard of it?'

She nodded and, looking past her, he gritted his teeth. Of course she'd heard of it. The tenth *arrondissement* was notorious for its sprawling concrete estates and for having a higher than average crime rate.

Even now he could still remember moving into the apartment, with its broken windows and graffiti-covered door. In no time at all his mother had retreated into herself, and he had begun truanting and dabbling in petty crime.

He gave a humourless laugh. 'It was a difficult time. Moving house, changing school, and then my mum being so crushed. I started getting into trouble at school—if I even went. Smoking, stealing, fighting… And then I surpassed myself and broke into Paul's office.'

Watching her face, he gave a sardonic smile.

'Don't worry! You're not married to a criminal. Weirdly, Paul came down and talked to the police and they let me off. And then he got me a job, helping out at his friend's vineyard. The first day I helped graft a vine and I was hooked. Five years later I ended up working for Yves, and the rest you know.'

He stopped abruptly. After the closeness of his confession the sudden silence was such a shock that all she wanted to do was to fill the void, so she said the first thing that came into her head. 'Why do you think Paul helped you?'

He frowned. 'I think he felt guilty about what he'd said to my mother, and how he'd treated her, and maybe even me too.'

Eyes narrowing, she nodded slowly. 'So he should.'

The indignation in her voice made him smile properly. 'And there I was, thinking you'd be all for putting me in handcuffs.'

Their gazes locked and a pulse of heat began to beat over her skin. 'Thinking or hoping?' she asked softly.

He breathed in sharply and she reached out for him and suddenly he was pulling her closer and burying his face into her hair. 'I'm sorry,' he murmured.

'For what? I was the one making stupid assumptions and even stupider accusations. And if you're talking about our marriage,' she added fiercely, 'then I meant what I said earlier. I walked into that chapel willingly. And I'd walk into it again now.'

As she spoke her heart gave a jolt, and she felt something inside her splitting apart and, with a mixture of fear and relief, she realised that for her their relationship was way more than physical. That at some unspecified point she had opened her heart to him.

For a moment she came dizzyingly close to telling him that she still loved him—more so even than she had before. And not just willingly, but unconditionally. But, glancing up at his set face, she knew that this was not about her and her feelings.

He stared down at her, his face still strained. 'That doesn't mean I'm not sorry for putting you in an impossible situation.' He hesitated. 'And that isn't the only reason I'm sorry.' Lifting his head, he looked down at her. 'When I met you, I was still a mess.'

She gave him a small, swift smile. 'You looked pretty good to me.'

His mouth curled upwards. 'On the outside, maybe. But everything had been so difficult for so long. When we got together I didn't want to be like my mum—just sitting around, waiting and wishing. I wanted to be in control.'

He frowned. It was the first time he'd ever articulated those thoughts to himself, let alone out loud, but for some reason—maybe the firmness of her arms around his waist, or the softness in her eyes—he wanted her to know them.

'Deep down, I think I knew it was too soon, and that you weren't ready, but I just wanted things to be definite between us—that's why I proposed. Only then Yves turned up, and he was so appalled and so opposed to even the idea of it—'

'He was shocked,' Margot said quickly. 'He felt the same way I did about our parents' marriage. I promise you, it would have been the same with any man.'

He frowned. 'I want to believe you, and maybe I can now. But he made me feel stupid and small, and you didn't say anything. I was angry and upset. So I told you that I'd only wanted you for your money. But I didn't. It was a lie. I just wanted to hurt you.'

Margot stared at him, misery swelling in her chest, seeing that moment as though from his perspective. Of course he'd been hurt. Yves had been brutal, and in her silence she had only condoned his brutality.

It was all such a mess.

They had both assumed the worst of each other. But by trying not to repeat the mistakes of the past they had succeeded in ruining their future together.

She bit her lip. 'I should have stopped Yves. If I'd said something—'

He looked down at her hand in his, and for a moment

she thought he was going to release his grip. But instead he lifted her fingers, tilting her rings up to the light.

'It wouldn't have made any difference. He was too angry and upset. We all were. And it doesn't matter any more, anyway. It might have taken us a long time to get here, but everything's worked out fine.'

His eyes on hers were soft, and she felt warmth spread over her skin.

'You're my wife, and we're together now. That's all that matters.'

She was breathless from his nearness. It was all she could do to stay standing as he cupped her face in his hands and kissed her. Her heart wanted to burst, for she couldn't ignore the facts. She might want Max to love her but he didn't. Not then and not now.

But as his fingers slid under her shirt all conscious thought was swept away. One hand splayed out over the skin of her back, the other tugged at her buttons until her shirt fell open and she felt cool air wash over her stomach and breasts. Her nipples tightened and, moaning softly, she reached out and touched his chest.

Breathing in sharply, he pulled her against him…

CHAPTER NINE

HER HEART WAS beating hard and fast. Her hands slid up through his dark hair and she moved backwards clumsily, his arm guiding her. Or was she pulling him? And then he was lifting her onto the desk, sweeping papers aside and lowering her to the gleaming wood.

For a moment he watched her, his eyes dark and glittering with desire, and then, breathing shallowly, he leaned over and kissed his way down her neck to her breast, rolling his tongue around first one rosy-tipped nipple then the other.

Arching upwards, she gasped, and then she collapsed back against the desk as he dropped to his knees and took her with his mouth.

Panting, she shifted against him, raising her hips, her body already starting to tremble, wanting more. And then her fingers tightened in his hair and she pulled him up. Her hands fumbled with the button on his trousers and suddenly she was pulling him free, her fingers closing around him in a fist.

He grunted, catching her hand with his. He pushed it away and, raising her up, thrust inside her, flattening her body with his.

'Look at me,' he muttered.

Wrapping her legs around his hips, she gazed up at

him as he pushed harder and deeper, the blaze in his eyes matching the burning heat between her thighs. Suddenly she was grasping his head in her hands, her muscles clenching as he surged into her again and again, and then, tensing, she cried out, her body joining his in a shuddering climax.

Feeling him bury his face in her throat, Margot closed her eyes and breathed out shakily. She couldn't move, certainly couldn't speak. And she didn't want to. All she wanted to do was lie there in his arms for ever, breathing in the air that he breathed.

She felt him shift above her and, feeling his gaze, she opened her eyes. He was gazing down at her, his face flushed, his breathing unsteady.

'Are you okay? I didn't hurt you, did I?'

She shook her head. 'This desk is actually more comfortable than it looks.'

Lifting her hand, she traced her finger along his jawline and over the shadow of stubble on his chin.

Frowning, he gently withdrew and pulled her upright, supporting her with his arm. 'I kept thinking we should go the bedroom, but I was desperate.'

She smiled. 'I don't know whether to be offended that you were clear-headed enough to think anything at all, or flattered that you were so desperate.'

Stroking her blonde hair away from her face, his gaze held hers. He smiled. '"Clear-headed" might be pushing it.' He kissed her lightly on the lips then, dipping his mouth to her throat, brushed the sensitive skin of her collarbone and the slope of her breast. 'I don't know what happens when I'm with you but it's got very little to do with thinking. Just wanting. And feeling.'

Her heart gave a lurch, but she knew that the feelings

he was talking about were physical, not emotional, and sexual desire was nothing like love.

Blocking the ache in her chest, and keeping the smile on her face, she said lightly, 'Me too.'

Breathing out, Max pulled her closer. Tipping her head back, he kissed her deeply, and as her nipples brushed against his chest he felt her stir restlessly against him. Instantly his body began to throb in response.

Moaning softly, she broke the kiss, and pressed a hand to the middle of his chest. 'Max...'

'Yes, Margot?' he said hoarsely.

'Do you think we could make it to the bedroom this time?'

He nodded slowly, his eyes on her mouth, and then, grabbing her wrist, he tugged her towards the door.

Later they swam in the pool and lay in the sun.

'Is this okay for you?' Margot glanced over at him, frowning slightly. *She* didn't actually want to go anywhere or do anything, but then she was in love. All she wanted to do was spend every minute of every hour with Max, savouring every moment, absorbing every detail.

But she wasn't ready to reveal her true feelings to him yet—in fact she wasn't sure that she would ever be ready. It had been hard enough to explore her own. Having to face up to the fact that Max couldn't and wouldn't ever share those feelings was not worth spoiling this new intimacy between them for. And besides, right now his body inside and beneath and on top of hers was enough.

She cleared her throat. 'I mean, we haven't actually left the villa once, and we've only got another five days. Is there nothing you'd rather do?'

His eyes rested intently on hers, and she shook her head, her mouth curving into a smile.

'You have a one-track mind.'

'It's not one-track,' he said lazily, reaching over to caress her hipbone in a way that made heat rush though her. 'It's just one destination.'

She reached for his hand, intending to still it, knowing that if she didn't she'd be begging him to take off her clothes—take *her*, full stop, out on the terrace. But his fingers curled around her wrist and he pulled her towards him, so that her stomach was pressing against the hot, toned muscles of his abdomen.

For a moment she stared at him, dry-mouthed. She loved what they shared, loved the press of his mouth on hers, the touch of hand and the weight of his body. Only, feeling as she did, she knew she should be careful. Wrapped in his arms, it was temptingly, dangerously easy for her to start fantasising about true love and happy endings, for that was when they were at their most intimate. But every time she thought about taking a step back she only had to look at him and she was struggling to breathe.

The trouble was that her hunger for him far outweighed her willpower, and each time she gave in to that hunger it got harder and harder not to tell him how she felt.

'What is it?'

He was staring at her, studying her closely so that for one terrible moment she thought she must somehow have revealed her thoughts.

'Nothing.' She gave him a casual smile. 'It just seems a shame to come all this way and not even have a look around. It's so beautiful... I'm sure there must be something stunning to see.'

His eyes slid slowly over the three turquoise triangles tied around her body. 'That bikini is pretty stunning.'

She rolled her eyes. 'I was talking about sightseeing.'

He grinned. 'In that case, now you come to mention

it, there is something I'd like to take a closer look at. You have this tiny little scar, just below your—'

Reaching over, she punched him lightly on the arm and he broke off, laughing.

'You're impossible!' She was laughing too. 'People do other things on their honeymoon beside tearing each other's clothes off.'

'And is that what you want to do? Other things? Like sightseeing.'

Assuming that he was still teasing her, and about to respond in kind, she looked up, her mouth curving at the corners. But as their eyes met she felt her heart start to pound. Max was smiling, but his eyes were serious, expectant, as though her answer mattered. Her smile seemed suddenly out of place. Why was he asking? Did he think that she was bored? Or that she wanted to be somewhere else, *with* someone else?

Meeting his gaze, she shook her head. 'No, I'm happy being here with you, relaxing,' she said carefully. 'I just wasn't sure if that was what *you* wanted.'

'I don't care what we do as long as I'm with you.' Leaning forward, he tipped her face upwards and kissed her softly on the mouth. 'That's all I want—to be with you.'

Letting her lashes shield her eyes, she kissed him back, feeling a shot of pure, sweet happiness. Maybe it was cowardly not to tell him the truth, but kisses were so much simpler than feelings—and even more so when his feelings were so far removed from hers.

Lying back on the lounger, Max stretched out his legs, closing his eyes to the beat of the sun. Despite his easy words he felt a ripple of unease snake across his skin, only he wasn't entirely sure why.

These last few days had been hard. Arguing with Margot, seeing her so upset and then confessing his past to her had been painful. But it had been worth it, for now he had everything he'd ever wanted. He was the biggest shareholder in one of the oldest and most prestigious champagne businesses in the world and, more importantly, Margot was his wife.

His life was complete, and he should be enjoying that fact. He *wanted* to enjoy it, but he wasn't. Instead he felt restless and uneasy.

Watching Margot turn the pages of her book, a tiny frown of concentration creasing her forehead, he knew that the problem was his alone. She seemed utterly happy—happier, even, than that slightly serious young girl he'd known all those years ago.

He, on the other hand, felt anything but relaxed. It didn't help that since they'd walked up to the terrace together their earlier conversation had been playing more or less on repeat inside his head.

Talking about his mother, remembering how devastated she had been by Paul's hurtful remarks and his lack of commitment, had made his muscles tense and a familiar feeling of anger and helplessness push against his ribcage.

For years those memories and feelings had been like fish in a pond over winter—there, but not there, still and silent beneath the ice. Now, though, it was as if he had smashed the frozen surface, and he couldn't seem to stop thinking about his mother and Paul. Himself and Margot.

He hadn't been consciously trying to rewrite history, and yet for the first time he could see that in so many ways his past had been driving his actions—pushing him to seek the certainty and legitimacy that his mother had craved. How else had he managed to build a global business worth billions in less than ten years?

His chest rose and fell.

Why else would he have proposed to Margot after seeing her in secret for just two months? And why else had he ignored logic and instinct and married her five days ago?

At the time, he'd justified his behaviour in any number of ways. Only he didn't care any more about the money he'd paid for the shares. Nor did he feel the need to take her business and turn it around, for he knew now that she hadn't judged him unworthy.

He breathed in sharply. Opening his eyes, he glanced over at where Margot was sitting, her sleek limbs gleaming in the sunlight. Always, right from the beginning, he'd seen their relationship from *his* point of view. It had been his past that mattered, his pride, his feelings—his motivation.

But this wasn't just about him.

'I had choices, and I walked into that chapel willingly.'

As her words replayed inside his head his thoughts slowed in time to his heartbeat, and suddenly and acutely he knew why he was feeling so uneasy.

Margot might be his wife, but the fact was there was no way she would have chosen to marry him if he hadn't forced the issue—forced her to choose between sacrificing herself or her family.

Really, what kind of a choice was that?

He had pushed her into this marriage, using the love she felt for her grandfather and her brother to get his own way. But now, having forced her to choose, where did that leave him—*them*?

'I was thinking about what you said earlier about doing other things.' Leaning forward, Max kissed Margot's bare shoulder. 'And I thought we might go scuba diving this morning. Danny can take us out in the boat, and we could spend a couple of hours in the water.'

They were eating lunch on the terrace. A delicate salad

of lobster and asparagus, followed by tuna carpaccio and a lime tart.

Gazing up at him, Margot felt her skin grow warm, a pulse of love beating through her veins. 'I'd like that.'

She loved the serenity and the slow-motion way of life beneath the waves. There was something intensely peaceful about slipping beneath the surface of the water, and the deeper you went the easier it was to forget your land-locked worries.

And that was exactly what she needed to do—what she had decided to do. Today she would concentrate on the good and stop dwelling on what she couldn't change. Most couples would envy the sexual connection that she and Max shared, and although he didn't love her he had confided in her, and that surely meant that he needed her for something other than sex.

It wasn't perfect, but few marriages were. And look how far they had come in just a few days.

She felt his fingers curl around hers.

'And you're okay swimming with sharks?' he asked softly.

She held his gaze. 'Isn't that what I've been doing all week?'

He grimaced. 'Is that how you see me?'

She studied his face. So much had changed in such a short time. A week ago she might only have noticed the ruthless line of his jaw, or the carefully guarded expression in his eyes. Now, though, she knew he was no shark. She'd experienced his softer side first-hand—not just when he was making love but in how he'd opened up to her.

'No, I don't think you're a shark.' Her eyes creased. 'You're more of a clownfish.'

There was a beat of silence, and then she shrieked with

laughter as he grabbed her onto his lap and buried his face in the hollow of her neck.

She was still laughing when she heard a distant rumble. 'What was that?'

Turning, they both gazed towards the ocean. On the horizon, so far away it looked almost like smoke, a loose dark cloud was hovering above the sea. Down on the beach, the waves were slightly choppier and more uneven than usual.

'Must be a storm.' His arms tightened around her and he smiled down at her easily. 'Don't worry, it'll probably miss us. But even if it doesn't it won't last long at this time of year.' Picking up his cup, he took a gulp of coffee. 'I'll go talk to Danny. He tracks all the weather for miles, so he'll know if we can still go out and—'

He broke off as his mobile started to ring.

Glancing down at the screen, his face shifted, the smile fading. 'Sorry, it's my mother. I'd better take it.'

Before she had a chance to speak he was tipping her gently off his lap onto her chair and standing up and walking swiftly across the terrace to the pool, lifting the phone to his ear as he did so. Watching him, she felt oddly bereft, almost hurt by his leaving, for it felt as if he was rejecting her…

But it wasn't that, she told herself quickly. He just wasn't used to sharing that part of himself.

It was impossible to hear what he was saying, and she couldn't see the expression on his face. But over the last few days she had become increasingly sensitive to the tiniest shift in his manner and, staring at his broad back, she knew something was wrong. His shoulders were pressing against the flimsy fabric of his shirt as though he was holding himself back—or holding something in.

She chewed her lip. Should she stay sitting or should she go over to him? Or maybe she shouldn't even be there.

She was just contemplating this new, third option when she heard Max hang up. For a moment she waited for him to turn round, her heart bumping nervously against her ribs. But he didn't turn round. He just carried on standing there in silence, his head slightly bowed as though he was praying.

Suddenly she could bear it no longer. It was probably a bad idea. Almost certainly it was. Only she didn't know any other way to be, for she cared that he was hurting. And so, standing up, she walked towards him.

'Max—is everything okay?'

She breathed out softly. Around them the air was heavy and motionless, and the birds were suddenly unusually quiet, as though sensing the sudden shift in tension on the terrace.

He turned slowly. 'Not really, no,' he said at last.

She felt cold on the inside. Trying not to think the worst, she said quickly, 'Is something the matter with your mum?'

He nodded. 'She needs me to come home, so I'm going to have to go back to France.'

'To France?' Whatever answer she had been expecting, it wasn't that.

He stared at her impatiently. 'Yes—that's where she lives.'

'But why? What's happened?'

'It doesn't matter. You don't need to worry about it.'

His voice was curt, but it wasn't his voice that made a chill settle on her skin. Moments before he'd answered the phone his eyes had been soft and teasing. Now, though, they were hard and flat and distant. And just like that time reversed, so that suddenly he was back to being the same remote man who had confronted her in the boardroom.

'But I am worried,' she said simply. 'I can see you're upset—'

He looked over at her blankly, almost as though he wasn't quite sure who she was, and then, running a hand over his face, he sighed.

'She's got the press camped out on her doorstep. Somehow they've found out about us. There are hundreds of them, all waiting outside, trying to get photos and hassling the staff. I can't expect her to deal with that.'

'Of course not.' She moved swiftly to his side, her hand reaching for his. 'We can leave now.' She glanced down at her bikini. 'I'll just go and get changed—'

His fingers tightened on hers, but even if they had been standing on opposite sides of the pool she would have known that she'd said the wrong thing, for she felt his entire body tensing beside her.

'You don't have to do that,' he said curtly, and then, as though hearing the harshness in his own voice, he softened his refusal by lifting her hand to his mouth and kissing it. 'In fact, it's probably better if you don't. They want a story, and it will be far easier for me to give them one if I'm on my own. So just stay here. I will fix this, and then I'll fly back.'

'But—' Margot started to protest but it was too late. He had already let go of her hand and was walking purposefully towards the house.

She stared after him in silence, her body quivering with a mixture of confusion and frustration. Theoretically, she'd accepted that Max would never love her, but now, faced with concrete evidence of that fact, she felt angry and hurt.

She sort of understood why he didn't want her to go back with him. Max knew how to handle himself, and she certainly didn't enjoy dealing with the *paparazzi*. Nor did she want to meet his mother for the first time with a pack of howling press slavering outside for a photo. So perhaps it would be better if she stayed here.

But if that was true then why did she feel as though he was only telling her part of the story? And, more importantly, why was she still standing here when she should be asking him that question?

Striding into his dressing room, Max yanked down a shirt and pushed his arms into the sleeves. He grabbed a tie and knotted it round his neck, then pulled his jacket on. After so long in beachwear, he felt as if his clothes were as unfamiliar and unwieldy as a suit of armour. But he wasn't planning on wearing them for long, or staying in France for any more time than it took to get whatever legal decision he needed to protect his mother. However, he sure as hell wasn't going to make the trip in swim-shorts and flip-flops.

Or with Margot there.

Remembering the hurt expression on her face, he closed his eyes. He didn't want to leave her behind, but how could he take her with him? The press were relentless, and with a story like this they would be like the sharks he had jokingly mentioned over lunch. Hungry, ruthless and unstoppable.

Without her, he could handle them, and that was why he would be going back to France alone.

Gritting his teeth, he walked back into the bedroom and picked up his wallet and his watch. Frowning, he stared down at the face. If he left in the next hour he would be back sometime after—

'I want to come with you.'

He turned. Margot was standing in the doorway, not quite blocking it but with a stubborn set to her chin that suggested she might be about to do so.

He sighed. Had he really thought that she would just give up?

Holding her gaze, he shook his head. 'It's not a good idea. If we go together it will only turn into a feeding frenzy—and, frankly it's bad enough that they're hounding my mother. I don't need them turning on my wife as well.'

She stared at him mutinously. 'I disagree. If we both go back then we can give them what they want. The two of us together. Mr and Mrs Max Montigny.'

He glanced away from her. She was saying everything he'd ever wanted to hear, offering him the kind of support and loyalty that he had always craved, and yet…

Something shifted inside him—a tectonic convergence of conversations and memories—and he heard not just her words but the calm acceptance in the voice.

'I'm a fixer-upper. I make it all look perfect.'

His heart was beating fast and uneven, as though he'd been running. Maybe because he was running away from a truth that he didn't want to face—away from facts that he could never change, no matter how much he wanted to.

He took a deep breath, his gut tightening, finally acknowledging the real reason why he couldn't take her with him.

Margot had spent all her life fixing her family: managing her parents' marriage, her grandparents' expectations and the demands of her brothers, sacrificing her plans and her hopes and dreams time and time again.

And here, on this archipelago, he had made her sacrifice herself to him. But knowing that, was he really going to ask her to do it again?

He felt her eyes on his face, and then the touch of her hand on his arm.

'I thought you wanted to be with me,' she said softly. 'That's what you said.'

Watching his face grow still and remote, Margot felt a chill spread over her skin. He might have spoken the words, but clearly he hadn't meant them. Like so much of what Max said, it bore little relation to what was going in that handsome head of his.

'I do—' he began.

Her pulse jumped and she took a step closer. 'So prove it. Take me with you. I should be there. I want to be there. I know it's been difficult between us, but I am your wife.'

Wife.

Remembering the vows they had taken, he felt suddenly unsteady, and a chill started to roll out over his skin. He had promised to love and to cherish her.

But he had lied.

Ever since the moment he had walked into the board-room at the House of Duvernay headquarters he had treated her with a ruthlessness that now sickened him. A ruthlessness that equalled—no, *surpassed* Paul's treatment of his mother, for he had exploited her misfortune to give, by proxy, his mother the happy ending she'd so wanted.

It was all such a mess.

He'd made Margot a pawn—bullying her, blackmailing her, rushing her into marrying him. Using her to solve the issues inside his head in the same way that Paul had used his mother for sex and to boost his ego. Using the real love Margot felt for her family to get his own way. He had hurt her and humbled her, deliberately and repeatedly, and she had risen above his treatment in ways he could hardly fathom and certainly didn't deserve.

Any more than he deserved her support now.

What she *did* deserve, though, was to have the freedom to choose. To be with the person she wanted. Not be saddled with a life sentence to a man she had been to all intents and purposes forced to marry.

Margot stared at him, her frustration shifting up a gear. 'You wanted this, Max. You wanted this marriage.

I thought you wanted—' Her insides turned over and abruptly she broke off, leaving the sentence unfinished.

He didn't want her.

She couldn't actually say the words out loud. Even thinking them was so painful that it hurt to breathe, but she knew she was right. The fact that he didn't want her to go with him told her everything she needed to know.

Had he trusted and valued her, then returning to France would have been the perfect opportunity for them to showcase their marriage in public. But he would rather go alone.

The thought ripped through her like a serrated knife.

Max stared down at her face. She had never looked more beautiful to him and he had never wanted her more. He felt a sudden warm rush of hope rising inside him. 'Okay, I'll take you with me,' he said slowly. 'But on one condition.'

He could feel the warmth fading, and in its place a chill spreading out as she looked up at him uncertainly.

'I want you to tell me the truth,' he said.

Outside the window he could see the darkening sky, feel the heaviness of the approaching storm, and yet it seemed feeble, even frivolous, compared to the tension swirling inside his chest.

'Okay.' She nodded, her brown eyes searching his face, her relief at his change of heart mingling with obvious apprehension at where the conversation was leading.

Holding her gaze, he cleared his throat. 'I want you to tell me why you agreed to marry me.'

Her face stilled, and she frowned. 'Well, because...'

She hesitated, and her eyes dropped as though she couldn't meet his gaze, and then he knew. He knew that it had all been worthless. He could never take Margot to meet his mother for she would know in an instant that it was a phony marriage. It would break her heart, and he could no more do that to her then continue to use guilt and financial threats to keep Margot as his wife.

Margot shivered. She wasn't sure what was happening, just knew that they were no longer simply talking about whether or not she should return with him to France.

She tried again. 'You know why.'

'But I want you to tell me in your own words,' he said softly.

Too softly, she thought a moment later, her throat drying as she looked up into his taut, set face. 'I needed the money—' she began, but he cut her off.

'So there was no other reason.'

Yes, there was—there were. So many reasons—too many—but she wasn't brave enough to start listing them now.

It took her a moment to realise that he wasn't asking a question, just stating a fact. For perhaps a minute he stared at her in silence, and then, just as she was about to protest, to tell him that it wasn't that simple, he lowered his mouth to hers and kissed her gently.

Her heart lurched with relief, her fingers curling around the muscles of his arm as he deepened the kiss, her longing for him stealing her words, her thoughts, even her fear.

Reaching up, she clasped his face. But as she tried to deepen the kiss she felt his hands on hers, and suddenly he was stepping away from her, breathing unsteadily.

'Don't follow me,' he said, and the finality in his voice cast a spell over her body, rooting her to the cold tiles.

She knew without asking that he didn't just mean out of the room. He meant to France, to wherever, and the shock knocked the air out of her lungs, so that before her stunned brain could even register what he was doing he had turned and walked swiftly out of the room.

CHAPTER TEN

IT TOOK THE first tiny clumps of raindrops slamming against the window to drag Margot's eyes away from the empty doorway. Hesitantly, as though she wasn't sure if her legs would respond, she took a step towards the bed and sank down onto it. Her body felt brittle, her breath leaden.

It hardly seemed possible, but Max had walked out on her. Not just out of the room, or even the villa, but out of her life. He hadn't actually said as much. But he hadn't needed to. She had seen it in his eyes. Something had happened between that phone call out on the terrace and her walking into the bedroom—some insight or decision that had turned him away from her, away from their marriage.

Curling her knees up to her chest, she hugged them against her body. Shock gave way to misery, and tears began sliding down over her cheeks, and then the shock returned and her heartbeat started to shake. Her body started shaking too, and she was glad suddenly that she was sitting down, for she knew that her legs were definitely not capable of holding her up, or of supporting the weight of misery in her chest.

She took a deep breath, striving for calm, but the pain in her chest was too loud, too demanding.

He'd left her. Max had left her.

After everything they'd been through, she'd thought for one brief, blissful moment that they had a chance, that maybe her love would be enough for the two of them to make their marriage work. But now it was all over before it had even got started.

She covered her mouth with her hand.

Was it really that surprising, though? The pull between them had only ever been sexual on his side, and what couple had ever managed to build a future on great sex?

Thinking about her parents' marriage, she felt her pulse quiver. Not a happy or healthy marriage, anyway.

Remembering his question, she felt her shoulders tighten. Would it have been any different if she'd told him the truth? That at first she'd told herself that she was marrying him for money, but that even then the real reason she'd agreed to his proposal was because she loved him, had never stopped loving him.

Love had been the reason she'd let him back into her life. And the reason why she had agreed to turn her life upside down.

Only now he was gone, and the idea of his not being there was unimaginable. Agonising.

Suddenly she felt exhausted. Her eyes were blurry with tears again and her head was aching. But the pain would pass. Maybe not today, or tomorrow, or even in a year... or five. Sometime in the future, though, it would be just a dull ache above her heart, like the pain of losing her mother and her grandmother and Yves.

She had survived losing Max once, and she would do it again. But first she needed to sleep, for she was just so tired.

Crawling up towards the pillows, she pulled the sheet over her body and closed her eyes. Soothed by the steady, soporific sound of the rain striking the ground, she fell asleep.

* * *

It was the sound of the birds that woke her. Not right away.
At first their cries were just background noise to the confused and unfinished dream she was having about Emile
and Max and that boat she had seen on the second day of
their honeymoon.

Opening her eyes, she gazed groggily around the room.
It was still daylight and, grabbing her phone, she realised
with shock that she had slept for nearly two hours. Judging
by the fact that the sky was no longer dark, but streaked
with palest pink and yellow, she had slept through the
storm too. Outside, the surf sounded reassuringly soft and
regular, and the air felt warm but fresh, as though it had
just come out of a tumble drier.

She felt fresher too—less tired and less desperate, both
her body and her mind revived by sleep. It wasn't that she
felt any better about Max's rejection, just that she could see
past it. Her heart might be in pieces, but that didn't mean
her life had to be too. She had recovered from breaking up
with him before, and the House of Duvernay had survived
wars and recessions. It would survive Max Montigny.

Only somehow she didn't think that he was going to
hang around anyway. He had walked out for a reason. Had
the company been prosperous, then perhaps it might be
different, but it was clear that he didn't want anything to
do with her, and she felt sure that his feelings would ex-
tend to their business relationship.

Her mouth twisted. Obviously he would feel that way.
To Max, all of this—including their marriage—had only
ever been about business. She had been the one to start
weaving fantasy through fact, letting the intimacy and intensity of the last few days sweep her away.

Perhaps for a short time it had swept him away too.
Only when it had come to returning to reality, to leav-

ing the perfect little self-contained bubble of their honey-moon, he'd come to his senses. And that was when he'd decided to walk.

Tears burned behind her eyes and she breathed out shakily. Even though accepting that fact felt like a knife being driven through her heart, in some ways she was glad of the pain, for it made her focus on herself in a way that she never had.

Before, there had always been a long list of people and problems: Colette, Emile, her grandparents, Yves, Louis, Duvernay. And each time she had put her own life on hold in order to find a solution.

But from this moment on that was going to change. *She* had changed.

Her heart might be broken, but her brain was working just fine, and she knew that it was time to stop fixing other people's lives. Even though she wasn't quite sure how she was going to do it, she was going to start living *her* life—not the life decided by those around her.

A life on her own...without Max.

She might have wed in haste, like her parents, but that was where the similarity between their marriage and hers would end. Right now a life without Max felt like a life without warmth and sunlight, but however agonising it was to imagine, she was going to divorce him.

If she was going to make good on this promise to change then she needed her name and her business back. And that meant divorcing Max—although she would leave the details to the lawyers. She might have found the strength to deal with the concept theoretically, but it would be a long time before she would be willing or able to speak to him again—if ever.

First things first, though. She needed to go home.

She packed methodically, the rhythm of folding and

layering her clothes helping her stay calm. Changing out of her bikini, she found a pair of skinny-fit jeans that she'd brought with her in case of a freakish cold spell, and a loose tobacco-coloured linen jumper. Her face was pale, and her eyes were slightly pink and swollen, and for a moment she wondered whether mascara and lipstick would make things better or worse. Deciding it would be easier just to wear dark glasses, she left her hair loose, picked up her bag and shoes and walked towards the door.

All that was left to do was thank the staff and make her way to the airport. But first she wanted one last walk along the beach.

Walking through the villa, she felt some of her self-control start to slip away, and suddenly she was fighting tears again. She had loved being here with Max, getting to know him, getting to know herself, but there was no point in thinking that way.

Swiping at her eyes, grateful that she hadn't bothered to apply mascara, she stepped out onto the terrace—and froze.

Max was sitting on the curved steps leading down to the pool. He was hunched over, his head in his hands, an empty glass lying on its side beside him.

She stared at him in stunned silence. What was he still doing here? Had the storm delayed his flight? And what exactly was she supposed to say to him now?

Glancing down, she felt her heartbeat skip erratically. He was still wearing the same charcoal-coloured suit, only it was soaking wet. She could see water dripping from the jacket, and the fabric was dark and swollen-looking. With shock, she realised that he must have been sitting out in the storm.

Carefully setting down her bag and shoes, she walked towards him. 'Max…?'

He looked up at her and she felt her heart twist, for his eyes were dull and colourless.

'I didn't know you were still here,' she said quietly.

He nodded. 'I couldn't leave.'

She bit her lip. 'Was it the storm?'

'The storm?' He frowned, as though he didn't understand her question.

'Did they close the airport?' Obviously they had. What other reason would he have for still being here? Although she wasn't sure why he hadn't sheltered from the rain.

His eyes fixed on her face, and then slowly he shook his head. 'I didn't go the airport. I couldn't—'

His voice cracked and, glancing down at his hands, she saw that they were shaking. Suddenly she was shaking too.

Forcing herself to lift her chin, she said stiffly, 'Why not? Why couldn't you go?'

Her heart was beating so hard that she felt light-headed. It didn't mean anything, him being here. There was probably some logical and simple reason. But—

She drew a breath, trying to calm herself.

Why else would he still be at the villa?

Don't even go there, she thought desperately.

But she couldn't help herself. From the moment she had walked out onto the terrace and seen him it had been there, hidden beneath the surface but still there, a longing and a hope that she knew was stupid and senseless. And yet she couldn't stop herself from feeling it.

'I couldn't leave you,' he said slowly.

She stared at him mutely, not daring to ask any of the questions milling around inside her head, not willing to have her hopes crushed again.

Suddenly she knew that she couldn't stay standing up. With legs that shook slightly, she sat down beside him. Up close, she could see that his shirt was drier than his suit, but still damp. She felt her throat swell.

Reaching over, she carefully righted the glass. 'Did you stay out here in the storm?'

Max shrugged, then nodded. 'I tried to leave, but I just couldn't.'

'What about your mother?'

Hearing the concern in her voice, he flinched inwardly. Even now she was thinking about someone other than herself.

'My lawyers got an emergency injunction so the photographers can't go within fifty metres of her house, so she's doing okay.'

He watched the tension in her beautiful face ease a little, and then she reached out and touched his jacket.

'And what about you? You're soaked through. Why didn't you come inside?'

For a moment he couldn't speak past the ache in his throat. And then he said, 'Because I knew if I saw you that I'd never be able to do it. I'd never be able to leave you. And I have to leave, Margot. I can't do this to you any more.' Clenching his jaw, he breathed out unsteadily.

'Do what?' Her brown eyes were searching his.

'All of this. Everything. I've treated you so badly, and I don't want to *be* that person.' He ran a hand over his face, suddenly struggling for words. 'I don't want to hurt you.'

Margot felt suddenly close to tears. 'So why are you leaving me, then?' She stared at him, frustration overriding her fear. 'If you don't want to hurt me then why are you doing this?'

He hesitated, his expression stricken. 'You did all this to protect your family. You're such a good person, Margot. And I'm not. You deserve better than me.'

Her chest tightened. 'Max—'

He shook his head. 'I want to be with you. That's all I want—all I've ever wanted.' His mouth twisted. 'That's why I came back to France. Why I bought the shares. Why I offered to marry you. For a long time I didn't want to admit it to myself, let alone you, but I need you to understand why we can't be together.'

Margot couldn't look at him. 'And why *is* that, Max?' Her voice split, the hurt and the longing rising to the surface. 'Why can't we be together?'

His hand slid over hers, and reluctantly she turned to face him.

'Because I love you,' he said softly. 'But I know you don't love me. I know you only married me because you love your family, and I'm sorry for making you do that. Sorry for everything else I've done and said.'

She gazed at him, feeling hot and dazed, as though she'd been sitting in the sun all morning, too stunned with shock and happiness to speak.

'You love me?' she croaked.

He nodded, his fingers tightening around hers.

'And what about if I love you?' she said shakily.

He stared down into her face. 'But you don't, do you?'

She couldn't reply, but she knew that she must be nodding, and smiling, because suddenly he breathed out raggedly and then he was pulling her onto his lap, wrapping his arms around her, holding her close, then closer still, as though he never wanted to let her go.

'You're such an idiot,' she whispered. 'Of *course* I love you, Max. I've loved you since I was nineteen years old.'

Lifting her face, she saw that his face was damp now too—but with tears, not rain.

'It nearly broke me, losing you,' he said, and his voice was hoarse with the emotions he was no longer trying to hide. 'I need you like I need air and water and food. Without you, nothing matters. Without you, I have nothing. I *am* nothing.'

Searching his face, she knew that he was telling the truth. 'Not to me,' she said softly. 'You're my husband, and my heart belongs to you.' She smiled up at him. 'And now I think we should get you out of that suit.'

He gazed down at her, his eyes gleaming in the sunlight, and she felt a rush of pure love for him as his mouth curved upwards.

'That has to be your most transparent attempt yet to get my clothes off.'

Reaching up, she curled her arm around his neck. 'Did it work?'

In answer to her question he scooped her into his arms and stood up, the burn of his gaze melting her bones and searing her skin.

'I think so. But you know I never like to leave anything to chance. So let's go and make certain.'

And, turning, he carried her back into the villa.

* * * * *

LET'S TALK
Romance

For exclusive extracts, competitions
and special offers, find us online:

f facebook.com/millsandboon

🐦 @MillsandBoon

📷 @MillsandBoonUK

Get in touch on 01413 063232

For all the latest titles coming soon, visit
millsandboon.co.uk/nextmonth